BEST NEW
PARANORMAL ROMANCE

BEST NEW
PARANORMAL ROMANCE

Edited by Paula Guran

BEST NEW PARANORMAL ROMANCE

For Peter Cannon and Jeff Zaleski
because they assigned me all those vampire romances

Juno Books
www.juno-books.com

For more information, contact Juno Books
info@juno-books.com

Printed in the United States of America

ISBN-10: 0-8095-5653-7
ISBN-13: 978-0-8095-5653-3

TABLE OF CONTENTS

INTRODUCTION:
WHAT IS "PARANORMAL ROMANCE"?

Paula Guran

"Paranormal romance" may not be what you think it is.

In standard romance publishing terminology, "paranormal romance" is a subgenre of romance. Romance, to *be* romance, must have a plot concerning a love relationship between two people (usually one male and one female) and have a positive satisfying ending in which the reader is assured the couple will remain together—if not "happily ever after" at least relatively happy for an extended period of time. (Romance fans shorthand this necessary "happily ever after" ending as "HEA".)

To be "paranormal" a romance needs involve the supernatural—magic, the occult, ghosts, shapechangers like werewolves, psychic powers, superhuman abilities, travel through time, fantastic or legendary creatures (vampires, fairies, gods and goddesses, angels, demons, and the like), a fantasy world or alternative-Earth or -reality setting, relationships that continue to exist over eras and eons, etc.—or have a futuristic or science-fictional element.

Pamela Regis, in *A Natural History of the Romance Novel*,[1] defines a romance novel as "a work of prose fiction that tells the story of the courtship and betrothal of one or more heroines" and there is no doubt that "romance novels end happily." (Regis also supplies a more complete definition that includes eight essential elements and three accidental elements characteristic of the genre.)

Gone with the Wind, then, is not romance and neither is Daphne du Maurier's *Rebecca*. *Pride and Prejudice* by Jane Austen and E.M. Forester's *A Room With A View* are romance.

True literary genres have limits. These are the limits of the romance genre. Despite my natural tendency to doubt definition and desire to expand boundaries, I have to agree with Regis: If it doesn't fit that definition then it isn't romance—at least to the people who have expectations of the genre. To keep things clear, let's style this genre from here on out as a proper noun and capitalize it: *Romance.*

As Regis writes, Romance "contains serious ideas. The genre is not about woman's bondage, as the literary critics would have it. The romance novel is, to the contrary, about women's freedom. The genre is popular because it conveys the pain, uplift, and joy that freedom brings." Romance is also the most underappreciated, disrespected, and misunderstood of all genres. It is also the most popular. [2]

But when it comes to the type of fiction referred to as paranormal romance, I contend that although *some* twenty-first century paranormal romance is still definitional Romance, another type of "paranormal romance" has emerged that is *not* Romance. Perhaps it is time to acknowledge this duality or at least explore the idea.

If there is no other reason for my musings, then my thoughts can at least apply to this anthology. Since *Best New Paranormal Romance* is, as far as I know, the first book to attempt to highlight some of the best short paranormal romance of the year, I suppose this alone makes it somewhat definitional. Of course, anyone having the audacity to point out examples of "the best" of anything is classifying. So, by compiling these stories in one volume, I am, by default, doing some defining.

But, don't worry; I'm not going to get very deep or profound here.

I've yet to discover when the term "paranormal romance" was first used or what book(s) it was applied to. I think, though, the first "big hit" for paranormal romance may have been Diana Gabaldon's time-travel title *Outlander.* It certainly wasn't the first paranormal romance novel ever published, but it seems to be the first to get a great deal of attention. It also had massive sales. The Romance Writers of America named it the Best Romance of 1991 and that same year the RWA introduced the "Futuristic/Fantasy /Paranormal" category for the organization's annual RITA Awards. [3]

Despite the award and the many Romance subgenre novels it inspired, no one can contend *Outlander* is Romance. Gabaldon's book does *not* conform to the conventions of any single genre. (The author herself feels the "best description is . . . 'the smartest historical sci-fi adventure-romance story ever written by a science Ph.D. with a background in scripting 'Scrooge McDuck' comics.'")[4] *Outlander* "was originally marketed as a historical romance because, although the book didn't fit neatly into *any* genre (and at the same time was certainly not 'literary fiction'), of all the markets that it might conceivably appeal to, romance was by far the biggest."[5] You often find *Outlander* (and the five novels that followed) shelved as "fiction" in many bookstores now.

It seems that books popularly referred to as paranormal romance (at least by some folks) have a history of not always being Romance.[6]

Looking (rather arbitrarily but coincidentally) at the Nielsen Bookscan Overall Adult Fiction Bestseller List (which includes hardcover, mass market, and trade paperback books) halfway through 2006 (the week ending 2 July 2006),[7] I found Laurell K. Hamilton's hardcover *Danse Macabre*, in its first week of release, listed as #2. Kim Harrison's *A Fistful of Charms*, just released as an original paperback, was #11. Also placing in the top 100 after one week of sales were Christine Feehan's *Dangerous Tides**(mmp original, #13), the mass market paperback reprint of the futuristic *Memory in Death* by [Nora Roberts writing as] J.D. Robb (#24), *The Vision* by Heather Graham (mmp reprint, #62); *Edge of Danger**(original mmp, #76) by Cherry Adair*, and *A Bite to Remember**by Lynsay Sands (mmp original, #92).

Switching to the "hardcover only" list for the week, we also find Sherrilyn Kenyon's first hardcover (after many mass market novels) *Dark of the Moon**at #34 after five weeks. The paperback-only list shows *Kitty Goes to Washington* by Carrie Vaughn as #47 after one week.

Readers, reviewers, and booksellers call *all* of these books *paranormal romance*.

Wondering what the asterisk (*) means? The books so marked are considered by Bookscan to be "Romance." J.D. Robb's *Memory in Death* is termed Mystery/Detective. *The Vision* by Heather Graham is listed as Horror/Occult/Psychological. The rest are listed as Fantasy.

How Bookscan determines category (I don't know), is not the

point. The point I am trying to make is that many of the most popular paranormal romance novels (as well as others less popular) are not Romances, yet they are often marketed as "paranormal-romance-the-subgenre-of-Romance." Further, although some paranormal romance readers prefer Romance, not all of them do. Some do not read Romance at all. Nor does the public as a whole nor the media think of pr specifically as Romance. Admittedly, neither the public nor media gives it much thought, but they do use the term paranormal romance.

Here's just one example. A recent *USA Today* article (tied to the release of Laurell K. Hamilton's *Danse Macabre*) addresses the popularity of vampire romance.[8] The article quotes Nicole Kennedy of Romance Writers of America: "It's a different twist on the bad-boy hero." The article then cites *Danse Macabre* as "the latest entry in a fast-growing trend that spans many genres."

Continuing to quote:

> At Borders stores, sales of novels with paranormal themes, which include vampires, are up as much as 30% over the past two years, particularly romance, says spokeswoman Sue Grimshaw. "Readers have embraced the genre."
>
> Nearly 20% of all romance novels sold in 2005 had paranormal story lines, compared with 14% in 2004, according to Romance Writers of America figures. "Vampires are one of the most popular trends in paranormal romance," Kennedy says.

Also mentioned are Charlaine Harris's six-book *Southern Vampire* series and Sherrilyn Kenyon's *Dark Side of the Moon*. Christine Feehan is called the "queen of the paranormal romance." MaryJanice Davidson is called "one of a growing number of authors writing in the vampire chick-lit genre."

Paranormal romance, to this reporter "spans many genres" and "novels with paranormal themes" need not be Romance.

I haven't read every single one of the books or authors I am about to mention, so I can't be absolutely certain I'm sorting them properly. But

I'll take a shot at separating Romance from paranormal romance to serve as an example. The following would probably be paranormal but not Romance: Kelley Armstrong's Women of the Underworld series, L.A. Banks's Vampire Huntress series, MaryJanice Davidson's Undead books, both of Laurell K. Hamilton's series, Charlaine Harris's Southern Vampire series, Kim Harrison's Hollow series, Katie MacAlister's titles like *A Girl's Guide to Vampires*, *Sex and the Single Vampire*, etc., and Carrie Vaughn's "Kitty" novels.

Examples of Romance writers who write paranormal (although not exclusively) are Amanda Ashley, Jayne Ann Krentz/Jayne Castle, Nora Roberts/J.D. Robb, Lynsay Sands, and Mary Jo Putney (but the books she writes as M.J. Putney are not). Christine Feehan, Sherrilyn Kenyon, and Maggie Shayne are probably a rather dark shade of Romance.

Kim Wilkins wrote novel *Giants of the Frost* knowing it crossed genres, but assuming (for several very good reasons) it would be identified as fantasy fiction. It was subsequently defined by publishers in Australia and the UK, reviewers, booksellers, and award panels as, among other labels, Romance, fantasy, and horror. The US publisher, Warner, published the novel as "fantasy" but positioned it, according to Wilkins, "as predominantly romance fiction" asking the author to change the ending as they were "concerned that readers would be so disappointed by my unhappy ending, that they would not recommend it to friends, nor buy anything else of mine subsequently." She complied and changed the ending.

Meanwhile, in Australia, the novel had been nominated as fantasy, as horror, and even as science fiction for various awards. But when Romance readers shortlisted it for a Romance award, Wilkins's publishers "withdrew the book from the shortlist," according to the author, "citing the marketing problems the romance-fiction shortlisting would create for my subsequent publications."[9]

Wilkins is an academic as well as a popular novelist. Using her experiences with *Giants of the Frost* and drawing on several literary theories of genre, she wrote a fascinating article: *The Process of Genre: Authors, Readers, Institutions.* (My two paragraphs here do not do

even the smallest amount of justice to it and I am greatly over-sim-
plifying.) She concluded "[G]enres are not given categories but interactions between text and reader . . . [but] these interactions are always
changing . . . genre itself is formed over time . . . *Giants of the Frost* is
[something] around which genres like romance fiction and fantasy fiction are defined and redefined, in a continuing process, at specific cultural moments."[10]

It is my theory (at least for now) that at this cultural moment a new
genre is being defined. Although some paranormals might be considered a subgenre of Romance, some cannot. There are paranormals that
would be best classified as belonging to a subgenre of fantasy or mystery or action/adventure or erotica or suspense or horror or historical
fiction . . . By combining the aspects of so many "types" of literature,
paranormal romance is becoming a type unto itself.

I did not come to paranormal romance from Romance. I suspect that
many other paranormal readers come from the same literary turf I
do—science fiction, fantasy, and horror. It's not that sf/f/h is devoid of
love stories or strong female characters, especially these days, but there's
also a long history and tradition of science fiction, horror, and yes, even
fantasy, having, well, let's just say "issues" concerning romance, sex, and
women. Readers of paranormal romance—male as well as female—may
find something in pr that they often find lacking in sf/f/h.

I have always been a voracious reader, but never inclined toward
Romance. Oh, I tried a few, but other than Barbara Michaels/Eliza-
beth Peters, Mary Stewart, and the romantic (but not Romance) novels
of Daphne du Maurier's *Rebecca* and *Frenchman's Creek,* I don't recall
reading much I liked. (It's probably significant that Stewart can be
considered the mother of modern suspense romance and that Barbara
Mertz—writing as Michaels or Peters—frequently wrote in both non-
supernatural and supernatural suspense romance. The latter is what
we'd now call paranormal.)

In the mid-1990s I started working with horror and dark erotica.
I came across one of the earlier Laurell K. Hamilton books not long
thereafter and wasn't terribly impressed. Those first paperbacks weren't

packaged very attractively, but I sampled one. Hamilton's writing just didn't grab me and get me reading. With so many other good books to read I wasn't inclined to read "vampire romance" anyway.

At the World Fantasy Convention in the fall of 1998, I was on an erotica panel with, among others, Cecilia Tan of Circlet Press. She enthusiastically mentioned that LKH wrote great sex scenes. The next time a Hamilton title came my way, I paid more attention. Cecilia was right.

Hamilton leapt from paperback novelist to hardcover author in January 2000 with *Obsidian Butterfly,* the ninth in her Anita Blake series. The novel made the extended *New York Times Bestseller List*. Later that year, Ballantine published *A Kiss of Shadows*, the first Meredith Gentry book. It hit #14 on the *New York Times Best-Seller List*. (It's rare for the first in any series to sell so strongly.)

On Labor Day Weekend 2001, at Dragon*Con, I was on a midnight panel with Laurell Hamilton that turned out to be just the two of us in front of a room overflowing with her fans. (By then I'd caught up with what she was writing.) These readers knew *all* her books and were intensely interested, truly involved with her characters. Fans may flock to any television or movie actor at Dragon*Con (a huge annual multi-media genre convention in Atlanta), but authors, even best-selling ones, seldom elicit this sort of devotion.

Hamilton's tenth Anita Blake book, *Narcissus in Chains*, was published in October 2001. It stayed on the *New York Times Bestseller List* for six weeks, reaching a high position of #5. Her best-selling status was no fluke. Editors began looking for "Hamiltonesque" writers.

Meanwhile, as a reviewer, I was being assigned a lot of "vampire romance." Many sf/f/h reviewers just didn't "get" why this stuff was so popular. Being genre reviewers they understood the appeal of space opera and monsters, but did not see the allure of paranormal romance. I thought I understood what enthusiasts saw. And, geez, there sure seemed to be a lot of these books being published—some good, some pretty bad—but a lot of somebodies were buying them.

I interviewed Hamilton in early 2003 and she mentioned that Robert E. Howard had inspired her writing. Her comment gave me the final clue I needed to theorize about at least one type of current paranormal romance. Adventure—books like Hamilton's were fantasy adventure stories for women. Robert E. Howard's Conan the Barbarian and Laurell K. Hamilton's Anita Blake, I realized, have quite a bit in butt-kicking common.

This type of paranormal romance novel adheres to the standard romance genre pattern in some ways, but also breaks away. It doesn't end with HEA and is often darker and/or grittier than Romance. Nor is it always focused primarily on "love". Like dark erotica, it explores sexual "secrets" and desires rather than just the "gender secrets" of Romance. The women protagonists are strong but often still finding themselves, or somewhat weaker and discovering empowerment.

Women see romance as part of life's adventure. The guys adventured with blood-drenched brawny swordsmen with sinewy muscles and big . . . weapons. Wipe out a horde of bad guys, grab a princess who adores you or a convenient wench, make whoopee, and depart to slaughter more monsters (or equivalents). James Bond was cosmopolitan, cool, deadly, and didn't spent much time discussing philosophy with his girls. A *female* Bond might love 'em and leave 'em (although women's adventure tends to seek soul mates rather than sequential lovers, but sequence sometimes leads to soul mate) but she's going to *talk* to her lovers. She's probably going to chat to her girlfriend (Ms. Moneypenny?) about her life and loves, too.

And, yes, adventure can even be found in one's own neighborhood.

Not all paranormal romance is adventure, of course. Sometimes the stories are about the journey taken that we call "love." Characters learn and grow on this journey and it can end in any number of ways. When it does end happily, "happy" may or may not mean life with someone else in a continuing monogamous relationship. Sometimes happiness comes after the sadness in recognizing a couple must part. "Ever after" is often impossible and sometimes "forever" can be a fearsome thing.

When I set out to select stories for this anthology and the novels for the entire Juno line, I did not confine myself to Romance. If forced to supply a label for all the stories selected for *Best New Paranormal Romance*, "fantasy" probably fits best—but that doesn't provide enough specific information. How about "supernatural women's fiction"?[11] That's not only awkward, it's inaccurate. These stories certainly weren't intended *only* for women. Most of them came from publications read by both men and women. "Paranormal fantasy"? What fantasy isn't paranormal? "Sf/f/h with an element of romance or vice versa" isn't too catchy and "sf, fantasy, and supernatural romance" is unwieldy, too. "Speculative Romance"? "Romantic fantasy"? "Fantasy romance"? (I tried that last one and got shot down.)

When looking at the projected cover for this anthology, a buyer for a major chain covered the word "Romance" with his hand and said he wished we could just drop it from the title. That would leave us with, of course, *Best New Paranormal*—and yes, you often hear pr called just *paranormal* or the novels termed *paranormals*—but in a bookstore, that might land us somewhere in nonfiction with "Mind, Body, Spirit" books near the Tarot cards.

Oh well. Paranormal romance it is. (For now anyway.)

There's one more aspect involved in considering a paranormal romance anthology—or paranormal Romance, for that matter—of the short form I'd like to mention. Twenty-first century Romance is overwhelmingly published in novel or short novel form. And, although sf/f/h writers complain at a lack of markets, Rich Horton, who reviews short fiction for *Locus* magazine and edits *Science Fiction: The Best of the Year* and *Fantasy: Best of the Year* "guesstimates" there are still at least 2500 sf/f stories "published in some at least vaguely semi-pro form each year,"[12] and I imagine he isn't counting all the horror. The tradition of "year's best"-type anthologies featuring short stories is well-established in science fiction, fantasy, horror, erotica, even "literary" fiction and poetry, but there is no equivalent for literate Romance. Some independent presses are producing anthologies, both print and electronic, but few offer professional-level writing. (One that was on the professional level in 2005 was *The Journey Home*, edited by Mary Kirk for ImaJinn Books.)

Quite a few anthologies are published by the major Romance imprints but they, in general, feature three or four novellas/novelettes in the 20,000-40,000 word range. *Best New Paranormal Romance* wouldn't be much of a showcase of "best stories" if it were confined to only three or four stories.

Such Romance anthologies are meant primarily to promote the publisher's books and authors. Nothing wrong with that. But, unlike other genres in which short (and shorter) fiction is more commonly published, these Romance novellas are not usually available to be re-printed elsewhere.

The situation in the sf/f/h field is just the opposite. Writers' contracts frequently stipulate that, despite other re-publication restrictions, a story may be re-published in a "best of" anthology. Some authors even command a financial "bonus" if their story is selected for such a compilation.

Different worlds.

Whatever you want to call them, here are a dozen excellent stories of love and wonder. They come from fantasy publications, literary publications, and fantasy, literary, and romance anthologies. (I read elsewhere, especially in erotica, but the final choices did not happen to come from elsewhere.) One unintentional subtext that arose by chance is that three of the stories, albeit greatly varied, deal with soldiers who have returned home from war. Considering the times in which we live, perhaps this should not be surprising.

Whether you read paranormal-romance-as-the-subgenre-of-Romance, paranormal romance, "regular" sf/f, or have never heard of any of it—I think that you will enjoy them.

Paula Guran
August 2006

Please share your views on paranormal romance and Juno Books at
www.juno-books.com or by e-mailing editor@juno-books.com

Notes

1. *A Natural History of the Romance Novel,* Pamela Regis (University of Pennsylvania Press, 2003) This is evidently the only work available that actually looks at the history of the genre as a whole and does not draw broad (negative) conclusions from a very narrow range of investigation. Regis may be the only person to present a valid discussion of contemporary romance novels at all. If you are interested in Romance, I highly recommend it.

2. Also from Regis.

3. Information is from the RWA Web site: www.rwanational.org. The RWA appears to have fought some definitional wars as well and, for 2004, introduced a "Novel with Strong Romantic Elements" category. Is this romance that is not Romance?

4. Quoted from Diana Gabaldon's website: www.its.caltech.edu/~gatti/gabaldon/. She is referring to an essay found at: www.salon.com/books/feature/1999/08/12/outlander/index.html.

5. Quoted from Diana Gabaldon's *The Outlandish Companion* (Delacorte, 1999).

6. Gabaldon, by the way, wrote Chapter 19 of *Writing Romances: A Handbook by the Romance Writers of America:* "Paranormal Romance: Time Travel, Vampires, and Everything Beyond" (Writers Digest, 1997, edited by Rita Gallagher and Rita Clay Estrada.

7. Nielsen Bookscan says it aggregates point-of-sale data from about 70% of US bookstores, including Amazon, Barnes & Noble, Borders, and many smaller chains and leading independent bookstores. It is generally accepted in the publishing industry that Bookscan undercounts mass-market books. Hearsay estimates of the number of mmp books that are counted vary from 33% to 50%.

8. "Romance fans: Vampires are just our type," *USA Today* article by Carol Memmott, 28 June 2006.

9. "The Process of Genre: Authors, Readers, Institutions," TEXT: Vol 9, No 2, October 2005, Kim Wilkins. [http://www.griffith.edu.au/school/art/text/oct05/wilkins.htm]

10. Also from Wilkins. Do read the article!

11. "Women's fiction does not have to have the happy ending that is synonymous with romance novels. Neither does it have to end with the heroine and hero developing a relationship. Women's fiction is simply that, fiction that appeals to women and is aimed at entertaining. Romance fiction ends in a way that makes the reader feel good and reinforces the idea of innate emotional justice—good things happen to good people the couple that struggles for each other and their relationship is rewarded. The conflict in the book centres on the love story. The climax of the book resolves the love story."—Definition from "The Social Significance of the Romance Novel" by "Cynthia" (www.aromancereview.com/columns/theromancenovelparttwo.phtml)

12. Quoting Rich Horton from the *Black Gate* website: http://www.blackgate.com/articles/years_best.htm

FOLLOW ME LIGHT

———

Elizabeth Bear

Pinky Gilman limped. He wore braces on both legs, shining metal and black washable foam spoiling the line of his off-the-rack suits, what line there was to spoil. He heaved himself about on a pair of elbow-cuff crutches. I used to be able to hear him clattering along the tiled, echoing halls of the public defender's offices a dozen doors down.

Pinky's given name was Isaac, but even his clients called him Pinky. He was a fabulously ugly man, lumpy and bald and bristled and pink-scrubbed as a slaughtered hog. He had little fishy walleyes behind spectacles thick enough to serve barbecue on. His skin peeled wherever the sun or the dry desert air touched it.

He was by far the best we had.

The first time I met Pinky was in 1994. He was touring the office as part of his job interview, and Christian Vlatick led him up to me while I was wrestling a five-gallon bottle onto the water cooler. I flinched when he extended his right hand to shake mine with a painful twist intended to keep the crutch from slipping off his arm. The rueful way he cocked his head as I returned his clasp told me he was used to that reaction, but I doubted most people flinched for the reason I did—the shimmer of hot blue lights that flickered through his aura, filling it with brilliance although the aura itself was no color I'd ever seen before—a swampy gray-green, tornado-colored.

I must have been staring, because the squat little man glanced down at my shoes, and Chris cleared his throat. "Maria," he said, "This is Isaac Gilman."

"Pinky," Pinky said. His voice . . . oh, la. If he were robbed with regard to his body, that voice was the thing that made up the difference. Oh, my.

"Maria Delprado. Are you the new attorney?"

"I hope so," he said, dry enough delivery that Chris and I both laughed.

His handshake was good: strong, cool, and leathery, at odds with his parboiled countenance. He let go quickly, grasping the handle of his crutch again and shifting his weight to center, blinking behind the glass that distorted his eyes. "Maria," he said. "My favorite name. Do you know what it means?"

"It means *Mary*," I answered. "It means sorrow."

"No," he said. "It means *sea*." He pointed past me with his chin, indicating the still-sloshing bottle atop the water cooler. "They make the women do the heavy lifting here?"

"I like to think I can take care of myself. Where'd you study, Isaac?"

"Pinky," he said, and, "Yale. Four point oh."

I raised both eyebrows at Chris and pushed my glasses up my nose. The Las Vegas public defender's office doesn't get a lot of interest from Yale Law School grads, *summa cum laude*. "And you haven't hired him yet?"

"I wanted your opinion," Chris said without a hint of apology. He glanced at Pinky and offered up a self-deprecating smile. "Maria can spot guilty people. Every time. It's a gift. One of these days we're going to get her made a judge."

"Really?" Pinky's lipless mouth warped itself into a grin, showing the gaps in his short, patchy beard. "Am I guilty, then?"

The lights that followed him glittered, electric blue fireflies in the twilight he wore like a coat. He shifted his weight on his crutches, obviously uncomfortable at standing.

"And what am I guilty of?"

Not teasing, either, or flirtatious. Calm, and curious, as if he really thought maybe I could tell. I squinted at the lights that danced around him—will-o'-the-wisps, spirit lights. The aura itself was dark, but it wasn't the darkness of past violence or dishonesty. It was organic, intrinsic, and I wondered if it had to do with whatever had crippled him. And the firefly lights—

Well, they were something else again. Just looking at them made my fingertips tingle.

"If there are any sins on your conscience," I said carefully, "I think you've made amends."

He blinked again, and I wondered why I wanted to think *blinked fishily* when fishes do not blink. And then he smiled at me, teeth like yellowed pegs in pale, blood-flushed gums. "How on earth do you manage that?"

"I measure the distance between their eyes."

A three-second pause, and then he started to laugh, while Christian, who had heard the joke before, stood aside and rolled his eyes. Pinky shrugged, rise and fall of bulldog shoulders, and I smiled hard, because I knew we were going to be friends.

In November of 1996, I lost my beloved seventeen-year-old cat to renal failure, and Pinky showed up at my door uninvited with a bottle of Maker's Mark and a box of Oreos. We were both half-trashed by the time I spread my cards out on the table between us, a modified Celtic cross. They shimmered when I looked at them; that was the alcohol. The shimmer around Pinky when he stretched his hand out—was not.

"Fear death by water," I said, and touched the Hanged Man's foot, hoping he would know he was supposed to laugh.

His eyes sparkled like scales in the candlelight when he refilled my glass. "It's supposed to be if you don't find the Hanged Man. In any case, I *don't* see a drowned sailor."

"No," I answered. I picked up my glass and bent to look closer. "But there is the three of staves as the significator. Eliot called him the Fisher King." I looked plainly at where his crutches leaned against the arm of his chair. "Not a bad choice, don't you think?"

His face grayed a little, or perhaps that was the alcohol. Foxlights darted around him like startled minnows. "What does he stand for?"

"Virtue tested by the sea." And then I wondered why I'd put it that

21

way. "The sea symbolizes change, conflict, the deep unconscious, the monsters of the Id—"

"I know what the sea means," he said bitterly. His hand darted out and overturned the card, showing the tan back with its key pattern in ivory. He jerked his chin at the spread. "Do you believe in those?"

It had been foolish to pull them out. Foolish to show him, but there was a certain amount of grief and alcohol involved. "It's a game," I said, and swept them all into a pile. "Just a child's game." And then I hesitated, and looked down, and turned the three of staves back over, so it faced the same way as the rest. "It's not the future I see."

In 1997 I took him to bed. I don't know if it was the bottle and a half of Shiraz we celebrated one of our rare victories with, or the deep bittersweet richness of his voice finally eroding my limited virtue, but we were good in the dark. His arms and shoulders, it turned out, were beautiful, after all: powerful and lovely, all out of proportion with the rest of him.

I rolled over, after, and dropped the tissue-wrapped rubber on the nightstand, and heard him sigh. "Thank you," he said, and the awe in that perfect voice was sweeter than the sex had been.

"My pleasure," I said, and meant it, and curled up against him again, watching the firefly lights flicker around his blunt, broad hands as he spoke softly and gestured in the dark, trying to encompass some inexpressible emotion.

Neither one of us was sleepy. He asked me what I saw in Las Vegas. I told him I was from Tucson, and I missed the desert when I was gone. He told me he was from Stonington. When the sun came up, I put my hand into his aura, chasing the flickering lights like a child trying to catch snowflakes on her tongue.

I asked him about the terrible scars low on the backs of his thighs that left his hamstrings weirdly lumped and writhed, unconnected to bone under the skin. I'd thought him crippled from birth. I'd been wrong about so many, many things.

"Gaffing hook," he said. "When I was seventeen. My family were fisherman. Always have been."

"How come you never go home to Connecticut, Isaac?"

For once, he didn't correct me. "Connecticut isn't home."

"You don't have any family?"

Silence, but I saw the dull green denial stain his aura. I breathed in through my nose and tried again.

"Don't you ever miss the ocean?"

He laughed, warm huff of breath against my ear, stirring my hair. "The desert will kill me just as fast as the ocean would, if I ever want it. What's to miss?"

"Why'd you come here?"

"Just felt drawn. It seemed like a safe place to be. Unchanging. I needed to get away from the coast, and Nevada sounded . . . very dry. I have a skin condition. It's worse in wet climates. It's worse near the sea."

"But you came back to the ocean after all. Prehistoric seas. Nevada was all underwater once. There were ichthyosaurs—"

"Underwater. Huh." He stretched against my back, cool and soft. "I guess it's in the blood."

That night I dreamed they chained my wrists with jeweled chains before they crippled me and left me alone in the salt marsh to die. The sun rose as they walked away singing, hunched inhuman shadows glimpsed through a splintered mist that glowed pale as the opals in my manacles.

The mist burned off to show gray earth and greeny brown water, agates and discolored aquamarine. The edges of coarse gray cloth adhered in drying blood on the backs of my thighs, rumpled where they had pulled it up to hamstring me. The chains were cold against my cheeks when I raised my head away from the mud enough to pillow my face on the backs of my hands.

The marsh stank of rot and crushed vegetation, a green miasma so overwhelming the sticky copper of blood could not pierce it. The pain wasn't as much as it should have been; I was slipping into shock as softly as if I slipped under the unrippled water. I hadn't lost enough blood to kill me, but I rather thought I'd prefer a quick, cold sleep and never awakening to starving to death or lying in a pool of my own blood until the scent attracted the thing I had been left in propitiation of.

Somewhere, a frog croaked. It looked like a hot day coming.

I supposed I was going to find out.

His skin scaled in the heat. It was a dry heat, blistering, peeling, chapping lips and bloodying noses. He used to hang me with jewels, opals, tourmalines the color of moss and roses. "Family money," he told me. "Family jewels." He wasn't lying.

I would have seen a lie.

The Mojave hated him. He was chapped and chafed, cracked and dry. He never sweated enough, kept the air conditioner twisted as high as it would go. Skin burns in the heat, in the sun. Peels like a snake's. Aquamarine discolors like smoker's teeth. Pearls go brittle. Opals crack and lose their fire.

He used to go down to the Colorado River at night, across the dam to Willow Beach, on the Arizona side, and swim in the river in the dark. I told him it was crazy. I told him it was dangerous. How could he take care of himself in the Colorado when he couldn't walk without braces and crutches?

He kissed me on the nose and told me it helped his pain. I told him if he drowned, I would never forgive him. He said in the history of the entire world twice over, a Gilman had never once drowned. I called him a cocky, insincere bastard. He stopped telling me where he was going when he went out at night.

When he came back and slept beside me, sometimes I lay against the pillow and watched the follow-me lights flicker around him. Sometimes I slept.

Sometimes I dreamed, also.

I awakened after sunset, when the cool stars prickled out in the darkness. The front of my robe had dried, one long yellow-green stain, and now the fabric under my back and ass was saturated, sticking to my skin. The mud seemed to have worked it loose from the gashes on my legs.

I wasn't dead yet, more's the pity, and now it *hurt*.

I wondered if I could resist the swamp water when thirst set in. Dehydration would kill me faster than hunger. On the other hand, the water might make me sick enough that I'd slip into the relief of fever and pass away, oblivious in delirium. If dysentery was a better way to die than gangrene. Or dehydration.

Or being eaten. If the father of frogs came to collect me as was intended, I wouldn't suffer long.

I whistled across my teeth. A fine dramatic gesture, except it split my cracked lips and I tasted blood. My options seemed simple: lie still and die, or thrash and die. It would be sensible to give myself up with dignity.

I pushed myself onto my elbows and began to crawl toward nothing in particular.

Moonlight laid a patina of silver over the cloudy yellow-green puddles I wormed through and glanced off the rising mist in electric gleams of blue. The exertion warmed me, at least, and loosened my muscles. I stopped shivering after the first half hour. My thighs knotted tight as welded steel around the insult to my tendons. It would have been more convenient if they'd just chopped my damned legs off. At least I wouldn't have had to deal with the frozen limbs dragging behind me as I crawled.

If I had any sense—

If I had any sense at all, I wouldn't be crippled and dying in a swamp. If I had any sense *left,* I would curl up and die.

It sounded pretty good, all right.

I was just debating the most comfortable place when curious blue lights started to flicker at the corners of my vision.

I'm not sure why it was that I decided to follow them.

Pinky gave me a pearl on a silver chain, a baroque multicolored thing swirled glossy and irregular as toffee. He said it had been his mother's. It dangled between my breasts, warm as the stroke of a thumb when I wore it.

Pinky said he'd had a vasectomy, still wore a rubber every time we made love. Talked me into going on the Pill.

"Belt and suspenders," I teased. The garlic on my scampi was enough to make my eyes water, but Pinky never seemed to mind what I ate, no matter how potent it was.

It was one AM on a Friday, and we'd crawled out of bed for dinner, finally. We ate seafood at Capozzoli's, because although it was dim in the cluttered red room the food was good and it was open all night. Pinky looked at me out of squinting, amber eyes, so sad, and tore the tentacles off a bit of calamari with his teeth. "Would you want to bring a kid into this world?"

"No," I answered, and told that first lie. "I guess not."

I didn't meet Pinky's brother Esau until after I'd married someone else, left my job to try to have a baby, gotten divorced when it turned out we couldn't, had to come back to pay the bills. Pinky was still there, still part of the program. Still plugging away on the off chance that eventually he'd meet an innocent man, still pretending we were and always had been simply the best of friends. We never had the conversation, but I imagined it a thousand times.

I left you.

You wanted a baby.

It didn't work out.

And now you want to come back? I'm not like you, Maria.

Don't you ever miss the ocean?

No. I never do.

But he had too much pride, and I had too much shame. And once I was Judge Delprado, I only saw him in court anymore.

Esau called me, left a message on my cell, his name, who he was, where he'd be. I didn't know how he got the number. I met him out of curiosity as much as concern, at the old church downtown, the one from the thirties built of irreplaceable history. They made it of stone, to last, and broke up petroglyphs and stalactites to make the rough rock walls beautiful for God.

I hated Esau the first time I laid eyes on him. Esau. There was no mistaking him: same bristles and thinning hair, same spectacularly ugly countenance, fishy and prognathic. Same twilight-green aura, too, but Esau's was stained near his hands and mouth, the color of clotted blood, and no lights flickered near.

Esau stood by one of the petroglyphs, leaned close to discolored red stone marked with a stick figure, meaning man, and the wavy parallel lines that signified the river. Old as time, the Colorado, wearing the badlands down, warden and warded of the desert West.

Esau turned and saw me, but I don't think he saw *me*. I think he saw the pearl I wore around my neck.

I gave all the jewels back to Pinky when I left him. Except the pearl. He wouldn't take that back, and to be honest, I was glad. I'm not sure why I wore it to meet Esau, except I hated to take it off.

Esau straightened up, all five foot four of him behind the glower he gave me, and reached out peremptorily to touch the necklace, an odd gesture with the fingers pressed together. Without thinking, I slapped his hand away, and he hissed at me, a rubbery tongue flicking over fleshless lips.

Then he drew back, two steps, and looked me in the eye. His voice had nothing in common with his face: baritone and beautiful, melodious and carrying. I leaned forward, abruptly entranced. "Shipwrack," he murmured. "Shipwrecks. Dead man's jewels. It's all there for the taking if you just know where to look. Our family's always known."

My hand came up to slap him again, halted as if of its own volition. As if it couldn't push through the sound of his voice. "Were you a treasure hunter once?"

"I never stopped," he said, and tucked my hair behind my ear with the brush of his thumb. I shivered. My hand went down, clenched hard at my side. "When Isaac comes back to New England with me, you're coming too. We can give you children, Maria. Litters of them. Broods. Everything you've ever wanted."

"I'm not going anywhere. Not for . . . Isaac. Not for anyone."

"What makes you think you have any choice? You're part of his price. And we know what you want. We've researched you. It's not too late."

I shuddered, hard, sick, cold. "There's always a choice." The words hurt my lips. I swallowed. Fingernails cut my palms. His hand on my cheek was cool. "What's the rest of his price? If I go willing?"

"Healing. Transformation. Strength. Return to the sea. All the things he should have died for refusing."

"He doesn't miss the sea."

Esau smiled, showing teeth like yellow pegs. "You would almost think, wouldn't you?" There was a long pause, nearly respectful. Then he cleared his throat and said, "Come along."

Unable to stop myself, I followed that beautiful voice.

Most of a moon already hung in the deepening sky, despite the indirect sun still lighting the trail down to Willow Beach. The rocks radiated heat through my sneakers like bricks warmed in an oven. "Pinky said he didn't have any family."

Esau snorted. "He gave it the old college try."

"You were the one who crippled him, weren't you? And left him in the marsh to die."

"How did you know that?"

"He didn't tell me. I dreamed it."

"No," he answered, extending one hand to help me down a tricky slope. "That was Jacob. He doesn't travel."

"Another brother."

"The eldest brother." He yanked my arm and gave me a withering glance when I stumbled. He walked faster, crimson flashes of obfuscation coloring the swampwater light that surrounded him. I trotted to keep up, cursing my treacherous feet. At least my tongue was still my own, and I used it.

"Jacob, Esau, and Isaac Gilman? How . . . original."

"They're proud old New England names. Marshes and Gilmans were among the original settlers." Defensive. "Be silent. You don't need a tongue to make babies, and in a few more words I'll be happy to relieve you of it, mammal bitch."

I opened my mouth; my voice stopped at the back of my throat. I stumbled, and he hauled me to my feet, his rough, cold palm scraped the skin of my wrist over the bones.

We came around a corner of the wash that the trail ran through. Esau stopped short, planting his feet hard. I caught my breath at the power of the silent brown river running at the bottom of the gorge, at the sparkles that hung over it, silver and copper and alive, swarming like fireflies.

And standing on the bank before the current was Pinky—Isaac—braced on his canes, startlingly insouciant for a cripple who'd fought his way down a rocky trail. He craned his head back to get a better look at us and frowned. "Esau. I wish I could say it was a pleasure to see you. I'd hoped you'd joined Jacob at the bottom of the ocean by now."

"Soon," Esau said easily, manhandling me down the last of the slope. He held up the hand that wasn't knotted around my wrist. I blinked twice before I realized the veined, translucent yellow webs between his fingers were a part of him. He grabbed my arm again, handling me like a bag of groceries.

Pinky hitched himself forward to meet us, and for a moment I thought he was going to hit Esau across the face with his crutch. I imagined the sound the aluminum would make when it shattered Esau's cheekbone. *Litters of them. Broods.* Easy to give in and let it happen, yes. But litters of *what*?

"You didn't have to bring Maria into it."

"We can give her what she wants, can't we? With your help or without it. How'd you get the money for school?"

Pinky smiled past me, a grin like a wolf. "There was platinum in those chains. Opals. Pearls big as a dead man's eyeball. Plenty. There's still plenty left."

"So there was. How did you survive?"

"I was guided," he said, and the blue lights flickered around him. Blue lights that were kin to the silver lights swarming over the river. I could imagine them buzzing. Angry, invaded. I turned my head to see Esau's expression, but he only had eyes for Pinky.

Esau couldn't see the lights. He looked at Pinky, and Pinky met the stare with a lifted chin. "Come home, Isaac."

"And let Jacob try to kill me again?"

"He only hurt you because you tried to leave us."

"He left me for the father of frogs in the salt marsh, Esau. And you were there with him when he did—"

"We couldn't just let you walk away." Esau let go of my arm with a command to be still, and stepped toward Pinky with his hands spread wide. There was still light down here, where the canyon was wider and the shadow of the walls didn't yet block the sun. It shone on Esau's balding scalp, on the yolky, veined webs between his fingers, on the aluminum of Pinky's crutches.

"I didn't walk," Pinky said. He turned away, hitching himself around, the beige rubber feet of the crutches braced wide on the rocky soil. He swung himself forward, headed for the river, for the swarming lights. "I crawled."

Esau fell into step beside him. "I don't understand how you haven't . . . changed."

"It's the desert." Pinky paused on a little ledge over the water. Tamed by the dam, the river ran smooth here and still. I could feel its power anyway, old magic that made this land live. "The desert doesn't like change. It keeps me in between."

"That hurts you." Almost in sympathy, as Esau reached out and laid a webbed hand on Pinky's shoulder. Pinky flinched but didn't pull away. I opened my mouth to shout at him, feeling as if my tongue were my own again, and stopped. *Litters.*

Whatever they were, they'd be Pinky's children.

"It does." Pinky fidgeted with the crutches, leaning forward over the river, working his forearms free of the cuffs. His shoulders rippled under the white cloth of his shirt. I wanted to run my palms over them.

"Your legs will heal if you accept the change," Esau offered, softly, his voice carried away over the water. "You'll be strong. You'll regenerate. You'll have the ocean, and you won't hurt anymore, and there's your woman—we'll take her too."

"*Esau.*"

I heard the warning in the tone. The anger. Esau did not. He glanced at me. "Speak, woman. Tell Isaac what you want."

I felt my tongue come unstuck in my mouth, although I still couldn't move my hands. I bit my tongue to keep it still.

Esau sighed, and looked away. "Blood is thicker than water, Isaac. Don't you want a family of your own?"

Yes, I thought. Pinky didn't speak, but I saw the set of his shoulders, and the answer they carried was *no.* Esau must have seen it too, because he raised one hand, the webs translucent and spoiled-looking, and sunlight glittered on the barbed ivory claws that curved from his fingertips, unsheathed like a cat's.

With your help or without it.

But litters of *what?*

I shouted so hard it bent me over. *"Pinky, duck!"*

He didn't. Instead, he *threw* his crutches backward, turned with the momentum of the motion, and grabbed Esau around the waist. Esau squeaked—*shrieked*—and threw his hands up, clawing at Pinky's shoulders and face as the silver and blue and coppery lights flickered and swarmed and swirled around them, but he couldn't match Pinky's massive strength. The lights covered them both, and Esau screamed again, and I strained, lunged, leaned at the invisible chains that held me as still as a posed mannequin.

Pinky just held on and leaned back.

They barely splashed when the Colorado closed over them.

Five minutes after they went under, I managed to wiggle my fingers. Up and down the bank, there was no trace of either of them. I couldn't stand to touch Pinky's crutches.

I left them where they'd fallen.

Esau had left the keys in the car, but when I got there I was shaking too hard to drive. I locked the door and got back out, tightened the laces on my sneakers, and toiled up the ridge until I got to the top. I almost turned my ankle twice when rocks rolled under my foot, but it didn't take long. Red rock and dusty canyons stretched west, a long, gullied slope behind me, the river down there somewhere, close enough to smell but out of sight. I settled myself on a rock, elbows on knees, and looked out over the scarred, raw desert at the horizon and the setting sun.

There's a green flash that's supposed to happen just when the sun slips under the edge of the world. I'd never seen it. I wasn't even sure it existed. But if I watched long enough, I figured I might find out.

There was still a hand span between the sun and the ground, up here. I sat and watched, the hot wind lifting my hair, until the tawny disk of the sun was halfway gone and I heard the rhythmic crunch of someone coming up the path.

I didn't turn. There was no point. He leaned over my shoulder, braced his crutches on either side of me, a presence solid and cool as a moss-covered rock. I tilted my head back against Pinky's chest, his wet shirt dripping on my forehead, eyes, and mouth. Electric blue lights flickered around him, and I couldn't quite make out his features, shadowed as they were against a twilight sky. He released one crutch and laid his hand on my shoulder. His breath brushed my ear like the susurrus of the sea. "Esau said blood is thicker than water," I said, when I didn't mean to say anything.

"Fish blood isn't," Pinky answered, and his hand tightened. I looked away from the reaching shadows of the canyons below and saw his fingers against my skin, pale silhouettes on olive, unwebbed. He slid one under the black strap of my tank top. I didn't protest, despite the dark red, flaking threads that knotted the green smoke around his hands.

"Where is he?"

"Esau? He drowned."

"But—" I craned my neck. "You said Gilmans never drown."

He shrugged against my back. "I guess the river just took a dislike to him. Happens that way sometimes."

A lingering silence, while I framed my next question. "How did you find me?"

"I'll always find you, if you want," he said, his patched beard rough against my neck. "What are you watching?"

"I'm watching the sun go down."

"Come in under this red rock," he misquoted, as the shadow of the ridge opposite slipped across the valley toward us.

"The handful of dust thing seems appropriate—"

Soft laugh, and he kissed my cheek, hesitantly, as if he wasn't sure I would permit it. "I would have thought it'd be 'Fear death by water.'"

The sun went down. I missed the flash again. I turned to him in a twilight indistinguishable from the gloom that hung around his shoulders and brushed the flickering lights away from his face with the back of my hand. "Not that," I answered. "I have no fear of that, my love."

Elizabeth Bear lives and works in central Connecticut, with a cat who is practicing to be Siamese. She writes science fiction and fantasy, and is the recipient of a Locus Award and the John W. Campbell Award for Best New Writer. Her recent and forthcoming releases include short story collection *The Chains That You Refuse*, a not-Edwardian alternate history mosaic novel entitled *New Amsterdam*, science fiction novels *Carnival* and *Undertow*, urban fantasies *Blood & Iron* and *Whiskey & Water*, and—with Sarah Monette—a dark Norse fantasy called *A Companion to Wolves*.

A MAZE OF TREES

Claudia O'Keefe

If you ever want to see a setting truly fit for a fantasy novel, it's best to come to West Virginia first. Like the state's motto, we are very wild here, wild in thought, sometimes wild in appearance, but always wild in landscape.

You notice it only a few miles after crossing the state line from Virginia into West Virginia. Our mountains aren't the type that jutted up out of the Earth during ancient upheavals. Our lands formed when water and ice dug down into the Earth, carved deeply and harshly through her plateaus to reveal her womb of smooth, solid rock. Rivers surge through nearly every low area, cold and broad and disdainful of man, yet invigorating to the eye, flowing with magic's clear blood. They call us the Mountain State, but what we really are is the land of secret valleys, of places where most people don't belong and soon leave, after remarking on their beauty.

I was one of those people who should have left. Unfortunately, I was in bad shape when I arrived, thinking a nice convalescence in these deceptively gentle hills would be just what I needed. I didn't need it. I should have run, dumped all my baggage, both real and imagined, and fled by any means possible, jet, train, bus, on a hog wearing a saddle and hackamore, whatever. I should have left, but I didn't. I became trapped. First by poverty, then by something much stickier, nearly impossible to transcend. Something that called to me with a voice I'd longed to hear my entire life, magic—real magic—the kind that doesn't care if you believe in it and gives you power whether you want it or not (I did at first), power that will drive you mad if you let it, and I'm afraid that I am. Just a little.

I was already half nuts by the time I met Landry. He served me my grilled sea bass with melon salsa at a new restaurant up at Frost Knob the last weekend in September. Being what I was, haunting the village at Frost Knob was like dining with the enemy, but I couldn't help myself. Frost Knob is the closest thing there is to civilization in my part of the Appalachians. It's the highest ski resort on the East Coast, and during the season the place sucks in well-heeled metropolitan types from D.C., New York, and across the south. Though I didn't ski and almost never talked with anyone on my visits to 4,900 feet, I could brush by tourists wearing Ralph Lauren sheepskin jackets or carrying the latest overnight tote by Prada and draw in tantalizing hints of halfway intelligent speech—a clause here, a truncated exchange there, mention of marketing meetings, the latest editorial in *The Times,* gossip about someone's botched eye job, or silly, fractious arguments over aborted play dates, what I call miscellaneous city talk. I walked through the resort's cobbled square, opening my ears like radar. As I passed candle and bookstores, restaurants, ski shops, and a Starbucks, I'd reel in these little snippets of civilization, like a fisherman on a sea so lonely he's reduced to holding one-sided conversations with the fish flapping and gasping in his net.

I wanted so badly to return to the world I once inhabited, have friends again, find a life, but I couldn't. *It* wouldn't let me.

"Would you like the fries, rice pilaf, or Jumpin' Jack black-eyed peas with that?" Landry asked me as he stood next to my table in the Gearhead Bar & Grill. He was memorizing my order as I gave it to him, rather than write it down. This either spoke well of his memory or poorly of the house count, most likely the latter. Snow hadn't yet begun falling up here, nor was it cold enough to make the white stuff artificially and keep it on the ground. Still, with this being the height of the resort's fall foliage season, the place should have been littered with almost as many tourists as dying leaves. It wasn't. I'd taken care of that.

Glancing up into Landry's troubled face, I felt bad about his lack of paying customers.

"Pilaf," I said.

"Alrighty," he said. "I'll go put this in and be right back with your Cosmo."

It was the *alrighty* that got me. That a man who stood over six feet and waited tables like a Grizzly practicing jeet kune do could use a word like that suggested a self-possession I immediately liked. The alrighty wasn't canned like the automatic responses you learn to use with the paying public. It was just him.

He returned with my Cosmo, heavy on the cranberry, in a frosted martini glass that could have served half a frat house.

"Wow," I said.

"Frost Knob invites you to ski happy," he said. "When we finally get snow, that is."

I concentrated a second or two before answering, "Next week about this time. A rare early blizzard."

"Is that the Weather Channel talking, or are you merely prescient?"

"Maybe it's just that there big toe I broke a ways back that acts up when the weather's a-changing," I said, doing my best, tasteless imitation of my hick neighbors over in Cherry Lick. I instantly felt a rush of PC-induced guilt, and smiled apologetically a moment later.

He assessed me and I studied him. I saw his name, LANDRY, spelled in machine-engraved letters on the gold plastic tag pinned to his uniform. I saw the confident way he wore the god-awful acrylic ski sweater they'd given him, his expensive haircut only just starting to grow out, nails that were still neatly manicured, teeth and fingers that were free of nicotine stains. I'd served food and drinks off and on most of my life and I knew he wasn't a waiter, not really.

"You don't belong here," I said.

After a moment, when he glanced down at the last scraps of city cool I still owned, my ten-year-old Betsy Johnson dress, which no longer fit well as it should, and the Okio sunglasses lying on the table next to my West Virginia driver's license, he smiled.

"Neither do you."

"Oh, yes," I said. "Unfortunately, I do."

Finishing lunch and deciding to give Landry my real phone number instead of one with an incorrect digit, I drove down the mountain to the base of the resort 1,700 feet below, just west of a T-intersection joining Frost Knob to the main highway leading back to parts known, I spotted four people climbing out of a Cadillac Escalade. It was parked next to a handcrafted billboard advertising a new five-hundred-unit development that would soon replace the hardwood forest beyond it. LUXURY IN CONCERT WITH NATURE, read the developer's slogan. This meant they'd leave a few landscape-quality trees behind when they clear-cut the rest to raise their condos.

I crossed the intersection and pulled my Tracker into the parking lot in front of the tiny grocery that served the people who stayed in condos already built. I felt It coming over me, into me, using me and me using It. It waited, curled inside me, watching the four as they flipped through their glossy brochures. The saleswoman in the group gestured at a seventy-foot sugar maple, its glorious crown torched by leaves just starting to turn, and then to an area on a plat map. Two of the visitors were husband and wife, and the husband tramped up the newly bulldozed ridge behind the sign to capture virgin terrain with his digicam.

This was the moment It could use to its best advantage, my magic. I couldn't help myself, didn't want to help It, but I had become It.

I took a soft, deep breath, then released my hold on the deep place within that understood and could manipulate both humans and forest effortlessly. I raised my left hand, cupped slightly around the object I created. If you could hold a solar eclipse in the palm of your hand—a black hole the size of a man's kidney, with a hundred snapping tentacles that sucked light and life toward it with the violence of a rip current—that would describe just one of the things my magic does. Though it wasn't necessary, since the thing could fly through my windshield without being altered, I rolled down the driver's side window and flung it gently into the air.

It shot with laser precision toward the man with the digicam. None of the four could see it, of course. I sighed, watching the thing go to work on him, hovering beside one ear and then the other, sticking its tentacles into each, wriggling and digging farther and farther inside his head, past eardrums deep into the part of the brain where mankind's most primitive reflexes reside. The man stiffened instantly, but didn't understand the shudder that raised the hairs on the back of his neck. Backing out of an ear, the writhing black ball went to work on the man's eyes next, prying up first one eyelid, then the next, sticking a tentacle underneath and smearing his eyeballs with an oily dark light. To the man, it would feel as if the forest had suddenly grown closer and darker. He would feel its lonely, claustrophobic embrace reaching out to smother him. When the thing stuck more of its tentacles up his nostrils, along the nerves and into his parietal lobes, the man would, to a lesser degree, smell the same type of panic that immobilized a horse in a burning barn.

Finally the black ball was finished with him. It floated toward the man's wife next. By the time it reached her, it was losing energy, moving less vigorously. It stuck a single tentacle into the woman's ear, and then as if pulled by a vacuum, its entire body was sucked, protesting and fading at the same time, inside her head.

Man and wife abruptly broke off what they were doing and looked around at the trees and the mountains crowding them in on all sides. Both tensed, their shoulders rigid, the complacent smiles they'd worn moments before gone. The man quit filming and stared worriedly into the shadows beneath the trees. Seconds later, he returned to the Cadillac while the wife distanced herself from the saleswoman, who noticed the change in her client's behavior, but didn't know what to make of it. A few polite yet terse exchanges later, all climbed into the Cadillac. The SUV remained a few minutes more, while the saleswoman struggled to salvage her deal, but it was useless.

They drove away.

I sat there in my car for another ten minutes, giving them a solid head start toward the safety of the sales office and human habitation. Then, thinking about Landry and his lack of paying business, I raised my left hand. On it was a tiny curl of misty light that moved up and away without my help, tendrils beating at the speed of a hummingbird's wings. It hurtled down the highway ahead of my Tracker on its way toward the interstate, the most popular route to Frost Knob. Bouncing from tree to tree, the tiny light dispelled the shadows my magic had placed there three weeks before, shadows the naked eye couldn't see, but that were sensed by the unconscious minds of all but the least sensitive.

I am the goddess of Lonely Spaces. Please bear in mind that I had to come up with this title by myself, as there's never been anyone to tell me who I've become. I may not be a goddess at all, but merely an oddity.

To explain what I do, let me tell you about my favorite road in these mountains. Route 7. Beginning at the turnoff from U.S. Highway 219 at Millerton, it stretches for fifty-eight miles, most of it through the Monongahela National Forest, until it reaches Freedom Forge. Winding and bending, climbing and climbing, it traverses the most sublime example of natural beauty in North America. If you've driven the snowy mountains and fjords of British Columbia's Highway 99 from Vancouver to Whistler, with its astonishing drop-offs to the pewter sea thousands of feet below, you may have thought you traveled the road to Valhalla. If you've ever been fortunate enough to take the ribbon of asphalt descending out of Los Alamos, New Mexico, with the whole of mystic Black Mesa to your northeast and the pink cliffs that become fuchsia at sunset guiding you to a dusty high desert freeway below, you might be tempted to think you're seeing exactly what the Zuni and Hopi saw thousands of years ago when they first came to the land. Take Route 7 from Millerton to Freedom Forge, however, and you'll discover a landscape so potent and unmolested it's enough to make you weep. Unlike these other roads, you can drive the entire fifty-eight miles and never pass another car, mobile home, gas station, or fast food restaurant. Instead you are immersed in a maze of trees reemerging triumphantly from the decimation of old growth forests during the previous two centuries. Your SUV flies like a private Lear jet through tunnel upon tunnel of green in the summer months, through chutes of molten red and orange leaves in the fall. You pass tiny waterfalls of stacked limestone that spray froth at your windshield and are so numerous and unplanned they appear like volunteer fruit trees springing up from carelessly thrown peach pits. You encounter a glacial bog that

exists nowhere else in the U.S. and is lush with wild cranberry and orchids and insect-catching plants. In the winter the entire road becomes
a black and white photographer's dream—black trunks, black ground,
white snow, and falls frozen into monumental ice sculptures. You drive
and twist and turn and marvel that there could still he a place like this
in the world and somewhere about mile twenty-three it hits you.

Loneliness.

This place is too lonely for you. It's gorgeous, but you want to see
something else, a town, a house, even a strip mall. You want to see
signs that you aren't totally alone here. To hell with the heavenly
mists weaving through the valleys and the tranquil, splashing Cherry
River that dogs the highway like a New Age fanatic who won't leave
you alone until you buy one of his idiotic healing energy crystals. You
want a goddamn McDonald's. Fifty-eight miles of peace and quiet
now seems like five hundred and eighty. You want out but you can't
make up your mind. Would it be better to turn around and go hack?
Or should you continue on in hopes that you'll regain civilization
sooner ahead?

To an extent. Nature performs this protective magic all on its own,
as it has for tens of thousands of years, keeping people who would destroy it at bay. In these modem times, however, with mankind wielding
the sword of technological superiority, human psychology alone isn't
enough to send men and women with chainsaws and Bobcats rushing
from dark glades and isolated valleys, back to the blare and growl of the
city, glancing nervously over their shoulders as they flee.

I have to do it.

Landry called the next morning, up much earlier than I would expect of someone in his business, since he probably didn't get off work
until close to midnight.

"Did business pick up at all after I left?" I asked.

"God, we were slammed. It was dead the rest of the afternoon and
even the first part of dinner. They were even ready to let me go early.
Then around seven all gustatory hell broke loose."

I calculated the time backward mentally. It's a good two-hour drive
from the Interstate to Frost Knob and the little tuft of light I released

at two-thirty would have cleared the darkness along the highway from the freeway to the resort by four. Instead of stopping to cancel their reservations in Lewisburg and turn around, as I'd encouraged them to do for weeks, the first of the hordes would have reached Frost Knob's check-in desk by six o'clock, and had an hour to get settled before descending on Landry in Gearhead. The timing fit.

"So what are you doing up at—" I checked the ghastly old plastic teapot clock on my kitchen wall, "—8:47? You must be exhausted."

"I couldn't sleep. I'm thrilled. I'm flush. After paying my first month's rent I've got an amazing wad of cash burning a hole in my pocket. Want to do something?"

"How big a wad?"

"Just a sec. Let me count." I waited, but he was quick. "Eighteen dollars!" he said.

"Good thing you called me," I told him. "If you're willing to leave campus, I can show you entire towns around here you could buy for that."

"With change leftover for dinner?"

"And breakfast," I said. I hadn't meant that to be a double-entendre, but I'm out of practice using the dialect from the land of my birth. Landry's voice held that mischievous grin I'd loved from the day before, like a bear caught with his nose in a fifty-dollar jar of Dean & DeLuca honey, but he opted to be a gentleman and instead pretended my slip had gone clear over his head.

"So where can we do the most damage with my eighteen dollars?"

I took him to a bakery in the middle of nowhere. That isn't much of a description, really, since everything around here is in the middle of nowhere, but I thought my bear would like the cinnamon sticky buns this place had to offer, baked in a genuine wood-fired oven. He did, devouring a six-pack of gooey rolls before we could finish our first cup of MauaJava.

"What is this place doing out here?" he asked, incredulous to find a gourmet-quality coffee and pastry spot on a vacant two-lane road an hour from even the least traveled tourist route.

I shrugged. "What is anyone doing out here?"

"What brought you here?" he asked, turning more serious than I liked.

"Probably the same thing that brought you to Frost Knob."

"Bankruptcy, foreclosure, and homelessness after your systems analyst job was outsourced to Pindladoor?" he asked.

"How'd you guess?" I said, favoring him with a sympathetic smile over his situation.

He waited patiently for my real explanation.

"Is there really a place called Pindladoor?" I asked.

"You're evading," he said.

I nodded, but I wasn't hiding, at least not from myself. I turned my reasons for being here over in my head every day, every hour, every few minutes, with the frequency the average man has thoughts of sex. I hated thinking about that stupid, stupid minute in the barn behind my house eight years ago that changed everything forever, but when your world narrows in on you as tightly as a dress that's now a size and a half too small, you tend to obsess.

It wasn't my house or my barn back then. They belonged to a man I'd never met named Ariel Walkrip. I grew up in southern California during the post-Brady Bunch Era. Los Angeles was still a demi-paradise, but starting to show a hipper urban edge. My family had lived there since the dawn of motion pictures, just a few hundred yards from where Charlie Chaplin built his studios on a then orange grove-lined Santa Monica Boulevard. When grown, the adults in my family habitually chose from two different professions, real estate or movies. I chose movies, as a writer, or rather a never-could-get-past-the-struggling-part writer. By the time the big earthquake came along in the early 1990s, demolishing my house on top of me, I was having daily work-related panic attacks and fought nightly with my coke-addicted agent boyfriend—who wouldn't represent my screenplays because he didn't want to look like he "subscribed to nepotism."

I left. I took what little remained unbroken from the earthquake, got on the Internet, and hunted up the cheapest place in the U.S. that I thought I could stand, where I could afford to sit and write the Great American novel.

Did I know that New York wasn't buying Great American novels anymore? No. Two years later, with an eviction notice thumb tacked to my door and urgently needing someplace even cheaper to live, I saw Ariel Walkrip's ad in the local throwaway.

Cute 1 br./l ba. with privacy on 80 ac. farm. $175 per month, utilities included, in exchange for light caretaking duties. 555-2419.

One hundred seventy-five dollars a month! How far I'd fallen. I remembered paying more than that for a cut and color in L.A.

Walkrip's farm was just outside an invisible Flying Brigadoon-like town called Cherry Lick. In the summer, the town mysteriously vanished into rampant overgrowth from the forest, houses fenced in by rats' nests of honeysuckle vines suspended from the trees, cut off by hillsides of weed-laced cornfields. At the end of October, the foliage died and voilà, the town reappeared.

I drove out to Walkrip's place the eighth of July, zipping by downtown Cherry Lick without realizing it, turned off where instructed and plummeted down a driveway so steep it should have had its own runaway truck ramp. At the bottom was the typical West Virginia pre-mobile home era abode, a one-and-a-half story farmhouse on homemade stone footings, recently reclad in rubbery vinyl siding. Instead of the traditional white, Walkrip had gone with cardboard brown. Various outbuildings were strewn about, a chicken coop made out of the back end of a retired U-Haul truck, a series of outhouses built one on top of another like successive civilizations in an archaeological dig, storage sheds, and a barn with an empty corral attached. No cute 1 br./l ba. guest houses in sight.

I called out the owner's name. Several times. Knocked on his doors, front and back, thinking he might be elderly and hard of hearing. I peered in the windows. No one. This left the barn as the only other logical choice.

I turned and walked hesitantly toward the rotting locust-wood structure. On the way I passed a disturbing kitchen garden. Though compulsively tidy and laid out like something on the best of HGTV, each of the mature vegetables in the garden had been . . . abused. Every cucumber, pumpkin, and squash had one or more strings tied tightly about their girths. They reminded me of a half-feral calico cat I'd once rescued. When it was still a kitten, some sicko had placed an industrial-strength rubber band around its midsection and then abandoned it to the wilds. The kitten grew into a cat, and as it did the rubber band restricted and distorted its growth. It probably could have survived this way indefinitely, but when it became pregnant, the result was horrifying. Walkrip's vegetables had received the same treatment.

I halted next to that garden and immediately knew I wasn't going to rent anything from this man. As soon as I found him, I'd let him know I wasn't interested.

Ariel Walkrip hung from a noose at the rear of the barn. He looked exactly how I'd pictured him during our phone conversation, an old farmer no different from a hundred other farmers out here, worn-out body in jeans, plaid shirt, and a John Deere cap. His eyes were nearly closed, his face bloated and purple, the fingertips on his arthritic hands pendulous and dark as well, like baby eggplant. His feet had swollen so badly with accumulated blood that his tightly tied shoes couldn't contain the flesh. It spilled over the constrictions, reminding me of the abnormally grown vegetables outside.

Instinctively, I knew he was dead, but I remembered something from research I'd done for a script involving a CSI team. You have to know what you're doing when you hang yourself, or else you won't snap your neck cleanly. Instead you can dangle and dangle until you suffocate instead, an agonizing way to go. I couldn't live with myself if I ran out of the bam without checking first to make certain Walkrip was really deceased and not simply unconscious and in need of emergency help.

Fighting every step before I took it, my toes dragging through the dust and straw, I approached.

"Hello," I said. "Mr. Walkrip?"

When he didn't respond, I dared myself, commanded myself, gingerly reached out and took one of his leather-clad toes between my forefinger and thumb to give his foot a little shake.

I couldn't see It, but I sensed It come awake at my touch. It had crouched there, inside Walkrip's body, just waiting for me to come along and rescue It. That power over loneliness. It jumped off the dead man faster than a flea and coated Itself to my skin. I went into agony, my body suddenly unable to breathe as if every inch of it were covered in metallic paint. Rays of silver light stabbed at my peripheral vision and I felt the thing bite into every last nerve ending I had and work its way upstream with its fiberoptic heat toward my brain. My body was wracked with minute convulsions. Choking, losing consciousness, I lifted one hand in front of my face and saw my flesh flaring jaggedly like video shot by a war correspondent on the run. I fell face first toward a dung-covered floor.

When I came to, I knew it was morning. Walkrip swung gently overhead in the breeze and I lay on the barn's rock scrabble flooring. Poised inches from my face was a green grasshopper, holding up a leaf from a pin oak. As I watched, the insect raised the leaf just a little higher over its head, then dropped it in front of me and slowly backed away, long, crooked leg by long, crooked leg.

Frowning, I fumbled for the leaf. The instant I touched it, I knew I was no longer me. The old me couldn't tell you exactly where to find the tree it had fallen from. The new me could tell you which branch.

Blundering through Walkrip's unlocked back door in search of a phone to call the authorities, I stepped into a kitchen just as bizarre as the garden outside. Gleaming new Corian countertops hugged the walls, installed above a set of dilapidated particleboard cabinets, two with doors hanging by a single hinge. Centered on the nearest countertop was a piece of paper, and beside that a plate of home-baked Tollhouse cookies covered with clingwrap.

SORRY, read the note, in oversized, shaky handwriting. I BAKED YOU SOME COOKIES.

I knew I couldn't tell Landry any of this. I'd never told anyone. For one, I had no family left, and my friends back in L.A. had all turned out to be of the fair-weather variety. I'd made acquaintances, but no solid friends in my decade lost in Appalachia. As desperately as I wanted someone to talk to about everything, I didn't want to send Landry running and screaming back to his mountaintop. I didn't just want I needed the connection he offered, like a lifesaving procedure or the human equivalent of a bottle of Zoloft.

"Carly?" He put down his coffee. "Are you okay?"

"Yes. I'm sorry. Just thinking about your question. Why I chose West Virginia."

"Why did you?"

"It's disaster-free. No earthquakes, no hurricanes, no terrorists, tornadoes, riots, or nuclear power plants to melt down. Sure, we have floods, but if you live on a mountaintop, you're pretty much safe."

"Safety, I can understand that," Landry said quietly, but his eyes didn't agree with his words. I knew he knew there was more to the story. I watched his eyelids flicker as he studied me, curious for the truth. He opened his mouth, then closed it, and touched my hand instead, stroking it softly with his finger, as the wheels inside him turned.

"How did you know?" Landry asked me over the phone. It was the fifth of October, and outside, the horror that is a West Virginia winter had set in two months early. Winter is dark and choking here. I hate it with a passion so overwhelming I can't think straight once it arrives. It comes at you like that stranger you dread at a roadside rest stop, the one who will abduct you and lock you in his trunk until you're dead and he can play with you.

The first snow of every year is like an unwelcome anniversary for me, reminding me that I am trapped with no hope of ever escaping.

"Carly?"

"*Farmer's Almanac,*" I said finally, explaining away my foreknowledge of the storm I'd predicted when we met the week before.

"You read the *Farmer's Almanac,*" he said. He sounded skeptical.

"No, but everyone else here does and is constantly blabbing about it."

"Incredible. I figured they used a random number generator to make their predictions," he said.

"Either that or threw groundhogs at dart boards."

"They probably do," I agreed.

We talked for more than two hours, until my phone went dead in the middle of one of his jokes. I never did find out how many Pindladoor programmers it takes to screw in a light bulb. Though I sensed he was doing his best to help lift me out of a depression I couldn't quite mask, I also suspected that he didn't really enjoy the joke himself, because it touched on a nerve he wished would go numb. He couldn't know how grateful I was just to hear his voice that bleak afternoon, warming me with his easygoing humor.

As a goddess, my territory is pitifully small. It covers portions of just five tiny counties along the West Virginia state line north of I-64, plus a narrow swath of three border counties in neighboring Virginia. I haven't been out of my territory in eight years, ten if you count the two years I lived here before my transformation. I'm tethered here by the magic that runs through me now. I am at its mercy. Profit-driven land developers may not be able to invade my territory, but as urgently as I want to go home, I can no longer set foot in their territory either.

I've never been able to figure out what exactly defines my boundaries, except that I can't enter a town with more than a certain number of dwellings, enough to house a population of three thousand or greater, without experiencing discomfort. Sixty-five hundred is the threshold at which I go into extreme distress. I don't want to think about what would happen if someone forcibly took me beyond my boundaries for longer than a few minutes. I know, more than suspect, that the magic inside me would rebel, and likely slip from my control, damaging many around me before it finally fed on and consumed my life.

Logically my territory makes little sense. Portions of both the Monongahela and Washington National Forests, not to mention many private and forested lands, extend well beyond it. What, if anything, protects those areas? I wonder. Does anything or anyone guard nature's other remote and hidden lands? I've never met another like me. Nor did I receive any postmortem clues from the late Ariel Walkrip. His will stipulated only that his house and property go to the first person to touch his body.

Landry made me feel like a human again that winter. God, how I loved him for being the kind of person he was. He taught me to ski under the stars and begged me to do ridiculous, even embarrassing things, like salsa dance underwater in the resort's indoor rock grotto pool. He hacked us into their reservation system, where he would appropriate empty condos for us, each complete with balcony hot tubs. We'd make feverish love in the open air and bubbling water, then afterward lie sated, wrapped in towels on the thick living room carpet. With our faces pressed against floor-to-ceiling windows, we watched Christmas and New Year's Day dawning through swirling snow that flecked the dead brown hills spread below us like spots on a sleeping fawn.

I showed him wonders as well, taking him trekking on snowshoes into the deepest wilderness I knew, a place no one, not even research scientists, loggers, or the forest service had been for more than a century. History claims that the last Eastern Woodland Bison was slaughtered in Randolph County in 1825 and that the last gray wolf in West Virginia was hunted down in 1900, also in Randolph. Crouching low on a granite spar overlooking one of my secret valleys, we spied on huffing, foraging buffalo whose shaggy manes tinkled with curtains of ice. Hidden downwind in a ring of birch saplings, we peered between the slender trunks while wolf pups entertained us unaware, roughhousing in fresh powder. Landry didn't realize my subspecies of buffalo were supposed to be extinct, nor the wolves disappeared from the wild. He assumed the wolves were officially introduced transplants from Canada and the buffalo escapees from a ranch raising gourmet steaks. I didn't correct him, but I worried that I had violated my own magic in revealing them to him. If it weren't for my power, I would never have known they were there. Someone before me, possibly pre-dating Ariel's tenure, had set up a type of invisible fence around them, allowing them just enough territory to roam and remain healthy, but herding them well away from exposure to hunters. I was meant to continue the guardianship. Would Landry tell people about them when he returned to civilization after the season was over?

"I was thinking about those wolves," he said to me one night a couple weeks after we returned from our weekend trip to the backcountry. I lay curled against his furry chest in our ill-gotten hotel room bed. The covers were tossed on the floor and our legs sprawled inelegantly on the king-size mattress. We'd been listening to pine logs pop and sizzle in the fireplace.

"What about them?" I asked, alarm ringing through me.

"Nothing really," he said. He absently fingered a lock of my hair hanging down into my face. "Just thinking about them."

He looked down at me then, gently tucking the lock of hair behind my ear. "You're such a wild child, Carly," he said.

"Hardly wild and a long time from being a child."

"You know what I mean. I'm not talking about parties and drugs and pissing in the face of authority. You *know* what I mean."

I wanted to sit up and pull away from him, but didn't dare let him see I was afraid. My heart raced and I was certain he could feel my pulse crashing blindly, thudding hard against his naked skin.

"How did you know where to find the wolves? How not to spook them? We were so close and they didn't even realize we were there. They should have, shouldn't they? They have powerful noses."

"I have a powerful nose, too," I said.

"I know you do," he said, momentarily playful. "You found me."

"And that's how I found them."

"Why is it then that I'm a ten times better skier than you, but you're the one who downhills flawlessly in the dark? You never hit anything, no near misses, no tripping. You're fearless out there. You even knew exactly when to turn back for home when that squall came up, but let us go just a little farther than we should have."

"I didn't know. I told you."

"You told me, but I think you kept us going until it was almost too late because you thought it was exciting."

"It was exciting, wasn't it?"

He frowned, searching my eyes for the answer he wanted and not finding it.

"Yes," he said at last. "I was scared shitless we'd get turned around and lost in the storm, but we didn't. We made it back." He paused. "How did you know where to find those wolves, Carly?"

"I've lived here a long time."

"How long?"

"Ten years."

He thought that over for several seconds, accepting what the answer contained rather than what it didn't.

"How often do you get back? To the city, I mean?"

"It's been ten years."

"What? You haven't left in a decade?"

"I don't make enough to go anywhere."

I realized how lame that sounded the moment it was out of my mouth. If I could afford the occasional meal at his restaurant, I could afford a tank of gas to take me to D.C. or at least as far as Charlottesville.

Rather than question my argument, however, he surprised me by asking, "What would you say if I asked you to come with me when I returned?" My breath halted in my throat. I was unable to speak as I fought off tears. A truth that isn't a lie. I need a truth to tell him that isn't a lie. "I would love it if I could go back to the city with you," I told him. I hadn't realized that his arms had tensed around me until I gave my half-baked answer. He relaxed then with a sigh. "Thank you," he said.

I made certain every moment of that season with Landry was as perfect as it could be. During his days on, business flowed into Frost Knob from all points of the compass and ended up at his restaurant. I didn't have any power over the tables he got or how much he was tipped, of course, but on the nights he worked the place was packed. On his days off, however, every highway leading to the mountaintop playground took on forbidding, unwelcome shadows and skiers who lingered too close to the treelines felt something watching them, a natural menace they couldn't explain, but which sent them hurrying to their condos to pack up and head back for the city. I didn't want it to be a ghost town, that would have been bizarre and upsetting to Landry, but I needed him to myself and didn't want him called in to wait tables because Gearhead got too busy. I'd also spent too much time in the village and the migraines I suffered at exposure to the development there worsened each time I visited. It was like an allergy on overdrive, like a poison taken in gradually larger doses until a lethal toxicity is nearly reached.

I begged off from staying in those free hotel rooms, but never once suggested that we go to my place. Landry didn't question me about it outright, but I could tell he thought this strange and he had every right.

"I live in a shack," I told him. "An honest to God hillbilly shack."

"Don't tell me. With an outhouse?"

"Three." I neglected to mention that they were no longer used and that my farmhouse had two perfectly usable bathrooms.

"What's the third one for?"

"The third one?"

"One for boys, one for girls. What's the third one for?"

"Around here? Lord only knows," I said.

And the topic was dropped, at least momentarily. I can't say why I didn't want to bring Landry home. Instinctively, I sensed there was danger for us there. From what, I couldn't say, but I knew it the way I knew where to find the missing boy who wandered off in early February, leaving the safety of his parents' condominium before the sun came up.

One afternoon I observed Landry scribble furiously on napkin after napkin he yanked from the dispenser on the window bar at Starbucks. Our seats looked out on the heart of the village. It was one of our favorite spots. That day, however, Landry was deep into his own head, inspired in a way I had never seen him before.

"What is that stuff?" I asked about his writings.

"When they let me go, after I was forced to train my Pindladoor replacement that was, they took away my whole life in the name of profit," he said. "I've been searching for a way to take that profit away from them, and this," he stabbed violently at the latest in his series of napkins with a happy, mad-computer-programmer gleam in his eye, "just may be the way to do it. A new service that makes theirs obsolete!"

"I was wondering why you fled from the city to our fair metropolis," I said.

He looked up at me then, really hearing me for the first time in half an hour. I saw that gleam in his eye wink out and die like a cheap light bulb from China. He stared at me, reluctance on his lips, and said nothing. The silence progressed until it was close to awkwardness. Then more than a dozen non-tourists, most in sheriff and rescue uniforms, rushed by our window. Next came a flurry of civilians, among them a fellow waiter Landry recognized from the restaurant.

Landry rapped on our window, calling the waiter's attention. The man pushed open the coffee bar's front door and leaned inside.

"Hey, Landry."

"What's up?" Landry asked.

"A kid's gone missing from Mogulmonkey." Mogulmonkey was a townhouse-style condo complex adjacent to the resort's snowtube park.

"They think he's been abducted, but they're mounting a search anyway," the waiter said.

Landry looked stricken.

"Okay," he said. "We'll be right there."

He hurriedly crammed his notes into his pockets and then grabbed me by the hand. I barely had time to lunge for my purse before I found myself rushing along with the others toward a command post erected under an E-Z UP tent outside the administrative offices. SUVs filled with searchers pulled up as if in a precision driving drill and two women dashed out of the admin building with stacks of photocopied photos of the boy. Radios squawked all over the parking lot.

"Landry, slow down a minute," I said. "Landry."

As if suddenly aware that he clutched my hand fiercely in his, he stopped so hard on the ice I skidded into him.

"Sorry. Do you want to go back to Starbucks and wait for me?" I studied his expression, trying to figure him out.

"No, of course not. You know how well I know this area. I want to help. It's just that—"

"Good girl," he said, squeezing my hand. We continued our sprint toward the command post.

He finally released me once he reached the line-up dividing the volunteers into search parties. I backed away into the trees. Landry didn't even notice. If the boy was still in my territory, I could find him. I only needed a moment.

Most people think of the forest as an insensate thing, but it feels just like the rest of us. I closed my eyes and touched the nearest spruce. The trees were frightened, absorbing the child's own terror and sending it outward in waves. They told me what I needed to know. Confused by the pre-dawn mist, the boy had walked off a cliff. When I returned to the E-Z UP, Landry already had our search assignment. He showed me our section of grid on the map. I shook my head.

"Who has that?" I pointed at an area well beyond the last black diamond run.

"No one, I think," he said.

"I think that would be the best place to look." Vertical lines appeared between his eyebrows and his lips turned down.

"Why?"

"There's an old mine down there."

"A mine. What kid would want to check out a mine in the middle of February?"

Landry was right. Besides, the mine was actually securely boarded and miles from where I sensed the boy at this very moment dropping exhausted into a shaded ice bank, immobile and curling into a fetal ball.

"Please, Landry," I said. "I have a hunch."

He sighed. "All right."

He went to speak to the search coordinator. A few minutes later we were in my Tracker, bombing down an officially closed road on the backside of the mountain. Snow heaped on the road in two- to four-foot drifts, and beneath that, rock-hard berms crisscrossed both lanes. As testament to the strangely grim mood affecting Landry, he made no mention of the road's condition or my outrageous driving. I saw a torment in him I didn't like. My sole concerns were to rescue the boy and relieve Landry's unexplained suffering.

Once we reached the only route accessible to us I knew we were even farther from the child than we had been at the top of the mountain. We'd find his bloody footprints in the snow approximately four and a half miles to the north-northeast.

How would I direct Landry where we needed to go without drawing his suspicion? As he trudged forward into the calf-high snow, I hesitated at the side of the road and glanced up at the sun's position in the sky. We wouldn't reach our destination before dark and Landry, as strong as I knew him to be, didn't have the energy to make it to the boy's side before nightfall. No one did.

What does it sound like when you're struck by lightning? People who imagine the event often think that the unlucky victim hears a crash, a bang, something on the order of a sonic boom, a fiery crackle from God's own hand. In reality it's nothing like that. The last thing you hear before you die is a simple *click*.

That's what Landry heard next. Behind his back, I lifted my hands to the sunny blue and whispered a single word.

Landry cried out, not in pain, but surprise. For a split second the skies over my miles and miles of territory went totally dark.

"What was—"

The borrowed light caught him in the breastbone like a lance as he turned to ask me if I'd just seen what he'd seen, a moment's pitch black.

He staggered back, gasping like a fish who has suddenly learned to breathe, and clutched at his chest. A second after that he sucked in a deep, confident breath. His cramped shoulders pushed down and back and he stood taller. His head came up, a near-delirious smile lighting his face, truly from within. His eyes and his cheeks warmed with a healthy, sure glow. He had no idea what had happened to him, wouldn't even be certain that something had happened to him, but he liked it.

I pretended frustration. "I'm sorry, Landry, now that we're down here, I'm not sure which way to go. All these trees and no path."

He turned in the direction we needed to go, beckoning me to follow. "Don't worry. This way."

His legs carved unfailingly through virgin snow crust, covering ground at a pace that I hoped he wouldn't compare to normal speeds. I also prayed he wouldn't wonder how I could possibly keep up with him. The light inside him touched the salt cedars as we swept past and the trees told the light inside him what it needed to know.

By twilight, he knelt by the crumpled body in its hollow of ice.

I gasped when I saw the boy, lips dark as frozen blueberries and his right foot nearly cut in half from his fall onto rocks at the bottom of the cliff. How had he managed to march so far with his foot flapping the wrong way at every step?

Humans amaze me, I thought with wonder.

The boy whimpered. Landry scooped him up and we took off at a run. At first Landry led the way unerringly back to the car as the child grew quieter and colder. Halfway there, though, we knew we were losing him. Landry ran faster, then began to wheeze, the light inside him rapidly leaking away. Not only did he slow dangerously, but—

"I don't remember which way," he said, faltering.

"I do," I prompted gently. "I remember."

I practically had to drag them. When Landry broke through the final knife-sharp stretch of ice between us and the car, he tripped and crashed to his knees, almost dropping the boy in his weariness.

This momentary weakness put a fear in him I didn't understand. He hugged the boy tighter to his chest, cradled him.

"Got you, got you, got you," he crooned, a mantra.

"Landry," I said.

"Got you, got you, got you."

I repeated his name. He didn't hear me. He let go of the boy with one hand and raised the hand to cover his eyes in a universal expression of anguish. The woods around us, previously lit by the light shining through him, dimmed. His golden skin grew as dusky as the twilight.

In the dark I said, "You have a son."

"Had," he answered. "A son."

"What happened?"

"My wife . . . . "

"Won't let you see him?"

"They're dead."

"Oh, Landry."

"It was after I lost my job. I didn't understand how much it affected her. The foreclosure, the prospect of living on the street. The house was hers originally. It had been in her family for generations. I didn't pay enough attention," he said. "I think she felt trapped. I think that was why she did it."

"What?"

He dropped his hand from his eyes and the sun looked up at me, with clouds in the way.

"Fire," he said. "She chose fire."

Though the boy's unexpected and miraculous return stunned the rescue crews, Landry never expressed doubts about how we managed to reach the boy in time, much less find him at all. Almost a week after we rushed the child to paramedics and his hysterical family, the event was old news. I believe Landry regretted his confession to me about his family and his part in their deaths and didn't want that day brought up again. I wished many times he would revive the topic so I could reassure him, but he never did.

We picked up our old routines. Though I was in agony much of the time, I joined him enthusiastically again in our pilfered luxury condos. March came, then April, but the slopes remained white and deep. Spring skiing season didn't want to end. Everyone at the resort remarked about the freakishly long season that looked as though it might stretch into May. It wouldn't. I had limits and should have known the forest wouldn't let me tamper much longer. It wanted to wake, to get the growing season up and running. Summers are pathetically short here, and the land needed every sunny or thunderously rainy day it could harvest from the sky.

On the last Sunday in April, we spent several hours hiking the Greenbrier Trail, reclaimed land along the Greenbrier River on which the C &. O Railroad used to transport timber and coal and isolated Appalachian families to the big city. Landry snapped photo after digital photo of Dutchman's breeches, bloodroot, Jack-in-the-pulpit, and trilliums that grew by the river, every wildflower sparkling with droplets that condensed out of the mist. Afterward, hungry, we stopped at a gas station that sold pizza and biscuits in its convenience store.

I knew the store well, because the owner was my neighbor nearly an hour away in Cherry Lick. I didn't like Vernice McCalder and she had been antagonistic with me from the day I moved into Ariel's place. She wouldn't admit it, but I suspected that the two of them had had a thing for each other. She'd probably been expecting to inherit his place.

"How much do you want?" Landry asked as he pulled my Tracker up to the pump.

"Better fill it," I said. "It's a long way back to the resort. I'll get us something to eat."

At the back of the store I chose a pizza from one of the two or three habitually boxed and waiting in the glassed warming oven, plus a couple of bottled teas out of the cooler.

"You know the only difference between a Methodist and Baptist, don't you?" an old farmer said to another man I recognized and knew dug wells for a living. His listener didn't answer.

"Methodists can read."

Both men chuckled. Incredibly, though his audience didn't grow, and no significant conversation had occurred in between, the farmer told the same joke a second time just seconds later. I tried to shut out their voices, but still heard the two laugh softly and mindlessly as if the joke were fresh.

I set the pizza box and drinks on the counter and reached into my purse for my wallet, when, as if caught in a time loop, the farmer by the beer nuts clapped his companion on the shoulder, and sucked in a breath to begin again.

"You know the only difference between a—"

I nearly bolted from the store. Vernice stopped me. At her post behind the counter, she'd faced the pumps, observing Landry filling up my gas tank. Now she turned and set something on the counter so she could take my money, which I realized I gripped convulsively in my fist. I looked down and saw what she'd been holding, a partially completed plastic canvas picture of a teddy bear holding a balloon that read W.W.J.D? *What Would Jesus Do?* Smoker's lines around her mouth puckered as she studied me.

"Not a good idea," she said, gaze flicking toward Landry. "Ariel would know better."

I was stunned. She *knew*. She'd always known what I was.

"Ariel played bondage games with his vegetables and then hung himself in his barn," I said. "Is he really an example to follow?"

"I'm warning you," Vernice said. "Don't use cuss words in my store, Carly."

I struggled to locate the expletive in my previous two sentences. "Bondage? Since when is that a swear word?"

She hissed at the repetition of the word and clutched her plastic stitchery to her breast. "God bless you, child. I'll pray for you at revival tonight."

"Please don't," I said and slammed out the door.

I have never since felt the way I did the night before Landry was due to leave. I understood my power better then than I had in all the years I'd possessed it. Loneliness is a fearsome enemy. Humans can stand any number of setbacks—poverty, starvation, the worst pain their bodies can inflict, homelessness, disaster, the moment before death, and the centuries upon centuries of life that remain once a loved one is gone forever. They can weather it and emerge from under the sledgehammer of it all as long they have one thing. Someone to go through it with them. Even if that person is not kind to them, they know at least that they are not alone.

What would you do if you were the last person on Earth? I know what I would do: shoot myself the instant I was certain no one else remained alive. Would I stop to write an epitaph? Something that extraterrestrial archeologists might discover thousands of millennia from now? Hell no. Over and done with. B'bye.

What would you do, however, if dragged off to an environment that was too different from your own for you to ever be happy? Not strange enough to make life impossible, but filled with a people whose mindset was so alien from yours that you would never, as long as you lived, find yourself laughing honestly again, had to guard who you were from them, censor everything you said or did, had no one, absolutely no one to talk to or walk with or run to when life was crap and something devastating happened? What if you knew you would never see home again?

Then, by miracle, a piece of home comes to you, not just a sliver or a suggestion or an empty memory, but a huge, comforting, bathrobe-sized piece of it. it wraps you up in its remembered cocoon. You sink back into its warmth, hug its security around you and for the first time in years you breathe the type of sigh that signals everything is right with your world.

That was Landry to me. Home and much more. If he and I had discovered each other before the earthquake, I never would have ended up in this breathtaking dump called Cherry Lick.

He expected me to go with him the next morning. We'll do this when we get back, Carly. We'll do that. *The start-up will take a lot of work at first, but you don't have to worry that I'll neglect you. I'll make certain we have ail the time we need together. I'll never lose track of us.*

I heard echoes of the tragedy with his wife and son, but I also heard the beginnings of something real for us. You can't fool the breeze that carries the words your heart speaks. It ferries your soul across spaces open or closed and not even the sturdiest door can keep it out. Only you can refuse to hear it. That is one of humankind's strongest powers, the ability to not hear another's heart.

I heard his heart. I knew my own. I couldn't go and I couldn't tell him why. I could change the course of floods, ask a valiant, forgotten apple tree to sacrifice itself so the forest could reclaim its place, calm a frenzied owl before it shredded its wing on a barbed-wire fence, but I couldn't face the man I loved and tell him good-bye.

Is it any wonder I did what I did?

Blinding rain savaged my mountains that night. Storms bloated the creeks, sent torrents of frigid mud sweeping down into the hollows. Below my farmhouse, the Greenbrier roared. Water sheeted from my chin. Ropes of it snaked across my breasts and down my arms.

I stood motionless in the downpour until I lost track of time. My teeth began to chatter and my skin grew icy.

It's time, I thought.

I sank my hand into my own chest and pulled out my heart.

For several minutes I held it, studying it without amazement, simply staring. It was a ghostly version, still pumping and bleeding ephemeral red mist. I hurled it at the ground with all the anger inside of me.

It hit, a sick thud that terrified the oaks nearby. The thing burrowed into the earth with lightning intelligence, planting itself. In my mind, I could see the thick tree roots under my feet recoiling at the bloody apparition's intrusion into their space. Within seconds, the invader anchored itself in the rocky soil. Less than a minute later it swelled and sprouted spectral mycelium as thick as my wrist, root-like structures snaking outward in all directions, handless forearms that grew and grew. They carried a red river of loneliness, thickening with it until they became as big around as second-year sycamores, then century maples, then old growth behemoths.

Around me trees thrashed in the wind, like waves crashing on invisible rocks. I sensed but could no longer feel my actual, physical heart continuing to beat. The center of me was calm. I was the eye, and storms seen and unseen raged along stalled fronts that would not move as long as I wanted to keep them in place.

Standing in the rain, I breathed quietly and waited. At last the voracious growth slammed up against my territory's boundaries and could go no further. A bloody fairy-ring hundreds of square miles in size lay under all and everything I controlled. Following nature, the phantom mycelium made a ninety-degree turn upward. Spores exploded from the ground, red, pulsing, veined lightballs that no longer resembled my heart, but carried a piece of it in each. One for every person who needed to leave.

Only I could see as they sought their targets, the cheerful hearts of the tourists, the thoughtless ones, musing ones, cruel ones, careless, self-involved, loving and hateful, thousands of hearts spinning in their own individual orbits suddenly touched by the unstoppable panic and fear I fought off daily.

"Go home," I said. "Now."

Turned and walked back to my farmhouse.

I stripped off my wet clothes. I curled up on the living room sofa under a blanket I had knit myself from wool purchased from a neighbor and watched television, mindless reality TV. Thunder made the house shiver and mountains cower. Though the village square at Frost Knob swam in frigid water, the asphalt along Route 219 was dry and welcoming. Rain clouds spared each and every road leading away.

Wouldn't want any accidents, would I? It would only delay their flight. It wasn't just the resort's residents I sent packing, however. My fairy-ring found all who weren't already firmly rooted here, those with the luxury of escape.

I smiled bitterly. A part of my mind watched the melee from afar, half zipped suitcases spilling clothing as they were flung into the backs of SUVs, condo and cabin doors left gaping, car doors barely closed before tires spun. Another part of my brain watched a woman on TV in a dirty bathing suit forcing down a bowl of live sand crabs. Arguments and altercations flared here and there throughout the rain-streaked Alleghenies, but they were soon overrun by the group gestalt, that primitive back brain drive to flee, lemmings to the sea of city lights awaiting them.

My forest cried. I apologized to it, assured it that this horrible human storm would blow over by dawn, but it cried. I no longer felt the loneliness. I'd given it all away. No other emotion took its place.

Please, the forest begged. I didn't understand. I couldn't be hurting it. I *was* the forest. I could only hurt the body to which it clung.

I thought about that. Ariel and his rope flashed in my mind, a vision opening before me with the gaiety of a Hallmark card pulled from its envelope. But not rope. I threw off the blanket and ran outside again into the deluge.

"Carly!" I heard Landry shout from uphill near the farmhouse. "Carly!" I shut out his voice. I made the thousands upon thousands of wildly beating hearts rage in my ears as cars hurtled along dark two-lane highways. I laughed. I laughed, cold, wet laughter with the tang of too many dead years, too much of my soul drained out of me. Joyless laughter smothered by the winds whipping the river in front of me.

I can ask the river to help me, I thought. I don't have to do it myself.

"Carly." I sighed, let all the breath out of my lungs as I prepared to command the black blanket lapping at my toes to reach up and let me sleep next to Mother Earth.

"Carly, stop it." His voice just steps behind me. "Carly." His hands on my shoulders. Turning me around. Making me look up into his face. He was afraid, of me or for me, I didn't know.

"Stop it."

"Stop what?"

"I know what you're doing."

"Doing."

"This. However you're driving them out. Stop it."

"I'm not."

"I know you are."

"How did you find me?"

"The woman at the store, the one you had words with. Now, stop. Someone's going to get hurt."

"I'm hurt."

"I know, honey."

He reached out to wrap me naked in his arms, but I stepped back up to my calves in the rushing water.

"You don't know anything," I shouted.

"I know. I've known for weeks."

"You don't know me."

"The blizzard you predicted, the wolves, the way we found that kid. Did you think I didn't realize what you did to me that day?"

"I didn't do anything."

"The gifts, Carly. Did you think I didn't see the gifts? At first I thought it was just some freak of nature, one perfect berry, an acorn, a single amazing feather left every morning we woke up together, right at our door. But then I saw them leaving them for you. Saw them making their offerings."

I'd forgotten about the gifts months ago. They still came, one every morning since I'd woken in the barn beneath a corpse, but I'd stopped looking at them. It had been years since I appreciated them.

"Landry, I—"

Like ripples in a pool, spreading outward from where I stood, the ghosts of my heart abruptly departed. They lifted from the thousands upon thousands of bodies they controlled, drifting upward into the night, thinning into nothingness the way smoke, gray and curling, disappears above a bonfire. I felt the people I'd wanted to chase away slow and regain their senses. I heard their pulses wind down. Clouds broke off their assault on the land. Skies cleared and leaves dripped.

Landry grabbed for and hauled me out of the river.

"I can't go with you," I told him. "I want to go, but I can't."

"What? Of course you can."

"No."

He started to protest further, ask why. He thought he knew what I was, but he didn't. So I spread my arms, and as I did, he saw what held me, who I really was.

I was never naked in my forest. My skin was my gown, bark thick and gnarled as hickories born before Thomas Jefferson made his brave journeys over the mountains from Virginia. Honeysuckle vines caressed and strangled my throat. Branchlets budded and flowered over and over again from my fingertips. I felt that pain and struggle of unending birth, quiet death. My head was pulled back viciously by my hair, grown over the years until it became trapped inside a hurl that hung behind my shoulders in the shape of a hood. Heavy, unyielding roots encased my thighs and ankles, hiding everything human in their drapes and folds. Larger, more intricate, thousands of times greater than the roots of the fairy-ring, they traveled out to touch every last growing thing in the mountains I protected.

Landry uttered a small, stunned noise. He fought for words, but to his credit, he didn't run. "Which one is the illusion?" he asked at last.

What he witnessed melted away to leave me the way he expected. The forest stopped weeping and I began. He watched me for several seconds and I had no idea what he was thinking.

"I don't know anymore." He picked me up and took me into the house, to my bed.

"Carly." He lay down next to me, wrapped us in the quilt that covered the bed, dried my face and thumbed away my tears with his gentle hands.

"I want to go," I said. "I'm so tired of being here."

"Shh," he whispered. "Let me take the pain away."

It was our last time together, so I gave him control. I trusted him to take me all the places I'd wanted so badly to go. I had dominion over the lonely places, but he owned all the rest, far, golden realms I barely remembered, open, noisy, crowded, landscapes dirty yet lived in, wanton human vistas set to a rhythm that lived for itself and thought of no one else, as we thought of no one. For one night. Just this one night they were mine, too. I was homesick, but he took it and spun my ache into pleasure. My desire for release became his reason. He sought redemption inside me. We were warmth and blistering heat, solace and cure for things that can never be completely healed. I dragged every memory of his world from behind the shutters in his eyes, distant sights and sounds that clung to the planes and angles of his face. My lips tasted everything he would see the next day, creative genius and traffic, jealousy and elevators, tandoori chicken, glittering storefronts, smog, and new hope. We were flesh on flesh on flesh and twining urgencies. We ate the moment whole. We gorged. We stole tomorrow out from under our feet and strained to keep it there with us as long as we could. Pushed. Clung. Rocked it between us. "Give me," he said. I gave.

"*Give* me."

I gave him everything that I had and was.

"Let it go, Carly."

I shared everything I knew and didn't, the pain, the power. "Let it all go!" he cried at the exact moment we touched perfection.

Light harsher and more cleansing than if I had borrowed a day's worth of sun blinded me. I closed my eyes and threw my head back. Ecstasy swept through me like heated syrup. A flash burn of relieved joy prickled the damp skin at my throat, the tender insides of my wrists. Landry cried out. At first I thought it was delight, but then as physical saturation turned to scorching pain, I knew something was wrong. I looked at Landry. The light around us continued to flare so brightly my shocked retinas saw only the black form of a man outlined by a corona.

"Landry!"

My back arched in surprise, my body suddenly not my own. I felt as if someone stuck a spoon into the back of my throat and dug out something that clung there fiercely by its roots. I struggled, gagging, shuddering uncontrollably, it went on and on until I knew I'd gotten the wish I'd made down by the river. Oblivion. Landry collapsed heavily atop me, his weight too much for me this close to death.

I blacked out.

It wasn't even dawn. No sunlight filtered into my room when I felt someone sit down beside me on the bed. I wanted to wake and speak, see if Landry was okay, if I had hurt him when we made love, but as hard as I tried I couldn't sit up. I didn't even have the strength to open my eyes.

"Sleep more," I mumbled.

"Sleep more," Landry agreed.

Minutes or hours later, I found myself being carried fully clothed outside. Heard gravel crunching under Landry's feet. Smelled the dew beginning to settle. I struggled to open my eyes, managed brief slits before the effort taxed me completely. Still dark.

"What's wrong?" I said, "It's not morning yet."

"Hush, little one," he said. He settled me in the passenger's seat of the Tracker, buckled my seat belt, and tucked the sleep-tousled hair that had fallen into my face behind my ear. "I want to show you something."

I drifted in and out as the car sped along. Why did I feel so strange? Why was I trapped in sleep? I dreamed I felt weak, weaker than I had felt in eight years, but also lighter, like someone who had lost fifty pounds surviving a deadly illness. As if I was unbothered by gravity. I could spring up stairs, climb like an eight-year-old, run and run until I fell down panting and laughing in the grass somewhere with . . . .

"Landry?" I found myself on my feet, standing next to the Tracker. What was going on? Landry passed his hand over my eyes and, slowly, I was able to open them. Disoriented, I didn't recognize where we were at first. I turned in a circle and realized we were at the farthest edge of my territory, where the forest touched the frontage road leading to the Interstate. I hadn't dared try and come this far in years.

"What is it? Why are we here?" I asked. "What did you want to show me?"

"Freedom," he said.

"What?"

I gazed up into his face. Lit by the rising sun, his eyes held pure wildness. Their feral mysteries confused me. His skin gave off the scent of bark and the musty fullness of birch leaves in May.

"Oh, God. *No.*"

He gestured at the Tracker behind me, loaded with packed suitcases and boxes of possessions, all of them mine.

"This is as far as I can take you. I can't go any farther than this. You understand, don't you?"

Panic filled my chest, my heart stuttered, but the anxiety, the strangling call of the mountains, the crushing weight on my chest were missing. I was so many things at once. Dazed, bereft, outraged, sad, lightheaded. I could breathe.

"The pain," I said.

He playfully touched his finger to the tip of my nose. "Gone," he said.

But I saw the grimace of pain tightening the corners of his own eyes, freezing the humor that once lived there.

Seconds after he stepped back from our last kiss I could still savor him, like a wine's finish. Within his aftertaste were two things, utter shock at a loneliness too heavy for any human to bear, and a regret to which he would never admit, the loss of his dream to build a new life in the city.

He turned toward the forest on foot.

"Landry," I cried and ran after him. "Landry!"

His trees cloaked him before I was more than a few steps into the wilderness. "Landry!" I cried again, frantic.

I stumbled on, but I couldn't read the branches or the leaves. The oaks no longer answered me and the breeze was just a breeze. Soon an unfamiliar feeling rooted itself at the back of my neck. Fear. Like the thousands I had sent fleeing the night before, I looked at the shadows and primitive hysteria flowered. Landry was responsible. My power had jumped to him, leaving me without the ability to fight him.

I came to a halt in a small clearing. No matter how much I tried,

I couldn't get my feet to take me deeper into the forest. He barred my way, forcing me toward escape and the bright new life his sacrifice was buying me.

In the center of the clearing stood a single white dogwood in full bloom. As I watched, the sun topped the evergreens and a ray of light reached the lonely tree.

"Landry," I said a final time.

My voice triggered a shower of white petals that floated back and forth lazily to the ground. When every last petal lay on the moss below, one of them unexpectedly fluttered up into the air. Not a petal, but a tiny bird. It flew toward me.

"I love you," it whispered as it passed.

Performed last fall not long after its publication, **Claudia O'Keefe**'s "A Maze of Trees" received a Book-It Repertory Theatre-style reading in Washington State. Her short fiction and nonfiction has appeared in *The Magazine of Fantasy and Science Fiction*, Salon.com, *Writers on the Range, American Libraries*, and *The World* in 2005, as well as numerous anthologies. She is the 2004 recipient of the Shell Economist Prize for essay. Among her five books are the novel *Black Snow Days*, and family-themed anthologies, *Mother, Forever Sisters*, and *Father,* which include original fiction by Winston Groom, Whitney Otto, Marilyn French, Jonathan Kellerman, Caroline Leavitt, and Joyce Carol Oates, among others.

THE SHADOWED HEART

Catherine Asaro

The colony Daretown on the planet Thrice Named, in the Year 2276

Night protected him. He ventured out only after the sun had set. Then he sifted through the ruins, searching for pieces of himself. Surely the parts of his soul he had lost were buried in this debris. A technology park had stood here before the Radiance War, but all that remained were shards of dichromesh glass, melted Luminex, and mounds of casecrete.

Once he had been a Jagernaut, a starfighter pilot. Harrick, they had called him. He and Blackwing, his jag fighter, had been one mind. Together, they blended with the rest of his squadron. Four pilots and four ships; they were a team without equal, able to deal with space combat in a way normal humans could never manage. That was why Jagernauts were empaths: they linked minds during battle. The difficult decision to send empaths into combat came from the desperate need of his people to counter the stronger forces of their enemies, the Traders. Nothing could match the versatility of a jag squadron. They lived, breathed, and fought together.

And when they died, they died together.

Except Harrick had survived. His ship had crashed, and he had crawled out of the wreckage into these ruins. He had stayed here ever since, looking for the pieces of his lost soul.

Rhose had wandered too far in her search. She had promised her family that she would bring back a supply of "remnants," energy sources from vehicles or spacecraft that had crashed during the war. When scavenged, they could provide heat and light for a house. The remnants near their home had all been taken, so she had ventured farther than usual, out here to what had once been a thriving technology park but now stretched into a smashed, desolate landscape.

As the sun set behind the broken towers, she sought refuge in a building with no roof. Most of the walls had fallen into rubble, but in one corner they reached above her head. The batteries in her lamp had failed, and like so much else in Daretown, her spares hadn't worked, either. With the sky overcast, she didn't have starlight. She doubted she could walk the twenty kilometers back in the dark, and after dark, gangs roved the outskirts of Daretown. Law hadn't broken down in the town, but at night certain areas were best avoided. Although she had a stun gun to protect herself, it would probably be safer to stay here for now and walk back to Daretown in the morning.

Rhose wished she had a comm to let her family know she was all right. Their old one had broken a month ago, and no one in town had new ones. Nor did her family have access to a vehicle. She couldn't even get equipment for her school. Daretown had never been affluent and now its people were barely surviving. It wasn't unheard of for a colonist to be out for the entire night, but she knew her family would fear the worst, that she had been kidnapped or murdered. Rhose shivered as she settled into the corner amid the hard chunks of casecrete. At least the gangs never came to these ruins, which were far from the city and supposedly haunted with cybernetic monstrosities.

Night fell gradually and left her in an oppressive darkness. When she held up her hands, she could make out their shape but little else. Cold seeped past her layers of sweaters and leggings. She folded her arms around her body and wedged herself farther back among the broken casecrete. Night lasted thirty hours at this time of year, which meant it was going to get a lot colder. She could sleep, wake, and sleep again before dawn lightened the world. She rummaged in a pocket of her outermost sweater. Good. Her meat roll and water tube were there. Although she would have to ration her food and she would be ravenous by morning, she wouldn't starve.

A cry echoed through the ruins.

"Saints," Rhose muttered. The wail sounded like an animal, but she couldn't be certain. She breathed in deeply. She had a curious sensation, as if she was aware of a disturbance in the air, yet she didn't hear, smell, or feel anything. She told herself that she had no need to worry about military assaults or land mines; the defending and invading ships had all destroyed each other in space. The enemy strikes against Daretown had come from orbit, a spiteful assault on a colony of civilians no one had any reason to attack.

Debris clinked across the room.

Rhose froze. She strained to hear, but the night had gone quiet. Too quiet. She hadn't realized how many whirs and clicks saturated the air until the tiny creatures that populated the ruins stopped their serenade.

"Who's there?" she asked.

No answer.

It's nothing, she told herself. Machine monsters didn't stalk this bleak place. Those were stories to frighten children.

Metal clinked.

She closed her fist around a chunk of casecrete and peered into the darkness. She couldn't see anything. With her other hand, she drew the taser from one of her sweater pockets. Bracing her arms on a boulder, she rose to her feet.

A scrape.

The noise seemed about twenty paces away, but she had no idea if it was friend or foe, alive or machine, big or small. If only she could see. An army of biomech creatures could be hulking out here, unnaturally silent in their mechanized lives. For all she knew, she was about to die.

A deep voice rumbled. "Who are you?"

So. It was a man. He spoke Skolian Flag, a common language taught many places and designed so that the disparate peoples of their far-flung settlements could communicate.

She switched into Flag. "I'm Rhose."

A light appeared—and revealed a stranger. He was huge, over two heads taller than she and at least twice her weight His arms strained the ragged cloth of his body-shirt. His face was hard to see with his hand partly covering his sphere-lamp, and also because of his dark, tangled hair. His clothes were black: a tattered shirt, form-fitting trousers, and heavy boots. A huge gun was holstered at his hip. He stood with his legs braced apart, a giant defending his territory.

Rhose spoke under her breath. "Gods almighty."

His heavy accent gave his words a harsh quality. "You aren't welcome. Leave."

Rhose wished she could leave, and fast. He was blocking the ragged opening she had used to climb in here. With the wall at her back and no light, she had only one option to get out: squeeze past him.

"I don't mean any trouble." Rhose inched along the wall, then stopped when she hit a pile of rubble. "I won't bother you."

Incredibly, he jerked as if she had threatened him just by moving forward. He lifted his glowing sphere, and light leaked around his large hand. He had long fingers, gnarled and slashed with either scars or recently healed wounds. She thought she saw injuries on his forearms, too, through the rips of his shirt.

"You're hurt," she said. "Did one of the gangs catch you?" She had thought they never came out this far.

He answered tightly. "If only."

If only? She couldn't imagine why he would say such a thing. Something was wrong here, something worse than marauding gangs.

"Do you need medical help?" she asked. Given the limited resources in the city, she often ended up treating children in the school.

"No." Gruffly, he added, "Your voice is shaking."

"It's cold. And it's too dark for me to go anywhere." *And I'm afraid of you.*

"Come over here." He sounded oddly reluctant. "Let me get a look at you."

Rhose edged forward, still holding the rock and taser, picking her way through the rubble. He watched intently, his hand clenched on the glowing sphere. She *felt* his troubled spirit. Although she couldn't tell what bothered him, it disquieted her that she could pick up so much.

Granted, she had always been good at reading people, but her awareness of him went beyond her usual sensitivity.

As she drew nearer, she noticed he was clean shaven. That he removed his beard despite living here suggested he wasn't normally a derelict.

She stopped in front of him. "Better?"

"Yes."

"Do you want me look at your injuries?"

"No."

"You've nothing to fear from me." Then she realized how bizarre that sounded, that a man of his size and obvious strength could possibly fear such a wisp of a woman.

"What do you want here?" he asked.

"Shelter," she said.

He didn't answer, but his silence had a different quality now, more thoughtful. She had always been a good judge of people's character and emotions, and her sense of his moods was even stronger than usual. It seemed tangible.

"Night here lasts a long time," he said.

Rhose blinked. The night was the night. It never varied much, only a few hours longer in winter than in summer.

"I guess," she said.

"You shouldn't have to freeze or starve because of that."

Rhose doubted she would do either. She didn't understand him. Nor did she know what to make of his monstrous gun. She wasn't even certain it was real. But it told her a great deal about him that his first concern, even when he didn't want her here, was for her wellbeing.

"I'll be all right." She kept her voice soothing, the way she might talk to a spooked cat. Humans had brought felines to this terraformed world, but since the war many had become homeless and gone wild—perhaps like this man.

In a low voice, he muttered, "Can't turn away someone in need."

Some of her tension eased. "What is your name?" she asked.

He watched her like a wild animal ready to bolt. "Harrick."

"My greetings, Harrick." She started to lift her hand, then realized she still held the rock. Although she stopped, it wasn't soon enough, and she accidentally brushed his frayed sleeve. He jerked away, but not before she saw the network of recent scars, puckered and red, that covered his arm, as if shattered glass had scored his skin.

"Saints," she murmured. "Who attacked you?"

"Don't ask." He regarded her with eyes as black as everything else about him, including his mood. Then he closed his hand around her hand, his large palm enveloping her fist with the rock. "Unless you plan to do so?"

"No." She kept the taser in her other hand down by her side. She had little doubt he knew she held the stun gun.

"Have you come to bedevil me?" he asked. "To make me think angels of redemption exist?" His words were ragged, but beneath their edge, his voice had a cultured, well-educated quality.

Rhose was acutely aware of his hand on hers. "If I'm an angel, I'm a terribly behaved one. I sleep late and I hate cleaning up." She knew she was talking too fast. "And I'm absent-minded."

He lowered his arm, still holding her hand. Then he abruptly let go of her, as if he had just realized what he was doing. Rhose dropped the rock, and it clattered on the ground at her feet.

"Are you cold?" he asked.

She pulled her sweaters tighter. "More so by the minute."

"Ah, hell," he said. "All right. You can stay with me. But you must leave in the morning."

Rhose waited for the fear to come, her anxiety about staying with someone who looked so dangerous. Instead she felt comforted to know she would be in his protection for the night. How she knew he meant her no harm, she had no idea. Was it something in his voice? His gestures and posture? His expressions? She couldn't say. It was as if she were picking it straight from his mind. But surely that couldn't be possible.

"Are you sure you don't mind if I stay?" she asked.

"If you promise not to shoot me with that gun of yours."

Startled, she smiled. "Fair enough."

"Well." His flush was visible even in the dim light. He stepped aside, making room for her to pass.

Harrick lived in another toppled skyscraper. He had built a lean-to from scraps of metal and crammed it into a corner. His home had almost nothing inside, just water tubes, vending-robot food, and a blanket. The slanted ceiling was so low, Rhose could barely stand up straight. Harrick squeezed in behind her, bending over, and used up what little space remained.

"It is small in here." He sounded embarrassed.

"Yes." Rhose was aware of his closeness. She noticed his well-built physique and the way his muscles strained his clothes. It was hard to make out his face in the dim light, but what she saw of his rugged features appealed to her.

"I can stay outside," he offered.

Although she appreciated the offer, she knew he could freeze without shelter. Her fingers had gone numb from the cold already. "Don't do that," she said. "With us crowded in here, it will be warmer." A nervous tickle started in her throat. Maybe she was naïve to think she was safe.

"I won't hurt you," he said.

How did he know she was worried? Probably because it was the obvious conclusion. Oddly enough, though, he seemed more in danger from her than the reverse, though she wasn't sure why. She wondered if he was experiencing her moods, too. He reached her in some way she didn't understand.

"I need to sleep," he added. "I didn't during the day."

"You stayed awake for thirty-two hours?"

His face was lit with dim orange light from the lamp. "Yes."

"But why?"

"I can't—. When I sleep, it all—it comes back."

"It?" She felt as if she were floundering.

"Nothing." He sat down and stretched out on the cracked floor. "You can have the blanket."

Self-conscious, Rhose knelt next to him. "Harrick, are you all right?"

Normally in a circumstance like this, she would have been too scared even to ask much, but she already felt as if she knew him well. On impulse, she laid her hand on his arm. "Can I help?"

His voice roughened. "I'm fine." He pulled away his arm.

Rhose understood his unspoken message: *Don't push.* With constrained motions, she lay on the blanket. Although it cushioned the hard floor, it was still uncomfortable. No wonder he hadn't slept.

Only a few hand-spans separated them. She was so sensitized to his presence, his tension seemed palpable. She felt too wound up to sleep, too nervous about the situation.

After a while his breathing settled into the deeper rhythms of sleep. Her mind synchronized with his, drifting, drowsy . . . .

A cry yanked her awake. Someone was looming over her and panic filled the night. She couldn't see—she raised her hands to shield herself—they hit someone's chest—

"Harrick?" she asked with a quaver. "Is that you?"

His voice wrenched out of the dark. "Who?"

"It's Rhose." She sat up slowly, careful not to bump him. "Remember?"

A pause. "I remember."

"Did you have a bad dream?"

He answered softly. "Oh, yes."

She felt him hurting as if his pain were a physical presence. Reaching out, she brushed his sleeve. He jerked, but then he curled his hand around hers. A shiver went through her. She felt wary, on edge, yet she also felt a connection with him, somehow, as if they had sat together this way on many other nights. Her first response with a stranger would have been to pull away, but she felt his need for comfort too much to deny it.

He smelled of soap-bots, another reason she didn't think he was a vagrant. It couldn't have been easy to find such cleansers in these ruins. She shifted position so she was sitting against the wall with him. "If company helps, I'm here."

He bent his head and pressed his lips against her hair. "Thank you," he whispered. The intimacy of his gesture should have felt strange, but that, too, was somehow right. He soon dozed off, sitting next to her. He stirred often, but if she stroked his hand or his forehead, he calmed.

Eventually she slept as well.

His muscles hurt.

It was Harrick's first waking thought. The darkness felt close, but for once it wasn't oppressive. He figured out why his body ached; he had slept sitting up. According to the atomic clock of his internal biomech web, he had been out for seven hours, the longest unbroken sleep he had managed since his crash here twenty-six long days ago.

A woven sweater scraped his arm. What? He had no such clothes.

It all came back then, the girl in the ruins, a waif with large eyes and gold hair wisping around her cheeks. He hadn't wanted to bring her here, but now he was glad she had come. Her presence comforted him.

He put his arm around her shoulders and leaned his cheek against the top of her head. She sighed without waking up, her body settling against his. The sweetness of her presence touched him. He marveled that she gave him this trust, because he sure as hell hadn't earned it.

Holding Rhose, he became aware of her shapely form through her sweaters. For the first time since the crash, his body reacted to the thought of a woman. He knew he should send her away. Hell, he could walk her back to town. He wasn't certain they could find the place at night, though, even with his lamp. Or maybe he just wanted to stay here, with her. She smelled good, like flowers and cinnamon.

Harrick knew about Daretown from conversations he had overheard among the people who foraged in these ruins. The looters only came in daylight. He did nothing to discourage the tales about monsters that frequented this place at night, stories that may have started when people had glimpsed him wandering around. The more they feared the ruins, the greater his privacy.

Every time he thought of going back, of contacting ISC, of letting anyone know he had survived, a protective darkness came over his thoughts. His squad had died. Their ships had died. His own ship had died. He had no right to live. A numb shell encased him, like a glass prison he could see through but never escape.

Except Rhose had come inside the glass. She didn't even seem all that frightened of him. He slouched down, bracing his boot heels against the opposite wall, and held her in his arms. Before he even realized what he was doing, he had pressed his lips against her forehead.

Rhose stirred in her sleep. He ought to wake her, find out more about her. If she kept unsettling him this way, his emotional defenses would weaken. When he turned his head, he misjudged her position and his lips brushed her nose.

"Harrick?" she asked, drowsy.

"Eh?"

"How are you feeling?" she murmured, her eyes still closed.

"In a glass shell." He hadn't thought the words strange until he heard himself say them.

"A shell?" Her face was only about two handspans from his own, but he could just barely make out the shape in the dark. She touched his cheek. "You feel trapped in a dark place where your life is suspended."

A flush spread through him. "How do you know that?"

"I feel as if you are . . . part of me."

Part of him. They were linking as empaths. Once he had shared a link with three other people—until their violent deaths burned out his spirit Tonight, those had joined her mind with his, never realizing the miracle she brought him. She was a salve on his torment, or water filling the scorched emotional void where he used to be part of a four-way link.

He had found a piece of his soul.

Harrick knew he shouldn't push. But even as he warned himself to stop, to pull back, to wait, he was lowering his head. He found her lips, full and warm, and kissed her with a gentle hunger he hadn't believed he would ever feel again.

Rhose braced her palms against his chest. He immediately started to let her go, angry at himself for taking advantage of someone who had sought his protection.

Then, incredibly, her lips softened under his. His loneliness poured in then, released by the simple act of touching another human being. Not just anyone, but this lovely girl who affected him so deeply. His pulse surged and he laid her on the ground, on her back.

Rhose turned her head to the side. "Please, slow down."

He silently swore, though he didn't know if his oath was directed at himself, for mauling this vulnerable girl, or at her, for breaching his emotional defenses.

He pushed up on one elbow. "Why aren't you afraid of me?" he growled. If she feared him, it would be easier to keep his distance. Then he would be less vulnerable to her. "You should be, you know. I have enhanced speed, strength, and reflexes, a microfusion reactor in my body for energy, and a node in my spine full of combat libraries. I'm a killing machine. I could crack you in two just like that." He snapped his fingers.

"Goodness." She didn't sound the least terrified.

Harrick wanted to growl more, but he couldn't when faced with her good nature and bravery. It was also difficult when he was so aware of her body. Their empathic link was also strengthening. She thought he was looped, eccentric, but she liked him. She savored the strength of his arms. She didn't understand what was happening to the two of them and made no attempt to hide her emotions.

Harrick let their link fade. He couldn't maintain an empathic connection that strong for more than a few moments.

Rhose cupped her palm around his cheek. "I wish I could see you better."

"I also, with you." It was an understatement. He lifted her sweater and found more sweaters underneath. "Are you cold?"

"Actually, I'm hot."

He tugged her sweater. "If you take this off," he said helpfully, "you won't be hot."

She laughed, a sparkling sound, and Harrick flushed. She knew perfectly well that he was trying to undress her. Yet she wasn't put off. Nervous, yes, because he was a stranger. Except they were no longer strange to each other. People could live together for decades and never blend their minds as much as he and Rhose were already doing.

"You've a beautiful laugh." He lay down and kissed her some more on her mouth, her cheeks, her nose. When she put her arms around him and pressed against his body, he groaned. Finally he found the bottom layer of her multitude of sweaters and slid his hand under them, across her bare skin.

"Ah . . . " Her breathing quickened.

Encouraged, Harrick explored further. He found her breasts, and they more than filled his hands. Her nipples hardened as he played with them. He pulled her sweaters up to her shoulders, leaving her torso bare. Saints, she felt good.

Rhose sighed and slid her palm down his chest, as if she wasn't sure where to put her hand. But she didn't tell him to stop. His pulse surged, and he fumbled with the tie at her waist until it came loose. She tensed as he pulled on her leggings, tugging the heavy cloth over her thighs, knees, ankles, and then all the way off. He slid his hand up her body. So curved and soft—

"Wait." Rhose caught his hand. "This is too much. Too fast."

Harrick felt as if he had hit a brick wall. Darkness shifted and flowed inside of him. "Do you want me to stop?"

"Y-yes. Please."

It took a great effort of will to still his hands, but he managed, one of his palms on her breast, the other on her thigh. She was so inviting, he thought he might expire of frustration. But damn it, he wasn't going to ravish her.

"Why?" he asked. "Why must we stop now?" The haunted feeling that had weighted his emotions since the crash crept back.

Her voice shook. "I guess I am scared, after all."

Well, hell. He knew that—or he should have. As an empath, he could pick up a vague sense of moods, though without the amplification provided by his ship, he had to be close to a person for it to happen. Even then, he couldn't maintain a link for long, and he couldn't manage that much unless he lowered his mental barriers, which he rarely did, both to protect himself and to respect the privacy of others. Since the crash he had hunkered behind his mental shields, locked away from all emotions.

Until Rhose invaded his sanctuary.

Harrick instinctively lowered his defenses during intimacy, which was one reason he rarely sought company. He was vulnerable to his lover's mood. If she found him lacking, he would know. What he picked up from Rhose was strong. Disconcerting. But good. She liked him, though she wasn't sure why. He understood better: as empaths, they produced pheromones targeted for each other, creating a strong physical attraction. It was one reason empaths managed to reproduce despite their rarity. Nor was it only chemical; if they started with any natural mental compatibility, their brain waves could resonate and intensify the effect, often almost immediately after they met. Poets called it "love at first sight," which sounded far more romantic than "a resonance of neural wave functions."

Then again, maybe he was just making arcane excuses for going at her like a rutting bull.

"I won't do anything you don't want," he said.

"I just—I need to take it slower."

Slower. That was a definite improvement over *stop*. He slid down her body so his weight didn't crush her. Then he took her breast into his mouth and suckled while he stroked her curves. Lovely curves. She wasn't such a waif after all. Her haze of arousal intensified, and she played with his hair. Her caresses made him warm in places she wasn't touching. He took his time, exploring, touching, kissing her everywhere.

After a while, he came back up and spoke near her ear. "Let me. You're ready. And so am I." *Saints,* but he was ready.

She spoke in a low voice, out of breath. "Yes. Now."

It was all he needed. He tugged at her sweaters, and she raised her arms so he could pull them off the rest of the way. He thought of undressing himself, but it made him feel open to attack. The last thing he wanted was for his spinal node to jack him into a combat mode and endanger her life. Knowing she wouldn't harm him didn't help; his need to protect himself went deeper than any physical threat.

Harrick opened his trousers and settled his hips between her thighs. She drew in a sharp breath as he guided himself into her. She felt so warm, so ready—what? He had hit a barrier.

"Oh," Harrick said. No wonder she wanted him to slow down. It astonished him that she trusted him enough to let him be her first lover. Perhaps it was the magic of this odd, surreal night and their unexpected affinity for each other, but he wanted to believe that he, and only he, was the reason.

"It is only you," she whispered.

He kissed her ear. "You're beautiful, Rhose."

She hung on to him and he felt her heartbeat. Her apprehension was there, yes, and bewildered surprise at her own desire, with a blur of sensuality that overlaid her thoughts. He pushed into her as gently as he could manage, though his control was slipping. When her barrier gave away, she moaned, but if it caused her pain, she gave no sign, either in her mood or body.

He tried to move with care, but it had been too long. When the shadows in his mind shifted and tried to darken his thoughts, the sheer, driving pleasure of their love-making obliterated the ghosts that haunted him. He lost control and thrust hard against her, his hands clenched in the blanket under them. The sensations exploded over him and his awareness of the world vanished.

Harrick began to think again. He was lying on top of her, sated and content. "Rhose?"

She let out a breath. "That was nice."

Nice was far more genteel than the words he would have used, but he agreed. "Are you all right?"

"Yes." She shifted beneath him. "You're heavy, though."

He rolled off her, onto his side, and felt around for his soap-bot cloths. He handed her one. "You can clean up with this, if you'd like."

Rhose took the cloth. "Thanks." She sounded half-asleep.

Harrick touched the soft skin of her breast and thought perhaps he was having a delusion. He stretched out against her side and closed his eyes. "Are you a phantasm?" he murmured. Maybe he truly had gone insane.

But such sweet insanity . . .

The cold awoke Rhose. She couldn't understand why one side of her body was freezing and the other side warm. And why had she fallen asleep on the floor?

It came back in a rush. Her face heated as she thought of what she had done, making love to Harrick and with such passion. She should be appalled at herself, but instead she felt . . . satisfied. This was so unexpected, so unreal, and such a sensually pleasing introduction to the ways of love. He was asleep against her side. The warm side. She pulled the blanket out from under her body and drew it over them both.

Harrick stirred. "Good morning," he said drowsily.

"Not for a while." She thought the night was probably about half over. "Maybe fifteen more hours."

He yawned and blew into her ear, making her tingle. "We'll just keep each other warm for a while longer, eh?"

"I would like that." She tugged at his body-shirt, trying to pull it over his head. "You don't need this."

He put his hand over hers as if to push her away. She could hardly see him in the dark, but his apprehension felt like a fog of sand against her face. Then he took an audible breath and said, "All right." He pulled off the shirt and dropped it behind her.

Rhose wondered at his hesitation. She stroked his chest, surprised and intrigued by its sculpted planes. Lying next to him, she moved into his arms as he pulled her close. It saddened her to think that when the sun rose, she would have to go home, leaving Harrick.

"Would you come to town with me tomorrow?" she asked.

His arms went rigid around her. "No."

"You might like—"

"No!" Then he said, "Stay here."

"I wish I could." She couldn't imagine it, though. Her family was poor, yes, their house small and rough, but it was home. She couldn't leave them or her students. "I can't, though. I have too many responsibilities."

After a moment, he said, "Responsibilities."

"You also?"

"I don't remember." In an oddly strangled voice, he added, "Can't remember."

She wasn't certain, but she thought he meant he couldn't allow himself to remember. "Does it hurt?"

His voice was low and subdued. "I used to go to a tavern with them. We would laugh and drink Urbanali beer."

"With who, Harrick?"

His voice caught. "They are gone."

She felt his grief. "I'm sorry."

"We still—we still have tonight."

She held him close. "Yes. We do."

This time when they made love, it was with bare skin against bare skin. Their minds blended—only vague impressions, no definite thoughts—but she sensed that in the simple act of undressing, he had fought a battle with himself and won.

In the early morning light, outside Harrick's lean-to, Rhose had a good look at the man who had turned her night into such a wonder. They had slept, made love, slept, and loved again. Now that she could see him better, her breath caught. He had strong features, rugged and bold, with dark eyes.

She stood with him in the watery light of an overcast sky, surrounded by the fallen tech-tower, with coils of wire and shattered Luminex piled on the ground. Chill wind tugged at her sweaters. So many dreams had ended with the destruction oils tech park. Its people had evacuated in time, but their livelihoods had been shattered.

Harrick was watching her intently. "You're even prettier in the light."

Her lips curved. "So are you."

"I most certainly am not pretty." His face flushed.

"Handsome, then. Big. Strong." She wanted to say *sexy*, but she was too shy. She felt his mood, though. She affected him the same way he affected her. "Are you sure you won't come with me?"

"I can't."

"Is it the gangs?" She had felt the scars on his body; now she could see the fine lines through rips in his body-shirt. "Harrick, what happened to you?"

He said only, "Will you come back?"

She let it go. "Yes. I will." She pushed back the hair around her face. Her mother called it a "riotous mop," and Rhose had been trying to tame it lately. She hadn't had much success, but she wanted to put on a good appearance for Harrick.

"I like your hair," he said.

Rhose froze. "How do you know what I'm thinking?"

"Can't you feel it?" He took her hands in his. "You're an empath, like me."

"Oh." She reddened. "Sure."

"I'm not crazy."

If he wanted to believe such things, it was all right with her. For all his strangeness, and the shadows lurking around the edges of his mind, she trusted him.

"I will see you soon," she said. "I promise."

"It's hard to believe." Darkness seemed to fall over him, though nothing had changed in the murky light. "You're an angel that drifted into my life. Perhaps a malicious god sent you as punishment, so my life would be even more wretched after you left."

Rhose stared at him. "Punishment? Whatever for?"

"For surviving." His voice was hollow.

"Harrick—"

"No." He pulled her into a hug and kissed her, silencing her questions.

Rhose didn't want to ruin their last moments by insisting on answers. She leaned into him, savoring the warmth of his lips and his embrace. He had boasted last night of arcane abilities, enhanced strength and speed, and a "microfusion reactor," whatever that meant. He had probably made it up, but that wouldn't put her off so much as make her wonder at his eccentricities. What drove a man like Harrick to hide out here?

When they finally separated, her body was flushed. She spoke softly. "Good-bye."

His voice rumbled. "Good-bye."

Rhose walked a few steps and turned. He started toward her, then bit his lip and stayed put.

She wanted to go back to him. But she had to get home as soon as possible. Her parents would be worried and her students upset. The children were already dealing with the aftermath of the colony's destruction. Most of the colonists had survived because Daretown had received warning in time to evacuate to the shelters, but many suffered from post-traumatic stress. It would destroy her family if they thought they had lost her, and she didn't want to add to the anxieties of her students.

Reluctant, she made her way through the debris. As she climbed a mound of broken casecrete, she looked back and saw Harrick watching.

She lifted her hand and he waved.

The next time she looked, he was gone.

By the time Rhose reached Daretown, the town had cycled through most of its first waking period, and people were sitting down to first-dinner. She was exhausted, empty-handed, and missing Harrick. Last night already seemed like a lost dream.

She trudged along the road. It was dirt and dust today, no mud. The day was already heating up despite the overcast, and they were only a third of the way through the thirty-two hours of sunlight.

The destruction here had been less than in the tech-park, and huts had sprung up on either side of the road, as people tried to rebuild their lives. Most of the important infrastructure of the colony had been salvaged, but it grieved her to see how few of their hard-fought gains had survived the beam strikes. Every crushed house symbolized a family with broken dreams. They worried about hazardous chemicals or gases leaking, huge capacitors that discharged with killing arcs of energy, and broken water mains that had undercut several streets and caused their collapse. Even the homes that still stood had mostly gone dark, their inhabitants gone, their solar tiles stolen. Gangs had looted many of them.

Up ahead, three children ran out of a huge white pipe that had fallen on its side. Their laughter reminded her that people recovered even after a disaster.

Rhose soon reached a familiar turn-off. She left the road and walked among broken furniture and the skeletal remains of an office lobby until she reached a plaza. Her family's house stood there, with a vegetable patch in front and lantern light behind the curtains. They had lost their old house and belongings, but they had rebuilt here from the remains of another fallen building that had been in better shape. As much as Rhose missed her home, she was immensely grateful her family was alive. Buildings could be replaced, but not people.

Inside the house, she stood unnoticed in the doorway of the kitchen and fondly watched her family. They were gathered around the big table: her parents, grandmother, sister, and younger brother. She had another brother two years her junior; he had married last year after he finished high school and moved to his own house. Usually there was a great deal of laughter and talking at meals, but today everyone was quiet.

"My greetings," she said.

Her parents twisted around, and her mother's face suffused with welcome. "Rhose!"

Her siblings knocked over their chairs as they jumped to their feet. Within moments they surrounded her. Her brother put his arms around her waist and her sister reached around him to hug Rhose, while her father put his hand on her shoulder, and her, grandmother squeezed her hand. Her mother cried as she tried to embrace Rhose around everyone else.

"Goodness," Rhose said, laughing, though her voice caught.

Her mother drew back and wiped her eyes. "We thought you were kidnapped! Or—or worse."

"I couldn't find any supplies," Rhose said. "I went too far and stayed in the tech-park last night." She wasn't ready to tell them about Harrick. She wasn't even sure yet how she felt about the encounter. "I'm sorry I didn't have any luck."

"No apologies!" her grandmother admonished. "We're just glad you're safe."

Rhose indicated a lantern hanging from the rafters. "You got more oil."

"I found a barrel outside town," her father said. "Closer to the port."

"We went to see the ships!" her sister exclaimed. She barely came up to Rhose's elbow and had a mop of curls very much like Rhose and their father. "We found out visitors are coming."

Offworld visitors? Rhose regarded her parents uneasily. "Is anything wrong?"

"It's good news," her mother said. "The Relief Allocation Service is bringing supplies, and Imperial Space Command is sending a delegation."

"ISC? Why? We have no military presence." Rhose heard the bitter edge in her voice. Daretown was an inconsequential colony that should never have been exposed to combat. It had been a fluke that a skirmish had been fought in orbit here, so far from the main engagements.

"Apparently none of the combatants survived," her father said. "ISC is sending people to investigate."

Rhose wished reinforcements had come *before* the fighting. An ISC squadron had been ambushed while traveling through this star system. She would always be grateful that they had managed to warn Daretown in time. Her people had made it to shelters before the invaders stabbed the populated areas of the planet. Shocked and bewildered, the colonists had struggled to recover since then. It wasn't until many days later that they heard the news: ISC had won the star-spanning war—just barely.

Rhose tried to smile. "Well, it is good if they can help with rebuilding, eh?" She squeezed her brother and sisters. "I hope you all left me some food."

Her grandmother clucked. "Come on, Rhosallina. Sit yourself down."

With relief, Rhose joined her family. She tried not to think about Harrick—or her inescapable sense that he was in danger.

He walked.

Harrick had never ventured beyond the tech-park, but he had an idea how to reach Daretown, having overheard foragers in the ruins talk about their home. The colonists seemed resilient, able to pick themselves up and start over regardless of the hardships they faced. Some had even searched the remains of his jag fighter. They found almost nothing to scavenge.

He shouldn't have survived, either. The ship had registered him as dead in the instant his squad's four-way link shattered. It had notified ISC of their loss. Harrick wasn't even convinced it had made a mistake in his case. He felt as if he were a wretched ghost. The living would have first priority with ISC, but eventually the military would come here to investigate the loss of his squad. He would float over them, a specter, dead and dark.

He shuddered and shook his head, trying to clear his thoughts. Before last night, he hadn't realized how bizarre his mental processes had become. Perhaps for Rhose, their love-making had been an exciting interlude, a time of sensuality to ease a difficult life, with the added spice of danger; for him, it had shaken his entire constrained life here. He thought she had felt more, too, but he couldn't be sure. He hadn't realized until last night that his mind was too injured to pick up emotions consistently. Only when the balm of Rhose's mind soothed his own did he realize how much he hurt.

His spinal node was making maps of the area as he followed the road. He had spent the day telling himself to stay in his refuge. But images of Rhose weakened his resolve. He wanted her. She endangered the shell of numbness that protected him. She was making him feel human again—and it hurt like hell.

He had suppressed his memories to keep his sanity, but now they were returning. Blackwing Squadron had been far more than four pilots and four ships. They had fought as one mind. It gave them a versatility, survival capability, and deadly accuracy beyond individual ships or pilots.

Mandi Jakes had flown with him for years. She had risen fast in the J-Force, commissioned as a Jagernaut Quaternary, promoted to Tertiary, and then to Secondary, a rank higher than most Jagernauts ever achieved. Usually they retired first. Mandi had stayed on, the Goldwing of his squad—until she died. His Greenwing, Benz Zannisteria, had been a Tertiary. And Sal. His Redwing. She had been a Quaternary, only one year out of the Academy, bright and fresh, proud to fly with Blackwing Squadron. They had been four parts of a whole. And he had failed them all.

He had no right to live, to walk to town, to seek out Rhose. But he couldn't stop himself. He had been injured on a deeper level than the physical wounds that scarred his body, but he was only now beginning to realize just how much he needed help.

When Harrick reached the outskirts of town, it occurred to him that he might look strange, with his tangled hair and torn clothes. ISC regulations required that its officers either crop their hair close to their heads or wear it pulled back in a warrior's queue. His was wild around his face and shoulders. Rhose's family might be put off, too, if he came to see their daughter with a Jumbler on his hip.

He stashed his weapon in an underground vault that had escaped destruction. The gun was keyed to his brain, so no one could use it except him, and he also hid it with care. Then he tried to neaten his hair. When he was more presentable, he resumed his trek.

The road was hardly more than a rut, but it seemed to be the main thoroughfare in Daretown. He thought about his home in Vyan City on the world Parthonia, a place where droop-willows hung over placid lakes and marble columns lined boulevards. Huddling in the ruins, he had forgotten he had a history, that he was a man as well as a biomechanical warrior.

He met no one. At first he thought they might all be inside, sleeping. But according to his internal clock, the midday sleep should be over and the town into its second waking cycle.

His skin prickled. They were watching him. Maybe he was paranoid, but he felt certain that gazes followed him everywhere. Had his biomech systems been operating properly he could have sensed the presence of watchers more accurately by picking up their vital signs, but he couldn't manage that now.

Harrick jerked his head several times, then realized he was acting strangely and made himself stop. His fingers twitched and he wished he were back in the tech-park. After another few minutes, he rounded a curve—and saw five men approaching him. One had an EM pulse gun, another carried a laser carbine, and two had clubs. Heavy muscles corded their forearms. They wore coarse shirts and trousers, though their clothes were in better shape than his uniform. All were young, probably in their twenties, measured in standard years. Although Harrick had an apparent age in his thirties, he was almost sixty. Nanomeds in his body repaired his cells and delayed his aging, but it seemed unlikely the colonists could afford such treatments.

Harrick slowed down. The men watched with hard faces as they surrounded him, forcing him to stop.

A thought came from his spinal node: **Combat mode ready.**

Stand by, he thought, with extra focus. Bioelectrodes in his neurons translated his thoughts into input for his node, and the reverse process changed the node's output into neural firings he interpreted as thoughts.

Waiting, it answered.

The tallest of the five men had blond hair razed close to his head. He stood in front of Harrick and idly swung his club, slapping it against his other open palm.

"You must have walked a long way," the club man said.

"From the tech-park," Harrick said.

"You weren't invited here." Club smacked his bat into his palm. "You got no sway. What I say, goes." Smack. "And I say, you don't belong."

"I don't want any sway," Harrick said, irritated. He didn't even know if he would stay. It depended on Rhose.

In his side vision, he glimpsed the other man with a bat. His node analyzed the man's posture, and his arm snapped up with enhanced reflexes. In the same instant, the man swung his club. Harrick easily caught the bat and wrenched it out of the man's hand, then cracked it in two over his leg and threw the pieces so hard, they sailed over the ruins. The entire scuffle lasted only seconds.

As one of the other men lunged at Harrick, Club drew his pulse gun, which would shoot serrated projectiles at accelerated speeds. Just one could tear a man apart and turn his insides into jelly. Using enhanced speed, Harrick dove to the side and rolled, coming up against a pile of broken mesh panels. The projectiles missed him and rammed deep into the road.

The man with the laser carbine unslung it from his shoulder.

Combat mode on, his node thought.

Harrick's mind accelerated.

He rolled to his feet just before the man fired his laser. Blinding light flared and the shot seared the ground, slagging rocks and dirt.

Harrick knew his body couldn't take the strain of accelerated movement for long, but he wouldn't survive this encounter without it. He sprinted into the ruins and ducked behind a huge white pipe. Pulse projectiles slammed the casecrete. He kept going, dodging in a zigzag pattern, driven by adrenalin. He couldn't have stopped now even if his attackers had disappeared.

Within seconds, he reached a thicket of barriers that had been hallways in a building and were now open to the sky. He darted among them until his node advised him to halt at a cracked wall. Looking through the crack, he saw his assailants stalking the ruins. They had attacked. He would defend. In combat mode, the world vanished. He felt nothing. He became pure Jagernaut, a human weapon.

The man with the laser was approaching the other side of the barrier. Harrick's node analyzed the cracks on the wall for weak points, then accessed his brain and created a translucent display he saw overlaid on the barrier. Several target areas glowed red. He waited until the man was on the other side of one target. Then he jerked back his arm and rammed the heel of his hand into the red area.

The wall shattered outward, showering the man with debris. Harrick sprang through the breach and tackled his enemy. It took only seconds to knock him out. He could have easily made the kill, but he let his assailant live. With his feet planted on either side of the man's body, Harrick reached down and took the carbine. It was an older model, army issue, probably stolen.

Scanning the area with augmented optics, he spied Club half a kilometer away, rummaging through another wrecked building.

Harrick crept nearer to Club's location until he reached part of a building that still stood. Crumbling stairs took him to a hallway on the second floor. The hall ended abruptly, where the building had collapsed, and he crouched in the shadows there, hidden.

He waited.

It took thirty minutes for Club to work his way to the area below Harrick's perch. Then Harrick aimed his gun. That slight motion was the final one needed to upset the balance of the broken hall, however. and the floor collapsed under him. He dropped in a shower of debris and landed on Club, the two of them falling to the ground in a tangle of limbs. Harrick easily absorbed the impact in his augmented body and jumped to his feet. Club recovered almost as fast—and fired his pulse gun. With no time to aim, he missed, but the tip of a projectile serration sliced Harrick's shirt.

You must have immediate medical attention, his node thought.

Pumped into combat mode, Harrick felt nothing. In his accelerated state, everything else slowed down. His swing arced toward Club, who was slowly ducking. Harrick's fist slammed into Club's head and a crack reverberated through the air. Club toppled in slow motion.

Harrick's time sense suddenly jumped to normal. He heaved in a breath, then dropped next to Club and felt for a pulse.

He found none.

Harrick felt as if he were caught in a loop that wouldn't stop. Couldn't stop. Couldn't stop. Standing, he looked around for his other would-be killers. Either they had spread their search so wide he could no longer see them or else they had fled.

I need my Jumbler, he thought.

You need a hospital, his node answered.

Can't stop.

Shall I take you out of combat mode?

No! Harrick set off jogging through the rubble. He couldn't settle his thoughts.

He knew only that he had to stay alive and destroy his enemies.

———

Rhose walked with her students to the community center. The West End was the only area of town with a sizeable number of intact buildings, including the center. Its main wing now hosted offices for the mayor and his staff. She used the south wing for a school, where she taught about twenty-five students, depending on who showed up. Attendance had dropped since the attack.

Today the children chattered and giggled, ranging from tots barely the height of her waist to teens on the verge of adulthood. They sounded so normal. But a day rarely passed without one or more of them breaking down in tears. Lately, though, it happened less often.

At the center, they entered a lobby with consoles and desks everywhere, all of the city offices crammed together. Rhose's assistant Dhanni was waiting, and the children waved as Rhose handed them off to the younger teacher.

Rhose crossed the lobby. Ten men and women were gathered in the mayor's "office," which consisted of a desk between two columns. The only person Rhose recognized was the mayor, Berni Ivers, a rotund man with a ruddy face and graying hair. The others all wore crisp green uniforms with the gold insignia of the Pharaoh's Army.

Rhose hung back, uncertain if she should interrupt. Berni was deep in discussion with one of the army men. From Berni's deferential behavior, she gathered this visitor ranked high in the ISC hierarchy. Seeing Berni scrape and simper gave her a certain satisfaction. Although Rhose considered him a good mayor, he wanted her to fawn all over him, which just wasn't her nature.

She hadn't thought anyone knew she was there, but when he and the army VIP finished, Berni beckoned her forward. Self-conscious in front of so many strangers, Rhose walked over to him. The army fellow was busy setting up a schedule with his assistant.

"Morning," Berni said.

"And to you," Rhose said. "I wondered if any new houses were available."

Curiosity sparked in his eyes. "You planning to move?"

"Not for me. For the school." She didn't mention Harrick. She had no idea if he would ever come out of the ruins. If he did, he would need a place to live, and if not, the school genuinely needed more space. "I've been getting more students lately."

"You'll probably have even more soon," he confided. "ISC is going to help us with the rebuilding."

It was good news. Rhose started to answer, but a commotion burst out across the lobby. She looked to see two boys running through the lobby, both of the youths about ten in standard years. They slowed when they saw the ISC contingent, but then they came on again, undeterred even by the presence of offworlders.

Berni frowned as they skidded to a stop in front of him. "You shouldn't be dashing around here like that."

"It's Blaster and his men!" one boy cried, out of breath.

"We're scrubbing out those gangs," Berni said firmly. "Put Blaster and his punks in the clink." Although he spoke to the boy, Rhose thought he was talking for the army VIP. Perhaps ISC could help. Gangs had preyed on Daretown since the post-war exodus had left the town with less protection. Most of the thugs only looted, but the worst of them had kidnapped, raped, and even committed murder.

"You c-can't scrub him," the second boy said. "He's dead!"

"*Dead?*" For a moment Berni looked as if he were going to rejoice. Then he caught himself and presented a more somber expression. "How?"

"Another gang-fanger pounded him," the first boy said.

"A new guy," the second boy added. "Tall. Even more muscles than Blaster. A mean fu—" He stopped, blushing as Rhose glared at him, then amended, "A mean guy."

"All, hell." Berni's face turned red, even his bulbous nose. "We've got another one now?"

"It was self-defense," the first boy said.

"No, he was a m-monster," the second boy said darkly.

"Black clothes, r-ripped up, and black hair all crazy. Big black boots."

Rhose blinked. "That sounds like Harrick."

Berni refocused his ire on her. "You hanging around gangs now, Rhosie girl?"

She hated it when he called her that. "Of course not."

"Harrick?" a deep voice asked. "Is that what you said?"

Rhose turned with a start. The army VIP had come back to them. A holo-badge on his chest read COLONEL W. COALSON.

Rhose spoke self-consciously. "Yes. He's someone I met."

"Jason Harrick?" Coalson asked.

Rhose twisted the hem of her sweater. "He just said Harrick."

"Can you give me more description?"

Coalson's intense concentration unsettled Rhose. "Just like the boy said. And Harrick has a lot of new scars."

"Any other features?" Coalson asked. "Insignia? Tattoos?"

Rhose's face heated. Harrick had a birthmark on his inner thigh, but she didn't want to speak about something so personal to a stranger. "I—I don't think so."

Coalson studied her. "I hope you aren't withholding information."

Mercifully, she remembered something else useful she could give him. "He had a gun. He called it a Jumbler."

"Saints almighty," one of Coalson's people said, a woman with a badge that read MAJOR KAMES. "Could he have *survived?*"

Berni crossed his arms and scowled. "You know this fanger? If I've another killer loose, I need everything you have on him."

For the first time Coalson showed an emotion. Incredulity. He spoke in an even voice. "Jason Harrick is a Jagernaut Primary. He is one of the most decorated heroes in any branch of ISC. He led the squadron that defended this planet, and he's the one who transmitted the evacuation warning to your people. If not for him, you would all be dead."

Berni's mouth dropped open. "A *Primary?* Good gods. Why would he come to town to kill people?" Then he added, "Not that he would be the first to want Blaster dead."

"I don't know," Coalson said. "We thought he had died."

Rhose recalled Harrick's words. "That's why he said the gods were punishing him for surviving."

"He told you that?" Coalson asked.

Rhose nodded. "He said a lot of things. I—well, I'm afraid I thought he was a little crazy."

Major Kames stepped forward. When Coalson nodded to her, she said, "If Harrick survived the violent death of his squadron, he could very well have gone insane."

"Just how dangerous is he?" Berni asked.

"We can't know until we find him." Coalson turned to the first boy who had told them about Blaster. "What is your name, son?"

The wide-eyed boy stood up straighter. "Jessie, sir."

"Jessie, did you see where this stranger went?"

"He took the laser carbine and ran out of town. East."

Coalson glanced at Kames. "Have the cruiser see if they can get a fix on his location." As Kames activated her gauntlet comm, Coalson turned his intent focus back to Rhose. "Did Harrick tell you anything else?"

She described their meeting, though she left out their love-making. "He didn't seem violent. Sad. Eccentric, maybe. But I never feared he would harm me."

Kames looked up. "Sir, I have a report from Tracking up in orbit."

"Go ahead," Coalson said.

"They've located the signature of what may be a Jumbler," Kames said. "It's buried in the noise of all the scavenged energy sources people are using here. If we hadn't advised them where to look, they probably wouldn't have found it. They can't identify its owner, but they have a location. It's just outside town."

"Good work," Coalson said. "Let's go."

"I'd like to go with you," Rhose said.

"I also," Berni said.

Coalson frowned at them. "Only if you stay back, out of the way. Let our people deal with him."

Rhose's pulse jumped. "You won't hurt him, will you?"

Berni spoke harshly. "He committed murder, Rhosie."

Jessie started to speak, then hesitated.

"Go ahead," Coalson told the boy.

"He was defending himself, sir. Blaster and them roughed him up.

They almost killed him. He was bleeding awful! He could have killed all of them, but he only did Blaster, because Blaster was shooting at him."

Coalson went very still. "Harrick is injured?"

"Real bad," the boy said.

"He's probably in survival mode," Major Kames said.

"What does that mean?" Berni asked. "Survival how?"

Coalson spoke grimly. "If he's off-balance, he'll attack anyone who approaches him. Right now, mayor, you may have one of the most consummate killers ever created loose in your city."

"No," Rhose said. "He wouldn't hurt people. You heard Jessie. It was self-defense."

Coalson considered her. "What exactly happened with you and Primary Harrick?"

Rhose's face flamed. "We, uh, were . . . together." She was almost stuttering. "Intimate."

Kames swore under her breath. "If he's fixated on you, ma'am, it could make him even more dangerous."

Rhose wished she had taken Harrick more seriously last night. Yet even now, she didn't believe he would hurt her. He had called the bond between them—the sense of knowing how the other felt—empathy. She had never believed psions existed, but it would explain so much. "Please tell me you won't hurt him," she said.

"We would like to bring him in alive." Coalson regarded her steadily. "But if he is out of control and threatening the lives of civilians, we may have to kill him."

Harrick was on the second floor of a gutted tower when he heard noise outside. He sidled up to a jagged hole and looked down at the road.

Enemies.

They were walking along the road from Daretown. According to his internal sensors, some carried nodes in their bodies similar to his, though apparently less extensive, he couldn't tell for certain with his damaged components.

I can identify the signatures of their nodes, his own node thought. **They are SC. Not enemy.**

Enemy, Harrick answered. They had tried to kill him.

Not enemy, his node persisted.

Silence!

It subsided. A node could never override the mind of the person who carried it. That security feature prevented opposing forces from hacking high-tech warriors and turning them against their own forces. His node obeyed only him. He had to protect himself. Protect Rhose. She lived here. He couldn't let his enemies hurt her.

Six invaders were on the road, which led to toward the plaza that separated this tower from the ruins of other buildings. It had to be a trick. They wouldn't leave themselves open. Sighting ahead of them, Harrick fired the laser. A brilliant flare of light burst out of his weapon and his optics filtered his vision. When it cleared, he studied the scene. The invaders had stopped. Although he had slagged a section of the road, the portion directly before them was untouched.

What protects them? he asked.

A reflector field, his node thought. **Effective against electromagnetic radioation.**

Harrick touched his Jumbler.

It can't reflect antimatter.

The gun was a miniature particle accelerator. It shot a stream of abitons, the antiparticle of the biton, a low energy sub-electronic particle. When abitons annihilated bitons, they produced harmless orange light. But bitons were part of electrons—and all matter contained electrons. A Jumbler beam annihilated anything it touched.

The invaders had deliberately drawn his fire to make him reveal his hiding place. He slung the carbine over his shoulder and sped down the stairs, then vacated the building, staying low behind broken casecrete walls. No one attacked the tower, though, which suggested his enemies were savvy to his strategy. He could no longer see them on the road. No matter. He was gone.

"Harrick!" The shout came from the ruins across the plaza. "We don't want to hurt you. Surrender and we won't shoot."

He peered through a crack in the wall. *Can you locate the source of that voice?*

A sensor shroud hides the source, his node answered.

What is its most likely location?

His node superimposed a display on the plaza, highlighting a jagged monolith that had once been a sculpture. Harrick concentrated on his Jumbler and felt a mental *click,* as if a switch had flipped in his mind. Only his brain waves could activate the gun. He drew the weapon—and fired.

A beam of orange sparks appeared in the air. When it struck the monolith, the slab flared a brilliant orange and vanished, turned into photons created by low energy particle-antiparticle annihilations. When the light faded, the sculpture was gone.

Harrick ran behind the wall, crouching down. *Did I get them?*

I don't know, his node said. **However—**

Suddenly the wall ahead exploded. Harrick froze and protected his head with his arms as rubble showered over him. Shards of casecrete cut his arms and shoulders.

Harrick, his node thought. **You are forcing your own people to seek your death.**

Enemies.

Friends!

I will hear no more. He raised his Jumbler and prepared to kill his enemies.

"No!" Rhose cried the word as the explosion tore apart the wall. But the blast hadn't killed Harrick. She would *know* if he died. The closer she came to him physically, the stronger their mental link.

A rubble-strewn plaza separated her from the tower where he had been hiding. She and Berni were crouching behind several upturned consoles a safe distance from the action. She didn't know how Harrick could have moved so fast from the tower to the ground, but she had no doubt he had fired both the laser and the orange beam. Yet even after Coalson's people had fooled him into shooting that monolith, they couldn't locate him.

Rhose wanted to shout at them to stop, but they would just send her away. At least they were targeting the wrong place; Harrick had outsmarted their sensors and gone in the other direction. They had meant it about wanting him alive; otherwise, they could have leveled this entire area with beams from one of their ships. But she could tell they thought he had gone insane. Sooner or later they would get him, even if they had to kill him.

"He's injured," Rhose said. "Not crazy."

"Tell the people he kills," Berni muttered.

Rhose pretended to shuddered. "I don't think I can watch this."

Berni gave her a look of sympathy. "Perhaps it's best if you don't, Rhosie girl."

"Will you let me know what happened?"

"Yes. Certainly." He patted her arm. "I'll come by your house later this evening."

"Thanks, Berni."

Rhose eased back into the clutter of melted consoles and scorched furniture. When she was out of Berni's sight, she slipped through the ruins, quietly, so she wouldn't alert Coalson, who had asked Berni to keep an eye on her. Finally she crouched behind a mess of casecrete blocks directly across the plaza from the wall where she thought Harrick was hiding. She couldn't be certain; she was depending on a nebulous impression of his mind that matched what she had felt last night.

She saw no way to reach him without going into the open. Taking a deep breath, she steeled herself. Then she stood and walked into the plaza.

The wind rustled her hair around her cheeks. She sensed Harrick watching her, and she went slowly, keeping her hands by her sides so he could see she had no weapons. A shout came from behind her, Berni, it sounded like. A bead of sweat ran down her neck. Harrick hadn't killed her. Yet.

"Rhose Canterhaven." The amplified voice rumbled. "Leave the plaza immediately."

She kept going. She knew so little about Harrick's condition. She had to trust her instincts that he wouldn't shoot.

Footsteps sounded behind her in the plaza. Rhose turned to see Kames striding after her.

"No!" Rhose said. "Let me do this."

A beam of orange sparks cut through the air and hit the plaza in front of Kames. As she jumped back, the ground vanished in a flash of light, leaving a ragged crater.

Kames watched her from across the crater. "Rhose, come back."

Rhose shook her head. "You have to go. He won't let you any closer."

"You've no guarantee he won't shoot you, either."

"I know."

"And you still want to do this?"

Rose's gaze never wavered. "Yes. Please don't try to stop me."

Kames pushed her hand through her cap of dark hair. Then she nodded reluctantly. "Good luck."

"Thanks." Rhose resumed her walk toward a broken wall as high as her waist. As she drew nearer, a rustle came from behind it and the clink of rubble.

Then Harrick stood up behind the wall.

Her pulse lurched. He had a carbine gripped in one hand and the black bulk of his Jumbler in the other. This wasn't he man who had kissed her last night, held her in his arms, teased her with his rare smile. He showed no emotion. This stranger was a machine.

She stopped a few steps away. "Harrick?"

"You are with my enemies." His voice was a monotone.

"I don't know them." Softly she added, "You came into town."

He stood motionless, a living statue.

"Did you come to see me?" She wanted to believe it was true.

No answer.

She walked to the wall and looked up at him. "Come back." Her voice caught. "Be the Harrick I knew last night."

His expression seemed to crumple. Then he gave a half-strangled groan. Still holding both guns, he reached across the wall for her, and Rhose went into his arms, embracing him, her cheek against his chest. He hugged her so tight, she could barely breathe. Blood had soaked his body-shirt, and he flinched when her arm scraped his side. But he never let her go. A blurred sense of his memories washed through her mind as he released his heightened combat sense and let himself remember his squadron.

"Gods," he whispered. The stock of his carbine was pressed along her back, aimed at the sky, and his other arm was tight around her shoulders. "I-I can't—"

"It's all right," she soothed. "You'll be all right."

His voice cracked. "Don't go away again."

"I won't." She drew back enough to look up at him. "But you must let these people help you."

He stared at her, his eyes dark. With a shaking hand, holding his Jumbler, he pushed back the hair that curled around her face. His gun brushed her skin, cold and hard. Then he looked over her head. Turning in his arms, Rhose say Coalson and Kames a few paces away.

"Primary Harrick?" Coalson asked. "Will you come with us?"

Harrick breathed out, long and slow. After an endless moment, he let go of Rhose and carefully dropped his guns. Moving stiffly, with great care, he climbed over the wall.

Rhose offered him her hand. He hesitated, then reached out and folded his large hand around her small one. Then he walked with her toward Coalson.

"I pray he'll be all right," Rhose said. She was waiting outside the infirmary that ISC had set up in the community center. Coalson was standing with her in the hallway.

His physical wounds will heal." Although Coalson spoke in a clipped style, his compassion came through. "The mental injuries will take more time."

"Will he stand trial?"

The colonel shook his head. "Our legal panel looked over the evidence for Blaster's death and the attack on my people. The download from Harrick's node matches the witness accounts. Could he have escaped without killing Blaster? Possibly. But how would he decide? He's designed to go into combat mode when attacked. If his mind hadn't been injured, he could have distinguished between the threat he faced here and a combat situation. But he *was* injured. Even then, the only time he shot anyone was when he was directly attacked." He spoke quietly. "They ruled his actions self-defense. But they also took him off active duty, until, or if, he recovers."

Rhose thought of the man she had held in her arms. "He hasn't been able to shut off being a soldier. He needs to relearn how to be a man instead of a weapon."

"Aye," Coalson said. "I think so."

The door slid open and a woman in the white jumpsuit of an ISC doctor looked out. "Rhose Canterhaven?"

"Yes?" Rhose asked.

The doctor had a shuttered gaze, giving away nothing. "Primary Harrick wishes to see you."

Rhose swallowed and nodded, suddenly nervous. As she entered the room, the doctor stepped outside and closed the door. Rhose stopped just inside. Harrick was lying on the bed, his eyes closed, his chest rising and falling in an even rhythm. Someone had cut his hair and given him a shave. The clean, chiseled lines of his features, his high cheekbones, his full lips and straight nose—he was a stunning man, truly fine to see, even more so than she had realized.

After a moment, he opened his eyes and gazed at the ceiling. Then he rolled his head to the side.

"Rhose!" He pushed up on one elbow. "How long have you been there?"

"Just a few moments. She went to the bed. "How do you feel?"

His grin flashed. "Better now."

A blush heated her cheeks. "A smile that gorgeous ought to be licensed. You could do damage with it."

Harrick laughed softly, the first time since they had met. She heard its undercurrents, his relief, as if he hadn't been sure he could ever laugh again. As he sat up, his hospital shift started to slip off one shoulder until the intelligent cloth contracted to keep itself in place.

"Come sit with me," he said.

As Rhose settled on the edge of the bed, he pulled her into his arms and laid his head on hers. She relaxed in his embrace and felt as if she had come home.

It was awhile before he lifted his head. He cleared his throat. "Rhose, I would like to ask . . . "

She waited. "Yes?"

"If you would stay with me." He lifted her hand and kissed her knuckles. "I know I have no right to ask for permanence yet. But empaths are so rare. Compatibility like ours is even rarer. I—well, I hope we can let that grow."

She spoke quietly. "I also, Jason."

His face gentled. "I like it when you say my name like that." He pulled her close and spoke softly near her ear. "Will you let me court you, Rhose Canterhaven?" Almost inaudibly, he added, "Will you let me love you?"

"Always," she murmured. "If you do the same for me."

His voice caught. "Yes."

Holding him, she thought of the first time she had seen him in the ruins, his hand half covering his lamp. He had hidden even from its dim light, but now he was willing to let his inner light chase away his shadows, even in those dark places where his loss and pain dwelled. Rhose felt certain they could mend, all of them: Harrick, her family, Daretown, her people.

For the first time since the attack, she looked forward to the future.

Catherine Asaro received her Ph.D. in Chemical Physics and MA in Physics, both from Harvard, and a BS with Highest Honors in Chemistry from UCLA. Once a physics professor, she's run Molecudyne Research for more than fifteen years. Her novel, *The Quantum Rose*, won the Nebula Award and she is a three-time winner of the Romantic Times Book Club award for "Best Science Fiction Novel." She has published seventeen novels, eleven of which belong to her Saga of the Skolian Empire. *Alpha*, a near-future sf thriller, is her most recent. Her short fiction has appeared in *Analog* and anthologies. A former ballerina, Asaro has performed on both coasts and in Ohio. She is married to an astrophysicist. They live in Maryland.

WALPURGIS AFTERNOON

Delia Sherman

The big thing about the new people moving into the old Pratt place at Number 400 was that they got away with it at all. Our neighborhood is big on historical integrity. The newest house on the block was built in 1910, and you can't even change the paint-scheme on your house without recourse to preservation committee studies and zoning board hearings.

The old Pratt place had generated a tedious number of such hearings over the years—I'd even been to some of the more recent ones. Old Mrs. Pratt had let it go pretty much to seed, and when she passed away, there was trouble about clearing the title so it could be sold, and then it burned down.

Naturally a bunch of developers went after the land—a three-acre property in a professional neighborhood twenty minutes from downtown is something like a Holy Grail to developers. But their lawyers couldn't get the title cleared either, and the end of it was that the old Pratt place never did get built on. By the time Geoff and I moved next door, the place was an empty lot. The neighborhood kids played Bad Guys and Good Guys there after school and the neighborhood cats preyed on its endless supply of mice and voles. I'm not talking eyesore, here; just a big shady plot of land overgrown with bamboo, rhododendrons, wildly rambling roses, and some nice old trees, most notably an immensely ancient copper beech big enough to dwarf any normal-sized house.

It certainly dwarfs ours.

Last spring all that changed overnight, literally. When Geoff and

I turned in, we lived next door to an empty lot. When we got up, we didn't. I have to tell you, it came as quite a shock first thing on a Monday morning, and I wasn't even the one who discovered it. Geoff was.

Geoff's the designated keeper of the window because he insists on sleeping with it open and I hate getting up into a draft. Actually, I hate getting up, period. It's a blessing, really, that Geoff can't boil water without burning it, or I'd never be up before ten. As it is, I eke out every second of warm unconsciousness I can while Geoff shuffles across the floor and thunks down the sash and takes his shower. On that particular morning, his shuffle ended not with a thunk, but with a gasp.

"Holy shit," he said.

I sat up in bed and groped for my robe. When we were in grad school, Geoff had quite a mouth on him, but fatherhood and two decades of college teaching have toned him down a lot. These days, he usually keeps his swearing for Supreme Court decisions and departmental politics.

"Get up, Evie. You gotta see this."

So I got up and went to the window, and there it was, big as life and twice as natural, a real Victorian Homes centerfold, set back from the street and just the right size to balance the copper beech. Red tile roof, golden brown clapboards, miles of scarlet-and-gold gingerbread draped over dozens of eaves, balconies, and dormers. A witch's hat tower, a wrap-around porch, and a massive carriage house. With a cupola on it. Nothing succeeds like excess, I always say.

"Holy shit."

"Watch your mouth, Evie," said Geoff automatically.

I like to think of myself as a fairly sensible woman. I don't imagine things, I face facts, I hadn't gotten hysterical when my fourteen-year-old daughter asked me about birth control. Surely there was some perfectly rational explanation for this phenomenon. All I had to do was think of it.

"It's a hallucination," I said. "Victorian houses don't go up overnight. People do have hallucinations. We're having a hallucination. Q.E.D."

"It's not a hallucination," Geoff said.

Geoff teaches intellectual history at the University and tends to disagree, on principle, with everything everyone says. Someone says the sky is blue, he says it isn't. And then he explains why. "This has none of the earmarks of a hallucination," he went on. We aren't in a heightened emotional state, not expecting a miracle, not drugged, not part of a mob, not starving, not sense deprived. Besides, there's a clothesline in the yard with laundry hanging on it. Nobody hallucinates long underwear."

I looked where he was pointing, and sure enough, a pair of scarlet long johns was kicking and waving from an umbrella-shaped drying-rack, along with a couple pairs of women's panties, two oxford-cloth shirts hung up by their collars, and a gold-and-black print caftan. There was also what was arguably the most beautifully designed perennial bed I'd ever seen basking in the early morning sun. As I was squinting at the delphiniums, a side door opened and a woman came out with a wicker clothesbasket propped on her hip. She was wearing shorts and a T-shirt, had fairish hair pulled back in a bushy tail, and struck me as being a little long in the tooth to be going barefoot and braless.

"Nice legs," said Geoff.

I snapped down the window. "Pull the shades before you get in the shower," I said. "It looks to me like our new neighbors get a nice, clear shot of our bathroom from their third floor."

In our neighborhood, we pride ourselves on minding our own business and not each others'—live and let live, as long as you keep your dog, your kids, and your lawn under control. If you don't, someone calls you or drops you a note, and if that doesn't make you straighten up and fly right, well, you're likely to get a call from the town council about that extension you neglected to get a variance for. Needless to say, the house at Number 400 fell way outside all our usual coping mechanisms. If some contractor had shown up at dawn with bulldozers and two-by-fours, I could have called the police or our councilwoman or someone and got an injunction. How do you get an injunction against a physical impossibility?

The first phone call came at about eight-thirty: Susan Morrison, whose back yard abuts the Pratt place.

"Reality check time," said Susan. "Do we have new neighbors or do we not?"

"Looks like it to me," I said.

Silence. Then she sighed. "Yeah. So. Can Kimmy sit for Jason Friday night?"

Typical. If you can't deal with it, pretend it doesn't exist, like when one couple down the street got the bright idea of turning their front lawn into a wildflower meadow. The trouble is, a Victorian mansion is a lot harder to ignore than even the wildest meadow. The phone rang all morning with hysterical calls from women who hadn't spoken to us since Geoff's brief tenure as president of the neighborhood association.

After several fruitless sessions of what's-the-world-coming-to, I turned on the machine and went out to the garden to put in the beans. Planting them in May was pushing it, but I needed the therapy. For me, gardening's the most soothing activity on Earth. When you plant a bean, you get a bean, not an azalea or a cabbage. When you see that bean covered with icky little orange things, you know they're Mexican bean beetle larvae and go for the pyrethrum. Or you do if you're paying attention. It always astonishes me how oblivious even the garden club ladies can be to a plant's needs and preferences.

Sure, there are nasty surprises, like the winter that the mice ate all the Apricot Beauty tulip bulbs. But mostly you know where you are with a garden. If you put the work in, you'll get satisfaction out, which is more than can be said of marriages or careers.

This time though, digging and raking and planting failed to work their usual magic. Every time I glanced up, there was Number 400, serene and comfortable, the shrubs established and the paint chipping just a little around the windows, exactly as if it had been there forever instead of less than twelve hours.

I'm not big on the inexplicable. Fantasy makes me nervous. In fact, fiction makes me nervous. I like facts and plenty of them. That's why I wanted to be a botanist. I wanted to know everything there was to know about how plants worked, why azaleas like acid soil and peonies like wood ash and how you might be able to get them to grow next to each other. I even went to graduate school and took organic chemistry. Then I met Geoff, fell in love, and traded in my Ph.D. for an M-R-S, with a minor in Mommy. None of these events (except possibly falling in love with Geoff) fundamentally shook my allegiance to provable, palpable facts. The house next door was palpable, all right, but it shouldn't have been. By the time Kim got home from school that afternoon, I had a headache from trying to figure out how it got to be there.

Kim is my daughter. She reads fantasy, likes animals a lot more than she likes people, and is a big fan of *Buffy the Vampire Slayer*. Because of Kim, we have two dogs (Spike and Willow), a cockatiel (Frodo), and a lop-eared Belgian rabbit (Big Bad), plus the overflow of semi-wild cats (Balm, Dwalin, Bifur, and Bombur) from the Pratt place, all of which she feeds and looks after with truly astonishing dedication.

Three-thirty on the nose, the screen door slammed and Kim careened into the kitchen with Spike and Willow bouncing ecstatically around her feet.

"Whaddya think of the new house, Mom? Who do you think lives there? Do they have pets?"

I laid out her after-school sliced apple and cheese and answered the question I could answer. "There's at least one woman—she was hanging out laundry this morning. No sign of children or pets, but it's early days yet."

"Isn't it just the coolest thing in the universe, Mom? Real magic, right next door. Just like Buffy!"

"Without the vampires, I hope. Kim, there's no such thing as magic. There's probably a perfectly simple explanation."

"But, Mom!"

"But nothing. You need to call Mrs. Morrison. She wants to know if you can sit for Jason on Friday night. And Big Bad's looking shaggy. He needs to be brushed."

That was Monday.

Tuesday morning, our street looked like the Expressway at rush hour. It's a miracle there wasn't an accident. Everybody in town must have driven by, slowing down as they passed Number 400 and craning out the car window. Things quieted down in the middle of the day when everyone was at work, but come 4:30 or so, the joggers started and the walkers and more cars. About 6:00, the police pulled up in front of the house, at which point everyone stopped pretending to be nonchalant and held their breath. Two cops disappeared into the house, came out again a few minutes later, and left without talking to anybody. They were holding cookies and looking bewildered.

The traffic let up on Wednesday. Kim found a kitten (Hermione) in the wildflower garden and Geoff came home full of the latest in a series of personality conflicts with his department head, which gave everyone something other than Number 400 to talk about over dinner.

Thursday, Lucille Flint baked one of her coffee cakes and went over to do the Welcome Wagon thing.

Lucille's our local Good Neighbor. Someone moves in, has a baby, marries, dies, and there's Lucille, Johnny-on-the-spot with a coffee cake in her hands and the proper Hallmark sentiment on her lips. Lucille has the time for this kind of thing because she doesn't have a regular job. All right, neither do I, but I write a gardener's advice column for the local paper, so I'm not exactly idle. There's the garden, too. Besides, I'm not the kind of person who likes sitting around in other people's kitchens drinking watery instant and hearing the stories of their lives. Lucille is.

Anyway. Thursday morning, I researched the diseases of roses for my column. I'm lucky with roses. Mine never come down with black spot, and the Japanese beetles prefer Susan Morrison's yard to mine. Weeds, however, are not so obliging. When I'd finished Googling "powdery mildew," I went out to tackle the rosebed.

Usually, I don't mind weeding. My mind wanders, my hands get dirty. I can almost feel my plants settling deeper into the soil as I root out the competition. But my rosebed is on the property line between us and the Pratt place. What if the house disappeared again, or someone wanted to chat? I'm not big into chatting. On the other hand, there was shepherd's purse in the rosebed, and shepherd's purse can be a wild Indian once you let it get established, so I gritted my teeth, grabbed my Cape Cod weeder, and got down to it.

Just as I was starting to relax, I heard footsteps passing on the walk and pushed the rose canes aside just in time to see Lucille Flint climbing the stone steps to Number 400. I watched her ring the doorbell, but I didn't see who answered because I ducked down behind a bushy Gloire de Dijon. If Lucille doesn't care who knows she's a busybody, that's her business.

After twenty-five minutes, I'd weeded and cultivated those roses to a fare-thee-well, and was backing out when I heard the screen door, followed by Lucille telling someone how lovely their home was, and thanks again for the scrumptious pie.

I caught her up under the copper beech.

"Evie dear, you're all out of breath," she said. "My, that's a nasty tear in your shirt."

"Come in, Lucille," I said. "Have a cup of coffee."

She followed me inside without comment, and accepted a cup of microwaved coffee and a slice of date-and-nut cake.

She took a bite, coughed a little, and grabbed for the coffee.

"It is pretty awful, isn't it?" I said apologetically. "I baked it last week for some PTA thing at Kim's school and forgot to take it."

"Never mind. I'm full of cherry pie from next door." She leaned over the stale cake and lowered her voice. "The cherries were fresh, Evie."

My mouth dropped open. "Fresh cherries? In May? You're kidding."

Lucille nodded, satisfied at my reaction. "Nope. There was a bowl of them on the table, leaves and all. What's more, there was corn on the draining-board. Fresh corn. In the husk. With the silk still on it."

"No!"

"Yes." Lucille sat back and took another sip of coffee. "Mind you, there could be a perfectly ordinary explanation. Ophelia's a horticulturist, after all. Maybe she's got greenhouses out back. Heaven knows there's enough room for several."

I shook my head. "I've never heard of corn growing in a greenhouse."

"And I've never heard of a house appearing in an empty lot overnight," Lucille said tartly. "About that, there's nothing I can tell you. They're not exactly forthcoming, if you know what I mean."

I was impressed. I knew how hard it was to avoid answering Lucille's questions, even about the most personal things. She just kind of picked at you, in the nicest possible way, until you unraveled. It's one of the reasons I didn't hang out with her much.

"So, who are they?"

"Rachel Abrams and Ophelia Canderel. I think they're lesbians.

They feel like family together, and you can take it from me, they're not sisters."

Fine. We're a liberal suburb, we can cope with lesbians. "Children?"

Lucille shrugged. "I don't know. There were drawings on the fridge, but no toys."

"Inconclusive evidence," I agreed. "What did you talk about?"

She made a face. "Pie crust. The Perkins's wildflower meadow. They like it. Burney." Burney was Lucille's husband, an unpleasant old fart who disapproved of everything in the world except his equally unpleasant terrier, Homer. "Electricians. They want a fixture put up in the front hall. Then Rachel tried to tell me about her work in artificial intelligence, but I couldn't understand a word she said."

From where I was sitting, I had an excellent view of Number 400's wisteria-covered carriage house with its double doors ajar on an awe-inspiring array of garden tackle. "Artificial intelligence must pay well," I said.

Lucille shrugged. "There has to be family money somewhere. You ought to see the front hall, not to mention the kitchen. It looks like something out of a magazine."

"What are they doing here?"

"That's the forty-thousand-dollar question, isn't it?"

We drained the cold dregs of our coffee, contemplating the mystery of why a horticulturist and an artificial intelligence wonk would choose our quiet, treelined suburb to park their house in. It seemed a more solvable mystery than how they'd transported it there in the first place.

Lucille took off to make Burney his noontime franks and beans and I tried to get my column roughed out. But I couldn't settle to my computer, not with that Victorian enigma sitting on the other side of my rose bed. Every once in a while, I'd see a shadow passing behind a window or hear a door bang. I gave up trying to make the disposal of diseased foliage interesting and went out to poke around in the garden. I was elbow-deep in the viburnum, pruning out deadwood, when I heard someone calling.

It was a woman, standing on the other side of my roses. She was big, solidly curved, and dressed in bright flowered overalls. Her hair was braided with shiny gold ribbon into dozens of tiny plaits tied off with little metal beads. Her skin was a deep matte brown, like antique mahogany. Despite the overalls, she was astonishingly beautiful.

I dropped the pruning shears. "Damn," I said. "Sorry," I said. "You surprised me." I felt my cheeks heat. The woman smiled at me serenely and beckoned.

I don't like new people and I don't like being put on the spot, but I've got my pride. I picked up my pruning shears, untangled myself from the viburnum, and marched across the lawn to meet my new neighbor.

She said her name was Ophelia Canderel, and she'd been admiring my garden. Would I like to see hers?

I certainly would.

If I'd met Ophelia at a party, I'd have been totally tongue-tied. She was beautiful, she was big, and frankly, there just aren't enough people of color in our neighborhood for me to have gotten over my Liberal nervousness around them. This particular woman of color, however, spoke fluent Universal Gardener and her garden was a gardener's garden, full of horticultural experiments and puzzles and stuff to talk about. Within about three minutes, she was asking my advice about the gnarly brown larvae infesting her bee balm, and I was filling her in on the peculiarities of our local microclimate. By the time we'd inspected every flower and shrub in the front yard, I was more comfortable with her than I was with the local garden club ladies. We were alike, Ophelia and I.

We were discussing the care and feeding of peonies in an acid soil when Ophelia said, "Would you like to see my shrubbery?"

Usually when I hear the word "shrubbery" I think of a semi-formal arrangement of rhodies and azaleas, lilacs and viburnum, with a potentilla perhaps, or a butterfly bush for late summer color. The bed should be deep enough to give everything room to spread and there should be a statue in it, or maybe a sundial. Neat, but not anal—that's what you should aim for in a shrubbery.

Ophelia sure had the not-anal part down pat. The shrubs didn't merely spread. They rioted. And what with the trees and the orchids and the ferns and the vines, I couldn't begin to judge the border's depth. The hibiscus and the bamboo were okay, although I wouldn't have risked them myself. But to plant bougainvillea and poinsettias, coconut palms and frangipani this far north was simply tempting fate. And the statue! I'd never seen anything remotely like it, not outside of a museum, anyway. No head to speak of, breasts like footballs, a belly like a watermelon, and a phallus like an overgrown zucchini, the whole thing weathered with the rains of a thousand years or more.

I glanced at Ophelia. "Impressive," I said.

She turned a critical eye on it. "You don't think it's too much? Rachel says it is, but she's a minimalist. This is my little bit of home, and I love it."

"It's a lot," I admitted. Accuracy prompted me to add, "It suits you."

I still didn't understand how Ophelia had gotten a tropical rainforest to flourish in a temperate climate.

I was trying to find a nice way to ask her about it when she said, "You're a real find, Evie. Rachel's working, or I'd call her to come down. She really wants to meet you."

"Next time," I said, wondering what on earth I'd find to talk about with a specialist on artificial intelligence. "Um. Does Rachel garden?"

Ophelia laughed. "No way—her talent is not for living things. But I made a garden for her. Would you like to see it?"

I was only dying to, although I couldn't help wondering what kind of exotica I was letting myself in for. A desertscape? Tundra? Curiosity won. "Sure," I said. "Lead on."

We stopped on the way to visit the vegetable garden. It looked fairly ordinary, although the tomatoes were more August than May, and the beans more late June. I didn't see any corn and I didn't see any greenhouses. After a brief sidebar on insecticidal soaps, Ophelia led me behind the carriage house. The unmistakable sound of quacking fell on my ears.

"We aren't zoned for ducks," I said, startled.

"We are," said Ophelia. "Now. How do you like Rachel's garden?"

A prospect of brown reeds with a silvery river meandering through it stretched through where the Morrison's back yard ought to be, all the way to a boundless expanse of ocean. In the marsh it was April, with a crisp salt wind blowing back from the water and ruffling the brown reeds and the white-flowering shad and the pale green unfurling sweetfern. Mallards splashed and dabbled along the meander. A solitary great egret stood among the reeds, the fringes of its white courting shawl blowing around one black and knobbly leg. As I watched, openmouthed, the egret unfurled its other leg from its breast feathers, trod at the reeds, and lowered its golden bill to feed.

I got home late. Kim was in the basement with the animals, and the chicken I was planning to make for dinner was still in the freezer. Thanking heaven for modern technology, I defrosted the chicken in the microwave, chopped veggies, seasoned, mixed, and got the whole mess in the oven just as Geoff walked in the door. He wasn't happy about eating forty-five minutes late, but he was mostly over it by bedtime.

That was Thursday.

Friday, I saw Ophelia and Rachel pulling out of their driveway in one of those old cars that has huge fenders and a running board. They returned after lunch, the back seat full of groceries. They and the groceries disappeared through the kitchen door, and there was no further sign of them until late afternoon, when Rachel opened one of the quarter-round windows in the attic and energetically shook the dust out of a small, patterned carpet.

On Saturday, the invitation came.

It stood out among the flyers, book orders, and requests for money that usually came through our mail-slot, a five-by-eight silvery-blue envelope that smelled faintly of sandalwood. It was addressed to the Gordon Family in a precise italic hand.

I opened it and read:

Rachel Esther Abrams and Ophelia Desirée Candarel
Request the Honor of Your Presence
At the
Celebration of their Marriage.
Sunday, May 24 at 3 PM
There will be refreshments before and after the Ceremony.

I was still staring at it when the doorbell rang. It was Lucille, looking fit to burst, holding an invitation just like mine.

"Come in, Lucille. There's plenty of coffee left."

I don't think I'd ever seen Lucille in such a state. You'd think someone had invited her to parade naked down Main Street at noon.

"Well, write and tell them you can't come," I said. "They're just being neighborly, for Pete's sake. It's not like they can't get married if you're not there."

"I know. It's just . . . It puts me in a funny position, that's all. Burney's a founding member of Normal Marriage for Normal People. He wouldn't like it at all if he knew I'd been invited to a lesbian wedding."

"So don't tell him. If you want to go, just tell him the new neighbors have invited you to an open house on Sunday, and you know for a fact that we're going to be there."

Lucille smiled. Burney hated Geoff almost as much as Geoff hated Burney. "It's a thought," she said. "Are you going?"

"I don't see why not. Who knows? I might learn something."

The Sunday of the wedding, I took forever to dress. Kim thought it was funny, but Geoff threatened to bail if I didn't quit fussing. "It's a lesbian wedding, for pity's sake. It's going to be full of middle-aged dykes with ugly haircuts. Nobody's going to care what you look like."

"I care," said Kim. "And I think that jacket is wicked cool."

I'd bought the jacket at a little Indian store in the Square and not worn it since. When I got it away from the Square's atmosphere of collegiate funk it looked, I don't know, too Sixties, too artsy, too bright for a fortysomething suburban matron. It was basically purple, with teal blue and gold and fuchsia flowers all over it and brass buttons shaped like parrots. Shaking my head, I started to unfasten the parrots.

Geoff exploded. "I swear to God, Evie, if you change again, that's it. It's not like I want to go. I've got papers to correct: don't have time for this"—he glanced at Kim—"nonsense. Either we go or we stay. But we do it now."

Kim touched my arm. "It's you, Mom. Come on."

So I came on, my jacket flashing neon in the sunlight. By the time we hit the sidewalk, I felt like a tropical floral display; I was ready to bolt home and hide under the bed.

"Great," said Geoff. "Not a car in sight. If we're the only ones here, I'm leaving."

"I don't think that's going to be a problem," I said.

Beyond the copper beech, I saw a colorful crowd milling around as purposefully as bees, bearing chairs and flowers and ribbons. As we came closer, it became clear that Geoff couldn't have been more wrong about the wedding guests. There wasn't an ugly haircut in sight, although there were some pretty startling dye-jobs. The dress code could best be described as eclectic, with a slight bias toward floating fabrics and rich, bright colors. My jacket felt right at home.

Geoff was muttering about not knowing anybody when Lucille appeared, looking festive in Laura Ashley chintz.

"Isn't this fun?" she said, with every sign of sincerity. "I've never met such interesting people. And friendly! They make me feel right at home. Come over here and join the gang."

She dragged us toward the long side-yard, which sloped down to a lavishly blooming double-flowering cherry underplanted with peonies. Which shouldn't have been in bloom at the same time as the cherry, but I was getting used to the vagaries of Ophelia's garden. A willowy young person in chartreuse lace claimed Lucille's attention, and they went off together. The three of us stood in a slightly awkward knot at the edge of the crowd, which occasionally threw out a few guests who eddied around us briefly before retreating.

"How are those spells of yours, dear? Any better?" inquired a solicitous voice in my ear, and, "Oh!" when I jumped. "You're not Elvira, are you? Sorry."

Geoff's grip was cutting off the circulation above my elbow. "This was not one of your better ideas, Evie. We're surrounded by weirdoes. Did you see that guy in the skirt? I think we should take Kimmy home."

A tall black man with a flattop and a diamond in his left ear appeared, pried Geoff's hand from my arm, and shook it warmly. "Dr.

Gordon? Ophelia told me to be looking out for you. I've read *The Anar-chists,* you see, and I can't tell you how much I admired it."

Geoff actually blushed. Before the subject got too painful to talk about, he used to say that for a history of anarchism, his one book had had a remarkably elite readership: three members of the tenure review committee, two reviewers for scholarly journals, and his wife. "Thanks," he said.

Geoff's fan grinned, clearly delighted. "Maybe we can talk at the reception," he said. "Right now I need to find you a place to sit. They look like they're just about ready to roll."

It was a lovely wedding.

I don't know exactly what I was expecting, but I was mildly surprised to see a rabbi and a wedding canopy. Ophelia was an enormous rose in crimson draperies. Rachel was a calla lily in cream linen. Their heads were tastefully wreathed in oak and ivy leaves. There were the usual prayers and promises and tears; when the rabbi pronounced them married, they kissed and horns sounded a triumphant fanfare.

Kim poked me in the side. "Mom? Who's playing those horns?"

"I don't know. Maybe it's a recording."

"I don't think so," Kim said. "I think it's the tree. Isn't this just about the coolest thing ever?"

We were on our feet again. The chairs had disappeared and people were dancing. A cheerful bearded man grabbed Kim's hand to pull her into the line. Geoff grabbed her and pulled her back.

"Dad!" Kim wailed. "I want to dance!"

"I've got a pile of papers to correct before class tomorrow," Geoff said. "And if I know you, there's some homework you've put off until tonight. We have to go home now."

"We can't leave yet," I objected. "We haven't congratulated the brides."

Geoff's jaw tensed. "So go congratulate them," he said. "Kim and I will wait for you here."

Kim looked mutinous. I gave her the eye. This wasn't the time or the place to object. Like Geoff, Kim had no inhibitions about airing the family linen in public, but I had enough for all three of us.

"Dr. Gordon. There you are." *The Anarchists* fan popped up between us. "I've been looking all over for you. Come have a drink and let me tell you how brilliant you are."

Geoff smiled modestly. "You're being way too generous," he said. "Did you read Peterson's piece in *The Review?*"

"Asshole," said the man dismissively. Geoff slapped him on the back, and a minute later, they were halfway to the house, laughing as if they'd known each other for years. Thank heaven for the male ego.

"Dance?" said Kim.

"Go for it," I said. "I'm going to get some champagne and kiss the brides."

The brides were nowhere to be found. The champagne, a young girl informed me, was in the kitchen. So I entered Number 400 for the first time, coming through the mudroom into a large, oak-paneled hall. To my left a staircase with an ornately carved oak banister rose to an art-glass window. Ahead was a semicircular fireplace with a carved bench on one side and a door that probably led to he kitchen on the other. Between me and the door was an assortment of brightly dressed strangers, talking and laughing.

I edged around them, passing two curtained doors and a bronze statue of Alice and the Red Queen. Puzzle fragments of conversation rose out of the general buzz:

"My pearls? Thank you, my dear, but you know they're only stimulated."

"And *then* it just went 'poof'! A perfectly good frog, and it just went poof!"

" . . . and then Tallulah says to the bishop, she says, 'Love your drag, darling, but your purse is on fire.' Don't you love it? 'Your purse is on fire!'"

The kitchen itself was blessedly empty except for a stout gentleman in a tuxedo, and a striking woman in a peach silk pantsuit, who was tending an array of champagne bottles and a cut-glass bowl full of bright blue punch. Curious, I picked up a cup of punch and sniffed at it. The woman smiled up at me through a caterpillary fringe of false lashes.

"Pure witch's brew," she said in one of those Lauren Bacall come-hither voices I've always envied. "But what can you do? It's the *specialité de la maison.*"

The tuxedoed man laughed. "Don't mind Silver, Mrs. Gordon. He just likes to tease. Ophelia's punch is wonderful."

"Only if you like Ty-dee Bowl," said Silver, tipping a sapphire stream into another cup. "You know, honey, you shouldn't stand around with your mouth open like that. Think of the flies."

Several guests entered in plenty of time to catch this exchange. Determined to preserve my cool, I took a gulp of the punch. It tasted fruity and made my mouth prickle, and then it hit my stomach like a firecracker. So much for cool. I choked and gasped.

"I tried to warn you," Silver said. "You'd better switch to champagne." Now I knew Silver was a man, I could see that his hands and wrists were big for the rest of her—him. I could feel my face burning with punch and mortification.

"No, thank you," I said faintly. "Maybe some water?"

The stout man handed me a glass. I sipped gratefully. "You're Ophelia and Rachel's neighbor, aren't you?" he said. "Lovely garden. You must be proud of that asparagus bed."

"I was, until I saw Ophelia's."

"Ooh, listen to the green-eyed monster," Silver cooed. "Don't be jealous, honey. Ophelia's the best. Nobody understands plants like Ophelia."

"I'm not jealous," I said with dignity. "I'm wistful. There's a difference."

Then, just when I thought it couldn't possibly get any worse, Geoff appeared, looking stunningly unprofessorial, with one side of his shirt collar turned up and his dark hair flopped over his eyes.

"Hey, Evie. Who knew a couple of dykes would know how to throw a wedding?"

You'd think after sixteen years of living with Geoff, I'd know whether or not he was an alcoholic. But I don't, he doesn't go on binges, he doesn't get drunk at every party we go to, and I'm pretty sure he doesn't drink on the sly. What I do know is that drinking doesn't make him more fun to be around.

I took his arm. "I'm glad you're enjoying yourself," I said brightly. "Too bad we have to leave."

"Leave? Who said anything about leaving? We just got here."

"Your papers," I said. "Remember?"

"Screw my papers," said Geoff and held out his empty cup to Silver. "This punch is dy-no-mite."

"What about your students?"

"I'll tell 'em I didn't feel like reading their stupid essays. That'll fix their little red wagons. Boring as hell anyway. Fill 'er up, beautiful," he told Silver.

Silver considered him gravely. "Geoff, darling," he said. "A little bird tells me that there's an absolutely delicious argument going on in the smoking room. They'll never forgive you if you don't come play."

Geoff favored Silver with a leer that made me wish I were somewhere else. "Only if you play too," he said. "What's it about?"

Silver waved a pink-tipped hand. "Something about theoretical versus practical anarchy. Right, Rodney?"

"I believe so," said the stout gentleman agreeably.

A martial gleam rose in Geoff's eye. "Let me at 'em."

Silver's pale eyes turned to me, solemn and concerned. "You don't mind, do you, honey?"

I shrugged. With luck, the smoking-room crowd would be drunk too, and nobody would remember who said what. I just hoped none of the anarchists had a violent temper.

"We'll return him intact," Silver said. "I promise." And they were gone, Silver trailing fragrantly from Geoff's arm.

While I was wondering whether I'd said that thing about the anarchists or only thought it, I felt a tap on my shoulder—the stout gentleman, Rodney.

"Mrs. Gordon, Rachel and Ophelia would like to see you and young Kimberly in the study. If you'll please step this way?"

His manner had shifted from wedding guest to old-fashioned butler. Properly intimidated, I trailed him to the front hail. It was empty now, except for Lucille and the young person in chartreuse lace, who were huddled together on the bench by the fireplace. The young person was talking earnestly and Lucille was listening and nodding and sipping punch. Neither of them paid any attention to us or to the music coming from behind one of the curtained doors. I saw Kim at the foot of the stairs, examining the newel post.

It was well worth examining: a screaming griffin with every feather and every curl beautifully articulated and its head polished smooth and black as ebony. Rodney gave it a brief, seemingly unconscious caress as he started up the steps. When Kim followed suit, I thought I saw the carved eye blink.

I must have made a noise, because Rodney halted his slow ascent and gazed down at me, standing open-mouthed below. "Lovely piece of work, isn't it? We call it the house guardian. A joke, of course."

"Of course," I echoed. "Cute."

It seemed to me that the house had more rooms than it ought to. Through open doors, I glimpsed libraries, salons, parlors, bedrooms. We passed through a stone cloister where discouraged-looking ficuses in tubs shed their leaves on the cracked pavement and into a green-scummed pool. I don't know what shocked me more: the cloister or the state of its plants. Maybe Ophelia's green thumb didn't extend to houseplants.

As far as I could tell, Kim took all this completely in stride. She bounded along like a dog in the woods, peeking in an open door here, pausing to look at a picture there, and pelting Rodney with questions I wouldn't have dreamed of asking, like "Are there kids here?"; "What about pets?"; "How many people live here, anyway?"

"It depends," was Rodney's unvarying answer. "Step this way, please."

Our trek ended in a wall covered by a huge South American tapestry of three women making pots. Rodney pulled the tapestry aside, revealing an iron-banded oak door that would have done a medieval castle proud. "The study," he said, and opened the door on a flight of ladder-like steps rising steeply into the shadows.

His voice and gesture reminded me irresistibly of one of those horror movies in which a laconic butler leads the hapless heroine to a forbidding door and invites her to step inside. I didn't know which of three impulses was stronger: to laugh, to run, or, like the heroine, to forge on and see what happened next.

It's some indication of the state I was in that Kim got by me and through the door before I could stop her.

I don't like feeling helpless and I don't like feeling pressured. I really don't like being tricked, manipulated, and herded. Left to myself, I'd have turned around and taken my chances on finding my way out of the maze of corridors. But I wasn't going to leave without my daughter, so I hitched up my wedding-appropriate long skirt and started up the steps.

The stairs were every bit as steep as they looked. I floundered up gracelessly, emerging into a huge space sparsely furnished with a beat-up rolltop desk, a wingback chair and a swan-neck rocker on a threadbare Oriental rug at one end, and some cluttered door-on-sawhorse tables on the other. Ophelia and Rachel, still dressed in their bridal finery, were sitting in the chair and the rocker respectively, holding steaming mugs and talking to Kim, who was incandescent with excitement.

"Oh, there you are," said Ophelia as I stumbled up the last step. "Would you like some tea?"

"No, thank you," I said stiffly. "Kim, I think it's time to go home now."

Kim protested, vigorously. Rachel cast Ophelia an unreadable look.

"It'll be fine, love," Ophelia said soothingly. "Mrs. Gordon's upset, and who could blame her? Evie, I don't believe you've actually met Rachel."

Where I come from, social niceties trump everything. Without actually meaning to, I found I was shaking Rachel's hand and congratulating her on her marriage. Close up, she was a handsome woman, with a decided nose, deep lines around her mouth, and the measuring gaze of a gardener examining an unfamiliar insect on her tomato leaves. I didn't ask her to call me Evie.

Ophelia touched my hand. "Never mind," she said soothingly. "Have some tea. You'll feel better."

Next thing I knew, I was sitting on a chair that hadn't been there a moment before, eating a lemon cookie from a plate I didn't see arrive, and drinking Lapsang Souchong from a cup that appeared when Ophelia reached for it. Just for the record, I didn't feel better at all. I felt as if I'd taken a step that wasn't there, or perhaps failed to take one that was: out of balance, out of place, out of control.

Kim, restless as a cat, was snooping around among the long tables.

"What's with the flying fish?" she asked.

"They're for Rachel's new experiment," said Ophelia. "She thinks she can bring the dead to life again."

"You better let me tell it, Ophie," Rachel said. "I don't want Mrs. Gordon thinking I'm some kind of mad scientist."

In fact, I wasn't thinking at all, except that I was in way over my head.

"I'm working on animating extinct species," Rachel said. "I'm particularly interested in dodos and passenger pigeons, but eventually, I'd like to work up to bison and maybe woolly mammoths."

"Won't that create ecological problems?" Kim objected. "I mean, they're way big, and we don't know much about their habits or what they ate or anything."

There was a silence while Rachel and Ophelia traded family-joke smiles.

"That's why we need you," Rachel said.

Kim looked as though she'd been given the pony she'd been agitating for since fourth grade. Her jaw dropped. Her eyes sparkled. And I lost it.

"Will somebody please tell me what the hell you're talking about?" I said. "I've been patient. I followed your pal Rodney through more rooms than Versailles and I didn't run screaming, and believe me when I tell you I wanted to. I've drunk your tea and listened to your so-called explanations, and I still don't know what's going on."

Kim turned to me with a look of blank astonishment. "Come on, Mom. I can't believe you don't know that Ophelia and Rachel are witches. It's perfectly obvious."

"We prefer not to use the W word," Rachel said. "Like most labels, it's misleading and inaccurate. We're just people with natural scientific ability who have been trained to ask the right questions."

Ophelia nodded. "We learn to ask the things themselves. They always know. Do you see?"

"No," I said. "All I see is a roomful of junk and a garden that doesn't care what season it is."

"Very well," said Rachel, and rose from her chair. "If you'll just come over here, Mrs. Gordon, I'll try to clear everything up."

At the table of the flying fish, Ophelia arranged us in a semi-circle, with Rachel in a teacherly position beside the exhibits. These seemed to be A) the fish; and B) one of those Japanese good-luck cats with one paw curled up by its ear and a bright enameled bib.

"As you know," Rachel said, "my field is artificial intelligence. What that means, essentially, is that I can animate the inanimate. Observe." She caressed the porcelain cat between its ears. For two breaths, nothing happened. Then the cat lowered its paw and stretched itself luxuriously. The light glinted off its bulging sides; its curly red mouth and wide painted eyes were expressionless.

"Sweet," Kim breathed.

"It's not really alive," Rachel said, stroking the cat's shiny back. "It's still porcelain. If it jumps off the table, it'll break."

"Can I pet it?" Kim asked.

"No!" Rachel and I said in firm and perfect unison.

"Why not?"

"Because I'd like you to help me with an experiment." Rachel looked me straight in the eye. "I'm not really comfortable with words," she said. "I prefer demonstrations. What I'm going to do is hold Kim's hand and touch the fish. That's all."

"And what happens then?" Kim asked eagerly.

Rachel smiled at her. "Well, we'll see, won't we? Are you okay with this, Mrs. Gordon?"

It sounded harmless enough, and Kim was already reaching for Rachel's hand. "Go ahead, " I said.

Their hands met palm to palm. Rachel closed her eyes. She frowned in concentration and the atmosphere tightened around us. I yawned to unblock my ears.

Rachel laid her free hand on one of the fish.

It twitched, head jerking galvanically; its wings fanned open and shut.

Kim gave a little grunt, which snapped my attention away from the fish. She was pale and sweating a little—

I started to go to her, but I couldn't. Someone was holding me back.

"It's okay, Evie," Ophelia said soothingly. "Kim's fine, really. Rachel knows what she's doing."

"Kim's pale," I said, calm as the eye of a storm. "She looks like she's going to throw up. She's not fine. Let me go to my daughter, Ophelia, or I swear you'll regret it."

"Believe me, it's not safe for you to touch them right now. You have to trust us."

My Great-Aunt Fanny I'll trust you, I thought, and willed myself to relax in her grip. "Okay," I said shakily. "I believe you. It's just, I wish you'd warned me."

"We wanted to tell you," Ophelia said. "But we were afraid you wouldn't believe us. We were afraid you would think we were a couple of nuts. You see, Kim has the potential to be an important zoologist—if she has the proper training. Rachel's a wonderful teacher, and you can see for yourself how complementary their disciplines are. Working together, they . . . "

I don't know what she thought Kim and Rachel could accomplish, because the second she was more interested in what she was saying than in holding onto me, I was out of her hands and pulling Kim away from the witch who, as far as I could tell, was draining her dry.

That was the plan, anyway.

As soon as I touched Kim, the room came alive.

It started with the flying fish leaping off the table and buzzing past us on Saran Wrap wings. The porcelain cat thumped down from the table and, far from breaking, twined itself around Kim's ankles, purring hollowly. An iron plied itself over a pile of papers, smoothing out the creases. The teddy bear growled at it and ran to hide behind a toaster.

If that wasn't enough, my jacket burst into bloom.

It's kind of hard to describe what it's like to wear a tropical forest. Damp, for one thing. Bright. Loud. Uncomfortable. Very, very uncomfortable. Overstimulating. There were flowers and parrots screeching (yes, the flowers, too—or maybe that was me). It seemed to go on for a long time, kind of like giving birth. At first, I was overwhelmed by the chaos of growth and sound, unsure whether I was the forest or the forest was me. Slowly I realized that it didn't have to be a chaos, and that if I just pulled myself together, I could make sense of it. That flower went there, for instance, and the teal one went there. That parrot belonged on that vine and everything needed to be smaller and stiller and less extravagantly colored. Like that.

Gradually, the forest receded. I was still holding Kim, who promptly bent over and threw up on the floor.

"There," I said hoarsely." I told you she was going to be sick."

Ophelia picked up Rachel and carried her back to her wingchair. "You be quiet, you," she said over her shoulder. "Heaven knows what you've done to Rachel. I told you not to touch them."

Ignoring my own nausea, I supported Kim over to the rocker and deposited her in it. "You might have told me why," I snapped. "I don't know why people can't just explain things instead of making me guess. It's not like I can read minds, you know. Now, are you going to conjure us up a glass of water, or do I have to go find the kitchen?"

Rachel had recovered herself enough to give a shaky laugh. "Hell, you could conjure it yourself, with a little practice. Ophie, darling, calm down. I'm fine."

Ophelia stopped fussing over her wife long enough to snatch a glass of cool mint tea from the air and hand it to me. She wouldn't meet my eyes, and she was scowling. "I told you she was going to be difficult. Of all the damn-fool, pigheaded . . . ."

"Hush, love," Rachel said. "There's no harm done, and now we know just where we stand. I'd rather have a nice cup of tea than listen to you cursing out Mrs. Gordon for just trying to be a good mother." She turned her head to look at me. "Very impressive, by the way. We knew you had to be like Ophie, because of the garden, but we didn't know the half of it. You've got a kick like a mule, Mrs. Gordon."

I must have been staring at her like one of the flying fish. Here I thought I'd half-killed her, and she was giving me a smile that looked perfectly genuine.

I smiled cautiously in return. "Thank you," I said.

Kim pulled at the sleeve of my jacket. "Hey, Mom, that was awesome. I guess you're a witch, huh?"

I wanted to deny it, but I couldn't. The fact was that the pattern of flowers on my jacket was different and the colors were muted, the flowers more English garden than tropical paradise. There were only three buttons, and they were larks, not parrots. And I felt different. Clearer? More whole? I don't know—different. Even though I didn't know how the magic worked or how to control it, I couldn't ignore the fact—the palpable, provable fact—it was there.

"Yeah," I said. "I guess I am."

"Me, too," my daughter said. "What's Dad going to say?"

I thought for a minute. "Nothing, honey. Because we're not going to tell him."

We didn't, either. And we're not going to. There's no useful purpose served by telling people truths they aren't equipped to accept. Geoff's pretty oblivious, anyway. It's true that in the hung-over aftermath of Ophelia's blue punch, he announced that he thought the new neighbors might be a bad influence, but he couldn't actually forbid Kim and me to hang out with them because it would look homophobic.

Kim's over at Number 400 most Saturday afternoons, learning how to be a zoologist. She's making good progress. There was an episode with zombie mice I don't like to think about, and a crisis when the porcelain cat broke falling out of a tree. But she's learning patience, control, and discipline, which are all excellent things for a girl of fourteen to learn. She and Rachel have reanimated a pair of passenger pigeons, but they haven't had any luck in breeding them yet.

Lucille's the biggest surprise. It turns out that all her nosy-parkerism was a case of ingrown witchiness. Now she's studying with Silver, of all people, to be a psychologist. But that's not the surprise. The surprise is that she left Burney and moved into Number 400, where she has a room draped with chintz and a gray cat named Jezebel and is as happy as a clam at high tide.

I'm over there a lot, too, learning to be a horticulturist. Ophelia says I'm a quick study, but I have to learn to trust my instincts. Who knew I had instincts? I thought I was just good at looking things up.

I'm working on my own garden now. I'm the only one who can find it without being invited in. It's an English kind of garden, like the gardens in books I loved as a child. It has a stone wall with a low door in it, a little central lawn, and a perennial border full of foxgloves and Sweet William and Michelmas daisies. Veronica blooms in the cracks of the wall, and periwinkle carpets the beds where old-fashioned fragrant roses nod heavily to every passing breeze. There's a small wilderness of rowan trees, and a neat shrubbery embracing a pond stocked with fish as bright as copper pennies. Among the dusty-smelling boxwood, I've put a statue of a woman holding a basket planted with stonecrop. She's dressed in a jacket incised with flowers and vines and closed with three buttons shaped like parrots. The fourth button sits on her shoulder, clacking its beak companionably and preening its brazen feathers. I'm thinking of adding a duck pond next, or maybe a wilderness for Kim's menagerie.

Witches don't have to worry about zoning laws.

Delia Sherman's first novel, *Through a Brazen Mirror* was published in 1989. *The Porcelain Dove*, her second novel, won the Mythopoeic Award for 1993. Her short fiction has appeared in *Fantasy & Science Fiction*, *Xanadu II*, *The Armless Maiden*, *Ruby Slippers, Golden Tears*, *A Wolf at the Door*, and *The Green Man*, among others. She lives with fellow author and fantasist Ellen Kushner (with whom she collaborated for novel *The Fall of Kings*, 2002) in a cozily cluttered old house in Somerville, Massachusetts, which has just enough garden for roses, lilacs, herbs, and a few vegetables. Sherman's latest novel is *The Changeling*.

A KNOT OF TOADS

Jane Yolen

"*March 1931: Late on Saturday night,*" the old man had written, "*a toad came into my study and looked at me with goggled eyes, reflecting my candlelight back at me. It seemed utterly unafraid. Although nothing so far seems linked with this appearance, I have had enough formidable visitants to know this for a harbinger.*"

A harbinger of spring, I would have told him, but I arrived too late to tell him anything. I'd been summoned from my Cambridge rooms to his little white-washed stone house with its red pantile roof overlooking St Monans harbor. The summons had come from his housekeeper, Mrs. Marr, in a frantic early morning phone call. Hers was from the town's one hotel, to me in the porter's room which boasted the only telephone at our college.

I was a miserable ten hours getting there. All during the long train ride, though I tried to pray for him, I could not, having given up that sort of thing long before leaving Scotland. Loss of faith, lack of faith—that had been my real reason for going away from home. Taking up a place at Gerton College had only been an excuse.

What I had wanted to do this return was to mend our fences before it was too late to mend anything at all. Father and I had broken so many fences—stones, dykes, stiles, and all—that the mending would have taken more than the fortnight's holiday I had planned for later in the summer. But I'd been summoned home early this March because, as Mrs. Marr said, father had had a bad turn.

"A *verrry* bad turn," was what she'd actually said, before the line had gone dead, her r's rattling like a kettle on the boil. In her understated way, she might have meant anything from a twisted ankle to a major heart attack.

The wire that had followed, delivered by a man with a limp and a harelip, had been from my father's doctor, Ewan Kinnear. "Do not delay," it read. Still, there was no diagnosis.

Even so, I did not delay. We'd had no connection in ten years beside a holiday letter exchange. Me to him, not the other way round. But the old man was my only father. I was his only child.

He was dead by the time I got there, and Mrs. Marr stood at the doorway of the house wringing her hands, her black hair caught up in a net. She had not aged a day since I last saw her.

"So ye've left it too late, Janet," she cried. "And wearing green I see."

I looked down at my best dress, a soft green linen now badly creased with travel.

She shook her head at me, and only then did I remember. In St Monans they always said, "After green comes grief."

"I didn't know he was that ill. I came as fast as I could." But Mrs. Marr's face showed her disdain for my excuse. Her eyes narrowed and she didn't put out her hand. She'd always been on father's side, especially in the matter of my faith. "His old heart's burst in twa." She was of the old school in speech as well as faith.

"His heart was stone, Maggie, and well you know it." A widow, she'd waited twenty-seven years, since my mother died birthing me, for the old man to notice her. She must be old herself now.

"Stane can still feel pain," she cried.

"What pain?" I asked.

"Of your leaving."

What good would it have done to point out I'd left more than ten years earlier and he'd hardly noticed. He'd had a decade more of calcification, a decade more of pouring over his bloody old books— the Latin texts of apostates and heretics. A decade more of filling notebooks with his crabbed script.

A decade more of ignoring his only child.

My God, I thought, meaning no appeal to a deity but a simple swear, *I am still furious with him. It's no wonder I've never married.* Though I'd had chances. Plenty of them. Well, two that were real enough.

I went into the house, and the smell of candle wax and fish and salt sea were as familiar to me as though I'd never left. But there was another smell, too.

Death.

And something more.

It was fear. But I was not to know that till later.

The study where evidently he'd died, sitting up in his chair, was a dark place, even when the curtains were drawn back, which had not been frequent in my childhood. Father liked the close, wood-paneled room, made closer by the ever-burning fire. I'd been allowed in there only when being punished, standing just inside the doorway, with my hands clasped behind me, to listen to my sins being counted. My sins were homey ones, like shouting in the hallway, walking too loudly by his door, or refusing to learn my verses from the Bible. I was far too innocent a child for more than that.

Even at five and six and seven I'd been an unbeliever. Not having a mother had made me so. How could I worship a God whom both Mrs. Marr and my father assured me had so wanted mother, He'd called her away. A selfish God, that, who had listened to his own desires and not mine. Such a God was not for me. Not then. Not now.

I had a sudden urge—me, a postgraduate in a prestigious university who should have known better—to clasp my hands behind me and await my punishment.

But, I thought, *the old punisher is dead. And—if he's to be believed— gone to his own punishment.* Though I was certain that the only place he had gone was to the upstairs bedroom where he was laid out, awaiting my instructions as to his burial.

I went into every other room of the house but that bedroom, memory like an old fishing line dragging me on. The smells, the dark moody smells, remained the same, though Mrs. Marr had a good wood fire burning in the grate, not peat, a wee change in this changeless place. But everything else was so much smaller than I remembered, my little bedroom at the back of the house the smallest of them all.

To my surprise, nothing in my bedroom had been removed. My bed, my toys—the little wooden doll with jointed arms and legs I called Annie, my ragged copy of *Rhymes and Tunes for Little Folks*, the boxed chess set just the size for little hands, my cloth bag filled with buttons—the rag rug, the over-worked sampler on the wall. All were the same. I was surprised to even find one of my old pinafores and black stockings in the wardrobe. I charged Mrs. Marr with more sentiment than sense. It was a shrine to the child that I'd been, not the young woman who had run off. It had to have been Mrs. Marr's idea. Father would never have countenanced false gods.

Staring out of the low window, I looked out toward the sea. A fog sat on the horizon, white and patchy. Below it the sea was a deep, solitary blue. Spring comes early to the East Neuk but summer stays away. I guessed that pussy willows had already appeared around the edges of the lochans, snowdrops and aconite decorating the inland gardens.

Once I'd loved to stare out at that sea, escaping the dark brooding house whenever I could, even in a cutting wind, the kind that could raise bruises. Down I'd go to the beach to play amongst the yawls hauled up on the high wooden trestles, ready for tarring. Once I'd dreamed of going off to sea with the fishermen, coming home to the harbor in the late summer light, and seeing the silver scales glinting on the beach. Though of course fishing was not a woman's job. Not then, not now. A woman in a boat was unthinkable even this far into the twentieth century. St Monans is firmly eighteenth century and likely to remain so forever.

But I'd been sent off to school, away from the father who found me a loud and heretical discomfort. At first it was just a few towns away, to St Leonard's in St Andrews, but as I was a boarder—my father's one extravagance—it might as well have been across the country, or the ocean, as far as seeing my father was concerned. And there I'd fallen in love with words in books.

Words—not water, not wind.

In that way I showed myself to be my father's daughter. Only I never said so to him, nor he to me.

Making my way back down the stairs, I overheard several folk in the kitchen. They were speaking of those things St Monans folk always speak of, no matter their occupations: Fish and weather.

"There's been nae herring in the firth this winter," came a light man's voice. "Nane." Doctor Kinnear.

"It's a bitter wind to keep the men at hame, the fish awa." Mrs. Marr agreed.

Weather and the fishing. Always the same.

But a third voice, one I didn't immediately recognize, a rumbling growl of a voice, added, "Does she know?"

"Do I know what?" I asked, coming into the room where the big black-leaded grate threw out enough heat to warm the entire house. "How Father died?"

I stared at the last speaker, a stranger I thought, but somehow familiar. He was tall for a St Monans man, but dressed as one of the fisherfolk, in dark trousers, a heavy white sweater, thick white sea stockings. And he was sunburnt like them, too, with eyes the exact blue of the April sea, gathered round with laugh lines. A ginger mustache, thick and full, hung down the sides of his mouth like a parenthesis.

"By God, Alec Hughes," I said, startled to have remembered, surprised that I could have forgotten. He grinned.

When we'd been young—very young—Alec and I were inseparable. Never mind that boys and girls never played together in St Monans. Boys from the Bass, girls from the May, the old folk wisdom went. The Bass Rock, the Isle of May, the original separation of the sexes. Apart at birth and ever after. Yet Alec and I had done everything together: messed about with the boats, played cards, built sand castles, fished with *pelns*—shore crabs about to cast their shells—and stolen jam pieces from his mother's kitchen to eat down by one of the gates in the drystone dykes. We'd even often hied off to the low cliff below the ruins of Andross Castle to look for *croupies,* fossils, though whether we ever found any I couldn't recall. When I'd been sent away to school, he'd stayed on in St Monans, going to Anstruther's Waid Academy in the next town but one, until he was old enough—I presumed—to join the fishing fleet, like his father before him. His father was a stern and dour soul, a Temperance man who used to preach in the open air.

Alec had been the first boy to kiss me, my back against the stone windmill down by the salt pans. And until I'd graduated from St Leonard's, the only boy to do so, though I'd made up for that since.

"I thought, Jan," he said slowly, "that God was not in your vocabulary."

"Except as a swear," I retorted. "Good to see you, too, Alec."

Mrs. Marr's eyebrows both rose considerably, like fulmars over the green-grey sea of her eyes.

Alec laughed and it was astonishing how that laugh reminded me of the boy who'd stayed behind. "Yes," he said. "Do you know how your father died?"

"Heart attack, so Mrs. Marr told me."

I stared at the three of them. Mrs. Marr was wringing her hands again, an oddly old-fashioned motion at which she seemed well practiced. Dr. Kinnear polished his eyeglasses with a large white piece of cloth, his flyaway eyebrows proclaiming his advancing age. And Alec— had I remembered how blue his eyes were? Alec nibbled on the right end of his mustache.

"Did I say that?" Mrs. Marr asked. "Bless me, I didna."

And indeed, she hadn't. She'd been more poetic.

"*Burst in twa*, you said." I smiled, trying to apologize for mis-speaking. Not a good trait in a scholar.

"Indeed. Indeed." Mrs. Marr's wrangling hands began again. Any minute I supposed she would break out into a Psalm. I remembered how her one boast was that she'd learned them all by heart as a child and never forgot a one of them.

"A shock, I would have said," Alec said by way of elaborating.

"A fright," the doctor added.

"Really? Is that the medical term?" I asked. "What in St Monans could my father possibly be frightened of?"

Astonishingly, Mrs. Marr began to wail then, a high, thin keening that went on and on till Alec put his arm around her and marched her over to the stone sink where he splashed her face with cold water and she quieted at once. Then she turned to the blackened kettle squalling on the grate and started to make us all tea.

I turned to the doctor who had his glasses on now, which made him look like a somewhat surprised barn owl. "What do you really mean, Dr. Kinnear."

"Have you nae seen him yet?" he asked, his head gesturing towards the back stairs.

"I . . . I couldn't," I admitted. But I said no more. How could I tell this man I hardly knew that my father and I were virtual strangers. No—it was more than that. I was afraid of my father dead as I'd never been alive. Because now he knew for certain whether he was right or I was, about God and Heaven and the rest.

"Come," said Doctor Kinnear in a voice that seemed permanently gentle. He held out a hand and led me back up the stairs and down the hall to my father's room. Then he went in with me and stood by my side as I looked down.

My father was laid out on his bed, the Scottish double my mother had died in, the one he'd slept in every night of his adult life except the day she'd given birth, the day she died.

Like the house, he was much smaller than I remembered. His wild, white hair lay untamed around his head in a kind of corolla. The skin of his face was parchment stretched over bone. That great prow of a nose was, in death, strong enough to guide a ship in. Thankfully his eyes were shut. His hands were crossed on his chest. He was dressed in an old dark suit. I remembered it well.

"He doesn't look afraid," I said. Though he didn't look peaceful either. Just dead.

"Once he'd lost the stiffness, I smoothed his face a bit," the doctor told me. "Smoothed it out. Otherwise Mrs. Marr would no have settled."

"Settled?"

He nodded. "She found him at his desk, stone dead. Ran down the road screaming all the way to the pub. And lucky I was there, having a drink with friends. I came up to see yer father sitting up in his chair, with a face so full of fear, I looked around mysel' to discover the cause of it."

"And did you?"

His blank expression said it all. He simply handed me a pile of five notebooks. "These were on the desk in front of him. Some of the writing is in Latin, which I have but little of. Perhaps ye can read it, being the scholar. Mrs. Marr has said that they should be thrown on the fire, or at least much of them scored out. But I told her that had to be yer decision and Alec agrees."

I took the notebooks, thinking that this was what had stolen my father from me and now was all I had of him. But I said none of that aloud. After glancing over at the old man again, I asked, "May I have a moment with him?" My voice cracked on the final word.

Dr. Kinnear nodded again and left the room.

I went over to the bed and looked down at the silent body. *The old dragon,* I thought, *has no teeth.* Then I heard a sound, something so tiny I scarcely registered it. Turning, I saw a toad by the bedfoot.

I bent down and picked it up. "Nothing for you here, puddock," I said, reverting to the old Scots word. Though I'd worked so hard to lose my accent and vocabulary, here in my father's house the old way of speech came flooding back. Shifting the books to one hand, I picked the toad up with the other. Then, I tiptoed out of the door as if my father would have minded the sound of my footsteps.

Once outside, I set the toad gently in the garden, or the remains of the garden, now so sadly neglected, its vines running rampant across what was once an arbor of white roses and red. I watched as it hopped under some large dock leaves and, quite effectively, disappeared.

Later that afternoon my father's body was taken away by three burly men for its chestening, being placed into its coffin and the lid screwed down. Then it would lie in the cold kirk till the funeral the next day.

Once he was gone from the house, I finally felt I could look in his journals. I might have sat comfortably in the study, but I'd never been welcomed there before, so didn't feel it my place now. The kitchen and sitting room were more Mrs. Marr's domain than mine. And if I never had to go back into the old man's bedroom, it would be years too soon for me.

So I lay in my childhood bed, the covers up to my chin, and read by the flickering lamplight. Mrs. Marr, bless her, had brought up a warming pan which she came twice to refill. And she brought up as well a pot of tea and jam pieces and several slabs of good honest cheddar.

"I didna think ye'd want a big supper."

She was right. Food was the last thing on my mind.

After she left the room, I took a silver hip flask from under my pillow where I'd hidden it, and then poured a hefty dram of whisky into the teapot. I would need more than Mrs. Marr's offerings to stay warm this night. Outside the sea moaned as it pushed past the skellies, on its way to the shore. I'd all but forgotten that sound. It made me smile.

I read the last part of the last journal first, where father talked about the toad, wondering briefly if it was the very same toad I had found at his bedfoot. But it was the bit right after, where he spoke of "formidable visitants" that riveted me. What had he meant? From the tone of it, I didn't think he meant any of our St Monans neighbors.

The scholar in me asserted itself, and I turned to the first of the journals, marked 1926, some five years earlier. There was one book for each year. I started with that first notebook and read long into the night.

The journals were not easy to decipher for my father's handwriting was crabbed with age and, I expect, arthritis. The early works were splotchy and, in places, faded. Also he had inserted sketchy pictures and diagrams. Occasionally he'd written whole paragraphs in corrupted Latin, or at least in a dialect unknown to me.

What he seemed engaged upon was a study of a famous trial of local witches in 1590, supervised by King James VI himself. The VI of Scotland, for he was Mary Queen of Scots' own son, and Queen Elizabeth's heir.

The witches, some ninety in all according to my father's notes, had been accused of sailing over the Firth to North Berwick in riddles— sieves, I think he meant—to plot the death of the king by raising a storm when he sailed to Denmark. However, I stumbled so often over my Latin translations, I decided I needed a dictionary. And me a classics scholar.

So halfway through the night, I rose and, taking the lamp, made my way through the cold dark, tiptoeing so as not to wake Mrs. Marr. Nothing was unfamiliar beneath my bare feet. The kitchen stove would not have gone out completely, only filled with gathering coal and kept minimally warm. All those years of my childhood came rushing back. I could have gone into the study without the lamp, I suppose. But to find the book I needed, I'd have to have light.

And lucky indeed I took it, for in its light it I saw—gathered on the floor of my father's study—a group of toads throwing strange shadows up against the bookshelves. I shuddered to think what might have happened had I stepped barefooted amongst them.

But how had they gotten in? And was the toad I'd taken into the garden amongst them? Then I wondered aloud at what such a gathering should be called. I'd heard of a murder of crows, an exaltation of larks. Perhaps toads came in a congregation? For that is what they looked like, a squat congregation, huddled together, nodding their heads, and waiting on the minister in this most unlikely of kirks.

It was too dark even with the lamp, and far too late, for me to round them up. So I sidestepped them and, after much searching, found the Latin dictionary where it sat cracked open on my father's desk. I grabbed it up, avoided the congregation of toads, and went out the door. When I looked back, I could still see the odd shadows dancing along the walls.

I almost ran back to my bed, shutting the door carefully behind me. I didn't want that dark presbytery coming in, as if they could possibly hop up the stairs like the frog in the old tale, demanding to be taken to my little bed.

But the shock of my father's death and the long day of travel, another healthy swallow of my whisky, as well as that bizarre huddle of toads, all seemed to combine to put me into a deep sleep. If I dreamed, I didn't remember any of it. I woke to one of those dawn choruses of my childhood, comprised of blackbirds, song thrushes, gulls, rooks, and jackdaws, all arguing over who should wake me first.

For a moment I couldn't recall where I was. Eyes closed, I listened to the birds, so different from the softer, more lyrical sounds outside my Cambridge windows. But I woke fully in the knowledge that I was back in my childhood home, that my father was dead and to be buried that afternoon if possible, as I had requested of the doctor and Mrs. Marr, and I had only hours to make things tidy in my mind. Then I would be away from St Monans and its small-mindedness, back to Cambridge where I truly belonged.

I got out of bed, washed, dressed in the simple black dress I always travel with, a black bandeaux on my fair hair, and went into the kitchen to make myself some tea.

Mrs. Marr was there before me, sitting on a hardback chair and knitting a navy blue Guernsey sweater with its complicated patterning. She set the steel needles down and handed me a full cup, the tea nearly black even with its splash of milk. There was a heaping bowl of porridge, sprinkled generously with salt, plus bread slathered with golden syrup.

"Thank you," I said. It would have done no good to argue that I drank coffee now, nor did I like either oatmeal or treacle, and never ate till noon. Besides, I was suddenly ravenous. "What do you need me to do?" I asked between mouthfuls, stuffing them in the way I'd done as a youngster.

"Tis all arranged," she said, taking up the needles again. No proper St Monans woman was ever idle long. "Though sooner than is proper. But all to accommodate ye, he'll be in the kirkyard this afternoon. Lucky for ye it's a Sunday, or we couldna do it. The men are home from fishing." She was clearly not pleased with me. "Ye just need to be there at the service. Not that many will come. He was no generous with his company." By which she meant he had few friends. Nor relatives except me.

"Then I'm going to walk down by the water this morning," I told her. "Unless you have something that needs doing. I want to clear my head."

"Aye, ye would."

Was that condemnation or acceptance? Who could tell? Perhaps she meant I was still the thankless child she remembered. Or that I was like my father. Or that she wanted only to see the back of me, sweeping me from her domain so she could clean and bake without my worrying presence. I thanked her again for the meal, but she wanted me gone. As I had been for the past ten years. And I was as eager to be gone, as she was to have me. The funeral was not till mid afternoon.

"There are toads in the study," I said as I started out the door.

"Toads?" She looked startled. Or perhaps frightened.

"Puddocks. A congregation of them."

Her head cocked to one side. "Och, ye mean a knot. A knot of toads."

A knot. Of course. I should have remembered. "Shall I put them out?" At least I could do that for her.

She nodded. "Aye."

I found a paper sack and went into the study, but though I looked around for quite some time, I couldn't find the toads anywhere. If I hadn't still had the Latin dictionary in my bedroom, I would have thought my night visit amongst them and my scare from their shadows had been but a dream.

"All gone," I called to Mrs. Marr before slipping out through the front door and heading toward the strand.

Nowhere in St Monans is far from the sea. I didn't realize how much the sound of it was in my bones until I moved to Cambridge. Or how much I'd missed that sound till I slept the night in my old room.

I found my way to the foot of the church walls where boats lay upturned, looking like beached dolphins. A few of the older men, past their fishing days, sat with their backs against the salted stone, smoking silently, and staring out to the gray slatey waters of the Forth. Nodding to them, I took off along the beach. Overhead gulls squabbled and far out, near the Bass Rock, I could see, gannets diving head-first into the water.

A large boat, some kind of yacht, had just passed the Bass and was sailing west majestically toward a mooring, probably in South Queensferry. I wondered who would be sailing these waters in such a ship.

But then I was interrupted by the wind sighing my name. Or so I thought at first. Then I looked back at the old kirk on the cliff above me. Someone was waving at me in the ancient kirkyard. It was Alec.

He signaled that he was coming down to walk with me and as I waited, I thought about what a handsome man he'd turned into. But a fisherman, I reminded myself, a bit of the old snobbery biting me on the back of the neck. St Monans, like the other fishing villages of the East Neuk, were made up of three classes—fisher folk, farmers, and the shopkeepers and tradesmen. My father being a scholar was outside of them all, which meant that as his daughter, I belonged to none of them either.

Still, in this place, where I was once so much a girl of the town— from the May—I felt my heart give a small stutter. I remembered that first kiss, so soft and sweet and innocent, the windmill hard against my back. My last serious relationship had been almost a year ago, and I was more than ready to fall in love again. Even at the foot of my father's grave. But not with a fisherman. Not in St Monans.

Alec found his way down to the sand and came toward me. "Off to find croupies?" he called.

I laughed. "The only fossil I've found recently has been my father," I said, then bit my lower lip at his scowl.

"He was nae a bad man, Jan," he said, catching up to me. "Just undone by his reading."

I turned a glared at him. "Do you think reading an ailment then?"

He put up his hands palms towards me. "Whoa, lass. I'm a big reader myself. But what the old man had been reading lately had clearly unnerved him. He couldna put it into context. Mrs. Marr said as much before you came. These last few months he'd stayed away from the pub, from the kirk, from everyone who'd known him well. No one kenned what he'd been on about."

I wondered what sort of thing Alec would be reading. The fishing report? The local paper? Feeling out of sorts, I said sharply, "Well, I was going over his journals last night and what he's been on about are the old North Berwick witches."

Alec's lips pursed. "The ones who plotted to blow King James off the map." It was a statement, not a question.

"The very ones."

"Not a smart thing for the unprepared to tackle."

I wondered if Alec had become as hag-ridden and superstitious as any St Monans' fisherman. Ready to turn home from his boat if he met a woman on the way. Or not daring to say "salmon" or "pig" and instead speaking of "red fish" and "curly tail," or shouting out "Cauld iron!" at any mention of them. All the East Neuk tip-leavings I was glad to be shed of.

He took the measure of my disapproving face, and laughed. "Ye take me for a gowk," he said. "But there are more things in heaven and earth, Janet, than are dreamt of in yer philosophy."

I laughed as Shakespeare tumbled from his lips. Alec could always make me laugh. "Pax," I said.

He reached over, took my hand, gave it a squeeze. "Pax." Then he dropped it again as we walked along the beach, a comfortable silence between us.

The tide had just turned and was heading out. Gulls, like satisfied housewives, sat happily in the receding waves. One lone boat was on the horizon, a small fishing boat, not the yacht I had seen earlier, which must already be coming into its port. The sky was that wonderful spring blue, without a threatening cloud, not even the fluffy Babylonians, as the fishermen called them.

"Shouldn't you be out there?" I said, pointing at the boat as we passed by the smoky fish-curing sheds.

"I rarely get out there anymore," he answered, not looking at me but at the sea. "Too busy until summer. And why old man Sinclair is fishing when the last of the winter herring have been hauled in, I canna fathom."

I turned toward him. "Too busy with what?"

He laughed. "Och, Janet, yer so caught up in yer own preconceptions, ye canna see what's here before yer eyes."

I didn't answer right away, and the moment stretched between us, as the silence had before. Only this was not comfortable. At last I said, "Are you too busy to help me solve the mystery of my father's death?"

"Solve the mystery of his life first," he told me, "and the mystery of his death will inevitably be revealed." Then he touched his cap, nodded at me, and strolled away.

I was left to ponder what he said. Or what he meant. I certainly wasn't going to chase after him. I was too proud to do that. Instead, I went back to the house, changed my shoes, made myself a plate of bread and cheese. There was no wine in the house. Mrs. Marr was as Temperance as Alec's old father had been. But I found some miserable sherry hidden in my father's study. It smelled like turpentine, so I made do with fresh milk, taking the plate and glass up to my bedroom, to read some more of my father's journals until it was time to bury him.

It is not too broad a statement to say that Father was clearly out of his mind. For one, he was obsessed with local witches. For another, he seemed to believe in them. While he spared a few paragraphs for Christian Dote, St Monans' homegrown witch of the 1640s, and a bit more about the various Anstruther, St Andrews, and Crail trials—listing the hideous tortures, and executions of hundreds of poor old women in his journal entries —it was the earlier North Berwick crew who really seemed to capture his imagination. By the third year's journal, I could see that he obviously considered the North Berwick witchery evil real, whereas the others, a century later, he dismissed as deluded or senile old women, as deluded and senile as the men who hunted them.

Here is what he wrote about the Berwick corps: *"They were a scabrous bunch, these ninety greedy women and six men, wanting no more than what they considered their due: a king and his bride dead in the sea, a kingdom in ruins, themselves set up in high places."*

"Oh, Father," I whispered, "what a noble mind is here o'erthrown," For whatever problems I'd had with him—and they were many—I had always admired his intelligence.

He described the ceremonies they indulged in, and they were awful. In the small North Berwick church, fueled on wine and sex, the witches had begun a ritual to call up a wind that would turn over the royal ship and drown King James. First they'd christened a cat with the name of Hecate, while black candles flickered fitfully along the walls of the apse and nave. Then they tortured the poor creature by passing it back and forth across a flaming hearth. Its elf-knotted hair caught fire and burned slowly, and the little beastie screamed in agony. The smell must have been appalling, but he doesn't mention that. I once caught my hair on fire, bending over a stove on a cold night in Cambridge, and it was the smell that was the worst of it. It lingered in my room for days.

Then I thought of my own dear moggie at home, a sweet orange-colored puss who slept each night at my bedfoot. If anyone ever treated her the way the North Berwick witches had that poor cat, I'd be more than ready to kill. And not with any wind, either.

But there was worse yet, and I shuddered as I continued reading. One of the men, so Father reported, had dug up a corpse from the church cemetery, and with a companion had cut off the dead man's hands and feet. Then the witches attached the severed parts to the cat's paws. After this they attached the corpse's sex organs to the cat's. I could only hope the poor creature was dead by this point. After this desecration, they proceeded to a pier at the port of Leith where they flung the wee beastie into the sea.

Father wrote: "*A storm was summarily raised by this foul method, along with the more traditional knotted twine. The storm blackened the skies, with wild gales churning the sea. The howl of the wind could be heard all the way across the Firth to Fife. But the odious crew had made a deadly miscalculation. The squall caught a ship crossing from Kinghorn to Leith and smashed it to pieces all right, but it was not the king's ship. The magic lasted only long enough to kill a few innocent sailors on that first ship, and then blew itself out to sea. As for the king, he proceeded over calmer waters with his bride, arriving safely in Denmark and thence home again to write that great treatise on witchcraft,* Demonology, *and preside over a number of witch trials thereafter.*"

I did not read quickly because, as I have said, parts of the journal were in a strange Latin and for those passages I needed the help of the dictionary. I was like a girl at school with lines to translate by morning, frustrated, achingly close to comprehension, but somehow missing the point. In fact, I did not understand them completely until I read them aloud. And then suddenly, as a roiled liquid settles at last, all became clear. The passages were some sort of incantation, or invitation, to the witches and to the evil they so devoutly and hideously served.

I closed the journal and shook my head. Poor Father. He wrote as if the witchcraft were fact, not a coincidence of gales from the southeast that threw up vast quantities of seaweed on the shore, and the haverings of tortured old women. Put a scold's bridle on me, and I would probably admit to intercourse with the devil. Any devil. And describe him and his nether parts as well.

But Father's words, as wild and unbelievable as they were, held me in a kind of thrall. And I would have remained on my bed reading further if Mrs. Marr hadn't knocked on the door and summoned me to his funeral.

She looked me over carefully, but for once I seemed to pass muster, my smart black Cambridge dress suitable for the occasion. She handed me a black hat. "I didna think ye'd have thought to bring one." Her lips drew down into a thin, straight line.

Standing before me, her plain black dress covered at the top by a solemn dark shawl, and on her head an astonishing hat covered with artificial black flowers, she was clearly waiting for me to say something.

"Thank you," I said at last. And it was true, bringing a hat along hadn't occurred to me at all. I took off the bandeaux, and set the proffered hat on my head. It was a perfect fit, though made me look fifteen years older, with its masses of black feathers, or so the mirror told me.

Lips pursed, she nodded at me, then turned, saying over her shoulder, "Young Mary McDougall did for him."

It took me a moment to figure out what she meant. Then I remembered. Though she must be nearer sixty than thirty, Mary McDougall had been both midwife and dresser of the dead when I was a child. So it had been she and not Mrs. Marr who must have washed my father and put him into the clothes he'd be buried in. *So Mrs. Marr missed out on her last great opportunity to touch him,* I thought.

"What do I give her?" I asked to Mrs. Marr's ramrod back.

Without turning around again, she said, "We'll give her all yer father's old clothes. She'll be happy enough with that."

"But surely a fee . . . "

She walked out of the door.

It was clear to me then that nothing had changed since I'd left. It was still the nineteenth century. Or maybe the eighteenth. I longed for the burial to be over and done with, my father's meager possessions sorted, the house sold, and me back on a train heading south.

We walked to the kirk in silence, crossing over the burn which rushed along beneath the little bridge. St Monans has always been justifiably proud of its ancient kirk and even in this dreary moment I could remark its beauty. Some of its stonework runs back in an unbroken line to the thirteenth century.

And some of its customs, I told myself without real bitterness.

When we entered the kirk proper, I was surprised to see that Mrs. Marr had been wrong. She'd said not many would come, but the church was overfull with visitants.

We walked down to the front. As the major mourners, we commanded the first pew, Mrs. Marr, the de facto wife, and me, the runaway daughter. There was a murmur when we sat down together, not quite of disapproval, but certainly of interest. Gossip in a town like St Monans is everybody's business.

Behind us, Alex and Dr. Kinnear were already settled in. And three men sat beside them, men whose faces I recognized, friends of my father's, but grown so old. I turned, nodded at them with, I hope, a smile that thanked them for coming. They didn't smile back.

In the other pews were fishermen and shopkeepers and the few teachers I could put a name to. But behind them was a congregation of strangers who leaned forward with an avidity that one sees only in the faces of vultures at their feed. I knew none of them and wondered if they were newcomers to the town. Or if it was just that I hadn't been home in so long, even those families who'd been here forever were strangers to me now.

Father's pine box was set before the altar and I kept my eyes averted, watching instead an ettercap, a spider, slowly spinning her way from one edge of the pulpit to the other. No one in the town would have removed her, for it was considered bad luck. It kept me from sighing, it kept me from weeping.

The minister went on for nearly half an hour, lauding my father's graces, his intelligence, his dedication. If any of us wondered about whom he was talking, we didn't answer back. But when it was over, and six large fishermen, uneasy in their Sunday clothes, stood to shoulder the coffin, I leaped up with them. Putting my hand on the pine top, I whispered, "I forgive you, Father. Do you forgive me?"

There was an audible gasp from the congregation behind me, though I'd spoken so low, I doubted any of them—not even Alec—could have heard me. I sat down again, shaken and cold.

And then the fishermen took him off to the kirkyard, to a grave so recently and quickly carved out of the cold ground, its edges were jagged. As we stood there, a huge black cloud covered the sun. The tide was dead low and the bones of the sea, those dark grey rock skellies, showed in profusion like the spines of some prehistoric dragons.

As I held on to Mrs. Marr's arm, she suddenly started shaking so hard, I thought she would shake me off.

How she must have loved my father, I thought, and found myself momentarily jealous.

Then the coffin was lowered, and that stopped her shaking. As the first clods were shoveled into the gaping hole, she turned to me and said, "Well, that's it then."

So we walked back to the house where a half dozen people stopped in for a dram or three of whiskey—brought in by Alec despite Mrs. Marr's strong disapproval. "There's a Deil in every mouthful of whiskey," she muttered, setting out the fresh baked shortbread and sultana cakes with a pitcher of lemonade. To mollify her, I drank the lemonade, but I was the only one.

Soon I was taken aside by an old man—Jock was his name—and told that my father had been a great gentleman though late had turned peculiar. Another, bald and wrinkled, drink his whiskey down in a single gulp, before declaring loudly that my father had been "one for the books." He managed to make that sound like an affliction. One woman of a certain age who addressed me as "Mistress," added, apropos of nothing, "He needs a lang-shankit spoon that sups wi' the Deil." Even Alec, sounding like the drone on a bagpipes, said "Now you can get on with your own living, Jan," as if I hadn't been doing just that all along.

For a wake, it was most peculiar. No humorous anecdotes about the dearly departed, no toasts to his soul, only half-baked praise and a series of veiled warnings.

Thank goodness no one stayed long. After the last had gone, I insisted on doing the washing up, and this time Mrs. Marr let me. And then she, too, left. Where she went I wasn't to know. One minute she was there, and the next away.

I wondered at that. After all, this was her home, certainly more than mine. I was sure she'd loved my father who, God knows, was not particularly loveable, but she walked out the door clutching her big handbag, without a word more to me; not a goodbye or "I'll not be long," or anything. And suddenly, there I was, all alone in the house for the first time in years. It was an uncomfortable feeling. I am not afraid of ghosts, but that house fairly burst with ill will, dark and brooding. So as soon as I'd tidied away the dishes, I went out, too, though not before slipping the final journal into the pocket of my overcoat and winding a long woolen scarf twice around my neck to ward the chill.

The evening was drawing in slowly, but there was otherwise a soft feel in the air, unusual for the middle of March. The East Neuk is like that— one minute still and the next a flanny wind rising.

I headed east along the coastal path, my guide the stone head of the windmill with its narrow, ruined vanes lording it over the flat land. Perhaps sentiment was leading me there, the memory of that adolescent kiss that Alec had given me, so wonderfully innocent and full of desire at the same time. Perhaps I just wanted a short, pleasant walk to the old salt pans. I don't know why I went that way. It was almost as if I were being called there.

For a moment I turned back and looked at the town behind me which showed, from this side, how precariously the houses perch on the rocks, like gannets nesting on the Bass.

Then I turned again and took the walk slowly; it was still only ten or fifteen minutes to the windmill from the town. No boats sailed on the Firth today. I could not spot the large yacht so it must have been in its berth. And the air was so clear, I could see the Bass and the May with equal distinction. How often I'd come to this place as a child. I probably could still walk to it barefooted and without stumbling, even in the blackest night. The body has a memory of its own.

Halfway there, a solitary curlew flew up before me and as I watched it flap away, I thought how the townsfolk would have cringed at the sight, for the bird was thought to bring bad luck, carrying away the spirits of the wicked at nightfall.

"But I've not been wicked," I cried after it, and laughed. *Or at least not wicked for a year, more's the pity.*

At last I came to the windmill with its rough stones rising high above the land. Once it had been used for pumping seawater to extract the salt. Not a particularly easy operation, it took something like thirty-two tons of water to produce one ton of salt. We'd learned all about it in primary school, of course. But the days of the salt pans were a hundred years in the past, and the poor windmill had seen better times.

Even run down, though, it was still a lovely place, with its own memories. Settling back against the mill's stone wall, I nestled down and drew out the last journal from my coat pocket. Then I began to read it from the beginning as the light slowly faded around me.

Now, I am a focused reader, which is to say that once caught up in a book, I can barely swim back up to the surface of any other consciousness. The world dims around me. Time and space compress. Like a Wellsian hero, I am drawn into an elsewhere that becomes absolute and real. So as I read my Father's final journal, I was in his head and his madness so completely, I heard nothing around me, not the raucous cry of gulls nor the wash of water onto the stones far below.

So it was, with a start that I came to the final page, with its mention of the goggle-eyed toad. Looking up, I found myself in the gray gloaming surrounded by nearly a hundred such toads, all staring at me with their horrid wide eyes, a hideous echo of my father's written words.

I stood up quickly, trying desperately not to squash any of the poor paddocks. They leaned forward like children trying to catch the warmth of a fire. Then their shadows lengthened and grew.

Please understand, there was no longer any sun and very little light. There was no moon overhead for the clouds crowded one on to the other, and the sky was completely curtained. So there should not have been any shadows at all. Yet, I state again—their shadows lengthened and grew. Shadows like and unlike the ones I had seen against my father's study walls. They grew into dark-caped creatures, almost as tall as humans yet with those goggly eyes.

I still held my father's journal in my left hand, but my right covered my mouth to keep myself from screaming. My sane mind knew it to be only a trick of the light, of the dark. It was the result of bad dreams and just having put my only living relative into the ground. But the primitive brain urged me to cry out with all my ancestors, "Cauld iron!" and run away in terror.

And still the horrid creatures grew until now they towered over me, pushing me back against the windmill, their shadowy fingers grabbing at both ends of my scarf.

Who are you? What are you? I mouthed, as the breath was forced from me. Then they pulled and pulled the scarf until they'd choked me into unconsciousness.

When I awoke, I was tied to a windmill vane, my hands bound high above me, the ropes too tight and well-knotted for any escape.

"Who are you?" I whispered aloud this time, my voice sounding froglike, raspy, hoarse. "What are you?" Though I feared I knew. "What do you want of me? Why are you here?"

In concert, their voices wailed back. "A wind! A wind!"

And then in horror all that Father had written—about the hands and feet and sex organs of the corpse being cut off and attached to the dead cat—bore down upon me. Were they about to dig poor father's corpse up? Was I to be the offering? Were we to be combined in some sort of desecration too disgusting to be named? I began to shudder within my bonds, both hot and cold. For a moment I couldn't breathe again, as if they were tugging on the scarf once more.

Then suddenly, finding some latent courage, I stood tall and screamed at them, "I'm not dead yet!" Not like my father whom they'd frightened into his grave.

They crowded around me, shadow folk with wide white eyes, laughing. "A wind! A wind!"

I kicked out at the closest one, caught my foot in its black cape, but connected with nothing more solid than air. Still that kick forced them back for a moment.

"Get away from me!" I screamed. But screaming only made my throat ache, for I'd been badly choked just moments earlier. I began to cough and it was as if a nail were being driven through my temples with each spasm.

The shadows crowded forward again, their fingers little breezes running over my face and hair, down my neck, touching my breasts.

I took a deep breath for another scream, another kick. But before I could deliver either, I heard a cry.

"Aroint, witches!"

Suddenly I distinguished the sound of running feet. Straining to see down the dark corridor that was the path to Pittenweem, I leaned against the cords that bound me. It was a voice I did and did not recognize.

The shadow folk turned as one and flowed along the path, hands before them as if they were blindly seeking the interrupter.

"Aroint, I say!"

Now I knew the voice. It was Mrs. Marr, in full cry. But her curse seemed little help and I feared that she, too, would soon be trussed up by my side.

But then, from the east, along the path nearer town, there came another call.

"Janet! Janet!" That voice I recognized at once.

"Alec . . ." I said between coughs.

The shadows turned from Mrs. Marr and flowed back, surrounding Alec, but he held something up in his hand. A bit of a gleam from a crossbar. His fisherman's knife.

The shadows fell away from him in confusion.

"Cauld iron!" he cried at them. "Cauld iron!"

So they turned to go back again towards Mrs. Marr, but she reached into her large handbag and pulled out her knitting needles. Holding them before her in the sign of a cross, she echoed Alec's cry. "Cauld iron." And then she added, her voice rising as she spoke, "Oh let the wickedness of the wicked come to an end; but establish the just: for the righteous God trieth the hearts and reigns."

I recognized it as part of a psalm, one of the many she'd presumably memorized as a child, but I could not have said which.

Then the two of them advanced on the witches, coming from east and west, forcing the awful crew to shrink down, as if melting, into dark puddocks once again.

Step by careful step, Alec and Mrs. Marr herded the knot of toads off the path and over the cliff's edge.

Suddenly the clouds parted and a brilliant half moon shone down on us, its glare as strong as the lighthouse on Anster's pier. I watched as the entire knot of toads slid down the embankment, some falling onto the rocks and some into the water below.

Only when the last puddock was gone, did Alec turn to me. Holding the knife in his teeth, he reached above my head to my bound hands and began to untie the first knot.

A wind started to shake the vanes and for a second I was lifted off my feet as the mill tried to grind, though it had not done so for a century.

"Stop!" Mrs. Marr's voice held a note of desperation.

Alec turned. "Would ye leave her tied, woman? What if those shades come back again? I told ye what the witches had done before. It was all in his journals."

"No, Alec," I cried, hating myself for trusting the old ways, but changed beyond caring. "They're elfknots. Don't untie them. Don't!" I shrank away from his touch.

"Aye," Mrs. Marr said, coming over and laying light fingers on Alec's arm. "The lass is still of St. Monan's though she talks like a Sassanach." She laughed. "It's no the drink and the carousing that brings the wind. That's just for fun. Nor the corpse and the cat. That's just for show. My man told me. It's the knots, he says."

"The knot of toads?" Alec asked hoarsely.

The wind was still blowing and it took Alec's hard arms around me to anchor me fast or I would have gone right around, spinning with the vanes.

Mrs. Marr came close till they were eye to eye. "The knots in the rope, lad," she said. "One brings a wind, two bring a gale, and the third . . . " She shook her head. "Ye dinna want to know about the third."

"But—" Alec began.

"Och, but me know buts, my lad. Cut between," Mrs. Marr said. "Just dinna untie them or King George's yacht at South Queensferry will go down in a squall, with the king and queen aboard, and we'll all be to blame."

He nodded and slashed the ropes with his knife, between the knots, freeing my hands. Then he lifted me down. I tried to take it all in: his arms, his breath on my cheek, the smell of him so close. I tried to understand what had happened here in the gloaming. I tried until I started to sob and he began stroking my hair, whispering, "There, lass, it's over. It's over."

"Not until we've had some tea and burned those journals," Mrs. Marr said. "I told ye we should have done it before."

"And I told ye," he retorted, "that they are invaluable to historians."

"Burn them," I croaked, knowing at last that the invitation in Latin they contained was what had called the witches back. Knowing that my speaking the words aloud had brought them to our house again. Knowing that the witches were Father's "visitants" who had, in the end, frightened him to death. "Burn them. No historian worth his salt would touch them."

Alec laughed bitterly. "I would." He set me on my feet and walked away down the path toward town.

"Now ye've done it," Mrs. Marr told me. "Ye never were a lass to watch what ye say. Ye've injured his pride and broken his heart."

"But . . . " We were walking back along the path, her hand on my arm, leading me on. The wind had died and the sky was alert with stars. "But he's not an historian."

"Ye foolish lass, yon lad's nae fisherman, for all he dresses like one. He's a lecturer in history at the University, in St Andrews," she said. "And the two of ye the glory of this village. Yer father and his father always talking about the pair of ye. Hoping to see ye married one day, when pride didna keep the two of ye apart. Scheming they were."

I could hardly take this in. Drawing my arm from her, I looked to see if she was making a joke. Though in all the years I'd known her, I'd never heard her laugh.

She glared ahead at the darkened path. "Yer father kept yer room the way it was when ye were a child, though I tried to make him see the foolishness of it. He said that someday yer own child would be glad of it."

"My father—"

"But then he went all queer in the head after Alec's father died. I think he believed that by uncovering all he could about the old witches, he might help Alec in his research. To bring ye together, though what he really fetched was too terrible to contemplate."

"Which do you think came first?" I asked slowly. "Father's summoning the witches, or the shadows sensing an opportunity?

She gave a bob of her head to show she was thinking, then said at last, "Dinna mess with witches and weather, my man says . . . "

"Your man?" She'd said it before, but I thought she'd meant her dead husband. "Weren't you . . . I mean, I thought you were in love with my father."

She stopped dead in her tracks and turned to me. The half moon lit her face. "Yer father?" She stopped, considered, then began again. "Yer father had a heart only for two women in his life, yer mother and ye, Janet, though he had a hard time showing it. And . . . " she laughed, "he was no a bonnie man."

I thought of him lying in his bed, his great prow of a nose dominating his face. No, he was not a bonnie man.

"Och, lass, I had promised yer mother on her deathbed to take care of him, and how could I go back on such a promise? I didna feel free to marry as long as he remained alive. Now my Pittenweem man and I have set a date, and it will be soon. We've wasted enough time already."

I had been wrong, so wrong, and in so many ways I could hardly comprehend them all. And didn't I understand about wasted time. But at least I could make one thing right again.

"I'll go after Alec, I'll . . . "

Mrs. Marr clapped her hands. "Then run, lass, run like the wind."

And untying the knot around my own pride, I ran.

For M. R. James

Jane Yolen, often called "the Hans Christian Andersen of America," is the author of almost 300 books that range from rhymed picture books and baby board books, through middle grade fiction, poetry collections, nonfiction, and up to novels and story collections for young adults and adults. Her books and stories have won an assortment of awards—two Nebulas, a World Fantasy Award, a Caldecott, the Golden Kite Award, three Mythopoeic awards, two Christopher Medals, a nomination for the National Book Award, and the Jewish Book Award, among others. Five colleges and universities have given her honorary doctorates. She has just sold two graphic novels, and among her newest books are children's fantasy novel *Troll Bridge* and the paperback of her YA historical novel *Prince Across The Water*. If you need to know more about her, visit her website at: www.janeyolen.com.

CALYPSO IN BERLIN

Elizabeth Hand

Yesterday morning, he left. I had known he would only be here for those seven days. Now, just like that, they were gone.

It had stormed all night, but by the time I came downstairs to feed the woodstove, the gale had blown out to sea. It was still dark, chill October air sifting through cracks in the walls. Red and yellow leaves were flung everywhere outside. I stepped into the yard to gather a handful and pressed my face against them, cold and wet.

From the other side of island a coyote yelped. I could hear the Pendletons' rooster and a dog barking. Finally I went back inside, sat and watched the flames through the stove's isinglass window. When Philip finally came down, he took one look at me, shook his head, and said, "No! I still have to go, stop it!"

I laughed and turned to touch his hand. He backed away quickly and said, "None of that."

I saw how he recoiled. I have never kept him here against his will.

When Odysseus left, he was suspicious, accusatory. They say he wept for his wife and son, but he slept beside me each night for seven years and I saw no tears. We had two sons. His face was imprinted upon mine, just as Philip's was centuries later: unshaven, warm, my cheeks scraped and my mouth swollen. In the morning I would wake to see Philip watching me, his hand moving slowly down the curve of my waist.

"No hips, no ass," he said once. "You're built like a boy."

157

He liked to hold my wrists in one hand and straddle me. I wondered sometimes about their wives: were they taller than me? Big hips, big tits? Built like a woman?

Calypso. The name means *the concealer*. "She of the lovely braids"—that's how Homer describes me. One morning Philip walked about my cottage, taking photos off the bookshelves and looking at them.

"Your hair," he said, holding up a picture. "It was so long back then."

I shrugged. "I cut it all off a year ago. It's grown back—see?" Shoulder-length now, still blond, no gray.

He glanced at me, then put the picture back. "It looked good that way," he said.

This is what happens to nymphs: they are pursued or they are left. Sometimes, like Echo, they are fled. We turn to trees, seabirds, seafoam, running water, the sound of wind in the leaves. Men come to stay with us, they lie beside us in the night, they hold us so hard we can't breathe. They walk in the woods and glimpse us: a diving kingfisher, an owl caught in the headlights, a cold spring on the hillside. Alcyone, Nyctimene, Peirene, Echo, Calypso: these are some of our names. We like to live alone, or think we do. When men find us, they say we are lovelier than anything they have ever seen: wilder, stranger, more passionate. Elemental. They say they will stay forever. They always leave.

We met when Philip missed a flight out of Logan. I had business at the gallery that represents me in Cambridge and offered him a place to stay for the night: my hotel room.

"I don't know too many painters," he said. "Free spirits, right?"

He was intrigued by what I told him of the island. The sex was good. I told him my name was Lyssa. After that we'd see each other whenever he was on the East Coast. He was usually leaving for work overseas but would add a few days to either end of his trip, a week even, so we could be together. I had been on the island for—how long? I can't remember now.

I began sketching him the second time he came here. He would never let me do it while he was awake. He was too restless, jumping up to pull a book off the shelf, make coffee, pour more wine.

So I began to draw him while he slept. After we fucked he'd fall heavily asleep; I might doze for a few minutes, but sex energizes me, it makes me want to work.

He was perfect for me. Not conventionally handsome, though. His dark eyes were small and deep set, his mouth wide and uneven. Dark, thick hair, gray-flecked. His skin unlined. It was uncanny—he was in his early fifties but seemed as ageless as I was, as though he'd been untouched by anything, his time in the Middle East, his children, his wife, his ex-wife, me. I see now that this is what obsessed me—that someone human could be not merely beautiful but untouched. There wasn't a crack in him; no way to get inside. He slept with his hands crossed behind his head, long body tipped across the bed. Long arms, long legs; torso almost hairless; a dark bloom on his cheeks when he hadn't shaved. His cock long, slightly curved; moisture on his thigh.

I sketched and painted him obsessively, for seven years. Over the centuries there have been others. Other lovers, always; but only a few whom I've drawn or painted on walls, pottery, tapestry, paper, canvas, skin. After a few years I'd grow tired of them—Odysseus was an exception—and gently send them on their way. As they grew older they interested me less, because of course I did not grow old. Some didn't leave willingly. I made grasshoppers of them, or mayflies, and tossed them into the webs of the golden orbweaver spiders that follow me everywhere I live.

But I never grew tired of Philip.

And I never grew tired of painting him. No one could see the paintings, of course, which killed me. He was so paranoid that he would be recognized, by his wife, his ex, one of his grown children. Coworkers.

I was afraid of losing him, so I kept the canvases in a tiny room off the studio. The sketchbooks alone filled an entire shelf. He still worried that someone would look at them, but no one ever came to visit me, except for him. My work was shown in the gallery just outside Boston. Winter landscapes of the bleak New England countryside I loved; skeletons of birds, seals. Temperas, most of them; some pen-and-ink drawings. I lived under Andrew Wyeth's long shadow, as did everyone else in my part of the country. I thought that the paintings I'd done of Philip might change that perception. Philip was afraid that they would.

"Those could be your Helga paintings," he said once. It was an accusation, not encouragement.

"They would be Calypso's paintings," I said. He didn't understand what I meant.

Odysseus's wife was a weaver. I was, too. It's right there in Homer. When Hermes came to give me Zeus's command to free Odysseus, I was in my little house on the island, weaving scenes into tunics for Odysseus and the boys. They were little then, three and five. We stood on the shore and watched him go. The boys ran screaming after the boat into the water. I had to grab them and hold them back; I thought the three of us would drown, they were fighting so to follow him.

It was horrible. Nothing was as bad as that, ever; not even when Philip left.

Penelope. Yes, she had a son, and like me she was a weaver. But we had more in common than that. I was thinking about her unraveling her loom each night, and it suddenly struck me: this was what I did with my paintings of Philip. Each night I would draw him for hours as he slept. Each day I would look at my work, and it was beautiful. They were by far my best paintings. They might even have been great.

And who knows what the critics or the public might have thought? My reputation isn't huge, but it's respectable. Those paintings could have changed all that.

But I knew that would be it: if I showed them, I would never see him again, never hear from him, never smell him, never taste him.

Yet even that I could live with. What terrified me was the thought that I would never paint him again. If he was gone, my magic would die. I would never paint again.

And that would destroy me: to think of eternity without the power to create. Better to draw and paint all night; better to undo my work each dawn by hiding it in the back room.

I thought I could live like that. For seven years I did.

And then he left. The storm blew out to sea, the leaves were scattered across the lake. The house smelled of him still, my breath smelled of him, my hair. I stood alone at the sink, scrubbing at the pigments caked under my fingernails; then suddenly doubled over, vomiting on the dishes I hadn't done yet from last night's dinner.

I waited until I stopped shaking. Then I cleaned the sink, cleaned the dishes, squeezed lemons down the drain until the stink was gone. I put everything away. I went into the back room, stood for a long time and stared at the paintings there.

Seven years is a long time. There were a lot of canvases; a lot of sheets of heavy paper covered with his body, a lot of black books filled with his eyes, his cock, his hands, his mouth. I looked up at the corner of the room by the window, saw the web woven by the big yellow spider, gray strands dusted with moth wings, fly husks, legs. I pursed my lips and whistled silently, watched as the web trembled and the spider raced to its center, her body glistening like an amber bead. Then I went to my computer and booked a flight to Berlin.

It was a city that Philip loved, a city he had been to once, decades ago, when he was studying in Florence. He spent a month there—this was long before the Wall fell—never went back, but we had spoken, often, of going there together.

I had a passport—I'm a nymph, not an agoraphobe—and so I e-mailed my sister Arethusa, in Sicily. We are spirits of place; we live where the world exhales in silence. As these places disappear, so do we.

But not all of us. Arethusa and I kept in touch intermittently. Years ago she had lived on the Rhine. She said she thought she might still know someone in Germany. She'd see what she could do.

It turned out the friend knew someone who had a sublet available. It was in an interesting part of town, said Arethusa; she'd been there once. I was a little anxious about living in a city—I'm attached to islands, to northern lakes and trees, and I worried that I wouldn't thrive there, that I might in fact sicken.

But I went. I paid in advance for the flat, then packed my paintings and sketchbooks and had them shipped over. I carried some supplies and one small sketchbook, half-filled with drawings of Philip, in my carry-on luggage. I brought my laptop. I closed up the cottage for the winter, told the Pendletons I was leaving and asked them to watch the place for me. I left them my car as well.

Then I caught the early morning ferry to the mainland, the bus to Boston. There was light fog as the plane lifted out of Logan, quickly dispersing into an arctic blue sky. I looked down and watched a long, serpentine cloud writhing above the Cape and thought of Nephele, a cloud nymph whom Zeus had molded to resemble Hera.

Why do they always have to change us into something else? I wondered, and sat back to watch the movie.

Berlin was a shock. We are by nature solitary and obsessive, which has its own dangers—like Narcissus, we can drown in silence, gazing at a reflection in a still pool.

But in a city, we can become disoriented and exhausted. We can sicken and die. We are long-lived, but not immortal.

So Arethusa had chosen my flat carefully. It was in Schöneberg, a quiet, residential part of the city. There were no high-rises. Chestnut trees littered the sidewalks with armored fruit. There were broad streets where vendors sold sunflowers and baskets of hazelnuts; old bookstores, a little shop that stocked only socks, several high-end art galleries; green spaces and much open sky.

"Poets lived there," Arethusa told me, her voice breaking up over my cell phone. "Before the last big war."

My flat was in a street of century-old apartment buildings. The foyer was high and dim and smelled of pipe tobacco and pastry dough. The flat itself had been carved from a much larger suite of rooms. There was a pocket-sized kitchenette, two small rooms facing each other across a wide hallway, a tiny, ultramodern bath.

But the rooms all had high ceilings and polished wooden floors glossy as bronze. And the room facing a courtyard had wonderful northern light.

I set this up as my studio. I purchased paints and sketchpads, a small easel. I set up my laptop, put a bowl of apples on the windowsill where the cool fall air moved in and out. Then I went to work.

I couldn't paint.

Philip said that would happen. He used to joke about it—*you're nothing without me, you only use me, what will you do if ever I'm gone, hmmmm?*

Now he was gone, and it was true. I couldn't work. Hours passed, days; a week.

Nothing.

I flung open the casement windows, stared down at the enclosed courtyard and across to the rows of windows in other flats just like mine. There were chestnut trees in the yard below, neat rows of bicycles lined up beneath them. Clouds moved across the sky as storms moved in from the far lands to the north. The wind tore the last yellow leaves from the trees and sent them whirling up toward where I stood, shivering in my moth-eaten sweater.

The wind brought with it a smell: the scent of pine trees and the sea, of rock and raw wool. It was the smell of the north, the scent of my island—my true island, the place that had been my home, once. It filled me not with nostalgia or longing but with something strange and terrible; the realization that I had no longer had a home. I had only what I made on the page or canvas. I had bound myself to a vision.

Byblis fell hopelessly in love and became a fountain. Echo wasted into a sound in the night. Hamadryads die when their trees die.

What would become of me?

I decided to go for a walk.

It is a green city. Philip had never told me that. He spoke of the wars, the Nazis, the bombs, the Wall. I wandered along the Ebersstrasse to the S-Bahn station; then traveled to the eastern part of the city, to the university, and sat at a cafe beneath an elevated railway, where I ate roasted anchovies and soft white cheese while trains racketed overhead. The wall behind me was riddled with bullet holes. If this building had been in the western part of the city, it would have been repaired or torn down. In the east there was never enough money for such things. When I placed my hand upon the bullet holes they felt hot, and gave off a faint smell of blood and scorched leather. I finished my lunch and picked up a bit of stone that had fallen from the wall, put it in my pocket with some chestnuts I had gathered, and walked on.

The sun came out after a bit. Or no, that may have been another day—almost certainly it was. The leaves were gone from the linden trees, but it was still lovely. The people were quiet, speaking in low voices.

But they were seemingly as happy as people ever are. I began to take my sketchbooks with me when I walked, and I would sit in a cafe or a park and draw. I found that I could draw Philip from memory. I began to draw other things, too—the lindens, the ugly modern buildings elbowing aside the older terraces that had not been destroyed by the bombings. There were empty fountains everywhere; and again, here in the eastern part of the city there had been no money to restore them or to keep the water flowing. Bronze Nereids and Neptunes rose from them, whitened with bird droppings. Lovers still sat beside the empty pools, gazing at drifts of dead leaves and old newspapers while pigeons pecked around their feet. I found this beautiful and strange, and also oddly heartening.

A few weeks after my arrival, Philip called. I hadn't replied to his e-mails, but when my cell phone rang, I answered.

"You're in Berlin?" He sounded amused but not surprised. "Well, I wanted to let you know I'm going to be gone again, a long trip this time. Damascus. I'll come see you for a few days before I go."

He told me his flight time, then hung up.

What did I feel then? Exhilaration, desire, joy: but also fear. I had just begun to paint again; I was just starting to believe that I could, in fact, work without him.

But if he were here?

I went into the bedroom. On the bed, neatly folded, was another thing I had brought with me: Philip's sweater. It was an old, tweed-patterned wool sweater, in shades of umber and yellow and russet, with holes where the mice had nested in it back in the cottage. He had wanted to throw it out, years ago, but I kept it. It still smelled of him, and I slept wearing it, here in the flat in Schöneberg, the wool prickling against my bare skin. I picked it up and buried my face in it, smelling him, his hair, his skin, sweat.

Then I sat down on the bed. I adjusted the lamp so that the light fell upon the sweater in my lap; and began, slowly and painstakingly, to unravel it.

It took a while, maybe an hour. I was careful not to fray the worn yarn, careful to tie the broken ends together. When I was finished, I had several balls of wool; enough to make a new sweater. It was late by then, and the shops were closed. But first thing next morning I went to the little store that sold only socks and asked in my halting German where I might find a knitting shop. I had brought a ball of wool to show the woman behind the counter. She laughed and pointed outside, then wrote down the address. It wasn't far, just a few streets over. I thanked her, bought several pairs of thick argyle wool socks, and left.

I found the shop without any trouble. I know how to knit, though I haven't done so for a long time. I found a pattern I liked in a book of Icelandic designs. I bought the book, bought the special circular needles you use for sweaters, bought an extra skein of wool in a color I liked because it reminded me of woad, not quite as deep a blue as indigo. I would work this yarn into the background. Then I returned home.

I had nearly a week before Philip arrived. I was too wound up to paint. But I continued to walk each day, finding my way around the hidden parts of the city. Small forgotten parks scarcely larger than a backyard, where European foxes big as dogs peered from beneath patches of brambles; a Persian restaurant near my flat, where the smells of coriander and roasting garlic made me think of my island long ago. A narrow canal like a secret outlet of the Spree, where I watched a kingfisher dive from an overhanging willow. I carried my leather satchel with me, the one that held my sketchbooks and charcoal pencils and watercolors. I wanted to try using watercolors.

But now the satchel held my knitting, too, the balls of wool and the pattern book and the half-knit sweater. When I found I couldn't paint or draw, I'd take the sweater out and work on it. It was repetitive work, dreamlike, soothing. And one night, back in the flat, I dug around in the bureau drawer until I found something else I'd brought with me, an envelope I'd stuck into one of my notebooks.

Inside the envelope was a curl of hair I'd cut from Philip's head one night while he slept. I set the envelope in a safe place and, one by one, carefully teased out the hairs. Over the next few days I wove them into the sweater. Now and then I would pluck one of my own hairs, much longer, finer, ash gold, and knit that into the pattern as well.

They were utterly concealed, of course, his dark curls, my fair, straight hair: all invisible. I finished the sweater the morning Philip arrived.

It was wonderful seeing him. He took a taxi from the airport. I had coffee waiting. We fell into bed. Afterward I gave him the sweater.

"Here," I said. "I made you something."

He sat naked on the bed and stared at it, puzzled. "Is this mine?"

"Try it on. I want to see if it fits."

He shrugged, then pulled it on over his bare chest.

"Does it fit?" I asked. "I had to guess the measurements."

"It seems to." He smoothed the thick wool, October gold and russet flecked with woad; then tugged at a loose bit of yarn on the hem.

"Oops," I said, frowning. "Don't worry, I'll fix that."

"It's beautiful. Thank you. I didn't know you knew how to knit."

I adjusted it, tugging to see if it hung properly over his broad shoulders.

"It does," I said, and laughed in relief. "It fits! Does it feel right?"

"Yeah. It's great." He pulled it off then got dressed again, white T-shirt, blue flannel shirt, the sweater last of all. "Didn't I used to have a sweater like this, once?"

"You did," I said. "Come on, I'm hungry."

We walked arm in arm to the Persian restaurant, where we ate chicken simmered in pomegranates and crushed walnuts, and drank wine the color of oxblood. Later, on the way back to the flat, we ambled past closed shops, pausing to look at a display of icons, a gallery showing the work of a young German artist I had read about.

"Are you thinking of showing here?" Philip asked. "I don't mean this gallery, but here, in Berlin?"

"I don't know. I hadn't really thought about it much." In truth I hadn't thought about it at all, until that very moment. "But yes, I guess I might. If Anna could arrange it."

Anna owned the gallery back in Cambridge. Philip said nothing more, and we turned and walked home.

But back in the flat, he started looking around. He went into my studio and glanced at the canvas on the easel, already primed, with a few blocked-in shapes—a barren tree, scaffolding; an abandoned fountain.

"These are different," he said. He glanced around the rest of the studio and I could tell, he was relieved not to see anything else. The other paintings, the ones I'd done of him, hadn't arrived yet. He didn't ask after them, and I didn't tell him I'd had them shipped from the island.

We went back to bed. Afterward, he slept heavily. I switched on the small bedside lamp, turning it so it wouldn't awaken him, and watched him sleep. I didn't sketch him. I watched the slow rise of his chest, the beard coming in where he hadn't shaved, grayer now than it had been; the thick black lashes that skirted his closed eyes. His mouth. I knew he was going to leave me. This time, he wouldn't come back.

If he had wakened then and seen me, would anything have changed? If he had ever seen me watching him like this . . . would he have changed? Would I?

I watched him for a long time, thinking. At last I curled up beside him and fell asleep.

Next morning, we had breakfast, then wandered around the city like tourists. Philip hadn't been back in some years, and it all amazed him. The bleak emptiness of the Alexanderplatz, where a dozen teenagers sat around the empty fountain, each with a neon-shaded Mohawk and a ratty mongrel at the end of a leash; the construction cranes everywhere, the crowds of Japanese and Americans at the Brandenburg Gate; the disconcertingly elegant graffiti on bridges spanning the Spree, as though the city, half-awake, had scrawled its dreams upon the brickwork.

"You seem happy here," he said. He reached to stroke my hair, and smiled.

"I *am* happy here," I said. "It's not ideal, but . . . "

"It's a good place for you, maybe. I'll come back." He was quiet for a minute. "I'm going to be gone for a while. Damascus—I'll be there for two months. Then Deborah's going to meet me, and we're going to travel for a while. She found a place for us to stay, a villa in Montevarchi. It's something we've talked about for a while."

We were scuffing through the leaves along a path near the Grunewald, the vast and ancient forest to the city's west. I went there often, alone. There were wild animals, boar and foxes; there were lakes, and hollow caves beneath the earth that no one was aware of. So many of Berlin's old trees had been destroyed in the bombings, and more died when the Wall fell and waves of new construction and congestion followed.

Yet new trees had grown, and some old ones flourished. These woods seemed an irruption of a deep, rampant disorder: the trees were black, the fallen leaves deep, the tangled thorns and hedges often impenetrable. I had found half-devoured carcasses here, cats or small dogs, those pretty red squirrels with tufted ears; as well as empty beer bottles and the ashy remnants of campfires in stone circles. You could hear traffic, and the drone of construction cranes; but only walk a little further into the trees and these sounds disappeared. It was a place I wanted to paint, but I hadn't yet figured out where, or how.

"I'm tired." Philip yawned. Sun filtered through the leafless branches. It was cool, but not cold. He wore the sweater I'd knitted, beneath a tweed jacket. "Jet lag. Can we stop a minute?"

There were no benches, not even any large rocks; just the leaf-covered ground, a few larches, many old beeches. I dropped the satchel holding my watercolors and sketchpad and looked around. A declivity spread beneath one very large old beech, a hollow large enough for us to lie in, side by side. Leaves had drifted to fill the space like water in a cupped hand; tender yellow leaves, soft as tissue and thin enough that when I held one to the sun I could see shapes behind the fretwork of veins. Trees. Philip's face.

The ground was dry. We lay side by side. After a few minutes he turned and pulled me to him. I could smell the sweet mast beneath us, beechnuts buried in the leaves. I pulled his jacket off and slid my hands beneath his sweater, kissed him as he pulled my jeans down; then tugged the sweater free from his arms, until it hung loose like a cowl around his neck. The air was chill despite the sun, there were leaves in his hair. A fallen branch raked my bare back, hard enough to make me gasp. His eyes were closed, but mine were open; there was grit on his cheek and a fleck of green moss, a tiny greenfly with gold-faceted eyes that lit upon his eyelid then rubbed its front legs together then spun into the sunlight. All the things men never see. When he came he was all but silent, gasping against my chest. I laid my hand upon his face, before he turned aside and fell asleep.

For a moment I sat, silent, and looked for the greenfly. Then I pulled my jeans back up and zipped them, shook the leaves from my hair and plucked a beechnut husk from my shirt. I picked up Philip's jacket and tossed it into the underbrush, then knelt beside him. His flannel shirt had ridden up, exposing his stomach; I bent my head and kissed the soft skin beneath his navel. He was warm and tasted of semen and salt, bracken. For a moment I lingered, then sat up.

A faint buzzing sounded, but otherwise the woods were still. The sweater hung limp round his neck. I ran my fingers along the hem until I found the stray bit of yarn there. I tugged it free, the loose knot easily coming undone; then slowly and with great care, bit by bit by bit while he slept, I unraveled it. Only at the very end did Philip stir, when just a ring of blue and brown and gold hung about his neck, but I whispered his name and, though his eyelids trembled, they did not open.

I got to my feet, holding the loose armful of warm wool, drew it to my face and inhaled deeply.

It smelled more of him than his own body did. I teased out one end of the skein and stood above him, then let the yarn drop until it touched his chest. Little by little, I played the yarn out, like a fisherman with his line, until it covered him. More greenflies came and buzzed about my face.

Finally I was done. A gust sent yellow leaves blowing across the heap of wool and hair as I turned to retrieve my satchel. The greenflies followed me. I waved my hand impatiently and they darted off, to hover above the shallow pool that now spread beneath the beech tree. I had not consciously thought of water, but water is what came to me; perhaps the memory of the sea outside the window where I had painted Philip all those nights, perhaps just the memory of green water and blue sky and gray rock, an island long ago.

The small, still pool behind me wasn't green but dark brown, with a few spare strokes of white and gray where it caught the sky, and a few yellow leaves. I got my bag and removed my pencils and watercolors and sketchpad, then folded Philip's jacket and put it at the bottom of the satchel, along with the rest of his clothes. Then I filled my metal painting cup with water from the pool. I settled myself against a tree and began to paint.

It wasn't like my other work. A broad wash of gold and brown, the pencil lines black beneath the brushstrokes, spattered crimson at the edge of the thick paper. The leaves floating on the surface of the pool moved slightly in the wind, which was hard for me to capture—I was just learning to use watercolors. Only once was I worried, when a couple walking a dog came through the trees up from the canal bank.

"*Guten Tag,*" the woman said, smiling. I nodded and smiled politely but kept my gaze fixed on my painting. I wasn't worried about the man or the woman; they wouldn't notice Philip. No one would. They walked toward the pool, pausing as their dog, a black dachshund, wriggled eagerly and sniffed at the water's edge, then began nosing through the leaves.

"Strubbel!" the man scolded.

Without looking back at him, the dog waded into the pool and began lapping at the water. The man tugged at the leash and started walking on; the dog ran after him, shaking droplets from his muzzle.

I finished my painting. It wasn't great—I was still figuring it out, the way water mingles with the pigments and flows across the page—but it was very good. There was a disquieting quality to the picture; you couldn't quite tell if there was a face there beneath the water, a mouth, grasping hands; or if it was a trick of the light, the way the thin yellow leaves lay upon the surface. There were long shadows across the pool when at last I gathered my things and replaced them in my satchel, heavier now because of Philip's clothes.

I disposed of these on my way back to the flat. I took a long, circuitous route on the U, getting off at one stop then another, leaving a shoe in the trash bin here, a sock there, dropping the flannel shirt into the Spree from the bridge at Oberbaumbrucke. The pockets of the tweed jacket were empty. At the Alexanderplatz I walked up to the five or six punks who still sat by the empty fountain and held up the jacket.

"Anyone want this?" I asked in English.

They ignored me, all save one boy, older than the rest, with blue-white skin and a shy indigo gaze.

"*Bitte.*" He leaned down to pat his skinny mongrel, then reached for the jacket. I gave it to him and walked away. Halfway across the plaza I looked back. He was ripping the sleeves off; as I watched he walked over to a trash bin and tossed them inside, then pulled the sleeveless jacket over his T-shirt. I turned and hurried home, the chill wind blowing leaves like brown smoke into the sky.

For the first few months I read newspapers and checked online to see if there was any news of Philip's disappearance. There were a few brief articles, but his line of work had its perils, and it was assumed these had contributed to his fate. His children were grown. His wife would survive. No one knew about me, of course.

I painted him all winter long. Ice formed and cracked across his body; there was a constellation of bubbles around his mouth and open eyes. People began to recognize me where I set up my easel and stool in the Grunewald, but, respectful of my concentration, few interrupted me. When people did look at my work, they saw only an abstract painting, shapes that could be construed as trees or building cranes, perhaps, etched against the sky; a small pool where the reflection of clouds or shadows bore a fleeting, eerie similarity to a skeletal figure, leaves trapped within its arched ribs.

But nearly always I was alone. I'd crack the ice that skimmed the pool, dip my watercolor cup into the frigid water, then retreat a few feet away to paint. Sometimes I would slide my hand beneath the surface to feel a soft mass like a decomposing melon, then let my fingers slip down to measure the almost imperceptible pulse of a heart, cold and slippery as a carp. Then I would return to work.

As the winter wore on, it grew too cold for me to work outdoors. There was little snow or rain, but it was bitterly cold. The pool froze solid. Ice formed where my watercolor brush touched the heavy paper, and the ink grew sluggish in my Rapidograph pen.

So I stayed at home in the studio, where the orbweavers again hung beside the windows, and used the watercolor studies to begin work on other, larger, paintings—oils on canvas, urban landscapes where a small, frozen woodland pool hinted that a green heart still beat within the city. These paintings were extremely good. I took some digital photos of them and sent them to Anna, along with the name of two galleries in Schöneberg and one in Kreuzberg. Then I went to visit Arethusa in Sicily.

I had planned on staying only a few weeks, but the Mediterranean warmth, the smell of olive groves and sight of flying fish skimming across the blue sea, seduced me. I stayed in Sicily until early spring and then returned briefly to Ogygia, my true island. I could not recall the last time I had visited—a steamship brought me, I do remember that, and the trip then took many hours.

Now it was much faster, and the island itself noisier, dirtier, more crowded. I found myself homesick—not for any island, but for the flat in Schöneberg and the quiet place in the Grunewald where Philip was. I had thought that the time in Sicily might give me other distractions; that I might find myself wanting to paint the sea, the bone white sand and stones of Ogygia.

Instead I found that my heart's needle turned toward Philip. I breathed in the salt air above the cliffs, but it was him I smelled, his breath, the scent of evergreen boughs beside shallow water, the leaves in his hair. I returned to Berlin.

I'd deliberately left my laptop behind and asked Anna not to call while I was gone. Now I found a number of messages from her. Two of the galleries were very interested in my paintings. Could I put together a portfolio for a possible show the following autumn?

I arranged for my most recent canvases to be framed. The sleeping nudes I had done of him back in Maine had arrived some months earlier; I chose the best of these and had them mounted as well. All of this took some time to arrange, and so it was mid-April before I finally took my satchel and my easel and returned to the pool in the Grunewald to paint again.

It was a soft, warm morning, the day fragrant with young grass pushing its way through the soil. The flower vendors had baskets of freesia and violets on the sidewalk. On the Landwehrcanal, gray cygnets struggled in the wake of the tourist boat as the adult swans darted after crusts of sandwiches tossed overboard. The captain of the boat waved to me from his cockpit. I waved back, then continued on to an S-Bahn station and the train that would bear me to the Grunewald.

There was no one in the forest when I arrived. High above me the sky stretched, the pale blue-green of a frog's belly. Waxwings gave their low whistling cries and fluttered in the upper branches of the beeches, where tiny new leaves were just starting to unfurl. I stopped hurrying, the sun's warmth tugging at my skin, the sunlight saying *slow, slow.* A winter storm had brought down one of the larches near the pool; I had to push my way through a scrim of fallen branches, yellow hawthorn shoots already covering the larch's trunk. I could smell the sweet green scent of new growth; and then I saw it.

The pool was gone: there had been no snow to replenish it. Instead, a cloud of blossoms moved above the earth, gold and azure, crimson and magenta and shining coral. Anenomes, adonis, hyacinth, clematis: all the windflowers of my girlhood turned their yellow eyes toward me. I fell to my knees and buried my face in them so that they stained my cheeks with pollen, their narrow petals crushed beneath my fingertips.

I cried as though my heart would break as the wind stirred the blossoms and a few early greenflies crawled along their stems. I could see Philip there beneath them. His hair had grown, twining with the white roots of the anemones and pale beetle grubs. Beneath rose-veined lids his eyes twitched, and I could see each iris contract then swell like a seed. He was dreaming. He was beautiful.

I wiped my eyes. I picked up my satchel, careful not to step on the flowers, and got out my easel and brushes. I began to paint.

Anemones, adonis, hyacinth, clematis. I painted flowers, and a man sleeping, and the black scaffolding of a city rising from the ruins. I painted in white heat, day after day after day, then took the watercolors home and transferred what I had seen to canvases that took up an entire wall of my flat. I worked at home, through the spring and into the first weeks of summer, and now the early fall, thinking how any day I will have to return to the pool in the Grunewald, harvest what remains of the windflowers, and set him free.

But not yet.

Last week my show opened at the gallery in Akazienstrasse. Anna, as always, did her job in stellar fashion. The opening was well-attended by the press and wealthy buyers. The dark winterscapes were hung in the main room, along with the nudes I had painted for those seven years. I had thought the nudes would get more attention than they did—not that anyone would have recognized Philip. When I look at those drawings and paintings now, I see a naked man, and that's what everyone else sees as well. Nothing is concealed, and these days there is nothing new in that.

But the other ones, the windflower paintings, the ones where only I know he is there—those are the paintings that people crowd around. I'm still not certain how I feel about exposing them to the world. I still feel a bit unsure of myself—the shift in subject matter, what feels to me like a tenuous, unsteady grasp of a medium that I will need to work much harder at if I'm to be as good as I want to be. I'm not certain if I know yet how good these paintings really are, and maybe I never will be sure. But the critics—the critics say they are revelatory.

Elizabeth Hand is the author of eight novels, including the forthcoming *Generation Loss,* and three short story collections, the most recent of which is *Saffron and Brimstone: Strange Stories.* Since 1988, she has been a regular contributor to the *Washington Post Book World,* among numerous other publications, and is a columnist for *Fantasy & Science Fiction* magazine. She lives on the coast of Maine.

HERO'S WELCOME

Rebecca York

Planet Thindar, four months after the Dorie-Farlian War

He was taking a risk. He could lose everything—the estate he'd been given and all the severance pay he'd invested in it. There was no guarantee he'd ever make a farmer. Still Ben-Linkman felt a rush of pleasure as he activated the breaker jets and eased the bulky air truck downward fifty more meters for a better view of his property.

"Mine. The spoils of war." He said the words aloud, savoring them as he swooped low over the small lake, winking in the greenish glow of the late afternoon sun, then circled the sprawling house. Catching his breath, he swung away from the landscaped grounds and roared over the broad, flat fields where oil-rich rokam had once grown.

Coming here was a huge gamble. He was betting everything that he could bring the land back to life. But could he? Did he have it in him? What if he failed? What if he—

Determinedly, he cut off the thought and set the air truck down behind the house. This was no time for second thoughts, and if he didn't want to lose the place to an enterprising thief, he'd better activate the security perimeter.

He rolled his shoulders, fatigued from flying the heavy government surplus ship eight hundred klicks from Spenserville, formerly Halindish. The city, which had been a Farlian provincial capital, had been recently—triumphantly—renamed after a legendary Dorre war hero.

Reaching behind his seat, he picked up his weapons and checked them: the small laser gun in the hip holster and the larger projectile rifle. High command had told him that gangs of deserters might be hiding in the hills. He wasn't about to let them catch him by surprise.

The hatch beside him swung open with a push, and he levered himself out of the opening, stifling a groan as cramped muscles stretched. The real pain came when he touched ground. He forgot to lock his bad knee, and it crumpled under him, sending a jolt of pain all the way down to the nonexistent toes. Gritting his teeth against a scream, he stood with his hands balled into fists.

The pills they'd given him were in his backpack. He could take one. Just one.

"No." He said it aloud.

He'd seen what happened when men started relying on the medication. They ended up needing more and more of the stuff, until their brains were so fried, all they could do was sit and stare into space. The pills were a one-way ticket to Farlian hell. He wasn't going that route.

Teeth still clenched, he walked to the back door of the large, well-proportioned house and worked the key pad with the combination they'd given him.

Inside, he paused to absorb the silence of the wide corridor before switching on a power light. Then he made his way to the central living area, where he took a quick look at the woven rugs and the graceful furniture. Expensive, he thought, running his hand over glossy Kardin wood.

Glancing toward the small window, he saw that the light was fading. If his people, the Dorre, had built the house, there would be skylights in the vaulted ceiling. The estate had been confiscated from Farlians, though, which meant it was constructed to allow only minimal outside light to penetrate. Like the caves Farlians had occupied to escape the predators on the planet where they'd first landed after leaving Earth. Hundreds of years of cave dwelling had changed their eyes, so that Farlians saw better in the dark.

A neat trick, but it hadn't won them the war.

Turning right, he headed for the control center. His father had been the maintenance supervisor in a rich Farlian household, so the equipment was familiar. In minutes he'd brought up the main computer and checked the circuits. About half the estate's power units, including the security perimeter, were working. He'd fix the rest tomorrow, after a good night's sleep. Tonight, he'd just do a sensor check.

First he scanned the grounds and detected nothing bigger than a tree sneep. When he checked the house, though, his hand froze on the controls. Eyes narrowed, he went through the drill again, but the screen didn't change. There was a Farlian in the house.

A wave of anger and hatred surged through him. Farlian and Dorre might come from the same human stock and claim Earth as their common ancestral home, but the only thing they had in common anymore was the war they'd fought for the right to rule Thindar.

Six months ago, just before the armistice, one of the slat-eating bastards had caught him below the knee with an energy blast that injected tissue poison. Amputation from the wound down had saved his life, but it hadn't stopped the pain that continually invaded the rest of his leg. Nor had it lessened his rage at Farlians.

If it weren't for the oppressive bastards, the Dorre never would have been forced to go to war. After abandoning the inhospitable planet where they'd lived, the Farlians had migrated to Thindar and colonized it. When the Dorre had arrived a hundred years later, on a generation ship from Earth that was at the end of its resources, the Farlians had saved his people's lives with food and medicine.

Then, when the newcomers had begun to prosper, the Farlians, afraid of losing power, had passed laws that made it impossible for Dorre to enter good schools, hold office, or even own property. A caste system had developed; his people were forced into the underclass—while the Farlians had consolidated relations with other space-traveling races, creating off-world trading partnerships, all the while growing ever richer and more arrogant.

Until the Dorre had risen in rebellion.

From the console, Link silently switched on some lights. Then he moved quietly toward the storage compartment where the sensors indicated the intruder was hiding.

His hand on the pressure trigger of his gun, he yanked open the metal door, nearly killing the Farlian behind it before seeing it was a female. A mane of red hair hid her face.

Grabbing her by the sleeve, he wrenched her into the open and tossed her onto the floor. She lay curled away from him, her ivory skin blotched by fear, her slender legs trembling visibly below a short tunic. Yet it was with regal bearing that she sat up and swept the fall of hair away from her exotic green eyes.

The sight of her familiar features knocked the breath out of him. "Kasimanda!"

She'd been beautiful as a child, more so as an adolescent. But now . . . by Atherdan, she was stunning. The pale skin, the cat-like eyes, and the wild red hair creating a vision that called to him with a familiar, forbidden longing. For an instant, he wondered if this was really her or some dream from his subconscious come to life.

Her gaze flicked from his face to the laser pistol in his hand. "Would you kill me, Link?" she asked in that musical voice he instantly discovered still had the power to stir his senses.

He pulled himself together. "Why shouldn't I? This is forbidden territory for a Farlian."

Doubt kindled in her eyes. "We were . . . friends."

"Friends." He threw the word back at her. Dorre and Farlian could not be friends. Yet he and the highborn Kasimanda of Renfaral had played together as children. And when they had reached adolescence, he had longed for more than friendship.

His eyes must have given him away, because he saw her relax a fraction.

"How did you get here?" he demanded.

She pushed herself off the floor and stood facing him defiantly. "Bribes."

"I hope you didn't spend too much, because you're leaving. Now," he said, emphasizing the last word.

She shook her head. "No."

He made his voice flat and hard. "You can't stay."

Her shoulders slumped. "Then kill me now."

"I don't kill women."

"No?" She raised her chin. "A Dorre raiding party killed my mother and sister. Are you so different?"

Sickened, though not surprised, by the news, he asked, "And they spared you?"

He saw her stiffen, swallow. "My mother pushed me into the refuse chute as they were coming through the front door. They didn't find me."

He tried to imagine Kasimanda of Renfaral hiding among the household garbage. Unthinkable. Yet he could see from her eyes that it was true—that and maybe worse.

"Why did you come here?" he demanded.

"To work."

He gave a short, sharp laugh. "You? Work?"

"Yes. The place was a mess. I cleaned it. I can keep it for you. I can cook. And I can help you with the rokam."

"Let me see your hands."

She kept her eyes on him as she held up her hands for inspection. He remembered them being soft and white, the hallmarks of a pampered woman. Now they were red and chapped.

Before he could comment, she went on quickly. "I was studying botany at the Grand Institute when the war started. I know about rokam. It's temperamental. You could lose the whole crop if you plant at the wrong time or if the minerals in the soil are out of balance."

He gave a tight nod. He knew the risks.

"I—"

"How did you get inside the house?" he interrupted her.

"I visited this estate several times before the war. I knew the access codes." With a gesture toward the south-facing window, she added, "I sold the ring my father gave me on my Passage Day—and some other things from the estate. With the last of the credits, I paid for a ride as far as the river."

His eyes narrowed. It was thirty klicks to the Little Jodda and two hundred klicks to the nearest settlement. "Some damn fool flyer pilot left you in the middle of nowhere?" he asked, his anger rising.

She gave a little nod.

"This is dangerous territory. You could have died if a storm had caught you on the plains. Or you could have run into a gang of deserters," he ground out, imagining the worst. "They're desperate. Dangerous."

"I have a laser gun."

"Weapons are forbidden to Farlians."

She met his gaze with steady eyes. "Are you going to turn me in?"

He heaved a sigh. "No." When she let out a little breath, he fixed her with a quizzical look. "How did you find me?"

"A woman who worked for my father is in the office where they keep information on troopers," she answered softly. "After . . . " She stopped, started again. "After I'd been on my own for a couple of months, I went to her, and she looked up your record."

"Why me?"

Her gaze dropped to the floor. "My parents and my sister are dead. So is my brother. There isn't anyone else. And my options are very limited."

"You're well educated. A lot better than me," he said. "Surely you can find something to do."

"Not many people are hiring ex-Farlian nobility." A shudder went through her. "There are houses where young women of my station entertain Dorre men. I would rather starve."

He struggled to keep his expression impassive as she continued.

"I won't beg you to let me stay, Link, but . . . I've brought something for your leg."

The blood drained from his face. Farlian hell, she knew about that, too.

"I bought some salve Farlian soldiers use," she whispered. "It draws out the poison."

His eyes widened. "There's a cure? Give it to me!"

"It's . . ." She stopped, shook her head. "They were testing it. I don't know if . . . "

He turned away so she wouldn't see the crushing disappointment in his eyes. An experimental drug. Probably it didn't work.

His jaw rigid, he stomped out of the room—to the extent that his limp allowed for stomping. He'd come here to hide his ruined body—from others or from himself, he wasn't sure. He didn't know how to cope with either the sudden reminder of the man he'd once been or with the false hopes she offered.

He threw his pack onto the floor in the hall and sprawled on the steps leading upstairs. Cursing under his breath, he rummaged in the pack. When his fingers closed around the tube of dried brew malt, he made a grateful sound. Not quite as good as pain pills, but it would do. He set the tablet in a plastic cup, poured in water from the bottle he carried, and watched the brew sizzle. Before the head rose, he began to drink. It was cheap beer, laced with brandy extract. In minutes he was feeling almost calm.

Almost calm enough to face Kasimanda as she came down the hall, carrying a small plate.

"You should eat," she murmured.

He acknowledged the advice with a grunt as she set the plate beside him. His resolve to ignore her wavered when he smelled nester cakes. Her family's cook had made them, and Kasi used to sneak them to him.

"You made these?" he asked.

"Yes."

He took a bite, wondering when and how she'd learned to cook. The cake was crisp and meaty, the way he remembered.

Tipping his head to one side, he peered at her through a brew-induced haze. "These are good. My compliments to the chef." His word slightly slurred, he asked, "But what if cooking and cleaning and tending rokam isn't enough? What if the one-legged man wants you in his bed?"

Her face went white.

"I see. The rules have changed, but I'm still not good enough for you."

She knitted her hands together in front of her. "I . . . can't."

The way she said it made him shudder. "Kasi?"

He turned toward her, but she was already darting out of his reach. She fled down the hall, and he stared after her long after she'd disappeared.

Finally, with a heavy sigh, he made another cup of the strong brew. A shame to waste good nestor cakes, he decided, cramming another into his mouth and licking his fingers. Sometime later he found the strength to get up and stagger down the hall to a bed chamber. Fumbling clumsily, he unstrapped his holster and shoved his gun under the pillow.

There was a mirror on the wall, and his reflection took him by surprise: A tall dark-haired man with broad shoulders, his face too young for the pain-etched grooves in his forehead. He couldn't remember the last time he'd looked at his own face. It was changed, and not for the better.

Turning quickly, he pulled off his trousers before easing off the prosthetic extension of his ruined leg. Freed of its constraint, the stump throbbed, and he bit back a groan as he flopped onto the bed.

He must have slept. The next thing he knew, he was awake and listening to stealthy feet moving in the darkness. His hand shot to the gun. The intruder was quicker, surer. He heard the weapon clank onto the stand beside the bed.

"It's all right," Kasimanda whispered.

Some of the tension went out of him. In the semi-darkness, he could see her only in outline. When he remembered she could see him a lot better, his stomach knotted. "What're you doing here?" he growled, trying to pull the bedding over the stump of his right leg.

Her hand covered his. "Lie still."

He felt the mattress shift as she came down beside him. "I'm going to take care of the wound."

"No." He tried to slide away, but one of her hands gripped his shoulder, stilling him. When the other hand touched his ruined flesh, he went rigid. "Don't."

"It's all right," she answered, a quaver in her voice. "I understand."

He uttered a short, humorless laugh. "Yeah? And how in Atherdan's name could you understand? What have you lost?" The instant the words left his mouth, he regretted them. Consumed by pain and humiliation, he'd forgotten what she'd told him only a short time ago, that, indeed, she'd lost everything.

She didn't reply, only stared at him. He couldn't hold her gaze, had to look away.

For several more moments, silence hung in the darkness between them. Then her fingers flattened against his hot skin.

"Let me see if this salve works," she whispered. "I want it to work. I want to give you that. Maybe it's all I can give you."

The soft sound of her voice kept him pinned to the bed as her hand glided over his leg, spreading some kind of cream. At first her touch brought him pain, and he clenched his teeth to keep from wrenching away. But in a few moments he felt something else: deep, comforting warmth, radiating through his skin, penetrating all the way to the bone.

Still, as her hand moved lower, toward the place where the energy burst had charred his flesh, he felt cold sweat break out on his forehead.

She kept talking to him in a low voice, words he couldn't quite catch. Yet they held him. He wanted to close his eyes, to pretend that the darkness hid his mangled body. At the same time, he wanted to turn on a light, so he could see her delicate features. He settled for straining his eyes, watching her bending over him, the long flow of her spectacular Farlian hair, with its rippling waves, curtaining her face.

"Is it doing anything?" she asked, her voice giving away her tension.

"I . . . think so."

"Good." The word eased from her lips like a long, satisfied sigh.

He reached toward her, but before his hand could connect with her flesh, she sprang away. For a moment she stood looking down at him, then she turned and ran out of the room.

The next morning, he might have chalked the whole thing up to fevered dreams, except that he could see the orange salve on his leg. He also felt a difference in the wound. The pain was less gnawing.

He limped to the bathroom, using the folding crutch they'd given him in the hospital, and took a quick shower, bracing his back against the curved wall and standing on one leg. When he had carefully dried the stump, he attached the prosthesis and braced for the hot pain that always came when he first put his weight on the damned thing.

It wasn't quite so bad.

He started down the hall, then, on second thought, stopped and went back. Standing in front of the mirror, he ran his hand over the dark stubble that covered his cheeks. He had intended to leave it. Instead he slathered hair-dissolving foam on the nascent beard and washed it away. The foam left his cheeks smooth and undisguised, forcing him to acknowledge the weight he'd lost. He looked lean and hungry and, in his own eyes, angry.

He tried to lighten his expression, to erase the frown, to make his lips curve upward in a smile. When he realized his attempts to rearrange his features only made things worse, he grimaced and turned away.

Kasimanda wasn't in the galley. But there was a plate of grain cakes on a warming square. And real coffee. Maybe the residents of the house had left it in long-term storage, he thought as he breathed in the wonderful aroma, then poured some into the delicate ceramic mug she'd set on the table for him.

Her grain cakes melted in his mouth, like the ones his mother had made, and he realized that she must have used a Dorre recipe. He wanted to tell her how good they were, but she didn't appear when he called her name.

"You don't have to leave," he said more loudly, hoping his voice conveyed a note of apology for his insensitivity of the night before. "You can stay here as long as you want."

No answer.

Half disappointed, half relieved, he went back to the power center and spent the morning on repairs. When the sun had reached its zenith and begun its slow fall toward the horizon, he headed outside to inspect the farm machinery. He wasn't going to look for her, he told himself as he limped his way to the large barn, where the equipment was kept.

After satisfying himself that the riding scour and harvester were in working order, he returned to the galley, where he found she'd put away most of the supplies he'd brought and prepared another Dorre-style meal. Like the fairy people in a children's story, he thought with a low laugh. An unseen helper.

Stomping down the hall, he began opening doors. In a wing off to the left, he found the small chamber where it appeared she had been sleeping. The bed was narrow, the storage bay small. Servant's quarters.

Why in the name of Far— He stopped himself, realizing suddenly how insulting the curse would be if he slipped and said it aloud in front of Kasi: his people defiling the name of hers.

He started over.

Why in the name of hell was she sleeping in here? She could have the master bed chamber for all he cared. He opened the storage bay. There were only a few tunics, all of them clean but made of cheap cloth. Wasn't there anything better in the house, he wondered as he fingered the coarse fabric, imagining it next to her soft skin. With a curse, he turned and stamped away.

He worked outside for the rest of the day. By evening, his leg was throbbing. Back in his room, as he pulled off his clothes and removed the prosthesis, he decided he could use some more of that orange stuff.

Would she come to him again? Or was one good look at his mangled leg enough, he wondered as he lay with his eyes half closed, too keyed up to sleep. An enormous sense of relief swept over him when the door finally glided open.

"Was your leg better today?" she asked softly as she tiptoed toward the bed.

"Yes."

"I'm so glad." In her voice was a hint of the music he'd always loved.

"I think more of that salve would help," he admitted in low, rough tones.

In one quick motion, she perched lightly beside him. He wanted to feel her touch. Still, he flinched when her fingers made contact with the leg. Teeth gritted, he ordered himself to relax as she began to soothe the magic salve over his poisoned flesh. Again there was warmth and sweet relief.

In the darkness, he began to talk, his tone flat and devoid of emotion. "I was on a mission to secure a farm house. There was a Farlian hiding inside. He burned my leg. I put a hole in his chest."

Her hand stilled, then started again.

"I killed a lot of your people."

"Are you bragging or asking for my forgiveness?" she asked, a little hitch in her voice.

He might have tossed out a cynical answer. Instead he gave her honesty. "Neither. I just . . . I just needed to say it. I'm not sure I'm fit company for anyone. I feel . . . uncivilized."

"The men you killed were uncivilized, too," she answered. "They would have killed you if you hadn't killed them first."

He made a low sound in his throat. "I started out as an idealistic boy fighting for my people's freedom. I didn't know what war was going to be like. I didn't know how it felt to look into a man's eyes and kill him."

"You did what you had to do. And your people are free."

"And yours?"

"We've paid the price for years of conceit and presumption."

Her answer shocked him. "That's what you believe?"

She sighed, a sad sound in the darkness. "When I think about it, I understand that when we raised the price of rokam oil too high, our buyers on Kodon Prime made a business decision to ally themselves with the Dorre and back them in a war against us." She sighed again. "But mostly I try not to think about it. I try just to survive, one day at a time."

She said it with such heart-wrenching simplicity that he struggled to draw a full breath. Her next words only added to the crushing feeling in his chest.

"Link, you're a man whose body and soul were injured by circumstances beyond your control. A man with the strength to heal the parts that can be healed."

"How do you know?" he asked in a hoarse whisper.

"Because you had the courage to tell me your doubts. Because you let me put my hands here." In the darkness, she lightly touched the stump of his leg. "There are things inside all of us that we find frightening. It's how we deal with the fear that counts."

When had she grown up, he wondered. Where had she gained this kind of wisdom?

"Doesn't it change the way you feel about me when I tell you I killed Farlian men?" he demanded.

"I never saw things in terms of Farlians verses Dorre. Our races evolved differently, because my ancestors came from Earth much longer ago than yours and adapted to a new environment that changed us. So my skin is very pale, and my eyes see better at night than yours. But those physical differences are superficial. Our hopes and needs and feelings are alike. We're all still people, and in all ways that matter, we're the same."

"Then why did you stop me that night, when you knew I was going to kiss you?" He blurted out the question, then immediately regretted it.

He thought she wasn't going to answer when she rose and took a step away from the bed. Then she began to speak in a low, rapid voice. "Because I knew my father was standing in the doorway, waiting for me to come in from the garden. And despite his liberal leanings, he would have killed you if you'd put your hand on his high-born daughter."

Before Link could respond, she turned and fled the room.

He lay for long hours in the darkness, remembering each word of the midnight encounter, each touch of her hands on his flesh. He especially remembered that she'd been motivated by a desire to protect him from her father, not revulsion for him, when she'd refused his kiss all those years ago.

Some time in the early hours of the morning, slumber finally took him.

Despite the short sleep, he woke feeling better than he had in months, as if a giant weight had been lifted off his body. He knew it was Kasimanda's doing. She was the first person he'd told how he felt—about the war, about his leg, about anything at all. Maybe it was because he'd known her longer than anyone still living. Maybe it was the gentle way she had about her. Whatever the reason, he felt he could talk to her, share himself with her. And with the talking and sharing had come a kind of freedom.

He wanted to tell her, but she had disappeared again. Anguish grabbed him when he considered that she might have fled the estate. Then he reminded himself that she'd said she had nowhere else to go.

He ate the food she had left for him, then headed outside. With the riding scour, he began to clear away rocks that had washed down from the nearby mountain with the season's rains. No one had tended the field since the war had started, and there was a lot of debris.

While he worked, he thought about Kasimanda. Kasi, he had called her when they were young. Things had changed abruptly when they'd grown into awkward adolescents. And more recently, changed again—in ways he was afraid to imagine. They both had been ground up and spit out by the war.

He sighed. On Laster of Renfarel's estate, where he and Kasi had grown up, Farlian and Dorre children had played together as near-equals—until they began to mature and were suddenly cautioned to remember their places in society.

Those places had changed, though. The Dorre, in waging war against their oppressors, had stood the world on its head, creating chaos in the process: cities renamed, rulers reduced to humiliation, civilians murdered. Families, like Kasi's, torn apart. Men, like him, maimed.

With a grimace, Link centered his mind on the task of clearing rocks. When the sun dipped low over the hills, he returned to the house and revived himself in a long cool shower. After eating the dinner Kasi had left him, he flopped into bed. But rather than lying down, he propped his back against a mound of pillows and left a small lamp burning in the corner of the room—as if he were expecting company. Then, as the silent minutes dragged by, his tension mounted along with the throbbing in his leg.

He had almost given up hope when the door slid open, and she stepped into the room. Stopping, she shielded her light-sensitive eyes, took a step back.

"Don't go."

"The light—"

"I need to see you."

He held his breath as she hesitated in the doorway, then felt the air trickle from his lungs as she crossed the space between them.

She was dressed in a short gown, not unlike her daytime tunics. As he watched, she opened a small medical kit and took out the salve. Easing gingerly onto the bed, she kept her eyes down as she began to work on his leg, the medicine and her touch bringing that same deep, healing comfort. This time, though, the sensation soon became more than mere comfort. With the absence of the pain, he was helpless to stop the response of his body to hers.

He sat there, feeling the heat gather in his loins as her hands worked their way down his leg and up again toward his thigh. And he knew the precise moment that she realized how her touch was affecting him.

Uttering a strangled cry, she scrambled off the bed.

"Kasi."

The name from their childhood stopped her. Still, she stood warily, poised to flee.

He gestured downward. "I'm not going to run after you. By the time I attached that pitiful excuse for a leg, you'd be gone—to wherever it is you hide during the day." He made a sound that was almost a laugh. "Or I could hop after you. I've never tried to see how fast I can hop." Nor had he joked about the leg, he thought with a kind of detached amazement.

Her features contorted.

"Kasi," he said again, very gently.

She held herself stiffly, as if she might break in two, and the question that had been gnawing at him for days worked its way to his lips and came out in a half-strangled growl. "The Dorre soldiers who came to Renfaral—did they find you?"

Her whole body jerked as if he'd slapped her, and he felt a sudden pain in his gut, like the twisting of a knife.

"Did they catch you?" he managed, praying he was wrong.

Her head gave the smallest of nods. When she spoke, her voice cracked. "In the woods. They didn't know I was Laster's daughter, so they didn't kill me."

The look on her face told him more than the words. He clenched his jaw to keep from roaring his outrage. He had heard soldiers bragging of catching Farlian women and teaching them a lesson in obedience to their new masters.

"I would never do anything to hurt you," he said, struggling to speak around the fist-sized obstruction in his throat.

"When I touched you, you got . . ." She stopped, gulped.

"Hard," he finished for her, then went on to admit, "I was aroused. Do you know what that means?"

"That you want to have sex with me."

The stark look on her face pierced though his chest to his heart. "That's only a small part of what I feel. When you touched me and talked to me, you made me feel things I didn't think I'd ever feel again. Good things. Things I thought had died inside me."

She stayed where she was, her gaze searching his face.

"Kasi, I would never hurt you," he repeated. "I swear that. On the altar of Atherdan."

Her head came up. "On Atherdan? The sacred place of your people."

"Yes."

Her small white teeth worried her lip.

"I can't get up. You have to come back here, so we can talk."

The breath froze in his lungs as he watched her stand unmoving. Then, in a rush she came to the bed and perched on the side, just out of reach, her face turned away from him.

"Can you tell me about it?" he asked.

"I haven't told anyone," she said in a ragged voice.

"Last night you made me face things I didn't want to face. And this morning I felt better."

"What happened to me was . . . bad."

"I know." He wanted to reach for her, take her in his arms. He kept his hands flat against the mattress.

"Four of them caught me," she choked out. "And they dragged me into the old toolshed."

She told him things, then, that he didn't want to hear, things that made bile rise in his throat, though he listened until she was finished, until she began to weep, until he wept with her. Finally, when he couldn't stand it any longer and reached for her, she slid away. When he called her name, she slipped out of the room.

And he was left alone on the bed with only his troubled thoughts for company. He had come to this place feeling sorry for himself, for what he had endured. But his wounds were of the flesh. Hers were of the soul.

Still, she had summoned the courage to tell him her secrets. He would do the same. If she was still there in the morning.

As tired as he was from his work in the fields, Link remained awake for a long while before sleep finally claimed him.

To his surprise and vast relief, he found Kasi the next morning, sitting at the table in the galley. Her eyes were red, as if she'd spent the whole night crying, and her hands were clenched tightly in front of her. But she was there.

He propped his hips against the counter, meeting her gaze with a steadiness that belied the pounding of his heart.

"So what do you think of me now?" she asked. "Kasimanda of Renfaral. The woman who served four Dorre soldiers against her will."

The calmness of her voice frightened him. He sensed he could lose her with a single wrong word. "I think you're as brave as any war hero, Dorre or Farlian," he answered from the depths of his heart. "Brave enough to keep going after you lost your whole family. Brave enough to go through what must have been hell to get yourself here. Brave enough to face me and my anger, and to take care of my leg, when I know what you wanted to do was run away."

She stared at him as if she couldn't believe the appraisal.

He ran a shaky hand through his hair, and fear made his words come out stiffly. "Kasi, when I first saw you here, I couldn't face what I felt. That's why I acted angry. I was terrified that you were going to hurt me."

Her lips parted, and her huge, gorgeous eyes opened wide in astonishment. "Me? Hurt you?"

"Oh, yes. The way you did that night seven years ago when you ran away from me in the garden." He swallowed, tried to gather some courage of his own to match hers. "Kasi, I have loved you since I was ten. A crazy, hopeless love. But now—" He gave a little laugh. "Now I guess I'm willing to wait for you until I'm a hundred, if that's what it takes."

Wildly conflicting emotions chased across her features.

"No pressure," he said, relieved that he had finally confessed the truth. "No demands or requests. No real expectations." He was lying, of course. Through his teeth. He had expectations, all right, enough to last several lifetimes.

Turning so that she couldn't see his face, he poured himself a mug of coffee. Then, without another word or even a glance in her direction, he grabbed a grain cake and headed for the fields.

She was waiting for him when he came in for dinner. While they ate the food she had prepared, they talked quietly about growing rokam and about the supplies she needed for the house.

He made his first wordless request when they were reclining on wide loungers beside the empty swimming pool. Moving his leg, he gave a small groan.

Her head swung quickly toward him. "Is it bad?"

He shrugged elaborately.

"You need more of the salve."

"I think you're right." He considered his options—his bedroom where she would be nervous, or out here where he would feel defenseless without his prosthesis. He chose her comfort. "We could use the lounger."

"Yes," she answered on a rush of breath that told him he'd made the right choice.

Still, his gaze slid away from her as he pictured himself taking off the leg. He wasn't ready to do that in front of her. Standing, he steadied himself against the wall. "I'll be back in a minute."

The sun had set by the time he returned. Overhead, stars winked in the black velvet of the sky, and the smallest of the four moons cast a blue radiance on the fields beyond the house.

He looked around anxiously for Kasi, afraid that she might have changed her mind. Then she moved, a shadow detaching itself from the wall of the house, and he watched her silhouette glide toward him. She was tall like most Farlian women, almost his height. But the blue light gave her a fragile, indistinct look. Long ago she had told him how things appeared to her in the moonlight. To her radiation-sensitive eyes, the light was soft and pink, giving objects a warmth he couldn't see.

Wearing a pair of short pants, with the folding crutch replacing his prosthesis, he limped slowly toward the lounger. He was rather amazed with himself, that he'd let her see him this way. But then, he decided, maybe it gave him an advantage.

The twisted logic brought a low chuckle to his lips.

"What's funny?" she inquired.

"I was thinking—how frightened can you be of a cripple?"

"Link, I can't think of you as crippled."

He snorted, disbelieving.

"You're a war hero."

"I'm no hero," he denied.

"Do they give rich holdings like this one to all the troopers?"

"No. But they knew my father was training me to run an estate, so they figured I had a better chance at producing rokam for them than some store clerk."

"It was more than that. They knew you had the will to succeed."

There was no point in arguing, he thought as he eased onto the lounger. Neither of them spoke as she sat on the edge of the cushioned surface and began to rub the healing medicine into his injured flesh. It wasn't long before her innocent caresses once again made his body grow hard.

He felt her touch falter, heard her breath catch.

He lay very still with his eyes closed and his arms at his sides, his fists clenched. And when he made no move to reach for her, she kept up her ministration.

"Thank you," he whispered, when she had finished. "Kasi, you've changed my life with that salve—given me new hope. But I'm not good at speaking the things in my heart. Words aren't enough. I can't tell you how I feel unless I touch you."

He heard her breath catch and went on quickly. "I'll keep my hands flat on the cushions. I just . . . I just want to kiss you. On the cheek."

She didn't draw back as he pushed himself up and brushed a

whisper-soft kiss against her tender flesh. When she stayed where she was, he stroked his way down to her jaw line, then back up to the corner of her eye. He felt a little shiver go through her.

He turned his head, moved his mouth gently against her lashes, feeling them flutter at the touch, feeling his own body tighten painfully in response.

He wanted more, but he was ready to deny himself further pleasure. "Thank you." He drew away from her, but she stayed where she was, her eyes closed.

"Would you . . . do it again?" she whispered, her voice shaky.

"Yes," he breathed. "Oh, yes." This time he nibbled gently at her neck, feeling her skin heat and her breath grow thready, and he had to grip the lounger beneath him to keep from reaching for her. Raising his head, he planted small kisses on her chin and cheeks. Her lips were moist and parted. He wanted to devour them. Instead he stroked the curve of one beautiful brow.

"Link." His name was a breathy sigh. For long moments she sat very quietly, then tipped her face toward him. "Do you know, no man has kissed me on the mouth?" she whispered.

He felt something catch in his throat.

"If you kiss me the way men and women kiss, it will belong only to the two of us."

He couldn't speak, could only nod as she slid millimeters closer to him. He kept his hands at his sides, leaning forward until his mouth touched hers.

He felt the tension in her. Slowly he brushed his mouth back and forth against hers, increasing the pressure by slow degrees, until her lips were sealed to his.

Heat leaped inside him as he felt the yielding softness of her, heard the low, purring sound in her throat. Yet he kept his hands where they were, the only contact point his mouth on hers as he opened her lips and gently probed the warmth and softness beyond.

When he lifted his head, her breath was ragged, and her eyes were soft and pleading.

"I want . . ." she whispered, the sentence trailing off.

"Anything," he answered, offering her his soul.

"I'm afraid of what I want."

"You don't have to be afraid. Not with me."

"I know that. At least, part of me knows. The other part is terrified that you'll grab me and . . . "

"I won't."

"How do I know?"

"Because a man doesn't get any more aroused than I am right now," he grated. "But the part of me that frightens you doesn't controls my actions. My brain does. And my brain knows that anything worth doing with you is worth waiting for."

Her gaze went to his face, searching. He kept his own gaze steady.

She laid her head against his shoulder, and they sat silently in the darkness.

When she began to speak, her voice was wispy. "Do you remember the day I put my pet palistan in a boat—and it drifted out into the lake?"

"I found you standing on the shore crying," he answered thickly.

"And you jumped in and towed the boat back to me. Your father came along and found you all wet, and you got a whipping."

He nodded, remembering.

"That was the day I fell in love with you," she breathed.

He stared at her, wondering if he'd heard correctly. She loved him?

"Until then you were just the big boy who was the leader of all the young people on the estate. That day, I lost my heart to you."

He started to reach for her, and her lower lip trembled though her eyes were soft and warm. Then her expression suddenly changed to deep alarm.

"What? Did I frighten you?"

"No. I saw something."

He turned, looked in the same direction, detected nothing but the blue moonlight on the stark hills. "What?"

"A man."

"Are you sure?"

"Yes." Her gaze stayed trained on the rise of ground as she sucked in a little breath. "Two men. Three. Dorre. Crouching, using the rocks for cover."

"How do you know they're Dorre?"

"By the way they're moving. They can't see where to put their feet. But they have weapons. A lot of weapons."

He swore under his breath, snapping into combat mode, his training taking over. The intruders weren't walking up to the front door. They were approaching by stealth—at night. Probably they were deserters, desperate men who wouldn't take prisoners.

"I guess they aren't here to beg food rations," he said aloud.

"What are we going to do?" she asked, the question coming out in a thin gasp, and he knew she was remembering what the soldiers had done to her.

"Make them wish they'd sneaked up on someone else."

"What if you can't?"

His hand closed over her wrist, feeling the blood thundering in her veins. "I will not let them get anywhere near you," he swore.

She sat still as a statue. He watched her rigid features and knew her terror might swallow her whole.

"Kasi, trust me to keep you safe."

At first he wondered if she were capable even of hearing his words. Then her shoulders straightened, and she raised her face to his. He saw the effort she was making to push away the terror and knew she was doing it for him as much as for herself.

Turning, she looked toward the intruders, then spoke with a detached, steely calm. "They have night viewers. But they haven't spotted us."

"Good." He gave her hand a quick squeeze. "Kasi, you're going to have to get my leg. And the laser pistol on the bed stand. I'll meet you in the computer room."

She nodded, darted into the building. Grabbing the crutch, he followed as fast as he could.

In the nerve center of the house, he scanned the alarms. Nothing. The intruders were too far away. They might have been there for days, watching, planning their move. If he got Kasi and himself out of this alive, he'd have to booby trap the hills.

If.

Bringing his mind back to the crisis, he activated the long-range scanners. He was rewarded by three sensor readings on the view screen. Three Dorre men, as she'd said, and they were moving this way.

Kasi came in with the prosthesis. It hurt to put the damn thing on so soon after he'd taken it off, but he ignored the pain, grateful that he could walk almost normally.

He kept his eye on the scanner. The raiding party had stopped. They must know he'd armed a protective ring around the house and the fields. Did they have torpedo launchers?

"I need them closer," he muttered.

"I know how to do that," she said with the same quiet calm that she'd summoned on the patio.

His head jerked toward her. "No!"

Ignoring the protest, she went on. "I can go outside—pretend I'm trespassing on the property. They'll jump at the chance to get their hands on me."

He stared at her, astonished. "Don't even think about it!"

"Do you have a better idea?" she asked, her voice remarkably steady.

He tried to think of one. Spenserville might send help. But he couldn't count on that—or on reinforcements coming in time. He looked in the weapons locker again. He had his own portable torpedo launchers. Not the most desirable of weapons, particularly since he'd bought them when he was almost out of money. He'd settled for the older models that the high command had taken out of service. Too bad he hadn't had a chance to test them.

Cursing under his breath, he thought about the tricky procedure for setting them up. He'd have to do it outside where the explosive gases couldn't collect. If he used a light, the intruders would see what he was doing. If he tried to work in the dark, he could blow himself up.

He raised his gaze to Kasi's. "I can't risk a light. If I tell you what to do, could you set up a torpedo launcher?"

She managed a little nod.

He pulled out the heavy case, opened it, and showed her the parts that had to fit together. Then he closed the carrier again and hoisted it to his shoulder. Outside, he picked a patch of ground partly screened by bushes.

He didn't tell her the danger of an accidental explosion. Instead, he explained each step while she fitted the parts together, her white fingers moving in the moonlight as she fit the launcher into the tripod and went through the check sequence. Holding his breath, he lifted a missile from the case and helped her guide it into the tube. Then he attached the computer cable. With a silent prayer, he pressed the activation button.

For heartbeats, nothing happened, and he thought it had all been for nothing. Then the screen flickered to life. As he tuned the probe, the same three blips he'd seen earlier came into focus.

A hissing noise overhead was followed by an explosion to the right. The slat-eaters were using rockets. Less sophisticated than computer-guided torpedoes—but just as lethal when they hit their target.

Kasi screamed as dirt and plant debris flew through the air. Link pushed her to the ground and worked the controls, adjusting the targeting. There was no time for fine-tuning, he realized as another explosion took off the roof above his left shoulder. All he could do was press the launch button and watch as the torpedo streaked into the sky.

The explosion was a lot more powerful than the previous two. The ground shook, and the night itself seemed to explode. Then, suddenly, everything went silent. He raised his head and looked at the targeting screen. Where the three blips had been there was only a concave depression—a crater twenty meters across.

It was over. The intruders were dead, and he'd killed them. His own people. At least he'd been spared from having to look into their eyes.

Beside him, Kasi whimpered, and when she raised her head, he saw blood seeping from a long gash on her temple.

"Damn the bastards!" he exclaimed, quickly moving to assess the extent of her injury.

"I'm all right," she told him, then slumped against his shoulder in a dead faint.

He managed to lift her, managed to carry her into the house without the leg giving way. His bed was the closest place he could lay her. Turning on the light, he examined the wound. It looked as if she'd been hit by a flying chunk of the building. Quickly he soaked a towel in water and cleaned the blood away—and sighed in relief when he saw that the cut wasn't deep. While he was dabbing on an antibacterial, her eyelids flickered open. She seemed confused for a moment. Then her beautiful green eyes focused on him.

"Did we stop them?" she whispered.

He nodded, captured by her gaze. "Yes. I thought I was through with killing, but . . . ." He drew a ragged breath. "Kasi, I'll do whatever it takes to keep you safe."

"We did what we had to," she answered, her gaze steady as it met his.

He'd thought he'd known her strength, but he realized he'd only scratched the surface. "You have more courage then half the men in my patrol."

She gave a little shrug. "I wanted us to be the ones who survived."

His throat ached as he found her hand and clasped it. "Yes. Us."

Her fingers tightened on his. "Stay with me."

"Here? In my bed?"

She tried to nod and winced. "Yes."

"You're sure?"

"Yes." This time the answer was stronger.

He turned off all but the small light in the corner and unstrapped the plastic leg before easing onto the bed. He planned to stay awake in case she needed him, but he was too exhausted to manage it.

When his eyes opened again, he could see a faint glow in the western sky. Kasi was awake.

"How are you?" he asked softly.

"Better," she said, her gaze fixed on the wall across the room. When she offered no more, he lay beside her in the big bed, listening to the thumping of his heart.

After a long time, she began to speak in a barely audible voice. "At first, I was afraid to tell you what happened to me. I was afraid you wouldn't want me here, in your home, if you knew."

"I hope by now you've figured out you were wrong." He turned toward her, his urgent gaze catching hers, holding. "I want you. For my wife. If you'll have me."

Tears gathered in her eyes. "Your wife?"

He nodded, but when he spoke, he couldn't quite keep the anxiety out of his voice. "Will you? Would you marry a Dorre?"

"Link . . . ." She smiled. "I would follow you to the end of the world." With a laugh, she added, "I did follow you to the end of the world. But what if . . . if I can't . . . " The question went unfinished, but he knew what she was asking.

"I want to know you're mine," he assured her. "On any terms I can get you."

"Oh, Link."

"Say yes."

He saw her even white teeth clamp her bottom lip.

"Say yes," he urged again. "We'll worry about the rest later."

"I can't . . . not until . . . " She swallowed audibly. "I want to . . . to love you. Your body joined with mine."

The words might be halting, but the look in her eyes told him she would only surrender on her own terms.

"I need to do everything—give you everything," she continued. "And I want to do it now."

"We will. But we don't have to do it all today," he answered, wishing she didn't have to push herself—or him.

"What are you afraid of?" she suddenly asked, and he knew she had read the hesitation in his expression.

He managed a rough laugh. "Not much, except that I haven't been with a woman since . . . the leg. It could make things a little awkward."

"Oh," she answered in a breathy whisper, and he knew that his doubts gave her a measure of confidence. Good. Score another one for the damn stump.

He turned toward her, gently stroking his knuckle across her lips, looking into her trusting but anxious face. "You're sure you want to do this now?"

"Don't you?"

"Only if you make me a promise—that you'll tell me if I do anything that frightens you."

"I promise."

He kissed her tenderly, then drew back and deliberately began to open the fasteners down the front of her tunic, watching her face, ready to call a halt.

She said nothing, but he saw the edge of panic in her eyes.

"Does it worry you when I reach for you, with my hands?"

"Yes."

"Then I'll show you how much pleasure I can give you with just my mouth."

Dipping his head, he kissed her neck, then the slender ridges of her collar bone, before edging toward the tops of her breasts.

Delicately he pushed the fabric of the tunic apart with his face, his kisses gliding over the soft warmth of her breasts until he captured one distended nipple between his lips.

She made a strangled sound, and her hands came up to cradle his head and hold him to her as he took his pleasure and gave it back to her in kind.

He kept the pace easy, demanding nothing of her. Between kisses, he talked to her quietly, ardently, as he stoked the fires of her arousal—first with his lips and then with only the lightest of fingertip strokes.

Her body was long and lithe and so beautiful. He could barely breath as he watched arousal bring a warm flush to her pale skin.

Aroused or not, when his hand drifted over the soft curve of her abdomen, downward to the triangle of fiery hair that covered her mound, she stiffened.

"Okay?"

Her face was tense.

"It's all right. We can stop any time you want," he promised, his words denying the clamoring of his body.

"I'm scared, but I don't want to stop."

"Good. Because I'm just going to touch you," he murmured. "Just my hand, stroking you, making you feel good."

"Yes . . . I already feel . . . "

"How?"

"Like a kriver flying too close to the sun."

"I promise, I'm not going to let you get burned."

"I know." Still, the breath hissed out of her, and she squeezed her eyes shut as his fingers slid downward, parting her silky folds and stroking her soft, sensitive flesh.

She was hot and wet to his touch, and he made a low sound of appreciation as he dipped one finger into her, moving his hand to give her maximum pleasure.

"That's good. So good," she gasped.

"Yes, love. Yes."

She was panting, rocking against him, and he whispered low, encouraging words while he pushed her higher, closer to climax, until all at once he felt her body go tense and ripples of sensation beat against his hand as she cried out his name.

He cradled her against him, feeling the aftershocks flicker through her. Gently he tipped her head up so that he could brush his lips against hers, seeing the wonder in her eyes.

"I didn't think I could let you get that close to me."

"But you did. And it was . . . "

"A trip to the center of the sun—and back," she finished.

He smiled down at her, glad that she had given him her trust. Yet it was impossible to completely hide the tension still gripping him.

She drew back, studying his face. Then, in a rush, she slid her hand down and found his erection. When she moved her palm against him, he couldn't hold back a shuddering gasp.

"We need to do something about this thing that's had me so worried," she whispered.

He gave a short laugh. "If you keep your hand there, it'll take care of itself."

She raised her head and searched his eyes. "Is that what you want?"

He thought about lying. Instead, he shook his head. "Not if I have a choice."

"Then what should I do?"

"Nothing complicated. Just let me kiss and touch you some more."

"But . . . I think I'm having most of the fun."

He chuckled. "I guess you don't know what a man in love considers fun." Leaning down, he nuzzled his lips against her breast. "The thing I want most," he breathed against her skin, "is to give you as much pleasure as I can, because my pleasure is tied to yours."

"Then we'll fly to the sun together," she whispered, her heartfelt tone making his throat ache.

Gently, he pulled the tunic off her shoulders, freed her arms from the sleeves.

"So beautiful," he breathed, as he looked down at her slender body before kissing her bare shoulders and working his way slowly down her body.

He kindled her need once more with his lips and hands. And when he knew he would die if he didn't feel her silky skin pressed to his, he dragged off his pants and eased her on top of him, his hands on her back, moving her against him as he rained kisses over her face. She was wet and slick for him again, and she made tiny noises in her throat as she moved against the swollen length of him.

"Raise your hips a little. Let me . . . "

A high sound escaped her throat as he eased himself halfway inside her. Going absolutely still, he watched her closely, steeling himself to stop. But she gave him a tremulous smile, and the smile turned to triumph as she tilted her hips and took him deep inside. For a trembling moment she looked overwhelmed. Then she began to move again, slowly at first, then driving in a frantic rhythm that captured him, sent him up and up toward the heavens, into the heat of the sun. His shout of satisfaction mingled with her cries as she followed him into paradise.

His arms went around her, clasping her tightly, holding her to him, knowing that he would never let her go.

When she raised her head, her eyes were shimmering. "Thank you. Not just for the pleasure. For the healing."

His throat was so tight that he could only answer with a nod.

She slipped down beside him, cuddled against him, and his arm came up to cradle her close.

"So now you can't back out on the marriage part," he said, more gruffly than he intended. "We can do it over the comm lines, with the records office in Spenserville."

"Rushing me into a signed contract?"

"Before you have time for second thoughts."

"You've already had my second thought—and third and fourth and countless others," she murmured. "I remember when my father sat me down and explained why I had to stop following you around. Until then, I didn't understand much about 'proper relations' between Farlians and Dorre. But my father made it very clear." She sighed. "Still, I couldn't stay away from you. That night when you found me in the garden, I ached to tell you to wait for me, so we could go off and be alone. I ached to be with you—to do all the things my father told me I could never do until I was married to a man of the proper rank—and race. But I understood that being with you would only make things impossible for both of us if anyone found out. So I walked away. Now I know what I was giving up."

"Oh, Kasi."

"After the soldiers—" Her voice hitched. "After the soldiers, I thought I could never let a man touch me again. But then, I started imagining someone holding me in his arms, comforting me, making me feel whole again—and the man was always you. Never anyone but you. So that's your answer. Yes, I want to marry you. I want to know you belong to me."

"Always," he breathed before kissing her, a long, sweet kiss of longing and wishes fulfilled.

When it was over, he looked down at her and vowed, "From now on, this place belongs to both of us. It's our home. And I'm going to keep you safe here." Then his face contorted. "But I've got to figure out where to get the money to buy more defenses."

She gave him an uncertain look. "Maybe we don't need more money. Maybe we just need more people."

His eyebrows drew together in a puzzled frown as he watched her eyes take on an excited glow.

"When I saw the estate," she said, "I started dreaming—about refugees living here. Orphans, Dorre and Farlians who've lost their homes. And good people who could make a community where all of us would be safe." She stopped, flushed as she anxiously studied his face. "Maybe it's a bad idea."

"No!" With the adrenaline of excitement flooding his veins and his mind suddenly alive with ideas, he said, "It's a wonderful idea! You're right—children will accept people for what they are. And maybe some of the men I met in hospital will want to join us. Men who never want another war. I'll send for a few of them first so we'll have a defensive force."

She gave him a tremulous smile that touched him to the depths of his soul.

"The war was a horrible thing," he said thickly. "But it brought you to me."

Wordlessly, she nodded.

He pulled her close. "I came here not caring whether I lived or died. Now, I'm going to thank Atherdan for every day I have with you—and for every day we can make a difference, at least, in our little corner off this damned, screwed up planet."

She stroked his damp hair back from his forehead. "Oh, Link, I know why I fell in love with you. You've always had vision and courage. You were a leader even when you were a boy."

"I forgot who I was," he muttered. "But you've made me remember."

And he clasped her tightly, the most precious thing in a world that had turned, overnight, from dark to light.

USA Today best-selling author **Rebecca York** (aka Ruth Glick) is the author of more than fifty romantic suspense novels, many with paranormal elements. The next book in her werewolf series, *New Moon*, will be published by Berkley in March, 2007. Her novella, "Bond of Silver," will be published by Berkley in *Unleashed* in December, 2006. Her website is http://www.rebeccayork.com.

SINGLE WHITE FARMHOUSE

——

Heather Shaw

Our house's frisky nature only became a problem after we'd wired her for the Internet. Before that our pretty white farmhouse's shameful ways had only led to a new doghouse or shed every few months, but we owned a lot of land and there was always room for her offspring. My family even had a decent side business selling off her pups, as she had a reputation for sturdy, handsome buildings capable of growing to many times their birth footage.

Sometimes, such as after the old barn burned down, she'd consent to be bred with buildings we picked out for her. To get Dad's new red barn we introduced her to Farmer Pierce's shiny silo, and after creaking about how big and shiny he was, she took him like he was nothing but a chicken coop. The barn was a difficult birth—her floorboards groaned and she rocked on her foundations, but she was very proud of Barny when he was born, as he was nearly full size.

Us kids were the ones wanting Internet access out at the farm. My older brother and I were both in high school and it was a long way back into town just to do our homework after supper. It also meant I couldn't sneak off to see my boyfriend while I was supposed to be at the library, which was why Mom joined us in convincing Dad to agree to the wiring. Dad said the house had been good to us—over the years, she'd grown from a one-bedroom cabin to a lovely two-story, six-bedroom farmhouse with a wrap-around porch and fireplace. Dad said it just wasn't nice to go threading wires between her walls after she'd given us a roof over our heads for so long, but he finally gave in.

Not one of us would have predicted the 'net sex.

The house consented to the wiring, and as soon as it was done she explored it carefully, like you or I would poke at a new tooth filling. Wasn't long before any unused terminal would be flashing from her zooms around the Internet. New bookmarks were always appearing in the browser files—architecture sites, construction sites, even some redecorating, *Better Homes and Gardens*-type sites were piling up in the history. Dad was disgusted by this—called it "house porn," which made me and my brother giggle.

It wasn't long before the house started spending all her time in chat rooms, flirting with buildings in far-off places such as New York and San Francisco. She left photos of the buildings she met on the desktop, and for a while we were all pretty proud of our little farmhouse. Every day a different landmark would send its picture—the Empire State Building, the Eiffel Tower, the Space Needle. Once she left a triptych of the Sydney Opera House, the Palace of Fine Arts, and the Taj Mahal on screen, and when Dad saw it he cursed, going on about how it was bad enough her catting around with skyscrapers online, but he wasn't living in a lesbian house, and she'd better lay off the other girl houses. She got real sad and shrunken after being yelled at like that, and we lost both our guest bedrooms over the fight. But she did lay off the other girls.

Wasn't long after that when she figured out how to order things over the 'net. Mom had been paying bills online, as it was a lot easier than writing a dozen checks every month, and the house picked up on it and snagged our credit card numbers.

At first it seemed like the only consequence of the house having access to the 'net and our credit cards was that we'd never have to worry about maintenance again. Exterminators showed up early one morning at our door. "Hi. Got a work order saying you've got a 'termite invasion in the southwest corner of the basement.'"

Dad scratched his head, torn between anger that he hadn't ordered this man to come out and pride over the farmhouse. Pride won out.

"Let me take you down there."

A little bit later, the exterminator was the one scratching his head as he had Dad sign off on the rather small bill.

"Sir, I don't know how she knew there were termites down there. It was just a pregnant queen and some workers . . . they didn't even have time to eat much, let alone set up their colony. I ain't never seen nothing like it; most houses don't notice till the infestation is much further along. Your house saved you hundreds of dollars of damage and I just can't figure out how she knew. She's got a lot upstairs, eh?"

Mom and I groaned and Dad made some evasive "aw shucks" noises, paid the man and showed him out. The man shook his head the whole way back to his truck.

Back inside, Dad stood in the foyer and said to the house, "Well, I guess that was all right, seeing as how you saved us money. Next time you ask first, though, you hear?"

Our house had never communicated directly with him, not even once we got her e-mail, so this was sort of a futile request. Mom always said it was because being silent was a powerful choice for certain women, but I thought she was just shy with people. She was starting to open up to me, though, gossiping with me over guys I met online, discussing the far-away big cities where they lived and, sometimes, the buildings they lived in. She was very popular online by then, a big flirt in the building scene, and pretty enough to pull it off.

She was clever, too. She waited until a school day when Mom was in town shopping and Dad was out in the back forty to have the house painters come. By the time everyone was home again, she was gleaming fresh white, her shutters painted a sultry shade of smoky blue. Sure enough, there was a hefty charge on the credit cards for a rush paint job.

Dad was livid about it, but instead of shrinking on him she gave back one of the guest rooms, Dad's favorite one, with all the furniture intact, and he forgave her.

Since I'd helped her pick the shutter shadow, I was relieved she got away with it. She was looking beautiful.

"She's learning fast," Mom said. She looked around in worry. "If you were my daughter, House, I'd be wanting to meet the young men you talk to and set curfews about now. These aren't the nice local boy-buildings you grew up with; you be careful, you hear?"

Mom was pretty proud of the house, though. When the gardeners showed up at the door a few days later, she not only let them landscape the front yard, but she paid them cash out of the cookie jar and told Dad she'd done it herself. Dad was a little skeptical about Mom's ability to carry and lay in the curving cobblestone path, let alone the flowering plum tree, but he let it go.

When Dad claimed that the new solar panels were his idea, my brother and I just rolled our eyes. It was cool to be off the grid, sure, but the house got away with everything!

I didn't tell them about my increasing communication with the house. She was getting to be a good friend of mine, actually, since she seemed to be the only one who realized how boring it was out on the farm or even in town. Looking back over those e-mails, I guess I should've realized what she was planning, but at the time I thought we were just daydreaming together.

By this time the house was looking very nice indeed. Her paint was fresh, the lawn green, and her window boxes overflowing with colorful flowers. She flattered Ma by sending her an e-mail asking for new lacy curtains in all the front windows. Ma bragged for a solid week about the house choosing to e-mail her instead of contacting a fancy interior designer.

When the house was all spiffed up and ready, I took pictures of her and scanned them into the computer system.

Turns out she'd been chatting online with a fancy skyscraper in San Francisco, and he had been pressuring her to send along a photo. She conveyed this to me while I was supposed to be doing my homework in my bedroom.

"Ah, so that's what you're up to! You should've told me sooner! Did he at least send you a picture of himself first?"

The screen fluttered and a photo of the San Francisco skyline flashed on the screen.

"Which one?"

The photo zoomed in on a tall pointy skyscraper in the right hand corner.

"Holy shit! That's the TransAmerica Pyramid! It's famous! Way to go, Housey!"

The lights in the bedroom dimmed and took on a rosy hue.

"Oh, quit blushing! We all know around here you're the best. Wait till he opens his shutters on you. If he wasn't in love before, he will be then."

The lights in the room fluttered excitedly as they brightened.

I sighed. "I'm jealous. I'd give anything to have a really sexy, sophisticated boyfriend instead of some farm dweeb who happens to be good at football and who my mom won't let me have any fun with anyway."

The lights dimmed and the floorboards sighed as a map flashed onto the screen. There was a star on our farm and another on San Francisco. A blue dotted line started at the farm and inched its way slowly to the coastal city.

"Yeah . . . that's true. A long-distance relationship sucks. After a while, letters aren't enough and you just want to rub skin . . . er, walls." The house groaned. "Poor Housey."

A few days later we heard a great creaking and groaning as the house rocked up from her foundations. Shutters flapped as her chicken legs unfolded beneath her.

We were shocked that she did this while we were all home, inside. Houses were notoriously shy about getting up and mating in front of humans. Dad ran out on the front porch, grabbing at the railing so he wouldn't fall off. The chicken legs had lifted the bottom step a clear fifteen feet off the ground.

"What the hell do you think you're doing?" Dad roared as the house took an unsteady step. It had been months since she'd moved last, and we'd never seen her so much as stand up in front of us before this. "I won't tolerate you mating while we're inside! You stop and let us off right now!"

Tilting back first so Dad slid down across the front porch and through the doorway, the house slammed the door shut, closing us inside. She took another step, then another, faster and faster until she was running across the landscape at a blurring speed.

When I gave her hell for not at least warning me that she was kidnapping us, she cringed and tried to distract me by pointing out that she'd waited until the crops were all in, and had picked a day after Mom had done a big grocery shopping run so we'd have food for the trip. Not that cooking is easy in a jogging house. Mom joked that the eggs flipped themselves, but it didn't take long before most of our meals were prepared in the microwave. Mom also wouldn't let any of us chop, saying we'd cut ourselves when the house leaped over the next creek, so we ate a lot of cereal and grits and had to tear off our meat in chunks. All the glassware was kept safely stowed away, so we had to use plastic cups. Dad hated this, saying the milk tasted funny in anything other than glass.

We passed a big cathedral in a small city the next state over, and when I made "hey-hey, check him out" noises about him, the house told me, rather primly, that cathedrals weren't sexual buildings, and that they were immaculately conceived. I wondered about that all afternoon.

Despite the cool new scenery just outside our windows, we were all getting grumpy, being cooped up together in a jolting house. After a few days, the house started sleeping during the day and traveling at night, probably to appease us. It was nice to have stillness, though for the first few hours every morning everyone staggered as if we'd been at sea for months, and towards the end of the eight hours everyone got jumpy, waiting for the house to start moving again. It still felt like we were at the mercy of the house, and for me it was weird not having her awake to chat with, so nothing felt normal.

"What I don't understand," Mom whispered on the fourth day of the trip while the house was sleeping, "is why she took us with her while running away." We were somewhere in the desert by then, and it was so hot we didn't do much but lay around in our summer clothes. The air conditioning automatically shut off to conserve energy while the house was asleep, so the still hours were practically pointless. It was too hot to do anything but sleep and we'd all gotten used to being rocked while we slept.

Dad grinned at us kids. "If you're gonna run-off, don't take us with you."

He was trying to be funny, but my brother snorted and I rolled my eyes.

"Dad!" I said, "Don't you get it? Housey's attached to us. She has to follow her heart, but she doesn't want to leave her family behind. I think it's sweet."

Mom and Dad exchanged a glance. My brother asked, "What the hell do you mean, 'follow her heart?'"

"Don't swear." Mom said. She always nagged more when she was too hot, even though it just made everyone more miserable.

"She's running off to see her shiny hot skyscraper in San Francisco! That one she's been chatting with?"

"You mean one of those online buildings has lured her out to—" Dad sputtered. "She's taking us out to the land of fruits and nuts?"

"We're going to San Fran? Cool!" my brother said.

"Oh, my goodness," Mom said. She kind of looked excited.

Dad stood up and pounded on the wall, waking the house before Mom could stop him. "Listen up, 'Housey'! Hear me good! There ain't no way in HELL you're taking my family out where all those 'people' live!" He even made the finger quotes when he said "people."

"Daddy!"

"Be nice, dear!" Mom said.

Dad muttered. "God damn liberal political correct . . . " He looked back up at the ceiling toward the entryway, which was usually where he looked when he spoke to the house directly. "You see what you done? You can't take my family there. My kids ain't going to see that. No way."

There was a pause and a sound like wind through floorboards while the house considered. Then the windows slammed down and all the outside locks in the house clicked closed with an audible "Clack!"

No one moved. Dad's eyes swiveled over to Mom's. I wondered if I looked as scared as my brother. Finally, I went over and tried to open the window. It wouldn't budge. Without speaking, my brother, Mom and finally Dad all came over and tried, without success. We moved soundlessly from one door or window until all outside entrances has been tested. Not one had moved an inch.

I glared at my father. "Great, thanks a lot Dad. Now we can't even get fresh air in here."

Dad mustered up his pride. "I think the house is agreeing with me that you all don't need to be catting around . . . that city."

Things were pretty tense after that. Everyone had been kind of curious about where Housey was going the whole trip. I'd been barely able to contain my excitement, let alone my Internet searches on cool stuff to do there. I spent the rest of the trip using this information to try and persuade my father that there were educational things to do other than going to drag queen shows, but even after I won him over the house showed no signs of opening up. She seemed piqued with us, as much as a house can, and it was strange for her to have a side in a family argument. My brother tried to freak me out by telling me that my bedroom was making creaking sounds, like it was going to disappear during the night. I hate it when he's a jerk like that.

We finally crossed the Sierra Nevadas and ran downhill through the valley toward the San Francisco Bay Area. We stayed one night on a big cattle farm that was all mud and no grass. The house seemed distressed by seeing cows staggering through the mud and scared a bunch of them by setting down in their midst for the night. The sound of cattle outside our window woke us before the stillness did. We left with one calf fenced in by Housey on the big porch. Housey let Mom open the kitchen window to feed it the last of our oats. Dad eyed the calf and muttered something about the difference between peace offerings and theft, but you could tell he was somewhat pleased by the house's thoughtfulness.

The next day we got to Oakland. If we'd thought Housey was upset by the cattle, it was worse in Oakland, where the houses seemed unnaturally still and colorless in many neighborhoods as we moved out of the hills. It took us a while to figure out that they were dead houses, full of people—crammed full of people in some places—but empty of their own spark of life. Housey shuddered and creaked, and even though it wasn't raining, the roof leaked. My brother made gagging noises to show his displeasure over the mildew smell. Me, I hugged my knees and rocked back and forth on my bed as I looked at the sad shells of houses outside my window.

"It's like a graveyard." Mom said to Dad, standing next to him at the big picture window in the front room. The house was moving slowly, almost reverently, along the streets. We watched people going into a particularly decrepit house and my parents shook their heads. "Can't people afford to put these to rest and buy some pups?"

"Don't know where they'd get 'em." Dad said. "Probably expensive to buy 'em out here where most of the buildings are long dead."

A little later he said, "At least we don't have to worry about her slumming."

Housey moved slowly to the bay, and she swam across to San Francisco as the sun set orange and yellow and pink above the water, which was dark silver with the approaching night. It was one of the most beautiful things I've ever seen. The houses were too close together in Oakland for us to sit down for the night anyway, not that we had hopes of room in a good neighborhood in San Francisco. We settled down on a vacant pier early so that Housey could get a night of "beauty rest" before meeting her skyscraper the next morning.

She rose early, and opened all her windows to let fresh air in for the first time in days. Mom's lace curtains fluttered in the salty breeze, and everyone went out on the porch and breathed deeply.

I was the first to wrinkle my nose. "Smells like . . . like fish!"

"Yuck!"

"Hm," Dad looked towards the water, "Probably low tide."

Mom waved a hand in front of her face and looked back towards the house. "You might want to move inland if your intention is to smell pretty, sweetheart."

Housey moved carefully inland, letting the wind whistle through her boards, making a merry little tune. Her excitement was palpable, and combined with the novelty of being allowed outside, it elevated everyone's spirits.

The city itself was a maze of narrow streets, and it was obvious that even the early morning traffic was annoyed by something as big as Housey wandering down the streets at such a slow pace. As we entered the business district, the honking got bad enough that we all went inside to let Housey pick up the pace.

We plastered our faces against the windows as we came out of the financial district into Chinatown. The streets were lined with strange shops and red buildings shaped like pagodas and a lot of the signs were in Chinese. "Holy shit, Mom, look! It's like being in China."

"Language—oh, my! Look! How strange and wonderful—" We were passing a little stall overflowing with beautiful Asian black lacquer boxes and huge paper fans and lanterns and a bin of leopard-print slippers for only three dollars a pair. "Look at the weird little shops! Oh, I wish I could stop and shop!"

As if on cue, the house stopped and kneeled down. There wasn't a basement to fold her legs into, so she had to gently lean forward to make the porch touch the ground.

"You're letting us off?" Dad asked from the porch. The house flapped her shutters towards the pointy skyscraper down the street. "You coming back for us?"

Once we were all outside the house nodded.

"Do you want me to come along, for moral support?" I asked. The house considered for a moment, then nodded again and knelt down to let me back on.

"Sweetheart, get back here!" Dad scolded.

"It's a girl thing, Dad. Don't worry, she won't let anything bad happen to me."

"I don't want you on board while that house—does her thing! Especially not with a skyscraper!"

"Da-ad! Jeez!" I couldn't believe him sometimes. "I'm just going along so she can meet him! What kind of house do you think we live in? She's not going to mate right away with a building she just met!"

Dad seemed embarrassed by this and muttered something like "Be good, then," and wandered off with Mom and my brother to explore.

The house and I went up the street, stopping at the foot of the big, pointy skyscraper. He was really tall, though not as tall as some of the other buildings we'd just passed in the financial district, where the Bank of America building had made Housey titter like a young schoolhouse, but he was kind of arrow-shaped, and I guess that pointy bit at the top was really hot to other buildings. I watched from my bedroom window as Housey fluttered her shutters at him. The shining building did not move. Housey creaked and groaned, demurely at first, then louder and louder until I finally suggested, "Try sending him an IM."

The terminal flashed as the message was sent. A short while later, words appeared on the screen and I read them out loud, "'You're here in the City? Now?'"

"Uh-oh." I said, glancing out at the still-oblivious skyscraper. "Oh, Housey, I'm sorry, sweetie, but that's not him out there. Find out which building he really is."

Turns out that another skyscraper—Housey called it, "a stumpy, artsy tower down the street, on a hill," but it was actually the Coit Tower—had sent along the TransAmerica Pyramid's photo as his own, hoping to impress Housey. After hearing the news, Housey walked us slowly into North Beach to see the real façade behind her Internet lover, and her lights went dim when she looked up the hill and saw the much smaller, and much less shiny, reality. She looked longingly towards Chinatown where we could still see the TransAmerica Pyramid glinting in the sunlight.

"Don't you like him, Housey?" I asked about the Coit Tower. "Think about it—he's all romantic, up on that hill like that! He's a landmark, too—just an older one."

The tower on the hill bent hopefully down towards the pretty white farmhouse at his feet, and she shuddered all over in response. I obviously don't get what's sexy to buildings, because I think the Coit Tower is pretty good looking—and famous! Coit slumped, obviously distressed. I read countless apologies from him flooding over the terminal, but Housey was deleting them almost too fast for me to read.

"Oh, Housey, look how sad he is! He was just insecure about his size and age! Why don't you give him a chance?"

Housey flashed a picture of my quarterback boyfriend, then a picture of the chess club president who had sent me countless, and eventually annoying, love e-mails last year.

I sighed. "Okay, point taken."

Housey flashed me another message.

I looked at the screen in surprise, then smiled up at the House. "Yes, yes, okay, lying is bad, too." I hugged a wall as best I could. "Sorry Housey."

After a moment, a photo of the Palace of Fine Arts flashed on the screen.

"Oooh, yeah, of course I remember her! She wrote you back? Excellent! You should totally go see her."

A photo of Dad flashed on the screen.

"Tell you what—you drop me in Haight Ashbury and let me explore the city for awhile on my own—and don't tell Dad where I was—and I won't tell Dad about that pretty lady you're going to go see in the Presidio. Deal?"

The lights flickered in assent and we skipped off toward the ocean.

Heather Shaw's short fiction has appeared in anthologies *Nine Muses, Polyphony 3* and *Polyphony 5, Strange Horizons, Fortean Bureau.* She co-edits the literary zine *Flytrap* with her husband, Tim Pratt. They live in Oakland with the requisite two cats. She has a website (http://www.hlshaw.com/) and a blog (http://www.journalscape.com/heather).

MAGIC IN A CERTAIN
SLANT OF LIGHT

———

Deborah Coates

"If you could wish for something magical, what would you wish for?" Jeff asks Nora as he enters the kitchen.

Jeff has been gone all day, helping a friend fix the plumbing in his basement. There's no "Hello," or "How was your day?" Just Jeff, in the doorway, asking about magic. "It can't be about yourself," he continues. "I mean, like making yourself immortal. Or about world peace. It has to be—"

"Talking dogs," Nora says.

Jeff smiles in that way he has that seems to change his face. He's wearing faded jeans and a sweatshirt that's been washed so many times its cuffs are all unraveled; it's a change from pin-striped suits and crisp white shirts. "You know, Dexter made a dog talk once and it didn't work out like he figured it would. That dog was annoying."

"Well, I don't know how to tell you this"—Nora chops onions under running water, then transfers them to the frying pan on the stove—"but I don't rely on Dexter's Laboratory for my scientific knowledge."

"Talking dogs are not scientific."

"Yeah, magical." Nora turns the heat up on the pan and looks through the cupboards for the spices that she needs. She swears that they're never where she put them, no matter how often she returns them to their proper place. "That's what we were talking about, right? Magic? You tell me, what would you wish for?"

"Zeppelins," he says without hesitation.

"Uhm, zeppelins actually exist."

He stands in the kitchen doorway, slouched against the frame, and she knows that he will leave her. There is something in the way he looks, a shadow in his eye, that wasn't there yesterday or even this morning. And it almost kills her, like being stabbed right through the heart, because he's the only one she ever really loved.

"Zeppelins," he says, crossing to her and putting his arms around her waist from behind as she turns back to the stove, "are a collective figment of the imagination."

"Zeppelins are totally possible. Plus, you can ride in one."

He kisses the back of her neck and it feels like the soft brush of sun-warmed honey. "Bring me a zeppelin," he says. His words murmur against her skin as he talks and she can feel his smile through the small hairs along the nape of her neck. "Then I'll believe you."

"Bring me a talking dog."

He pulls her away from the stove and kisses her again, this time on the lips. After a minute, she turns off the stove and they go into the bedroom where they make love under the covers for hours until hunger drives them back to the kitchen at midnight to eat cold noodles and ice cream from the container. Then he kisses her again with lips that taste like vanilla beans and curry and laughs when she wrinkles her nose at him. He plants a line of kisses along her nose and down her chest, setting up a cool shiver along her spine. She wants him more than ever, wants him right now on the kitchen table. She grabs the waistband of his sweatpants to pull him toward her and kisses him so hard that it feels entirely possible for the two of them to meld completely.

But she still knows, before the year is through, that he will leave her.

The students in Physics 101 call her Dr. No, as in Dr. Nora, but also Dr. Knows-All-Sees-All, and possibly the James Bond villain, because she can tell Susan in the twelfth row back to stop necking with her boyfriend, Gianni, without ever looking up from her notes. She tells them it's just fun with mirrors; half-seen images that reflect against the whiteboard and the metal edges of things in the room. They don't tell her what she doesn't even know herself, that no matter where they sit, whether she's looked up from her notes or has her head turned to the whiteboard, she knows where each and every student sits and calls on them by name.

Today's lecture is on thermal energy and she's given it enough times before that she only half-thinks about it as she talks. Her eyes scan the room, her right hand writes notes, mostly on the overhead, but sometimes on the board. She thinks about Jeff and wonders what he's doing. He works at a small but very prestigious law firm downtown. Indications are that he will make partner soon and she wonders if that will be it, the thing that makes him leave her. Occasionally she thinks that she will ask him—I know that you will leave, she'll say, but I don't know why.

"Nora Holt! Where have you been keeping yourself?"

In the faculty dining hall, Sara Long, professor of English, approaches Nora's table. She wears flowing clothes that sweep back from her body when she walks as if she's always facing into the wind. Many years ago at another university, Sara and Nora were roommates, an unlikely mismatched pair, but they have remained friends ever since, eventually meeting up again when they both got professorships here.

Nora smiles up at her. "I don't think I'm the one who's been hiding," she says. "I eat here every day."

Sara is pregnant but she doesn't know it yet. Nora can tell by the glow of her skin and the extra bit of brightness in her eye. She was married last year to a man seven years younger than herself and she radiates happiness down to her toes.

"How's the research going?" Sara asks her.

"It's a dead end," Nora says. Though she knows it will be at least six months before she proves this, she can see it in the way her charts shade over time, in the way light refracts when she enters her lab, in results that aren't quite anything yet, except a trend she has no name for.

Back in her office, Nora sits at her desk and attempts to map out her relationship with Jeff. He is not the first lover she has ever lost. It is not the first time she has ever known. Nora always knows; she reads the smallest signs. But Jeff is the first one who will break her heart.

They met at a party just over a year and a half ago, the kind of thing Nora never goes to. She doesn't pay much attention to him at first; he is too tall, too thin, too well-dressed. She likes short, straight-shouldered men who wear loose-fitting blue jeans and clay-colored polo shirts. Late in the evening, past the time when Nora's usually politely bowed out, she finds herself next to him leaning against the railing of the backyard deck listening to the increasingly desperate laughter of three women in the living room whose husbands will divorce them before the year is over.

"My name is Jeff," he says to her.

At the very same moment, Nora says, "Leslie Walker is about to explode all over her husband."

"Literally explode?" Jeff asks.

Nora looks at him for what may be the first time that evening. "It will be very messy," she says with a straight face, "and they will be picking pieces out of the carpet for months."

Jeff grins, but before he can say anything further, Leslie Walker, who is standing by the open sliding glass doors, suddenly shouts in the kind of angry voice that simply stops every other conversation in the room, "Jack, you son of a bitch! You shut up! Shut up right now or I'll kill you where you stand!"

Jeff lays his hand on Nora's bare arm. "How did you know?" he asks her.

"Know what?" Nora asks him.

"That she would do that?"

"I could tell by the tone of her voice, by the way she was standing, by the other conversations in the room around her."

"You couldn't tell by the other conversations," Jeff says.

Nora looks at him. His hand is still on her arm. "Right," she says, "I meant the unspoken tensions."

"Ah," he says, "the unspoken tensions." And she is sure he doesn't notice that his hand runs down her arm and his thumb gently strokes her wrist.

He doesn't say much of anything else to her; five minutes later he's saying his goodbyes to the host and hostess and offering to drive Jack Walker home. Nora watches him walk out the door, not-quite-guiding Jack's unsteady progress, and isn't sure why she's watching him or why she can still feel a tingle across the bones of her wrist as if he's somehow been in contact with more than just her skin. There are eight bones in the wrist—pisiform, triquetrum, lunate, hamate, capitate, trapezoid, trapezium, and scaphoid. The scaphoid is the one that usually breaks. Nora doesn't know which one is tingling—it's possible they all are— maybe it's muscle or nerve instead of bone. But it's a new feeling for Nora, warm and cold, both at once. She isn't sure she likes it.

He's too tall, she tells herself, too thin and too well-dressed. She doesn't want him. She doesn't picture him standing at the base of her bed, pulling a faded red T-shirt off over his head. She doesn't imagine him touching her, making her whole body tingle the way her wrist does. She doesn't. He's not her type at all.

At dinner, Jeff brings up talking dogs again.

"Say I could invent talking dogs," he says. He's still wearing his shirt and tie from work though the tie is loose and hanging crooked. Jeff, the professional, always looks perfectly put together, perfectly cool when he leaves the house in the morning to go to work. Nora prefers Jeff at home, slouched and casual, like a secret only she has access to.

"Okay, see," she says to him, leaning on the table, "if you invent them it's not magical. It's science."

"If science says they can't exist," Jeff counters, "and I still manage to invent them . . . "

"If science says they can't exist, you can't invent them," Nora tells him. "Science makes life simple. Things that can't happen don't."

"Science makes life simple for you, you mean," Jeff says, but with a smile that erases any bite the words might have.

No, Nora wants to tell him, it doesn't. It doesn't make life simple at all.

"What about my zeppelin?" he asks later. "I hope you're working on that."

"Zeppelins exist," Nora says somewhat absentmindedly, working out a problem for tomorrow's class.

"Where's the magic?" Jeff asks her.

And it doesn't occur to Nora until later that he might have left off talking about zeppelins right then.

———

Nora goes running in the morning. She used to run every day, back before Jeff, before she had anything much to think about besides science and her next class and maybe ducking committee meetings. Now, she runs once a week, maybe. She enjoys it. She can feel the world open up when she runs. Possibilities become endless. It's only after she stops, after she takes a quick shower and dresses for the work day, that she knows that Jeff will leave her, that her department chair is going to announce his retirement in the next three weeks, that she will catch three students cheating on her next exam.

Between classes, she gets on the Internet and searches for "the science of love" and then doesn't visit any of the websites her search pulls up.

"Why do men leave women?" she asks Jeff that night after dinner is over and the dishes are washed. She asks it as if it's a big question—all men and all women and all the things they do—as if it has nothing to do with them. They are sitting on the couch together, she against one arm and he propped against the other, their legs intertwined.

Jeff is reading the evening paper and his reply is absentminded. "Which men?"

"Any men. Ever." Nora is exasperated. It has taken courage and planning to ask this question, as if asking manifests reality. And he isn't taking her seriously.

Jeff folds down the newspaper. "People leave," he says seriously. "Men. Women. It's all the same. They leave because they leave. Most of them think they can explain it—we never agreed on anything, he was too controlling, she never listened. But nearly always the real reason is both smaller and larger than any of those things. It's—"

"Research says," Nora begins earnestly.

"Oh, research." Jeff shrugs and the motion rustles his paper. "Research can tell you anything."

Nora bites her tongue on a long speech about scientific method and framing questions and double blinds and statistics because she knows it won't help the current situation.

"I'm still working on that talking dog thing," Jeff says five minutes later from behind the paper.

Nora doesn't really hear him. She's thinking about what he said—"she never listened." What was that about? Does he mean her? If she asked him, she knows he would say it was just an example. But it must be true. Why else would he say it? She thinks she listens. She intends to listen. But maybe she doesn't. Maybe this is why he leaves her.

"What did you just say?" she asks him, a shade of desperation in her voice.

"What?" He lowers the paper.

"What did you just say?"

"About what?"

"Never mind."

The next morning as Jeff is tying his tie, he asks her casually, "If I bring you a talking dog, will you get me my zeppelin?"

Nora's throat is suddenly dry; she has to clear it before she speaks. This is it, she thinks, the test she will fail, the path by which he will leave her. "Zeppelins are easy," she says.

"That's what you think," Jeff replies.

Nora thinks she sees a zeppelin directly overhead as she's driving to her office, a blinding flash of silver that makes her stop flat in the middle of the road and climb out of her car. She stares up at the sky as if staring is the answer, until a battered orange pickup truck, swinging wide around the corner, almost takes her arm off.

She is more absentminded than usual in her morning class. One of the students asks her how time works in a black hole and she tells him that "time" and "black" and "hole" are all just symbols of actions and objects. "In a way, they can be whatever you want," she says.

"I don't think that's right," he says cautiously. "I mean, the book says—"

"Yes," she says hastily, "of course." She can't tell him that she was thinking about Jeff, wondering whether he was playing word games with her, cleverly redefining "I'm leaving you" into zeppelins and talking dogs.

After class, instead of heading back to her office, she exits the building and crosses the busy quadrangle to the low, ivy-covered brick building that houses the English department. Though it won't be announced for at least six months, Nora knows that the Provost is maneuvering to demolish the three old buildings that house English, Foreign Languages, and History. She knew at convocation by the way he leaned on the podium, by the words he used to welcome them back, by the interplay of shadows on the wall just past his shoulder. She finds Sara in her office sitting cross-legged in a battered leather armchair, talking to one of her students, who is perched nervously on the edge of a straight-backed chair. "Look, it's quite simple really," Sara is saying to the student. "Find out what your character wants most, and then take it away from them."

"What?" the student asks, a frown creasing her earnest forehead.

"What will they do?" Sara asks. "When what they want most in the world is gone, what will your character do?"

Nora stands in the doorway, her breath caught in her throat. Jeff cannot possibly be what she wants most in the world. She wants the Nobel Prize, an endowed chair, the next great radical rewriting of the rules of the universe. She wants . . . oh god, she wants to own her place in the world.

A memory six years gone flashes into Nora's head: her first postdoc in Finland. "Why would you want to go there?" her mother asked her nearly every time they talked on the telephone in the weeks before she left.

"For the lights," Nora told her.

"The lights? What lights? Are you insane?"

"I mean the research," Nora said.

"All right, then," said her mother.

Nora has been telling people she means the research ever since.

She's halfway down the stairs when Sara catches up with her. "Nora," she calls, "did you want to talk?"

"What do you think a zeppelin costs?" Nora asks her.

"Millions," Sara answers without hesitation, the only evidence of surprise a half-raised eyebrow.

Nora nods as if considering. "What about a talking dog?"

"I don't think you can actually buy one of those," Sara tells her.

Nora looks up the stairs at Sara. There is a crispness in the air, as if winter is coming early. Nora can feel her life, her careful, controlled, scientific life sliding down through the soles of her feet and tumbling, broken, down the stairs.

"I don't want Jeff to leave me," she says as if that's what their conversation has been about all along.

Sara appears more stunned by this uncharacteristic confession than by talk of zeppelins and talking dogs. She recovers quickly, though, and descends the stairs to grasp Nora's shoulder. "Oh, honey. I don't think he'd—why would he leave you?"

"I don't know."

"Then you don't know that he'll leave."

When Nora doesn't answer, Sara sighs and says, "Look, just ask him."

Nora understands that asking would be simple for Sara. "What's up?" Sara would say. "Are you leaving me or what?" But for Nora it would be like ripping her own heart from her chest—because what if the answer is something she can't fix? "The thing is," Nora says, "if I don't ask, then I can't get the wrong answer. Like Schrödinger's cat, you know."

"Is that the cat that doesn't die unless you look at it?"

Nora rolls her eyes. "Sort of."

"You need to get over the science thing," Sara says prosaically. "Thought experiments are not going to help you here."

Nora knows that this conversation will eventually inspire Sara to write a series of short stories dealing with the domestic lives of scientists, played out against the background of historic events. Characters will lose what they want most in all the world and science will not help them win it back.

"Science explains the world to us," Nora says.

"How's that idea working out for you?" Sara asks wryly.

"I have to go now," Nora says, backing away.

"Just ask him," Sara says to the back of Nora's head as she hurries out the door.

Nora sees flashes of silver in the sky when she's walking across campus, when she's in the parking lot getting into her car, when she's driving through downtown. She stops, gets out of her car and looks up at the sky. Red light from the setting sun slants across the clouds. Nothing silver, nothing big, nothing like an airship. She looks away and there it is—a flash of silver—out of the corner of her eye, just out of sight, just out of reach.

Nora gets back in her car and drives to the park, where she parks in the nearly empty lot and walks out into the middle of the open green. She stands there for twenty-seven minutes until the sun has completely faded from the sky, until the shadows have spread from horizon to horizon, until the moon rises.

Nora leaves her car behind and walks across the park. The moon is three-quarters full and the light it casts is so silver that it turns the shadows blue. There's a nip in the air, like the promise of winter, but the breeze is warm. She crosses a dry creek bed and climbs the bank to a large open field. She puts her hand down on a half-liter plastic soda bottle someone has tossed and picks it up. Nora has never walked this way before, though she knows where her home is from here, like a beacon lit by rooftops. Scattered throughout the field are tall stalks of dried grass that look silver in the moonlight.

In the center of the field, Nora drops to her knees and gathers silvery dry stalks of grass in her hands. The moon shadows and brightens as clouds like wispy cobwebs filter across the sky. Nora winds strands of grass around the plastic bottle in her hands, weaves silver in and out, length to length. She discovers to her surprise that she is crying, as if what she's doing is both destroying and creating the world.

When she's finished she holds the long cylinder, woven all around with grass from the field, up to the moonlight. It is very light and seems to nearly float in the soft breeze. It glows like bioluminescent plankton, like the afterglow of rocket engines, like the eyes of wolves in wilderness. She walks the rest of the way home, which seems to take longer than it should, carrying her prize gently in her hands.

She comes to the house from the back and stands for a moment on the porch looking into the kitchen through the window. Jeff is standing at the counter, his jacket off and his tie askew. His hands are flat against the counter and his head is hanging as if he's staring at his own hands. Nora wonders what he's thinking. Is he wondering where she is or has he not yet noticed that she's gone?

She wipes dried tears from her cheeks, takes a deep breath and walks into the kitchen, holding her woven-grass-soda-bottle-zeppelin in one hand behind her back. Jeff looks up when the door opens and smiles, that breathtaking smile that Nora can scarcely bear—it slams her heart like a hammer, like a promise and a threat, and she's not sure which one's a good thing.

"Where have you—" Jeff begins.

"I brought you something," Nora says at the same time. She brings it out from behind her back and shows him what she's created. "Your zeppelin."

There's a moment of silence. Jeff takes the grass and soda bottle creation and holds it at arm's length, turning it slightly in his hands.

"You may have to squint," Nora says, tilting her head to the side. "Or look at it in moonlight, maybe."

Jeff just stands there silently and looks at the object in his hands. It looks so crude, just broken stalks of grass, that Nora wants to cry. She has rarely been so foolish—so fooled—because it really looked, out in the moonlight, like something magic and silver and—

Jeff takes her hand and pulls her outside.

On the open back porch, moonlight slants across the whitewashed plank floor. Jeff holds the woven-grass-soda-bottle in the open palm of his right hand. In the moonlight the awkward strands of dried grass seem to knit themselves together into a smooth whole that swallows the shape-holding soda bottle and becomes something that encompasses the world, something so right in the space and time in which it exists that it becomes more than its components, an extension of the moonlight, and seems to float on its own just above Jeff's hand.

Jeff stares at it for several minutes, his other hand still clasping Nora's as if the connection is as important as the silver object in his hand. Eventually, he sets the zeppelin carefully on a rail post and brushes Nora's hair gently away from her face. He doesn't say anything, just kisses her. Nora wraps her arms tightly around his neck and kisses him fiercely back.

Sometime later, he says, "I haven't had a lot of luck with the dog thing yet."

Nora laughs. "Don't worry about it," she says.

Nora knows that within the next six months Jeff will take on a pro bono property case for a family in Montana he's never met. He will hike through three canyons on the border between Montana and Canada with a local survey crew, lose track of the arbitrary lines between one country and the next, and find an entire valley that no one has ever mapped. He will return from that trip with a dog that never barks or cries, though occasionally, when the two of them have been arguing about money or chores or other things that don't actually matter, the dog will jump onto the kitchen table and stare at them each in turn until they are forced to see the world reflecting back at them through its eyes.

Deb Coates lives in Ames, Iowa with two large dogs. She has had stories published in *Asimov's, SciFiction,* and *Strange Horizons.* A new story, "Chainsaw on Hand" will be published in *Asimov's* in March, 2007.

FIR NA TINE

Sandra McDonald

Greg Schweinfurth was her first Fir Na Tine. Fourth grade, June of 1973, and the morning was so hot that after just fifteen minutes of recess Lisa Sheldon's pink polyester pants clung to her damp skin and made her thighs itch. She was retrieving a soccer ball from the corner of the playground when she saw Greg vomit fire into a trash barrel.

"It's okay," Greg said, wiping his lips with the back of his hand. "It happens—"

Flames shot from his mouth again. Lisa sprinted toward the school, her sandals slapping against the asphalt. She dodged crowds of boys and girls and skidded to a stop at the picnic bench set aside for teachers.

"Miss Flaherty! You have to come see!"

Miss Flaherty frowned. "What did we say about loud voices, Lisa?"

"Greg's throwing up fire. I saw him!"

"Fire? Where, child?"

Lisa led her back to the spot, but Greg was nowhere to be seen. Miss Flaherty poked around the inside of the barrel and asked, "What fire? I don't see anything."

"It was coming out of his mouth!"

Mrs. Flaherty folded her arms. "Little girls shouldn't tell fanciful stories."

Lisa stomped her foot. "I'm not making it up!" But when she told her parents and sisters they didn't believe her either. A few days later school ended for the year and the Schweinfurth family moved away from Massachusetts. Lisa never saw Greg again.

"Smell that?" Lisa whispered. Six years had passed since that day on the playground. She had grown breasts and started her period. She liked disco dancing and glittery nail polish and hadn't been enjoying the family trip to Florida until this particular evening in Key West. "That's pot."

"You're too young for that," her sister Meg whispered back. Meg was only a year older than Lisa but thought she was the queen of knowing everything because she'd already kissed three different boys.

Their older sister Jill, her face protected by a wide-brimmed hat, leaned close. "What are you two whispering about?"

"Girls, look." Lisa's father pointed down the seaside pier to a man juggling fire. "Remember, don't try that at home."

Lisa asked, "Can I go watch, Mom?"

"Don't get lost," her mother said.

She jostled her way through the crowd to stand closer to the juggler. Tall, sinewy and bare-chested, he had a bald head and wore a silver hoop in his left ear. Heat poured off his torches along with the smell of burning gas.

"People ask me how I learned to do this," the juggler said to the crowd. "One third-degree burn at a time."

He pretended to almost drop one. The people around Lisa let out a nervous sound and backed away, but she stood her ground. The juggler caught two of the torches in his left hand and then deftly plunged the third down his throat. When he pulled it out the flame was extinguished. He blew out a long stream of air and fire shot up into the sky.

Lisa joined the crowd in loud applause. "Don't be too impressed," said a barefoot teenager at her elbow. His pooka shell necklace gleamed against his tan, and his blond hair had been bleached nearly white by the sun. "If he was really good, why work down here at the end of nowhere for crappy tips?"

Lisa cocked her head as the audience moved on to other performers. "What do you know about it?"

The boy smirked. "There are people who do tricks, and people who really have fire inside them. See?"

He snapped his fingers and produced a small blue flame. Lisa reached toward it, felt genuine heat, and pulled her hand away.

"It's a trick," she said. "You coated your fingers with gas and used a hidden lighter."

"Maybe. But isn't it more fun to believe in magic?"

He leaned forward and kissed her. Heat shot from her lips to her hips. He was burning hot—drenched by sun, baked by it, burned by it all the way to his bones, and for a few fevered seconds she thought maybe he was made of the same fiery atoms as the sun itself. Something unfamiliar stirred deep inside her, a wild and wonderful spasm that shook her insides and then faded, leaving her weak-kneed and off balance.

The teenage boy searched Lisa's expression as if hoping to find something. She could only gape at him, dumbfounded, as an aftershock made her shudder.

"Mom," she heard Meg say, "Lisa's kissing strange boys."

He melted away into the crowd. Lisa never saw him again, but that kiss—ah, that kiss! She sought a repeat of it throughout high school, aching to find another boy with the sun in his bones. By the middle of her freshman year at Boston University she had kissed dozens of boys, none of whom held a candle to Key West Boy. By day she concentrated on staying on the Dean's List. By night she combed the bars on Commonwealth Ave., looking for someone with sparks in his eyes and fire between his fingertips.

"You sure this guy in Key West was really that good?" her roommate Beth asked one night after they'd both drunk too much.

Dizzy, Lisa leaned her forehead against the window of their high-rise dorm room. The lights across the river in Cambridge looked like stars, always twinkling out of reach. "You can't possibly imagine."

Beth burped. "And what if you never find someone like him again?"

"Not an option," Lisa said.

Sophomore year she dated a fellow history major who seemed so enthralled by the Great Boston Fire of 1872 that she let him take her to bed. For years she would remember him grunting, "Here? Are you sure?" between sheets that smelled like potato chips. Not the experience she'd hoped for, certainly. Maybe Key West Boy had been an illusion brought on by the tropical heat or pot fumes. She almost began to lose faith. Then, in the autumn, she took a Modern European History seminar and met Steven Hogan. Tall, dark-haired and intensely serious, he came late the first day, tried to slip into the seat beside her and accidentally brushed her arm.

Warmth flashed up her arm to the base of her skull. Lisa immediately lost track of the professor's lecture and swiveled in her chair. Steven had ducked his head over his notebook but when he finally looked up she gave him a smile full of promise and innuendo. He blushed and turned away. Not easily deterred, she was ready for him when class ended.

"Aren't you Phil Guarneri's roommate?" Lisa asked.

He shook his head and stuffed his notebook into a frayed green backpack.

"Maybe we met last Christmas. The History Department social?"

Steven headed for the door. "I'm a Spanish major."

On Thursday he came late again. After class she asked, "Didn't we meet at the Student Union? You borrowed money for the vending machine."

He gave her a sideways look. "That wasn't me."

The weekend dragged by. She dreamed of Key West Boy's kisses and woke in damp sheets with an ache her fingers couldn't satisfy. At the end of class on Tuesday she asked, "Didn't we meet at the movies last month? That new Michael J. Fox one?"

Steven looked perplexed. "We haven't met."

She offered her hand. "I'm Lisa."

After a moment he took it. Heat poured down her hand into her whole body, and she smiled.

Their first date was pizza and soda at a little campus cubbyhole. Steven was busy with the track team and a part-time job, but she wrangled a second date out of him and then a third. He walked her back to her dorm, both of them perspiring in the heat of Indian summer. Students crowded the sidewalk under the not-so-dark sky and cars were double-parked up and down Bay State Road. The aroma of grilling hamburgers hung heavy in the air, along with auto exhaust and the muddy smell of the river.

She asked, "Would you like to come up? My roommate's staying with a friend."

"I shouldn't." Steven studied his shoes. "There's stuff you don't know about me."

"We can just talk," she said.

Once upstairs, Lisa put Fleetwood Mac on the turntable and lit the rose-scented candle on her dresser. She draped a red scarf over the table lamp. Steven sat stiffly on the edge of her bed and tried to move away when she put a hand on his knee.

"I know what's inside you," she said.

Steven's voice cracked. "I don't know what you mean."

She told him about Greg Schweinfurth and Key West Boy, the latter not in lurid detail. Steven's gaze remained fixed on her face, relieved but still wary.

"You're like them, aren't you?" she asked.

"You tell me," he said, and kissed her, and pleasure sang through her body. She had found the sun again.

By Halloween she was spending weekends at the small apartment Steven shared with nerdy Alan, an engineering major who was usually hunched over the green and black screen of an Apple IIe computer. Steven had slept with girls before, he told her, but in bed he was tentative, almost unsure.

"I don't want to hurt you," he said.

"You won't," Lisa told him.

She bought a copy of *The Kama Sutra,* ignoring the wide-eyed interest of the bookstore clerk. They leafed through the pages together, tried a few positions, and ended up nearly breaking the old springs of Steven's bed. More than once the neighbors pounded on the walls. Lisa walked around campus in a permanent afterglow, daydreaming about the bright flares of Steven's kisses, the heat in his hands, the way he made her simmer with pleasure. Orgasms made her see explosions of red and blue so fierce that her eyes felt damaged afterward.

"When did you first know you had this thing inside you?" she asked one Sunday morning as they shared bagels and the Sunday newspaper.

Steven was sitting up in bed, profiled by the gray daylight falling through the room's only window. "When I was two years old, I burned down our house in Newport."

Lisa blinked. "You did? How do you know?"

"My parents told me. The fire started in the nursery, they didn't smoke, and there were no electrical problems. We lost Grandma's piano, Dad's war collection, things that couldn't be replaced."

"But no one saw it happen, did they?"

"They knew it was me." He put the sports section aside. "There'd been fires before—little ones when I didn't get what I wanted or I was hungry or something. When my brother was born they said if there were any more, I'd have to go live in an orphanage."

Lisa imagined a small boy trembling as his parents threatened to take away all he knew and loved. "That was wrong."

"It didn't stop the fires, but it stopped me from telling anyone about them." Steven gazed out the window. "I used to collect stories about people who burned up in their armchairs for no good reason. You ever read those stories? Maybe the fire got out of them. They all of a sudden lost control."

"You don't lose control," she said.

Steven snagged the travel pages. "Not usually."

He planned to take a year off after graduation in the spring, perhaps to tour and live in Spain, and then return to Boston to get his master's degree. Though Lisa told herself they were awfully young to wed, she thought maybe they could live together when he came back. Through the holidays she made secret plans for their future, but one evening at the beginning of March she was sitting by the library windows when Steven crossed the quad holding another girl's hand. Lisa rose to her feet, her notes sliding to the floor, and watched as the blonde hooked her hand around Steven's head and pulled him into a passionate kiss.

For several moments she could do nothing but stand in shock, her limbs like ice. Blindly she gathered her notes and ran back to her dorm, arriving breathless and teary-eyed.

"He wouldn't do that to me, would he?" she asked Beth.

Beth's face showed a curious mix of compassion and relief. "All those nights you spent apart, and you didn't get suspicious?"

After an hour's worth of tears Lisa grabbed her coat. The night was bitterly cold, the campus hushed as students crammed for midterms. Lisa kept her head down against the wind and reached Steven and Alan's apartment just after ten o'clock. She saw the three of them, Steven and Alan and the girl, drinking beer in the kitchen. She pushed their buzzer so hard her finger ached.

"Yeah, who's there?" Alan asked over the intercom.

"It's Lisa. I know Steven's there."

Silence. She tried to imagine what lies they were concocting.

"Lisa, he's kinda busy—"

"He's a fucking asshole! Tell him to get down here."

More silence. She kicked at the ice-encrusted phone books that had been left in the doorway and pushed the buzzer again. She would stand there all night if she had to, keep them awake, wake the neighbors, cause the police to come, it didn't matter—

Steven appeared on the stairs, nearly stumbling in a pair of unlaced boots. His hands shook as he unlatched the door. "Lisa, what's wrong?"

"What am I, the idiot girlfriend? The one for when you have nothing better to do?"

"It's not that bad—"

"It's not that bad? You fuck her and it's not that bad?" Lisa punched him in the arm and stalked away. Steven dogged her footsteps, his voice high and quick.

"Will you please stop—"Steven pulled her to a stop. "I can explain!"

"I hate you," she said, her face wet and cold.

"I have to do it." He hadn't put on a coat, and she could see him shiver. "It's too much inside me. It builds and it builds, and I get scared that I can't control it. If I'm only with you, you'd get hurt."

"You are so full of shit." Lisa broke his grasp and dashed across the street. A driver beeped at her and she gave him the finger. Steven didn't follow her, but she felt his gaze burning into her back as she hurried away.

Back at the dorm, her phone rang every ten minutes until Beth yanked it out of the wall. The next day Lisa walked around raw and wounded, sure that everyone on campus could see her humiliation. She started crying in Philosophy class and had to excuse herself. She cried again while eating lunch and abandoned a whole tray of food. When she returned to her dorm a dozen roses were waiting for her. She threw the bouquet into the trash.

"Come on," Beth said. "Let's drown your sorrows."

Three bars and eight beers later Lisa vomited on a grimy restroom floor and let Beth haul her into the cold night air. A trolley chugged by, the noise of it making Lisa's head throb. When they stumbled back to the dorm Steven was waiting outside.

"Stay away," Lisa said.

"She's in no condition to talk to you," Beth said.

"I just—" Steven's voice caught. "I want to make it right."

Lisa said, "Liar." To Beth she added, "Best sex you'll ever have, and then they break your heart."

She might have said more, maybe even thrown in Key West Boy, but in the morning, hungover with bile in her throat, the memories escaped her. She stumbled to the shower and tried to eat, but finally curled up in bed with a cold cloth draped over her head.

"You look pathetic," Beth said when she returned in the late afternoon. "How do you feel?"

"Lukewarm dead. Did I totally humiliate myself last night?"

"I don't know if you humiliated yourself, but you did a number on him. You shouted up and down the street that he burned down his parents' house. Is that true?"

Lisa pulled her pillow over her head. "Shit."

On Sunday she took a campus shuttle to the athletic center for the last big event of the indoor track season, where almost fifty teams had gathered to compete. Whether Steven sensed her presence or was simply scanning the large audience, she didn't know, but his gaze locked on her and she forced herself not to squirm. He looked away, his lips tight, and then took his position. When the race started he took off down his lane faster than she had ever seen him run. He was a blur as he circled round the far end of the track, and when he crossed the finish line he'd shattered the school record.

The crowd was still applauding when Lisa noticed smoke rising from his sneakers, fine gray wisps of burning rubber.

Someone by the judge's bench pointed his finger. Lisa heard a shout and then a yell, and someone dumping a cooler of water over Steven's feet. She went down to the railing but a guard asked her to stand back and she could only chew on her thumbnail while the competition paused and confusion reigned. When the races ended for the day she intercepted Steven in the parking lot. He came out with a few friends, all of them ribbing him about setting the track world on fire. When they were gone Steven stood awkwardly beside her and fidgeted with the strap of his bag. The sun had finally come out, weak and small in the spring sky.

"I'm sorry for what I said," she told him. "I was out of line."

Steven only shrugged.

Lisa looked down at his feet. "Did you burn yourself?"

"No. Not even blistered." He stared across the street. "Lisa . . . "

"You only need me," she blurted out. "No other girls."

"It won't work."

"If it gets too much you can take care of it yourself," she said. "Masturbate."

His ears turned red. "It's not the same."

"If I mean anything to you, you can at least try."

Try they did, for the rest of that month. Steven didn't stray, as far as she could tell. Sex became better than ever, so good it almost hurt to simply gaze on him, but a curious lassitude began to steal over her. She did poorly on two papers. Despite the cold spring weather she slept with the windows wide open and the blankets tossed aside. Her concentration fragmented into little sparkling bits and her skin tight and hot, as if she had an invisible sunburn.

"Lisa, it's me that's doing this," Steven said one afternoon as she lay listlessly on his sofa. He put a cold cloth on her forehead. "We can't stay together this way."

"Don't be silly," she said. "It's just the flu."

The physicians at the student clinic couldn't find make a diagnosis. She took cold showers, sucked on cups full of ice cubes and ate pint after pint of vanilla ice cream. She craved Steven's touch more than ever, but one evening he entered her and the heat was so intense she got lost in the fire. She woke with two paramedics standing over the bed.

"You had a seizure," they told her.

At the hospital they ran tests that revealed nothing. "Fever of unknown origin," the E.R. doctor decided, and after a couple hours of observation discharged her with instructions to follow up with the campus clinic. Steven arranged for a cab to take them back to his apartment. She got out first and saw a man standing in the doorway of Steven's building as if waiting for someone. He was in his late thirties, dark-haired, with a square face and square jaw.

"Who's that?" she asked.

Steven finished paying the cab driver. "Who?"

Lisa nodded her head but the man was already moving away down the sidewalk, in a hurry to be somewhere else. In the doorway Steven bent to pick up a piece of folded newspaper.

"I think he dropped this." Steven unfolded it and blanched. "It's about what happened at the track meet last month. My sneakers."

Lisa gazed down the sidewalk, but the man had disappeared. "Maybe he's a reporter."

"Coming around at midnight?" Steven shook his head but said no more. He ushered her upstairs and sat her in an armchair while he changed the bed sheets. Alan was tapping away on his keyboard in the other room, tap-tap-tap, and she wondered what was so damn engrossing about computers.

"Come on, get some rest." Steven pulled her into his bedroom. She lay with the window open, streetlight substituting for moonlight, and he sat in the corner with his knees drawn to his chest.

"It's not you," she murmured, but they both knew it was a lie. The next day she went back to her dorm room and crawled into bed. On their third day apart her fever broke.

"We have to find a way to be together," she said to Steven on the phone.

"You think you love me, Lisa, but there's more to love than just sex," he said.

"It's not the sex!" she protested. It was the fire. It was touching the sun, and being touched in return.

"Goodbye, Lisa," he said. Three weeks later he graduated, and four months after that she got a letter postmarked from New London, Connecticut. He had dropped plans of graduate school and become a firefighter instead.

"Fighting fire with fire," he wrote, and signed it, "Love always, Steven."

After her own graduation Lisa took a job working for her aunt in the Elders Affairs department at Melrose City Hall. Her job consisted of fielding complaints from senior citizens and connecting them to various city or state resources. The work was rewarding and sometimes interesting, and within a few years she took over her aunt's position. A few years after that she became the director of a small non-profit that serviced seniors across the county.

She lived alone in the second-floor apartment of an old Victorian with a Scottish terrier and rooms crammed full of heavy cherry furniture inherited from her grandmother. The men she took to her four-poster bed often admired the woodwork and craftsmanship. She dated no one longer than a month or so, but considered her romantic life no worse than that of her sisters. Meg married at twenty-six and divorced three years later with a toddler and a newborn to care for. Jill moved to San Francisco and announced she was a lesbian.

"Still," she confided to Lisa, "even out here, it's hard to find someone to really connect to, you know?"

Lisa knew. Lisa had memories of the sun embedded in her brain, and no lover after Steven came close to triggering that same melting response in her bones and muscles. Although she knew no good could come of it, she began looking for that heat again. She dated local firemen, but though all of them had soot under their fingernails, none of them had fire in their souls. She dated the local newspaperman who covered fires, but he was an uninspired lover who muttered dirty words to himself while she did most of the work. She even dated a firebug, a tall, well-mannered insurance executive who listened obsessively to emergency scanners and showed up at every three-alarm and higher.

"Professional curiosity?" Lisa asked.

"I just like fires," he said, and there was no arguing with that.

Beth, who'd taken a job as a corporate attorney in Manhattan, offered unsolicited advice. "You're never going to find someone who makes you feel the same way Steven did. Move on, okay? Enjoy yourself."

Lisa tried. By the time she was thirty she had dated a doctor with a commitment problem, a car mechanic with money woes, a professional poker player who never seemed to win and a car salesman who liked her to wear high-heels to bed. Nice men, most of them, but easy to forget. When she was thirty-one she and Beth took a Caribbean cruise. There were only ten single women on the entire ship, and the dining room maître d' seated them all at the same table as objects of either admiration or pity. She turned thirty-two and donned a maid of honor dress for her sister Meg's second marriage. She turned thirty-three and met an electrician named Joe, who walked his terrier Oswald in the same park where she walked Hephaistos.

"Nice furniture," he said when she invited him home.

One hot summer day one of Lisa's case workers called in sick, and she took it upon herself to keep an appointment with a pair of elderly Irish sisters. The inside of their small cottage was immaculate, not a single lace doily out of place. Mabel Flaherty was seventy-nine years old and suffering from macular degeneration. Alice Flaherty, slightly younger and wheeling an oxygen tank behind her, had a familiar mole on her cheek.

"You used to teach at the Mary Ronan School, Miss Flaherty," Lisa said. "I was in your fourth-grade class."

Alice peered over the rims of her glasses. "That was many years ago, child."

"I told you once that a boy was throwing up fire, and you told me I was making it up."

"Fir na Tine." Mabel fumbled at the plate in the center of the kitchen table. "Would you like another cookie?"

"Fir na Tine?" Lisa asked.

"Myths and fables," Alice said.

Lisa's pulse sped up. "There are myths of men made of fire?"

Alice rolled her eyes but Mabel leaned forward, her face intently serious. "The villagers back home used to tell stories about men forged from fire. The Fir Na Tine. They could burn down a field with the tips of their fingers, or set a forest afire with one cross look."

"But I looked in libraries—"

"They're not a people who want to be known," Mabel said. "Like you and me, they are, but very careful about who they marry."

"Poppycock and lies," Alice said. "Don't fill the child's head with nonsense."

Lisa went back to the library. The only references she could find to Fir Na Tine were in the logos of American fire departments with strong Irish ties. She contacted one of her old professors, a man who specialized in Irish and Celtic myths.

"Heard of them," he said. "Oral bits here and there, nothing written down, not enough for a paper or journal. The French have their own version, if I remember right. *Hommes de feu?* Something like that."

Fir Na Tine, *Hommes de Feu,* Men of Fire. Lisa dreamt of Steven standing calmly in a sea of flames, reaching for her with a sad look on his face. The next morning her phone rang and the caller identified himself as Captain David Baresse of the New London Fire Department in Connecticut.

"I'm very sorry to have to tell you," he said. "But Steven left a list of people to call in case anything happened to him."

Joe the electrician offered to come to Steven's funeral with her. Lisa told him she would be fine. She drove down to Connecticut and a family-run funeral home near the Thames River. The wake began at four o'clock in a whitewashed front parlor and by four-fifteen the room was crammed full of firemen in somber blue uniforms. Two air conditioners hummed in the windows but so many mourners made it almost as sweltering inside as the August evening outside. Lisa knew only Alan, Steven's old roommate, who had gone almost completely bald and had done well for himself with Microsoft stock. They stood near the closed white and gold casket, staring at Steven's official portrait on an easel.

"I don't believe it," Alan said. "Drowning while rescuing a kid from the river. He never did like to swim, but who expects that? Who dies at fucking thirty-four years old?"

Lisa didn't answer. She didn't know if she had any tears left in her. The thought of his body in the closed casket only a few feet away made her nearly sick to her stomach. She had loved that body, had lain with it, had held and made love to it, and now it would go to the ground for only worms to enjoy. And what of the man himself, his intelligence, his dreams and hopes? Gone, she thought, all gone.

"Lisa," Alan said, "this is Captain Baresse. The fire chief."

Lisa looked at Baresse's face and felt as if she'd stepped back in time to a cold winter street.

"Miss Sheldon," the square-jawed captain said. If he remembered her from the night Steven brought her home from the hospital, he gave no indication. "Steven spoke of you fondly."

Perfunctorily she shook his hand. "Thank you—" she said, and then broke off as a tiny bit of heat shot up her arm. Just a flicker, barely perceptible, but there wasn't the slightest acknowledgment in his eyes, not a single slip of control. He was steel, she thought, welded and strong under his jacket and medals. He might have been an inferno, a red-hot furnace so hot it glowed white, steam boiling past the pressure point, but his palms were cool and callused, the fire tightly self-contained.

Lisa stayed in a motel that night, sleepless with grief and a shameless fantasy of Baresse and the heat in his hands. She sat stoically through the funeral mass the next morning, ignoring Jesus on the cross and the saints in their stained glass windows. The burial itself, in a well-tended cemetery overlooking the river, was picture-perfect.

"See you in the afterlife, pal," Alan said, and dropped a handful of dirt into the open grave.

Lisa let a red rose fall down to the coffin and whispered, "It wasn't just the sex."

Baresse had invited everyone back to his house after the funeral. Lisa followed Alan's Lexus to a small white Colonial on a quiet cul-de-sac. The dim, cool house was full of photos of Baresse and his friends hiking across winter ridges. No frills, flowers or lace for this bachelor, she decided. On the back lawn, buffet tables bowed under the weight of hamburgers, fried chicken, ribs and fudge brownies. Baresse held court at the grill, drinking beer alongside other men from the department. She couldn't imagine confronting him with her questions. And what was the point, really? What good did it do to know that men of fire existed if they were unattainable to those who most desired them?

Instead of going out to the lawn she drifted to a framed photo of Baresse, Steven and three other men. Judging from the soot and grime on their faces, they had recently put out some raging inferno. They looked tired but proud, and Steven was grinning ear-to-ear. Fresh grief tried to wake inside her, but all she could manage was a little sniff.

"Were you a friend of Steven's?" a dark-haired woman asked. She was pretty and petite, and despite the hot summer day wore a dark blue cardigan over her sundress.

"We knew each other at college." Lisa offered her hand. "Lisa Sheldon."

"Maria Lopez." The woman's fingers were icy cold. "Everyone's going to miss Steven terribly."

"You knew him?"

"I know all of David's men. Steven was the one everyone trusted and liked. He was that kind of guy, you know?"

"I know."

Lisa stayed only for a few more minutes. Before she left, she saw Maria go to Baresse's side by the grill and slide under his arm. Baresse kissed the top of her head and smiled fondly at her. Lisa shook her head. The relationship would never last, of course. It had been doomed long before it ever started.

"Marry me," said the note in Lisa's fortune cookie.

"Joe," she said, looking across the restaurant table, "we've been through this before. Why ruin a perfectly good relationship with a ring?"

He smiled nervously. Chinese music played in the background and an immense koi fish swam in a tank beside their booth. "Because we've been seeing each other for four years and I'm tired of commuting between your place and mine, Lisa. Because the dogs miss each other when we're apart. Because I want to wake up every morning next to your smiling face."

"You hate my morning breath," she reminded him.

"And if we're going to have children, we'd better start now."

She bristled at the implication. "I'm not forty yet."

"I am. I'll be on Social Security by the time our first kid gets out of high school."

"We'll talk about it when I get back from my sister's, how's that?" Lisa signaled for the check. "I can't concentrate on anything until I know she's better."

She tried not to think of Joe's proposal on the flight out to San Francisco. She knew her parents would be delighted if she married him. "He's a good man," her father had said, right after Joe helped him replace a circuit breaker box. "Handsome, too," Lisa's mother added, "and always so neat." Lisa could list his many fine attributes all day long but she still didn't know if she wanted to spend her whole life with him.

"Why does everyone think you have to be married to be happy?" she had once asked Meg, who'd divorced for the second time.

"They don't," Meg replied. "But at least when you're a couple, you get to share the misery."

By the time the plane landed in San Francisco, Lisa was no closer to an answer then she'd been at take-off. Jill and Jill's lover Naomi met her at the gate. Dark-haired Naomi was carefree and quick to laugh. Jill didn't look sick at all. She had made herself fashionably thin, spent far too much money on chic haircuts and blonde dye jobs and was fussy with everything from the cut of her business suits to the position of a small vase on an end table.

"I worry about everything," Jill said over dinner in their large, sculpture-filled condominium near the Castro. "Every little detail."

Naomi patted her hand. "That's why you have me, sweetheart. To remind you about the big picture."

Two days later the nurses wheeled Jill into an operating room. Lisa sat and read the same magazine for six hours. Naomi phoned friends, paced the halls, went home to feed the cat and returned with a box of gourmet cookies for the nursing staff. Jill's oncologist and surgeon came out to report that the tumor had been large and unwieldy but, in the final analysis, benign.

"That's one fucking important detail," Naomi said, and broke down in tears.

While Jill recovered, Naomi showed Lisa around the city. They took a walking tour of Nob Hill, spent several hours at the maritime museum, had dinner in Chinatown and then made the rounds of upscale gay and straight clubs. At one crowded, very loud place near Fisherman's Wharf, Lisa downed two margaritas in quick succession, relishing the bite of salt and lime.

"You better hold your booze better than your sister," Naomi warned.

"I hold it very well." Lisa let her gaze travel over gyrating dancers with bare midriffs and six-pack abs. "How old do I look?"

Naomi threw back a shot of bourbon. "That's a terrible question to ask."

"My boyfriend wants to get married. How do I know he's the right one?"

Naomi ordered more drinks. "How does anyone?"

Lisa leaned back in her chair and watched a man in a black turtleneck and leather jacket take a seat at the bar. He looked tight and unhappy, one of those brooding types, and showed no interest in the pretty young Tammies and Michelles flitting about in their tight pants. If cigarette smoking hadn't been outlawed in all San Francisco bars she imagined he'd be smoking something long and European. Not gay, she decided, though she'd been mistaken before.

"Do you love him?" Naomi asked.

The man at the bar toyed with his napkin. It burst into flame, but he scrunched it into the palm of his hand before anyone could notice.

"Oh, Christ." Lisa lurched to her feet.

"What's wrong—"

"I know that guy," she said, a lie, but she didn't have time for explanations. The stranger was standing and finishing the last of his beer. She pushed through the crowd of dancers and almost toppled a waitress's tray. Hot, damp bodies blocked her way and conspired against her. Lisa caught the man halfway to the door and grabbed his jacket.

"Wait!" Lisa said. "I can help you!"

Up close, she could see he was much younger than she—mid-twenties, perhaps, certainly not much older. Anger poured out of him in all directions like dark, toxic smoke.

"Who the hell are you?" he asked.

"I know what you are!" Lisa tried to grab his hand but he shrugged her off. "I know about the fire!"

"Fuck off," he said, and went outside.

Lisa followed. The chill night air reeked of fish and diesel as she teetered after him on her clumsy high heels. "There are others! You're not alone!"

He paused in the act of mounting a Harley. A muscle in his cheek twitched. A Ferrari zoomed by, its radio pounding out a bass line.

"You're not alone," she said.

"Tell me," he demanded.

Lisa rubbed her arms. "Take me to your place."

She had never ridden a motorcycle before. He helped her climb on, gave her his helmet to wear and then, without warning, they were off, the engine deafeningly loud and vibrating between her legs, the streets slipping under the wheels like magic. He took her up a steep hill and down the other side of it to a converted factory and his studio apartment, which was filled with half-finished paintings and fire extinguishers. His only furniture was a mattress, a battered old kitchen set and a TV sitting on a milk crate. The refrigerator in the kitchen rattled and whined.

"I'm Mark Chang," he said.

"I'm Lisa." The loft was cold and dark, with street light spilling in through the towering windows. Going off with a strange man in an unfamiliar city suddenly didn't look like such a smart idea. Mark Chang pulled two green bottles from the dying refrigerator and handed her one.

He gulped down half of his and asked, "What did you mean? Others?"

"Fir Na Tine." She stepped closer to him, aching for the heat of his touch. "You're like them. Maybe you burned your house down by accident when you were a kid. Maybe you set things on fire all the time, and don't know why."

His dark eyes bored into her. "Who else?"

Lisa touched his arm. Blessed warmth tingled through her fingers. "Make love to me."

"I don't even know you."

No doubt he'd had women his own age, pretty girls with smooth, unlined faces. Insecurity washed through her at the thought she could no longer seduce at will, that her moment in the sun had passed.

"How long have you been alone, thinking you were the only one?" she asked. His breathing hitched but he didn't move a muscle. "How long have you been afraid and angry?"

"You don't want me," he said. "I can't control it."

Lisa stroked his dark hair. "I can help."

His mouth closed on hers. Heat roared down her throat and she cried out in welcome. Mark Chang fumbled at her blouse and bra but she ripped them off for him, finesse forgotten, and they tumbled onto cold cotton sheets. When his hands cupped her breasts, pleasure ignited all the way to the base of her spine. He pulled at her jeans as she dug at his back, desperate for more. He slid between her thighs and she arched up, nearly consumed, the supernova inside her now, scorching her, scalding her vagina, too much, too much, like a welding torch to her loins, she was roasting from the inside out, screams torn from her throat as she tried to push him away, god, away, and when he collapsed beside her she crawled off the mattress and curled up on the cold wooden floor.

"I'm sorry," he whispered, and didn't touch her. Lisa didn't know how long she lay there, hurting in the darkness. Tears stung her cheeks and the back of her throat. When the sky outside the windows turned gray she pulled herself to her feet. Her thighs felt blistered and seared, but the skin was smooth and white, untouched. She pulled on her clothes and fumbled for the telephone.

"Directory assistance for New London, Connecticut," she said to the operator. "Steven Baresse."

"I have no listing for Steven Baresse," the operator said. "I have a David and Maria Baresse on Lincoln Street, will that do?"

She realized her mistake. "I'm sorry. Yes, that's fine."

Although it was three AM on the East Coast, David Baresse answered, sounding alert and ready for disaster.

"Fir Na Tine," Lisa said. "I have someone who needs your help."

She handed the phone to Mark Chang and went out into the cold morning rain to find her way home.

Lisa stayed in San Francisco for two more weeks on the pretense of helping Naomi care for Jill. When she finally did return home, she said yes to Joe's proposal. They eloped to Hawaii, where their hotel room overlooked the nightly luau show and men juggling fire sticks.

"Let's go watch," Joe said.

Lisa pulled the curtain. "Let's not."

She didn't think of Mark Chang if she could help it, but one detail from that unfortunate night stayed with her long past the point when she should have let it go. She checked the phone listings for New London again and yes, she'd heard it correctly, David and Maria Baresse. They had married. On the anniversary of Steven's death she went down there for the dedication of a firefighters' memorial and decided to ask the question. David Baresse, his hair gone silver and a new scar on his cheek, was as unapproachable as ever during the ceremony on the lawn of the town library. Instead Lisa cornered Maria in the small ladies room in the library basement.

"You're Steven's friend," Maria said, and Lisa nodded.

"I have to ask you something, and I'm sorry if it's personal." Her voice came out louder than she'd intended and she lowered it. "I know David's like Steven was. I know about the Fir Na Tine."

Maria gazed solemnly at her. Hot air wafted in through the window, bringing with it the sound of children playing. Lisa thought of a long ago playground and a little boy bent over a barrel.

"I tried all my life, and I could never—they were too much. I learned my lesson. But how do you do it? How do you stand the heat?"

Maria didn't answer.

"Please," Lisa said. "I have to know."

Another long moment passed. Finally Maria reached over and touched Lisa's arm with icy fingers. "In my mother's village, the old folks spoke about men with fire boiling in their blood. *Los hombres del fuego*. They could only marry a special kind of woman, *las mujeres del hielo*. All their lives these men and women would look for one another, trying to find a perfect balance. Maybe your mother or grandmother was like that, maybe you have a little of their blood. You recognize these men when you see them, but you don't have enough *hielo* in you to match their fire. Do you understand?"

Steven had been the Spanish major. Lisa knew only English, and the language of loss and longing. She shook her head.

"*Las mujeres del hielo*," Maria said. "Women of ice."

Sandra McDonald's first novel *The Outback Stars* (Tor, April 2007) is about romance, duty and really big Australian spaceships. Her short fiction has appeared in *Realms of Fantasy, Strange Horizons, Twenty Epics*, and other markets. Visit her website at www.sandramcdonald.com.

A TREATISE ON FEWMETS

Sarah Prineas

Shortly after 7:30 in the morning, the phone rang, waking Assistant Professor Esme Quirk from a very uncomfortable nap. She peeled her face from the surface of her desk and looked blearily around the lab. *Ring*. On the desk sat her quantum thaum computer, a stack of photocopied journal articles, a mug of cold tea, a pile of Elemental Studies 101 midterms waiting to be graded, and the phone. *Ring*.

Too much to do. The tenure track was going to kill her, she just knew it. She bent over and rested her forehead on her desk. The phone stopped ringing. She gave it a look. Good. One less thing to worry about.

The phone began again to ring. Esme groaned and fumbled it off the hook.

"What?" she mumbled. Her neck was stiff and her mouth tasted like stale tea.

"I must speak with a professor," began a hurried voice on the other end of the wire. "Somebody who knows something about elemental magic."

Esme picked up the cup of cold tea, decided it looked all right. "I'm a professor in the Elemental Studies Department." Taking a sip of the tea she grimaced, but began to feel more lively. "Can I help you with anything?"

"Well, you might." He continued hesitantly, "You see, there's something very strange going on, and we thought—" Somebody on his end of the line interrupted the caller, and he paused. "Yes, yes, Aunt Maude, it is a woman professor, just as you wanted. All right, I'll tell her that, too," he said. "Sorry," he addressed Esme again. "My aunt. She thinks, well . . ." He took a deep breath. "What's your name, by the way?"

"Esme. Professor Esme Quirk." Perhaps the 'Professor' would calm him down.

"I'm Ned Slithers. Here's the thing, Professor Quirk. There are monsters lurking in my aunt's back garden." Before she could comment, he continued quickly, "I know what you're going to say: she's old, she's batty, there are no monsters running about in Hertfordshire, but I-I-I'm fairly sure she knows what she's talking about."

As he spoke, Esme sat up straight in her chair, the crick in her neck and the nasty taste in her mouth forgotten. Monsters? In a Hertfordshire garden? "Oh, no, I believe you," she said hastily, interrupting Slithers's protestations.

Ha! One of her looming deadlines was to finish a presentation on nexuses for the upcoming Elemental Research Conference. Her colleagues had laughed at the idea, but all her calculations indicated that one of the world's last undiscovered nexuses might exist in Hertfordshire.

Trouble was, she had no empirical evidence to support her calculations. The magical element was elusive; it didn't seem to like getting involved in experimental observations. This time, though, just maybe . . .

She glanced at the papers on her desk, at the cinder-block walls of the lab, at the fluorelemental lights buzzing overhead. Then she nodded briskly. "All right, Mr. Slithers. I'll be on the morning train out of London."

Ned Slithers, when she met him, was about what she had expected: English twit. Nervous. Tweedy. Spectacles. She sighed, adjusted her black cape, and shook Slithers's hand when he offered it to her.

"Thank you so much for coming to Briar Hall, Miss Quirk," he was saying. He took her bag and gestured to a Volkswagen beetle that seemed about to fall apart under the weight of its own rust.

She shot him a glare. "*Doctor* Quirk."

He blinked. "Oh. Sorry. It's just, you know, well, you don't really look much like a doctor. Er, a professor, I mean." She continued to stare stonily at him. To her surprise, he blushed, then continued. "You're too young. I mean, you look young and, you know, too—"

"Just call me Esme, all right?" She sighed and shook her head, climbing into the car. Evidently not much going on upstairs at Ned Slithers' house. "You said on the phone that your aunt's been seeing monsters?"

"Er, yes," Slithers replied.

"Have you seen them as well?"

"Not exactly." He slammed his door and started the engine.

Esme narrowed her eyes. "Then how do you know they're there?"

"Oh, you know. Crushed branches. The occasional footprint. Droppings. Fewmets, that is."

Fewmets? Esme shook her head. What the hell was a fewmet?

As they pulled into the gravel drive, Esme realized that there was more 'Briar' than 'Hall' to Aunt Maude's home. An ancient castle had melted away, leaving behind chunks of stone and crumbling walls, all covered with heavy curtains of brambly bushes. Only a single turret remained of the original structure, and though its age was apparent in the mossy stone walls, flowered curtains fluttered in the arrow slits and pots of geraniums stood by the arched front door.

Esme climbed out of the car, prepared to meet the great aunt.

Maude Slithers was very tall, broad shouldered, spoke in the loud monotone of the partly deaf, and was accompanied by two enormous, leaping, grey-furred dogs with lolling red tongues. And she was, quite clearly, a witch.

"Welcome to Briar Hall," Maude bellowed, slamming the front door behind her and wiping her hands on an apron which she wore over a ragged pair of denim overalls. She turned to Esme, who was fending off one of the dogs, and stuck out her hand. "Down, Prancer! Professor Quirk, I presume?" She gave Esme a disturbingly thorough look over. "A little pale, Neddy, but she'll serve the purpose very nicely. Well done!"

Esme pushed a wet doggy nose away from her crotch, shook hands, and mumbled a greeting—"Nice to meet you, Mrs. Slithers"—and then tried to rub the tingling shock from her hand. Yes, the woman was sparking with magical element, which meant there had to be a nexus around here somewhere . . .

"Now come on in for tea! And call me Maude; everybody does. Prancer, *down!* Watch your step here, the stone's a bit crumbly!"

Esme followed Ned and his aunt into the turret, turning left into a hemispherical room outfitted as a formal parlor. The dogs went immediately to lie down on a rug before the hearth, though no fire was lit.

Esme accepted a cup of tea. "Mrs. Slithers," she began, "Can you—"

"Maude!" shouted her hostess. "Have a scone!"

"Thanks, er, Maude," Esme said gruffly. She shot a sideways look at Ned Slithers, who had perched on a chair and was gnawing at a biscuit. Esme froze with her mouth open, about to bite into a scone. She blinked. Ned Slithers was, she realized with a shiver, rather wonderful. Quite the Greek god, in fact: tall, blond, brown-eyed, strong-chinned. And that was a very fine set of muscles he was hiding away under a worn tweed jacket. Esme gave herself a brisk mental shake. Why was she drooling over this unexpectedly lovely man? He would never be attracted to a frump like her, with her dumpy figure, mousy brown hair, thick glasses. She took a sip of lukewarm, watery tea and addressed Ned's aunt. "Can you tell me about your back garden?"

"It's more of a jungle than a garden," Ned interjected in a murmur.

Maude did not appear to hear. "There's lizards in the back garden," she announced. She plunked an iced cake into her mouth. "A couple of 'em, right, Neddy?"

At that, Esme's ears pricked. Odd things abounded in nexuses, which were imbued with elemental magic. "I'd like to have a look, if it's all right," she said.

"What's that?" Maude shouted. The dogs lifted their heads from their rug, alert. "Speak up, girl!"

"She said she'd have a look at the back garden, Aunt Maude!" Ned explained.

Esme forced out a smile. Just as well, she thought, that he didn't know she hadn't come all the way to Hertfordshire to help his dear old witchy aunt, but to unearth some evidence to prove her hypothesis about the nexus.

"Or worms!" Maude shouted.

Esme and Ned turned to stare at her. "I beg your pardon, Aunt Maude?"

The older woman beamed. "The lizards in the garden, Neddy. They might be worms!"

Ned was right, Esme realized. The back garden was actually a jungle. It had once, perhaps, been an orchard, but the abnormally tall apple trees were covered with jubilant swags of ivy. Between the trees, thick clumps of weeds and grass grew up higher than Esme's head. Overgrown bushes with enormous, suspiciously shiny leaves crowded close to a narrow trail, and leggy rosebushes sprawled amongst the undergrowth. There was a feeling of closeness and of sweltering green life. Esme shivered.

After walking for a quarter of an hour, they reached a rickety-looking shed surrounded by a relatively clear area. Ned leaned into the shed and pulled out a sharp-edged gardening implement.

"What's that for?" Esme asked.

Ned looked off into the trees. "It's a scythe. In case we, you know, meet any dangerous, er, plants. I'll go first, if you don't mind."

"Go right ahead." Esme wrapped her cape about her and prepared to follow. She knew next to nothing about flora and fauna, but even she could tell that the plants here were not normal and might possibly be, as Ned had said, dangerous. The air felt unnaturally thick, and she heard none of the sounds she might have expected: no birdsong, no scuttling in the bushes, no breeze rustling the branches overhead. Ned paused to hack at a clump of tangled vines that hung across the path.

They made their way slowly down the path, Ned hacking away as they went, across a sluggish stream, and deeper into a grove of bramble bushes overshadowed by stands of bamboo mixed with apple trees. Ned paused to pick a clot of weeds from the blade of his scythe. He had removed his coat and rolled up his sleeves; with his tousled blond hair and smoothly-muscled forearms he looked, Esme thought, quite distracting. Mmmm. She caught her breath—he'd never be interested in her, they never were—and turned away to admire a patch of sun-dappled greenery. How nice, she thought. Real wildlife. It glows just like emeralds and gold in the sunlight.

Then the patch shifted. Esme's gaze was drawn up—and up—until she realized she was staring not at a pretty patch of leaves and vines but at the massively muscled haunch of a—

"*Dragon,*" she whispered.

It blended almost indistinguishably with the trees and sunlight, its body winged and serpentine and covered with smooth gold-and-emerald scales and a crest that flowed like a silken banner from its horned and bewhiskered head to the tip of its spiked tail. Its eyes were turned away as if it was surveying, above the treetops, the domain over which it lorded. It would, Esme realized, certainly see them when it turned back.

"Ned," she croaked.

"Yes?" he answered in a normal tone of voice, stepping up beside her. "What is it?"

She didn't have to answer, for at that moment the dragon's head swiveled around. Ned dropped his scythe and stood staring upward, transfixed by the dragon's regard.

The dragon's eyes were blue, Esme noted, mesmerized, but oddly opaque, like smudged windows looking out at a crystalline sky. They were the color of the magical element. She gave herself a mental shake. Think like a scientist, she told herself. Obviously the dragon was an elemental creature. Aunt Maude had been correct; she had simply meant *wyrms,* not *worms.*

"Do something," Ned squeaked.

The dragon shifted and cocked its head as if to see them better. Its long neck snaked down, and down, until they smelled the hot, thunder-and-lightning smell radiating from its scales and felt the rush of its intaken breath as it snuffed the air.

"Esme, please *do* something!" Ned whispered. The dragon's attention twitched toward the sound, and he froze.

"I think we'd better run." Esme grabbed Ned's limp hand and jerked him away. At the same moment the dragon reared back on its haunches, raised its snout into the air, and trumpeted a call that shook the tree branches and sent leaves whirling about their heads. Esme didn't look back to see what the dragon did next; she held on as Ned took the lead, dragging her back through the jungle.

"The tool shed!" he shouted. They burst from the overgrown path, shedding leaves and trailing scarves of vines, and raced for the rickety building. Ned pulled her inside and slammed the door. Safe!

For the moment. Inside the shed was very dark after the sunlight of midday; they stood gripping each others' hands in the close, velvety darkness, trying not to breath too loudly, listening to the not-so-distant crashing of a very large creature making its ponderous way through a riot of trees and bushes.

The crashing came closer, and still closer. Finally it stopped. Slowly their eyes adjusted to the dimness; light crept in through cracks in the board walls and filtered through a dirty window overhung with ivy.

Esme blinked and looked down at her fingers, which were getting a cramp. She was clinging to the front of Ned's shirt, and he, in turn, was clutching her as if she were the only thing keeping him on his feet. His chest panted for breath beneath her fingers. She looked up to find him looking down at her, eyes wide with surprise.

With a gulp, she straightened and reached up to pull at a clump of burrs that had gotten tangled in her hair. In the dim light she saw that Ned wore a crown of vine-strangled leaves. He looked lovely, like a greeny-gold elven prince.

"I thought you could protect us," he whispered. "We could have been killed. Why didn't you do anything?"

"You mean magic?" When he nodded she gave an exasperated sigh. Why did so many people assume that every member of the faculty of the College of Magic was a practitioner of magic? Grrr. "I'm an experimentalist, Ned, but I don't actually *do* magic, I only study it." He stared at her. "I'm not a witch, all right?"

"Then what are we going to do?" He gestured at the door. "The dragon's out there, waiting for us. And—" even in the dim light, she could see his face turn pale. "And Aunt Maude said lizards. More than one."

"Well then, we'll just have to figure out another way to deal with it. Them." She looked around the shed: rubbish bins, rakes, hoes, other sharp-looking tools, a bucket, all of it covered with dust and with cobwebs that twitched ominously, as if unnaturally large spiders were waiting in the dark corners to see what might stray into their parlors. Esme shivered. She hated spiders.

Better spiders than dragons, though. As Ned had pointed out, more than one of the creatures might be out there waiting. But the shed wasn't much protection, rickety as it was; they couldn't stay here. They'd have to do their best to sneak past the dragon, arming themselves in case of confrontation. She thought again of the dragon's smudged blue eyes and recalled how it had bent down to smell them.

"Hmmm." Ned turned toward her, expectant. "You know, I think it might be short-sighted."

"The dragon?"

No, Ned, the field mouse. Lovely but dim, as she'd thought. "Yes, the dragon. If we're quiet we might be able to creep right under its nose to your aunt's tower."

Ned nodded. "That sounds like a good idea. There are porphyric metal spikes on the tower's battlements. We'd be safe from anything elemental. But what if it isn't myopic?"

Esme shrugged. "Then it'll catch us, fry us up, and eat us for afternoon tea, like kippers."

"How can you make jokes at a time like this?"

She hadn't been joking. She glanced around at the dusty contents of the shed and picked up a hay fork. "This might do." She seized a plastic rubbish bin lid and held it up. "And this, for a shield."

"That will do you no good at all, Esme." Ned shook his head soberly. He tapped the bin lid's plastic surface. "It's made from high density polyethylene. Hmmm." He sat down on an overturned bucket and put his chin in his hand. "I assume the dragon will be burning a gas to create its flame. Methane, possibly, which burns at around 1200 Celsius. Natural gas burns at about 1600 Celsius. Oxygen and acetylene, like a welder's torch, give a flame temperature of 3200 degrees Celsius."

"What?" Esme said. Where was this stuff coming from?

Ned gave a sympathetic nod. "Yes, I agree that acetylene is unlikely. Let's assume a dragon flame temperature of between 1200 and 1600 degrees C. Now, HDPE melts at 130 C. You can see for yourself, Esme. The plastic bin lid has no chance. Under dragon flame it would melt immediately and turn to pure carbon ash, allowing the flame to pass on to you. Kippers in short order, I'm afraid."

Esme looked at the plastic bin lid, then tossed it into the corner. "What do you suggest instead?"

Ned stood up and looked around. "This." He plucked a metal lid from another rubbish container. "Steel melts at closer to 1600 C. Betters your odds." He cocked his head and gave her a quirky smile. "Unless, of course, we could come up with an anti-dragon-fire blessing, like the one the Faerie Queen put on St George's shield."

Esme stared up at Ned. God, he was lovely. Never mind dragon flame; she was melting already. "I take it you're a hobbyist?" Oh please, Esme thought. Not one of those weirdos who dresses up like a medieval knight, bashes at other knights with a replica sword, and then quaffs ale from a pewter tankard made in Taiwan.

"A physicist, actually."

"Oh." What a relief. They stood in awkward silence for a moment. Esme cleared her throat. "Steel bin lids it is, then."

"Unless the dragon burns magical element," Ned said thoughtfully. "In that case, I couldn't begin to predict the outcome. It could transform us into anything, really."

"Well, I don't fancy becoming anything else."

"I wouldn't like that either," Ned said.

Esme took a deep breath, grasped her steel bin lid and her hay fork and made what she hoped looked like a fearless move toward the door. "No sense waiting, then. Let's go."

Ned took up his bin lid and another scythe and waited while she cracked open the door and peered out. All she saw were overgrown apple trees, tall weeds, and blue sky. "All right," she whispered. "Go quietly. You watch our rear."

"Ummm—"

"Watch behind us, I mean," she added quickly, with a glance over her shoulder. She almost smiled: he was blushing again. She had never had this effect on a man before. Maybe it was the nexus; maybe, in Ned's vision, her pale, ordinary face and dumpy figure had been transformed in some way by the magical element. She shrugged, setting her speculations aside for later. First she had dragons to deal with.

They had covered half the distance between the shed and Maude's tower when the dragon spotted them. Its horned, crested head popped out above the trees off to their right and slightly ahead, then disappeared. A moment later Esme saw its scaly back crest over the treeline, like a sea monster swimming on the surface of the ocean.

"Faster!" she screamed.

They flew down the path, hearing the crash and rumble as the dragon approached. There was a pause in the noise and then a trumpeting call rang out; it was answered a moment later, then a second crashing approach was heard.

They crossed the stream and fled on, vines and branches lashing their faces, roots reaching up to trip their feet. They felt the ground shaking and heard, once again, one dragon's bellowing call and the other dragon's answer, this time from right behind. Aunt Maude's tower lay just across a grassy field, less than two hundred yards away. Ned and Esme burst from the jungle and raced toward it.

Esme felt a shadow pass over them and heard a rush of wind; she looked up to see the dragon's pale green belly and the vast sweep of its leaf-green wings overhead. It landed with a violent thud on the path before them.

Ned skidded to a halt. Esme crashed into his back and they clung together to avoid falling over, out of breath, still clutching their weapons and shields. One dragon crouched ahead of them, blocking their route to the tower; the other reared up at their backs—they were trapped.

"E-Esme," Ned whispered. The dragons cocked their heads, as if measuring the firing distance to their prey.

They were beautiful creatures, Esme found herself thinking, like glorious sailing ships with banners and flags flying. The second dragon was green and gold, like the first, its eyes the same opaque blue, but its crest blushed a lovely rosy pink and it seemed slightly more delicate in form. It looked like an illumination from an ancient manuscript, come alive. Beautiful.

"Esme!" Ned repeated, more urgent than before.

She tore her gaze away from the dragon crouched between them and Aunt Maude's tower. Drat. Just one hundred yards more and they would have made it. But now it was kippers, for sure.

Ned grasped her shoulders. "It's me they want. I'll draw their attention so you can get away, all right?"

"What?" Surely chivalry is dead, Esme thought. He couldn't be doing what she thought he was.

"I distract, you run." Ned bent down, kissed her soundly on the lips, then shoved her away.

She stumbled, head spinning, then whirled and broke into a run. Behind her, she heard Ned shout a challenge.

For a moment she thought it would work, that the dragons would leap on Ned—poor, lovely, brave, elven-prince Ned—and leave her to find safety in the tower. But her flight was short.

Both dragons twitched toward the sound of Ned's yelling; then, as one, they abandoned him to pursue Esme, catching up to her in one earth-shaking leap. Esme darted one way and a bejeweled claw slammed down like a portcullis. She darted the other way and a graceful, spiked tail slithered across the path, blocking her escape. Two massive, snakelike bodies circled her once, twice, then thumped to the ground, where they ringed her with an impenetrable wall of emerald and gold scales.

Esme clutched her hay fork and bin lid, ready to defend herself. As if from far away, she heard Ned shouting. What was it he had said about flame temperature? 1600 Celsius? And the melting point of steel was— oh, god. Even her bin lid shield wouldn't be much protection. Esme closed her eyes, prepared for the worst. Good-bye, lovely Ned, smart-physicist Ned. Sprinkle my ashes over England's pastures green.

Nothing happened. Esme cracked open her eyes. The dragons' heads were poised above her, but they did not attack. The larger dragon snaked its head down slowly; its more delicate, pink-crested companion did the same, until both enormous heads hung before her, close enough to touch, if she wanted to. Two sets of finely-etched nostrils twitched. Esme felt the rush of wind as the dragons snuffed. The dragons breathed out again, ruffling her hair and cape, then inhaled again, then again, and yet again. Their breath smelled of ozone and thunder, the tang of magical storms, and it moved over her body like a caress, soft and tingling. Esme found herself relaxing, having to cling to her hay fork to stay upright. The dragons took one, last snuffling sniff. Languidly, langorously, their blue eyes half lidded, they drew away and lay their heads down along each others' scaly sides. They each took a few shuddering breaths and fell asleep.

Esme stood still, staring at the sleeping dragons that encircled her. Tentative, she reached out with the butt of her hay fork and prodded one dragon's scaly tail. Not even a twitch. Then she heard Ned shouting and the barking of Aunt Maude's dogs. A moment later, Ned's blond head appeared above the rosy-crested dragon's haunch.

"Esme, quick!" He reached down toward her; without hesitating, she climbed atop one clawed foot and grasped Ned's hand. As he pulled her up, she slid against the dragon's scales, which were slippery and glowing with a heat she could feel even through her clothes. Ned heaved her onto the dragon's back. For a moment they sat holding hands. Ned smiled and Esme sighed, overcome with the languorous warmth of the scales, feeling also surprisingly tingly, as if every inch of her skin had suddenly awoken from a long sleep.

A shout interrupted her thoughts. Ned, predictably, blushed and Esme looked away. As they turned to climb down the dragon's other side, Esme saw Maude Slithers standing wide-eyed and open-mouthed before the tower, holding the gray-furred dogs' collars while the dogs barked in a frenzy.

"Come on, Esme." Ned turned onto his stomach and climbed to the ground, then held up his arms, as if to catch her. Esme slid down the dragon's smooth flank, enjoying the hot, silken feel of its scales against the palms of her hands and the skin on the back of her legs. Ned staggered as she landed in his arms.

"Come on," she said, pulling down her skirt, which had ridden up during her slide down the dragon's side. "Before they wake up."

Ned—blushing yet again, she noticed—took her hand and they ran together away from the entwined and sleeping dragons to the tower. Aunt Maude hustled them inside—"Down, Prancer!"—and slammed the door.

The dragons slept for most of the afternoon. After a call to the authorities was attempted—"phone's on the blink!" said Maude—they settled down in the hemispherical sitting room to decide what to do.

Maude Slithers settled herself in an armchair; Ned and Esme sat together on the sofa. Esme had to keep herself from edging closer to him. And, she noticed, he'd forgotten to release her hand once they'd come inside.

"Well now," Maude said loudly. "It seems to me we've got a variable nexus here."

Esme sat bolt upright and pulled her hand from Ned's grasp. Of course! A variable nexus. No wonder her calculations had never been supported by observation. What a scholarly paper it would make. And elemental dragons! She sat up straighter. Maybe Ned would co-author it with her. Something this big could come out in *Elemental Studies Review B* or even *UnNature*. She might be offered tenure after all.

Ned looked confused. Esme explained. "The elemental unpredictability factor increases tremendously in a variable nexus, Ned, so that exceptionally rare transformations are manifested. Such as the dragons." She smiled, thinking of the dragons' delightful, tingly warmth. "The dragons are a wonderful example of their kind. Almost unique, I should say."

Ned nodded. "What I want to know is, why did the dragons go after you, instead of me? And what did they do, while they had you in there with them?"

"They, um . . . " To her chagrin, Esme found herself blushing. "They sniffed at me."

"Ah!" said Maude, her eyebrows raised.

"And then they went to sleep."

"I see." Maude Slithers nodded, beaming again.

The dragons chose that moment to awaken.

The dogs noticed first, rising from their hearth rug with stiff legs and rumbling growls. Everyone turned toward the windows. Esme saw the dragons approaching, then darkness fell abruptly over the room.

"I'll get the lights!" Maude shouted. Esme heard the sound of a switch being flipped, but no lights came on. "Electric's on the blink! I'll get the lamp." There was a sound of fumbling at the mantle above the fireplace, the flare of a match, then the soft glow of lantern light filled the room.

They sat staring at each other in silence. Maude was the first to speak. For the first time her voice sounded strained. "Neddy, please go and see if all of the windows are covered."

Ned got up and left the room. In a few minutes, he returned. "They are."

"What's going on?" Esme asked. The dogs had lain down again, this time on Maude's feet, as if both protecting and seeking protection.

"The dragons have coiled themselves around the tower, Professor Quirk," Maude answered. "As it happens, I know a few things about elemental magic. We witches are not as ignorant as you academics would like to think! The dragons smelled you and then went to sleep, is that right?"

Esme nodded, wary.

A note of amusement crept into the witch's voice. "There's something about elemental dragons that is not very widely known. And that is that they are particularly fond of the smell of . . . well, of a virgin. They'll take males if they can get them, but there's nothing they like better than the smell of a female human virgin."

Oh, god, Esme thought. If you're going to take me, take me now. She stared down at her hands, face burning, afraid to look up and see

Maude's amusement or Ned's—whatever. Surprise, disappointment, disgust . . .

"Is that the way it is, Professor?" Maude's voice sounded kind, but Esme didn't want kindness. Death by dragon flame would be better. "Are you a virgin?"

Without looking up, Esme nodded.

Ned made a choking sound.

Maude went on to explain. "The smell of a virgin is absolutely compelling to them, you see, which is why—"

Esme shut her ears to the rest of Maude Slithers's lecture on the long history of dragons and virgins. At some point, Ned put a glass of some very strong alcoholic beverage into her hands, which she drank. Then she had another, but it still didn't make her feel better, so she had another.

"The question is," Maude concluded at last, with a keen look at Esme and Ned, "what are we going to do about these dragons? Hmmm?"

By midnight, the dragons still lay in tangled coils around the tower, Maude Slithers sat snoring in her armchair, the dogs were asleep on their rug, and Ned lay on the sofa, an empty glass resting on his chest. An almost-empty bottle of whiskey stood on the side table. Esme sat on a hard chair, a drink in her hand, watching the room orbit around her. Now and then the tower walls shook, as if caught up in some kind of spasm.

Esme watched as Ned shifted on the couch. He sat up and cocked his head, listening to the low grunts and growling purrs coming from outside.

"You know what they're doing out there, don't you?" Ned asked, as the dragons shifted and the tower shivered.

"Mmhmmm," Esme answered. And apparently they were going to keep doing it all night long. Because of her. How mortifying.

Ned stretched. "What are we going to do about it?"

"No idea," Esme said. Well, she had one idea, but she wasn't going to mention it. Especially since she had the feeling that Maude Slithers, snoring away innocently in her chair, had just that solution in mind.

Ned shot Esme a nervous glance, then looked down at the floor. "I wondered, um, if you had wondered, Esme, why the dragons came here in the first place."

Esme blinked. Now that she thought about it . . .

"Right." He was blushing again, she noticed. "I'm one, too. A—you know."

Esme stared. How could it be that someone as lovely as Ned had never . . . ?

"I think," he said, still not looking at Esme, "well, I mean, I think I'm going upstairs. To bed." He stood up, a bit unsteady from the drink, and carefully set his empty whiskey glass on the side table.

Oh, Esme thought, and swallowed another mouthful of her whiskey. He's off to bed. No lovely blond Ned for me. Just Aunt Maude and her snoring dogs. Alas.

He hesitated in the doorway. In the lantern light he looked like a hero prince from a troubadour's ballad.

Ah, she thought, and shivered with longing. The warmth from the dragons tingled under her skin. Think about tenure, she told herself. That'll cool you down, right quick.

"Esme," Ned said.

"What?"

He gave her a shy smile and held out his hand. "Aren't you coming?"

The tingling blossomed into expectant heat. They could do more than publish a treatise on fewmets together. Esme went.

By morning, the dragons were gone.

Sarah Prineas lives near the Iowa River in Iowa City, Iowa, where she works at, you guessed it, the University of Iowa. Her stories have appeared in various print and online magazines, including *Realms of Fantasy, Strange Horizons, Paradox, Flytrap,* and *Cicada,* and have been honorably mentioned in several "Year's Best" anthologies. Sarah thanks Eric Marin of *Lone Star* Stories, who did a fabulous job editing "A Treatise on Fewmets" before it first appeared in print.

THE HARD STUFF

John Grant

We saw things in Falluja that people shouldn't be expected to see and want to carry on living. People fused together by the flames, pregnant women with their guts splayed out and the unborn child among them, infants with their limbs blown away. All the time our superior officers kept telling us it was the insurgents who'd done this with their car bombs and their mortars, and all the time we knew they didn't even believe this themselves. We'd rained high explosives and incendiaries and hell upon these people. Some of them had probably been ready to kill us; the vast majority of them were just ordinary men and women and kids who'd been caught underneath the technology we'd let fall on them; none of them deserved what we'd done to them. What made it worse was that we all of us knew by then there was no real reason for us to have done any of this. We'd been lied into this place by people who used human beings' lives as rungs on a ladder of personal greed.

We moved forward through the smoke and the stink of burning masonry and people's flesh. Some of us threw up, some of us did terrible things to the occasional survivors we encountered, all of us had no expectations that we'd ever be the same again.

I don't remember anything about the moment when the ghosts of the dead took their revenge on me. Their tool might have been a home-made incendiary that somehow hadn't detonated earlier, during the bombardment. It could have been one of our own bombs. All I knew was that one moment I was probing through the smoking hinterlands of Hell, my rifle at the ready, and the next I was . . . somewhere else, a place there was nothing to be seen or sensed except the agony that devoured me. Every cell of my body had been replaced by a flame. The whitest heat of the fire was in my arms; from there it spread to fill everything.

Then there was a time when the world was a polychromatic fan of constantly shifting images, none of which made any sense at all even though they seemed like memories I might once have had. But this time of release couldn't last for long—never long enough—before the fire returned to claim me. There was a thunder in my ears that was either the roaring flames or my own bellows of pain and terror. Occasionally I had fleeting glimpses of faces that were trying to look kindly but succeeded instead only in looking routinely resigned.

Someone told me I was lucky still to be alive, to have all my senses and my "good looks" intact, but it was only later that I was able to stitch those words together, like someone painstakingly repairing a ripped piece of lace. At the time they were just stray torn threads that didn't seem to have any relation to each other, dancing along in a gale of raw heat. Then I was told, repeatedly, that I was going home. That didn't make sense to me either. Didn't these people realize that I had no home? That all I had was that I was. I had no past, unless my past was an infinity of the fire that was the present. I wasn't a human being at all, just a construct woven from filaments of eternal pain.

But one more thing I didn't have was any words with which to say any of this. So I just carried on through the tunnel of eternity until at last I noticed things were different.

"Your trouble, Quinn," said Tania, "is that you're forever filling your head with all the things you can't do any longer. It makes you think there's nothing you can do."

We were sitting on the porch watching a late-Fall sun head toward the horizon. The sky was painting the tree-splashed hills the colours of toasted bread. It was the end of another day marked by little except the fact that I'd lived through it.

I made no reply to her. Most of the time I didn't.

"You should wipe those thoughts out of your head, Quinn," she continued, nodding as if I'd said something. She was standing with her hands on the porch rail, and was looking out defiantly toward the sunset. There was enough of a breeze to press her dress against her legs. "If you don't, you're letting them be the bars to the prison cell you've locked yourself into."

She turned to face me, and I tried to meet her gaze. I couldn't, so instead I looked down at my own arms, what was left of them. The months had etiolated them. They looked like empty denim shirt-sleeves hanging on a line, one of them tucked up by the wind more than the other. The people with the resigned faces had saved my left arm down as far as the wrist, my right not so far as that, only to a few inches below the elbow. Freakishly, the explosion hadn't harmed the rest of me at all beyond a few superficial shrapnel wounds that had soon healed, leaving scars that looked like nothing more serious than long pale crinkly hairs plastered by sweat to my skin. My "good looks", as the medics had called them, were still the way they'd always been, except for the waking nightmares that seethed behind my face.

I didn't have much use for mirrors, but sometimes Tania made me look into them as she shaved me, or trimmed my hair, or brushed my teeth.

As the sun came into laborious contact with the cut-out hilltops I spoke at last.

"Time for a drink," I said as I always did this time of the evening. "An aperitif. Fuck the meds."

Tania slapped her hands against her cotton-covered thighs and let out a gasp of exasperation.

"Have you been listening to a single word I've been saying?"

"Yes. You've been telling me I should look on the bright side, think positive, all that."

She sighed.

It was a constant bone of contention between us, like my refusal to wear the clumsy prosthetic hands I'd been given, which lay in their box upstairs. If I wanted a more sophisticated pair we were going to have find the money for them—a lot of money for them—from somewhere. All the government would spring for were lumps of pink plastic that looked ridiculous because of their colour and chafed my stumps to agony within minutes. That was all the country could afford, they said. There were, after all, tax breaks to pay for.

"But I'm a stupid self-pitying bastard," I said, "so I just carry on wallowing in my misery and bitterness, or dreaming up crazy schemes about what I'd like to do to the fatcat fuckers who made me like this." I raised my shorter arm, the one that seemed always to be wanting to hide itself within the sleeve of my T-shirt. "The trouble is, I can't nuke Crawford, Texas, and fry Il Buce and the Stepford Wife alive because how the fuck without any fingers could I set the"—I formed the word fastidiously—"*device?* I can't strangle Rumsfeld in his own intestines, which is what I'd dearly love to do, because he hasn't left me with any hands to strangle him with. As for that fucker Cheney . . . So all I have left is talking about how I'd like to do every one of those things and more, and getting my jollies by dreaming about those bastards' screams and them begging for a mercy I won't give as they choke on their own severed genitals, because every time I ask you for your help making my dreams real you just look disgusted or your face twists up in pain or you pretend you've not heard me, which is probably the worst and cruelest thing you could do to me. And somehow in the middle of all that I can't find room to cram in a Dale Carnegie course on encouraging my positive thoughts."

It wasn't one of my longer speeches. I was just getting started. I could go on for hours, when the spirit took me, detailing the medieval tortures I wanted to inflict on the shits who'd stolen my hands and put me here.

"I'll get you that beer," said Tania, heading for the screen door. "And something a bit stronger for myself," she appended under her breath, thinking I couldn't hear her.

She came back out a few minutes later and plonked the beer down on my chair arm. In her other hand she had something cheerily red and toxic-looking with a cherry lurking menacingly at the bottom of the glass and a parasol sticking out the top. My beer was in a plastic beaker with a screw-on top and a straw. The condensation wouldn't form properly on the plastic sides, which looked blotchy and diseased rather than enticingly misted. Nonetheless, I bowed my head and sucked and the liquid was tart and cold, like the ice no one had been able to put on me when the fire possessed me.

Tania flopped into the other chair on the porch, and let her free hand dangle as she took a sip—a gulp—of her drink. Two chairs were all we needed out here any longer because we didn't have visitors very often any more, and most of them didn't want to stay very long. I thought it was because they were sickened or embarrassed by my deformity. Tania thought the same, only it was different deformities we were thinking of.

Dad didn't come here at all any longer. A soldier without hands isn't a soldier any longer. He'd made himself forget about me.

"I'm taking you away on a trip," she announced abruptly in an alcoholcoloured voice.

"Yeah. Right. Another psych checkup by those terribly nice people at Newark General?"

"Nope." She put her glass carefully down on the armrest of her chair and stared at it. "I'm taking you to see my folks." That caught my attention. Her folks hadn't come across from Scotland for the wedding, although they'd sent a bunch of tartaned ethnic objects for us to fill the attic with. We'd kept planning to go over to what Tania called, with a curious twist of her lip, "the old country," but somehow as the years passed we'd never gotten around to it. And then, of course, there'd come my Iraq posting, the murderer of all plans, real or otherwise.

I looked at her, questioning.

"I think I need their help," she said. She was still staring at her half-emptied glass of red stickiness. For once she seemed doubtful of her words.

"Their help with you, Quinn," she added, as if the glass didn't know already that this was what she meant. "I've booked us tickets for Friday. Return tickets from Newark to Glasgow. We're going for a week, just over."

"You didn't think this was something we should discuss?" I said, purely for the sake of saying it. She was the one who took my decisions for me—I was happy enough about it, because it was one less thing for me to make a mess of. But that didn't mean I couldn't voice a few words of false independence from time to time.

"I knew you'd just argue about it for days, so I thought I'd pre-empt you."

She winced. "Pre-empt" wasn't the most popular of words around our house. She gave a flutter of her hand as apology, then took another swig of her drink to distract my attention.

"I think it's a good idea," I said, surprising her. "I just wish you'd asked me first."

She grinned at me, for the first time in days. For the first time in weeks or years, I managed a grin back.

"Just remember who's the boss, woman."

"Yes, boss."

My good mood was covered over by the usual black tar before she'd finished the second word. I stood nine inches taller than her, but she'd be the one carrying the baggage or struggling with the trolley. I wondered how many times during the trip I'd reach instinctively with my left arm toward my inside right jacket pocket for the tickets and the passports or the money before realizing that of course these days they resided in Tania's pocket, not mine. I wondered how many times I'd force that embarrassed little "silly me, it doesn't really matter, honestly" laugh for the benefit of the people around me.

I didn't say anything more that evening until after she'd led me inside and fed me fried chicken and microwaved sweet potatoes and praline caramel ice cream, and then taken me into the bathroom and unzipped my trousers and pulled them down around my knees so I could have a shit.

When I finally spoke it was just to say thank you after she'd wiped my ass for me.

The one time I wished my pride would take a holiday so I could use my cheap, wrongly-coloured, hated prosthetics.

My dad made it to be a five-star general, unlike his farm-labourer father before him. He wanted lots of sons who'd all make it to be five-star generals, so the family tree would glow in the night like some spiral galaxy and impress the hell out of the Hubble Telescope.

It didn't turn out that way, because my mother never properly recovered after giving birth to me. I have vague recollections of the smell of soap and soft skin and summery cloth; there are other memories, too, of the smells being not so good, but by then my father had decreed it was probably best if "his little man" was kept out of the sickroom. Clear as a colour photograph in my head is what I saw when, at the age of three and a half, I was held aloft for one final look at my mother, framed by the oblong of her coffin. I gazed down at the face of a stranger who bore a casual resemblance to someone I'd once known.

Dad never married again. He had a succession of lady friends, one or two of whom he succeeded in coaxing out of their military uniforms when he thought I was asleep. But their visits were few and far between. Mainly it was just him and me.

And his ambitions for me. If he couldn't have a passel of sons, then the one son his weak vessel had borne to him should fulfill a passel's worth of his dreams. I was a soldier from even before my mother died. I could get my bedclothes as tight as a drumskin by the time I was five.

Tania shouldn't have found me, but she did. Why her eyes ever alit on the stuffy youth with the micrometer-precise haircut, whose personality was hardly more than the uniform he wore, is something I've never been able to fathom. But she bubbled up to me at my cousin's wedding and introduced herself, asking me if I agreed with her a cow had probably sneezed into the *vol-au-vents*. Young women were a slight mystery to me at the time, although I'd read all the usual magazines, gazing with a sort of astonished fascination at the glistening revelations; and so I didn't know quite what to do with myself during that first conversation. But she was persistent, and without my ever understanding quite how it had happened I had a date with her the following week.

The years didn't change Tania. The faint accent she had, which wasn't so much an accent as a startling lack of one, never went. She had a face you'd dismiss as nothing special, really rather plain, except that at the same time you'd find yourself thinking it was maybe the most beautiful face you'd ever seen. Around that oval hung straightish blonde or muddy-mousy hair that was either lank or aethereally fine, like the flimsy webs that billow across the blackness between the stars. Her eyes were green, or perhaps brown, or perhaps even darker than that. Her skin was pallid; her skin was deliciously porcelain-pale. I wasn't so dazed during our first meeting that I didn't notice, with the highly trained reflexes of military men everywhere, that she significantly lacked the generous frontal rations enjoyed by the women in the magazines. Curiously, this made her seem far more feminine than they were.

(No, there was one thing about her that changed. She gave up smoking after she'd been properly introduced to him. Dad had moral compunctions about women smoking.)

What else did she look like?

She looked like Tania. That's all the description necessary. Certainly it's the only real description I can come up with.

Born in Scotland, midway between Glasgow and Edinburgh and a bit to the north of both, she'd been raised in a village that sounded more like a few houses, a shop, a pub and a post office than anything you'd recognize as a settlement. About the family business she was always charmingly imprecise: I got the impression her father wasn't really a farmer and not really a trader, but somewhere midway between both and a bit north, just like where they lived.

Somehow she'd ended up training as a dancer in London, and had come to New York as an understudy to a touring production of something by Chopin, or maybe it was Delibes. But then she'd sprained her knee (did I not mention the slight limp with which she walked ever after? it was something I had a hard job remembering, even as I watched her) and after that there could be no more question of her pursuing a career as a dancer, except perhaps along Eighth Avenue, a performance art she wasn't prepared to countenance. So she turned instead to production. She already had a work visa, and she was able to wangle that into an assistant position somewhere far enough off Broadway it was probably in the middle of the Hudson.

That was not too long before she found me.

Dad and the army laid on a hell of a military wedding, I'll give them that, even though he hid his disapproval of this "Bohemian" so deeply and effectively that it was the first thing strangers became aware of when they first met him. She turned to costume design so that we could be together as I finished college and then wherever around the country the army's whim took me.

My posting to Iraq represented the first time we'd spent more than a day apart since our wedding.

Dad's eyes were watery with pride as he wished me bon voyage. He put on all his old medals, the better to show off the puffing of his chest.

"Go serve your country and kill those heathen motherfuckers, son."

I'm surprised the stare Tania gave him didn't boil the flesh from his bones.

"I don't care what you say, sir. I think that's liquor."

Tania and I looked at each other in frustration. Behind her face, the depth of the moulded plastic window frame gave me the illusion that I was looking out not upon sunset-painted clouds but upon the ocean floor, where weirdly coloured coral formations sprouted. The last time we'd flown by Continental Airlines we'd sworn we'd never do so again, and yet we had, and now we were discovering why we shouldn't have. The chief stewardess, who looked like an advertisement for the Aryan race after a teenager had doctored it with Photoshop, had spied the plastic bottle full of glucose solution sitting on the fold-down tray in front of me and gotten it into her head that I was sipping scotch or brandy through the bottle's built-in straw. On these planes, she'd informed us coldly, it was a Federal Offense to drink any alcohol except that sold to us at great cost by the cabin crew.

"I strongly advise you, sir, not to drink any more out of that bottle," she concluded, fixing us in turn with a stare borrowed from an old Gestapo movie. "Know what I mean?"

She flounced off down the aisle, doubtless to phone her mother for a good weep.

Tania began to giggle. So, after a few moments, did I. My laughter felt very distant from me, but the emotion was perfectly genuine. Adversity was bringing Tania and me closer together than we'd been in months.

We'd navigated Newark International with the usual dehumanizing and, in my case, emasculating hindrances. The clerk at check-in had seemed sickened by my vulgarity in putting my elbows on the counter in front of him. The security people had taken one look at my dark face and my truncated arms and decided I was obviously a mad Arab suicide bomber—who else would go around with his hands missing, after all? We'd dissuaded them from the full body-cavity search, but they'd done just about everything else they could think of. We'd discovered the eateries and drinkeries behind the security gates all worked under the assumption that their customers could carry their own plates and glasses; burdened by our duty-free bags and our carry-on luggage, Tania had done her best to cope for two, but even so there was a corner of the hall that was going to be forever beer-stained. After she'd fed the both of us, there were still two hours to go before departure; I got through the first hour okay but eventually confessed I needed a leak, so there was a whole round of further complication when we found the disabled bathroom was closed for repairs . . .

I was dreading our arrival in the airport at Glasgow, where presumably we'd have to go through the entire rigmarole all over again.

"Put it this way," said Tania, reading my thoughts, "it couldn't possibly be any worse."

"You bet?" I said, though in fact I agreed with her.

"Have a nice glug of glucose, Quinn. It'll make you feel better. If that nasty lady comes back I'll deal with her."

I chuckled again. Tania was grinning. Before Iraq, her grin had always made me chuckle. It was one of our countless ways of making love.

Time passed.

We watched a movie in which Cameron Diaz waggled her rear end at the camera. No change there. I slept for a while. A different stewardess, younger, woke me up to ask me if I wanted a breakfast that I took one look at and didn't, although I accepted the coffee and the plastic demitasse of orange juice.

"I'm lucky," I said to Tania as she peered out the window into the beginnings of sunrise to see if Scotland were visible yet.

She turned from the window, surprised. "It's been a long time since I've heard you say that, Quinn."

I knew she was expecting me to tell her I was lucky because I had her, so instead I said: "There are countless other poor assholes who've come back who would envy me for having got off so lightly."

Her face fell, but she rallied. "Taken you a while to realize that, hasn't it?"

"And at least we've got enough money to cope," I went on. Dad might have decided I was a lost son, but either he'd forgotten to cancel his monthly allowance to us or it was his way of canceling out his guilt for the abandonment.

"That certainly makes it easier," she said, nodding, her eyes narrowing.

I felt the corners of my mouth twitch, even though I was trying to stop them doing so.

She saw.

"You're a bastard, Quinn Hogarth," she said, the disguised offendedness draining out of her eyes, leaving behind sparkle. But she took one of my ears in each hand and dragged my head towards her for a kiss. "I knew that when I married you."

"Say it," she whispered in my ear.

"Those are the least important things of all," I murmured back to her. "You're my luckiness, Tania, and always will be."

"You don't know the half of it," she said.

The airport in Glasgow was a bit of a disappointment—which was to its credit. Our adrenaline levels had geared themselves up for another dose of Newark International, only worse because of being in a foreign country. Instead, we were greeted with smiling courtesy all round. The place was about a tenth the size of its Newark counterpart, which might explain some of this—but not all. There was neither subservience nor bored resentment and suspicion on display. The attitude of the various uniformed officials seemed to be that we were all equal colleagues in achieving a common aim, which was to get arrivals through the bureaucracy as quickly and comfortably as possible.

Tania joined me in the All Other Passports line at immigration. When the guy at the counter saw her UK passport he frowned and was halfway through pointing her toward the queue for EU nationals when he realized why she was here.

"The business in Iraq?" he said, nodding toward my stumps. His accent was quite thick, and totally different from Tania's non-accent, but I had no difficulty understanding him.

"Yes." I tried to soften my curtness with one of those instant smiles in which I specialized.

"I'm sorry you had the misfortune to be sent there," he said offhandedly, shrugging as he stamped my passport.

I caught my breath. It was exactly the right thing he'd said. No overweening sympathy. No gung-ho denunciations of towel-heads. Just a sort of acceptance and sharing of my bad luck.

He looked me in the eye, smiling. "I hope you're bringing the lady back home to stay," he said. "It's an ill thing when all the best and prettiest ones get taken away from us."

I laughed. "Just a holiday, I'm afraid."

He shrugged. "Ah, weel."

"Is everyone in Scotland like this?" I asked Tania later, jerking my head toward the terminal building we'd just come out of.

"No," she said with a smile, looking around her for the taxi rank. We'd decided beforehand that it'd be silly to try negotiating the buses into the city centre, me with my handlessness and Tania with all the luggage. "But a lot of them are. It's a more laid-back country than you're used to, Quinn. And freer."

As the taxi driver loaded our cases and bags into the trunk of his big black vehicle, he told us he'd take us to Glasgow Central, where our hotel was, for twenty pounds.

"Twenty pounds?" I hissed to Tania as we settled ourselves into the back seat and she reached across me for the tongue of my seat belt. "That's well over fifty bucks! It's only about ten miles, isn't it? He's ripping us off."

"Some things are more expensive here," she replied, jiggling the belt's tongue into its socket. "A lot of things. Just get used to it."

"But . . . "

"Think of it as your payment for medical insurance."

That ended the discussion.

Everything in Scotland seemed to be smaller, more enclosed-feeling than at home, I mused during the drive into the city. The dinky little airport. The threelane highway whose lanes seemed narrower than I'd have expected. Most of the cars were actually cars: there were hardly any SUVs on the road. The transport trucks and buses seemed half the size of real ones. The overall effect was to make me feel as if I'd strayed into a model of the world, somewhere slightly enchanted. I recognized the sensation. It was the same as I'd felt when visiting miniature villages as a child. There was more than a difference of scale involved when, rather than being dwarfed as usual by adults, one stood towering above rooftops and even the church tower: there was a magic that sprang from the dislocation.

Tania and a uniformed valet whipped us from the taxi into our hotel, which was not so much next to as half-inside Glasgow Central Station, through registration and up to our room. As she stowed away our clothes in drawers and a wardrobe I gazed out the window onto a vista of the railway station, sensing again that odd magic, this time because the double-glazing muffled into silence all but the very loudest of noises. I could hear the announcements over the loudspeakers, but only very faintly and fuzzily, as if they were a long way away and I were wearing faulty earplugs. There was far more grime than would have been tolerated in a station back home. From where I stood, high above, the passengers scurrying around in obedience to their own motivations were as incomprehensible as ants on an unswept kitchen floor.

"Are you tired?" said Tania from behind me.

I turned and saw that she was sitting on the bed, hands between her knees, all our kit and caboodle safely tidied away into appropriate places where I'd be unable to find any of it unassisted. On the bedside table, beside the telephone, lay a stick pen; there was one beside every phone at home, too. It was there for me to pick up in my teeth and dial with if ever I had to, in the event of emergency. Next to the pen she'd put one of the bottles of bourbon we'd got at the duty free in Newark, as well as a carton of cigarettes I hadn't realized she'd bought. She'd opened the carton. A pack of Basics lay on the coverlet beside her.

"Smoking?" I said. "I thought you gave that up."

The edge of her mouth quirked. "Your father's three thousand miles away."

"Even so."

"Even so, I've not got anything to light the damn' things with. And I'm too shagged out to go downstairs and get a box of matches from the lobby."

I nodded toward the table underneath the window. Alongside the slightly creased advertisement-stuffed tourist guide to Glasgow, the hotel stationery and the anachronistic blotter were a book of matches and an ashtray.

"Compliments of the house," I said, trying to keep any judgemental note out of my voice.

"Just be a dear and bring . . . " She stopped. Resignation crossed her face as she heaved herself to her feet. "Sorry, I forgot."

She tossed the book of matches onto the bed and went into the bathroom, where I could hear the clattering of glass. A moment later she emerged with a tooth-glass.

"Cigs. Booze. Sleep," she said, gesturing at the bourbon. "The recipe for a happy wife, right now.

We kicked off our shoes and lay side by side on the bed, drinking the raw whiskey. Tania had rinsed out my plastic cup, getting rid of the remains of the glucose drink and replacing it with neat bourbon—to the brim; she wasn't a woman who believed in doing chores twice when once would do. I don't know why we hadn't bought scotch in Newark. Maybe it would have seemed blasphemous, or something, to bring a bottle of scotch to Scotland. I made a resolution to rectify the situation in the morning, or, if we woke early enough this evening, tonight. But just at this moment, lying together in what was for me a brand-new country and for Tania a long-abandoned homeland, the bourbon seemed perfectly in keeping. It was a symbol. We were using up, so that we would eventually piss away, the last vestiges of all the emotional and intellectual encumbrances we'd brought with us. I even smoked a couple of her cigarettes—the first time I'd smoked since the stolen guilts of adolescence—although they made my head spin and she laughed at my coughing.

Later, a little clumsily, we got off the bed and I watched her as she bent to pull back the sheets. She undressed me for sleep, and then undressed herself. I don't know if it was the booze or the tiredness or the fact that we were shedding our old selves just as we'd shed the noises of America, but for the first time in four months we made love.

We did this a little clumsily too, but that didn't matter.

Two days later, we were driving away from Glasgow, heading roughly northeastward. Tania seemed far more at ease behind the wheel of the rental car than she ever did driving the Nissan at home. Maybe it was that the driver seat was on the opposite side; maybe it was just because the car was that little bit smaller in every respect. I don't know. Whatever the case, I myself had found the differences initially disconcerting, then within a few minutes strangely liberating. They were part and parcel of the past forty-eight hours or so. We'd spent most of one day just wandering around, picking up a few things (including a bottle of Laphroaig) in the Glasgow shops; we'd spent most of the second day in the Burrell Collection, where I gazed at the foreignness of the Scottish exhibits while Tania gazed at the foreignness of everything else. In between, we'd eaten two excellent Indian meals and a bad hamburger meal. We'd also made love half a dozen times more, another rediscovery of the ancient arts.

"Where are we going?" I asked for the thousandth time.

"You'll find out when we get there," she said, laughing at the repetition of the exchange.

I glanced sideways at her, watching suburbs speed backwards past her face. There was a shiny vivacity in her eyes, focused on the road ahead, that I'd not seen in far too long.

"Second glen on the right, then straight on 'til morning, sort of thing?" I said.

She began to speak, then paused, then spoke. "That's probably a more accurate description than most," she said primly.

I brushed my hair back from my forehead with my smaller lump of pink plastic. There was still novelty in the gesture. Since Iraq I'd let my hair grow, and it was now longer than I'd ever had it. The other, larger, prosthetic was still in their shared case, somewhere in the trunk behind us.

Unknown to me, Tania had packed the plastic hands for the trip to Scotland, "just in case." When I'd discovered this, instead of flying into a temper I'd asked her to strap on the left one for me—just the one, as a form of compromise with my arrogance. The thing itched like hell sometimes if I kept it on too long, but the agonies of my previous experience were just a memory. We'd discovered, in one of the Indian restaurants, that if Tania wedged a spoon firmly between the useless thumb and the equally inflexible fingers, I could feed myself—messily and sloppily at first, as the biriani-streaked front of one of my shirts testified, but I'd improved rapidly with practice. Spaghetti was a distant dream, but perhaps the day would come.

The waiters in the restaurant had watched the performance with a friendly amusement, once or twice pointlessly offering help. This was the curious thing I'd discovered in Glasgow: the complete acceptance by everyone of my disability as just a part of who I was, nothing special. There was the occasional startled glance when people first encountered me, but otherwise it was as if handless men were on every street corner. At home in Jersey, on the rare occasions when I allowed Tania to take me out, I received looks that could be pitying, or sickly fascinated, or even derisory. Once in a supermarket, as I'd dawdled aimlessly behind Tania and her shopping cart, a trio of prepubescent boys had seen fit to follow me, taunting. Their parents, nearby, hadn't intervened until Tania, when she'd finally cottoned on to what was happening, had laid into the kids with a few—quite a lot of—well chosen and acidly delivered words. One of the mothers, springing to the defence of her little angel, had angrily retorted: "Well, what can you *expect?*"

There was none of that in Glasgow. Nor, either, was there any perceivable reaction to our being a "racially mixed couple." I suppose the fact that we were both Americans outweighed any differences there might be between us.

In Scotland it doesn't take you long to drive anywhere. The kind of journey I was accustomed to at home would have had us driving into the sea before it was halfway through. Even so, it seemed to take a good while to leave the urban smear behind. At last, though, the road narrowed from four lanes to three, the central reservation being discarded. Then we were down to two lanes, and ultimately to what seemed to my American eye to be more like one and a half. The countryside we went through was at first rather drab, in terms of its landforms and its vegetation both; the greens were duller and more muted than at home, as if they'd forgotten to wash their faces this morning.

And then things finally began to change. The road became twistier, its progress punctuated by lots of small rises and falls—some of them not so small. The engine of the Morris laboured in a few places as we struggled to reach a crest. The hills were taller and rockier, crowding around us; when we saw them ahead of us in the distance, they had that mysterious purple colour I'd read about but only rarely seen at home. We had the way more or less to ourselves; on the rare occasions we came across a tractor or another car, Tania slowed down as the two vehicles manoeuvred carefully past each other. Each time, she and the other driver would say a few words of greeting to each other, usually about the weather, in one case about a lost sheep. As far as I could gather—the accents were becoming less intelligible to me here, directly counter to Tania's predictions—it was an extremely interesting sheep.

"Tell me something more about your folks," I said when we'd left him and his battered paint-free zone of a truck. She'd never mentioned anything except the basics: Dad, Mom—"Mum," I mean—sisters Alison and Jenny, brother Alan. Unlike me, who had two fat albums filled with badly focused snapshots and stiff formal portraits of my family, she possessed no photographs of her kin. There were phone calls every week or two—in the old days I'd been called upon to say a few phatic words to one in-law or another, but not since Iraq—and letters from her mother at least as often, although I'd never noticed Tania writing back. My wife's memories seemed to begin when she'd moved to London. It wasn't as if she were particularly secretive—far from it, in fact. I once joked that I knew more about what her boyfriends before me had been like in bed than I did about her family. She'd given me a cold look and asked me to pass the potatoes, and the conversation had drifted in other directions.

"I'm going to be meeting them soon enough," I added. "You might as well warn me what to expect."

She thought this over for a few moments, frowning to herself, tilting her head to one side while still watchfully regarding the next curve in the road, letting her foot ease off the pedal a little as if that would help her deliberations.

"They're the kind of people that you just need to take them the way they are, Quinn. You've got a vile habit of trying to mould people into what you want them to be—you got it from your dad, although heaven be thankful you're not as bad as he is. My folks, they're . . . they're not *mouldable,* if that's a proper word. If you try to think of them as anything other than what they are, they won't change. But maybe you will."

It wasn't much of a description, and she refused to add to it. I had images of a commune of merry left-over hippies, passing the joints around and forgetting to wash.

Well, I could cut it—of that I was sure. Despite what Tania had said, I was as adaptable as anyone. There'd been plenty of dope in Iraq—it was the only way most of us knew how to get through what was happening—so the prospect of the drugs didn't bother me. Might take a toke or two myself, if it seemed appropriate to do so.

We came to a place where the road faded out, just beyond a small, dilapidated farmhouse that seemed to be entirely populated by mangy-looking dogs, who watched with suspicious boredom as we drove by. The metal and the low roadside walls stopped abruptly, but two confident-looking ruts carried on across the fields. Tania didn't slow the car or otherwise seem to notice the change in surface.

"It's pretty remote where they live, is it?" I said.

She giggled, and now she did slow the car a little. "I can't see too many townships around here, can you, Quinn?" She nodded ahead of us, where there was little to be seen except sheep-spattered browny-green slopes and, beyond, two greater hills seeming to intersect in a pronounced V-shaped notch. "That's where we're heading. To the—

what was it you called it? Ah, yes. To the second glen on the right, straight on 'til morning."

"Not literally, I hope?"

"Hm?"

"'Til morning, I mean. That's about fifteen, sixteen hours away."

She threw back her head and laughed. If it hadn't been for the ruts we might have driven off the track.

"No," she said. "Mornings are the last thing you'll need to worry about."

It was a puzzling remark, but then a lot had been puzzling me since—oh, since about the time we'd said our goodbyes to the man who'd lost his sheep. Tania was changing, changing even as I sat beside her in the car. We'd pulled into a layby at one point so we could both have a pee (an operation whose mechanics were made possible for me, just, by the lump of plastic at the end of my arm). She went first, and as she emerged from the scraggly bush there'd been no earthly reason to hide behind, I observed the way her stride had changed. It was as if she'd lost about half her weight and was in danger of floating off the ground if she didn't remember to tether herself there. And there was a glow about her that wasn't entirely explicable by the prospect of her seeing her family for the first time in years. I had the odd illusion that the land across which we moved was feeding her, somehow—and doing so with a full willingness. This was her country. She reigned here with the contented respect of her great, silent subject. There was a communion between her and the very soil unlike anything I could imagine myself experiencing back home in my own native land.

As she'd climbed back into the car and I rocked myself to and fro in my seat, preparing to swing myself out for my own pee, I'd noticed how many birds seemed to be singing around us. God knew where they'd been perching—the trees in this region weren't anything to write home about, being largely of the variety that are obviously not dead yet, but thinking about it. As we bumped along the rutted track, now, I wondered if, were I able to roll my window down—no electronic controls in this car, just a handle—I'd hear the songs of just as many birds, even though we were in the middle of nowhere.

"How long to go?" I asked after a few more minutes' silence.

"We'll be there very soon, Quinn," she reassured me, adopting the voice of mothers everywhere when the brats in the back are being a pain in the ass.

"Yes, Mommy," I responded, joining in the game, "but how soon?"

"You haud yer wheesht, Jimmie, or your dad'll stop the car and gie ye a good skelping."

"Huh?"

For the next half-hour or so, as the ground beneath us got less and less kempt and the sun, poised midway down the afternoon sky, pondered whether or not to call it a day, she regaled me with Scotticisms. Before giving me the translation in each case, she insisted I make a few guesses myself. The laughter between us got louder and more uncontrollable as my guesses grew progressively more obscene.

"No, Quinn"—this in schoolmistressly tone—"'fit rod?' does not mean a healthy . . . "

She suddenly paused. We'd gone round so many twists and turns since leaving Glasgow that I'd lost my orientation, but it seemed we were now heading more or less due west. Directly in front of us, the sun was settling into the notch I'd seen earlier between the two hills.

When Tania spoke next, her voice was different—quieter, lower, slower, barely more than a breath

"Ohhh, Quinn, we're almost there." This seemed to be as much to herself as to me. "The sun's opening the gates for us."

I squinted at her, wondering what in the hell she was talking about. She didn't notice my attention.

And, as I watched, she quite deliberately lifted her hands off the steering wheel, leaving the car to guide itself.

In any other circumstances I'd have panicked entirely. No way was I able to grab the wheel, not with a singly chunk of badly sculpted, lifeless plastic in place of hands. As it was, there washed across me like calming warm air the conviction that her action was a perfectly natural one, that everything around us was as it should be, as if ourselves and the cheap little car scuttling along the now nearly invisible track were tucked inside a cocoon where things were . . .

Where things were *done differently.*

That was how it was as we drove through the gateway that the blood-red sunlight filled.

The blinding glare of the sunlight shattered, revealing itself to me as clouds of rusty-winged insects that fluttered away, their group interest caught by something else as I waved my arm, shooing them.

How could I have imagined they were sunlight? The sun was at its noon height in an unblemished silver sky. Tania and I were walking hand-in-hand through ankle-deep grass and little black-button-eyed wildflowers across a gently curving foothill. The flowers were mainly pink and white, though there were blues and yellows scattered here and there, as well as some distinctly more exotic colours, ones that I couldn't quite find a name for. The grass was the unnatural green of Astroturf, but its fresh smell told me it was real, not plastic. There was a curious blur across the ground; it took me a few moments to realize that the tip of each blade of grass was stained a faint, airy violet, the colour that ultraviolet might have if you could see it, the colour of the faint breeze that both warmed and cooled my face.

And all around us there was birdsong, although I could see no birds.

My mind hopped back a pace or two.

Real, not plastic, I had been thinking.

I could feel Tania's fingers curled around mine.

I glanced down at the hand that was holding hers, then at the other.

"I'm . . . " I began.

"Hush," she said quietly. "There's no need to be saying anything, Quinn."

Again her voice had changed. The precision of her non-accent had become more than it had ever been, so that I had the impression I was listening not to a voice but to pure language. At the same time there was a sense of the archaic about the timbre.

I dragged my eyes away from the hand of mine that was in hers and followed the line of her bare arm up to her face. Gone were the blue jeans and the sensible striped blouse she'd been wearing for driving. She was wearing a dress the same colour as the tips of the grass-blades, and as insubstantial-seeming. The neck of it was high, prim, so that the bareness of her arms was a near-uncanny incongruity. The hem of her dress, I saw out of the corner of my vision, brushed the grass we walked upon, and trailed out behind her like half-seen downy feathers.

She trod the ground as lightly as the feathers rustled, as if her body had given up all of its matter to the sky.

Tania turned her head slowly toward me, meeting my gaze.

These were the eyes of my wife I was looking into, of my Tania, and yet they were no eyes I'd ever seen before. I was gazing into shady green corridors that retreated infinitely far back, into places and times where I was not entirely certain I wanted to go. Her lips were thinner, her mouth a little wider, and was there a trace of an unaccustomed cruelty in the laughter lines at the corners? The porcelain whiteness of her skin had become almost opalescent. Her hair was the pale, pale colour of highly polished pure gold, where the yellowness is more of an idea than a hue. In it she wore a coronet plaited of the variously coloured field flowers that sprinkled the field we walked through. Her forehead was unmarked. The eyebrows beneath it, darker than her head hair, were fine lines that seemed to have been painted on rather than grown; one was raised a little above the other, giving her an expression that I might have interpreted as cold cynicism had it been on any other face.

"Who are you?" I said so softly that I'm not sure I spoke the words aloud. "Where are we?"

She laughed.

"Less of your questions, questions, questions all the time, darling Quinn." She lifted my hand as if it were a plaything and skipped forward a step or two, pulling me into the dance with her. "You know you have always wanted to see my folks. Well, now you shall. They have been waiting so long and eagerly to meet my lover from the west, and to share with him the love they have for me. They have a ripe welcome waiting for you, my Quinn. But do not pester them with your questions, the way I allow you to pester me. They might not be so gracious if their tempers fray."

Again she glanced at me. Her eyes were wide, mocking.

I suppose I should have begun to get frightened around now. Who was this stranger I'd thought I knew through and through? Where was she leading me? Who were these enigmatic people who might harm me if their "tempers frayed"? Had I entered some hallucinatory madness? Was the madness even my own?

But, gazing into those antiquity-coloured, teasing eyes of Tania, I trusted her entirely—trusted far more even than I ever had. Wherever I was, I was here because of her love for me. This world was an extension of her. I could no more come to any real harm here than she would strike me a fatal blow with her own hand.

"Watch where you're going, Quinn," she said lightly. "If you trip and fall I'm not sure if I could hold you."

Obediently I turned my head forward. The curved rim of the hillside was approaching us faster, it seemed, than the steps we took could account for.

"Where are we . . . ?" I started to say, then remembered her stricture.

"Stop asking," she said anyway. "There is nothing you know how to ask about. Just *be*, Quinn."

And then we were over the breast of the slope and looking down from its small height onto a little valley. A stream curled along the bottom. By the stream's side there gathered like idly curious spectators a collection of small stone houses with grassed roofs—they looked like pictures I'd seen of Highland crofts. A white horse grazed unfenced. Two dogs cavorted together, warring over something I couldn't see from here that floated in the air above them. A ram looked up towards us as if it had been observing our arrival, its twin horns like hard nails. Smoke coiled up from the chimney of the largest of the houses, which was still small.

"The second glen on the right," I said quietly.

Just a few yards ahead of us, a notice had been stuck into the ground—a flat sheet of wood nailed to a stake. The untidily painted letters read:

ABANDON YOURSELF
ALL YE WHO ENTER HERE

There was no sign of another human being but us.

"Everyone's inside," explained Tania before I could break her rules again. "They're preparing for us."

"No need for them to dress up specially," I said, making a joke of the remark's inadequacy.

"Oh, but they will, they will," she assured me. "Come on, Quinn. Time to meet the folks."

Much later, although it was still noon, there were ten of us crammed into the only room of what I was told should properly be called the Bothy. In Tania's absence, her sisters and her brother had both wed; Alison was showing a generous bulge and had proudly informed us the baby was due in under four months. We'd had plenty of beer to drink as we ate what seemed to be an entire sheep, with potatoes and a coarse kind of beet called a turnip. The noise level was getting high. Faces were getting red. Eyes were getting bloodshot and watery.

I'd expected Tania's family to be as aethereal as she herself had become while we were approaching this place, but instead they were of big-boned, broadshouldered country stock, as assuredly physical as an ox. And Tania herself was no longer the unworldly creature she'd seemed to be on the hillside. As we'd descended into the valley she'd shed her strangeness like steam; by the time we reached the Bothy she was the same Tania who'd long ago seduced me, then married me. But perhaps not the same Tania who'd left America with me, for this one bore smiles that seemed to come all the way up from the soul.

All that was left of the hillside Tania was her dress, which was made of a fabric that fascinated me. As I sat on the floor at her feet, leaning against her knees—there weren't enough chairs to go around, and we'd eaten off big wooden plates on the floor—I repeatedly, however hard

I tried to stop myself, took a fold of the garment's hem between my fingers and rubbing it back and forth. It felt as if it were made of woven water. I couldn't decide if it was the peculiarity of the fabric's texture that drew me again and again, or just the fact that I had fingers against whose skin I could feel it. Her calves beneath the cloth were slender and smooth and cooler than they should have been in the heat of the room. Whenever I thought no one was looking I'd covertly caress them, making her stir in her seat.

Outside, it was still broad daylight. Inside, it was night, and we depended on the guttering flames of half a dozen oil lamps placed strategically around the room. We could see the sunshine through the Bothy's half-open door and its three or four small grimy windows, but it seemed to be unable to penetrate more than a few inches into where we were, as if the air itself snuffed out the brightness.

For the third time that evening I needed to go take a leak. I was apparently the only one of the company who had any such requirement, but earlier Tania's father, James, had pointed out a tiny stone shack, like an upright sarcophagus, inside which I'd sure enough found an earth privy. The pit was perfectly clean, when I glanced down into it. My guess was it had been specially dug for me just a few hours ago.

Explaining quietly to Tania, who was busily occupied in laughing at one of brother Alan's more ribald jokes—my scatologies earlier in the car had been as nothing compared to the stuff this family regarded as commonplace—I hauled myself to my feet, marvelling for the thousandth time at the way my hands obeyed the commands I gave them. Taking exaggerated care not to trip over the bakelite elephone which sat anachronistically in the middle of the floor as the room's centrepiece, or the flex that snaked off into an unexplored corner, I made my way haphazardly out into the daylight. I'm sure they all of them knew of my going—knew precisely which muscles I'd moved and the number of breaths I'd taken—but not one of them gave the slightest sign of registering any change. Indeed, there was something quite unnatural about the way the hubbub of excited chatter and laughter stayed totally unaltered, I thought woozily as I shut the door behind me and made my way to the privy. It sounded somehow . . . orchestrated, somehow pre-recorded, like the laughter track on a bad television sitcom. What were they really thinking, these people? What were they in fact communicating to each other under the cloak of smutty jokes and oddly un-pin-downable reminiscences?

What did they truly look like?

Tania had told me they'd been preparing themselves for my arrival, and I'd assumed they were putting on finery, adding final touches to make-up or hair. But that most certainly hadn't been the case. The men were in farm-soiled loose trousers, James's held up despite the overhang of his belly by a piece of hairy string knotted around his waist; their shirts were coarsely woven cotton. The women were in smock-like dresses with torn hems and cooking stains. If any of them had brushed their hair—or their teeth—in a week there was no evidence of it. All the men needed a shave, and, although I'd never dream of saying a word about this to Tania, so did her mother, Ellen.

If they'd not been dressing up for me, was it conceivable they'd been dressing *down*? Could it be that Tania's family, in their natural state, resembled the loved; the lovely; yet the, in some measure, terrifying creature who'd accompanied me across the grassed hillside to reach here? Had they donned solidly corporeal bodies, convincingly detailed right down to Alison's pregnant swelling, in order to make me feel less of a stranger?

Or might they have had some other motive for adopting their guises? Was their intent, less benevolently, to deceive?

I shivered as I creaked the privy's wooden door open. For a while up there on the hillside I'd been certain that the place to which Tania was leading me was Fairyland, and I still wasn't sure this conclusion had been too far askew. The face I'd gazed into on the slopes, the face with the eyes of a lost and ancient time, could have been the quintessence of La Belle Dame Sans Merci. At military school we'd studied Shakespeare's *A Midsummer Night's Dream* as one of our few concessions to culture, and I'd learned enough to know that fairies weren't the cute little bundles of mischief the Victorians had turned them into. They had cruel ways with mortals who strayed into their realm.

Again, I should have been frightened, but I wasn't. Wasn't Tania here? In both of her guises, I knew, she loved me. She'd not let grief befall me.

When I returned to the Bothy and pushed on the door, the sound of raucous laughter was cut off abruptly. The daylight followed me as I slowly entered the room, which was now as silent and empty as if it had been deserted for decades by all except spiders. The dust on the floor showed no foot-trails except my own. What had been gravy-streaked platters just a couple of minutes ago were now loose boards warping up from the floor's level. The picked bones of the sheep's carcase had become a grey skeleton so desiccated it looked as if it would collapse into dust if I trod too heavily.

Where the quaint heavy old telephone had sat, the chrome of its dial mottled by the corrosion of at least one generation's fingertips, there was a glass bottle, with the hipflask shape and about the size of a pint of liquor. The bottle's shoulders were the only thing in this room that still gleamed. I moved to pick it up, pausing reflexively for a moment as I bent toward it and then remembering that here, in this land of Tania's, I had the fingers with which to grip it.

It felt chilled in my hand.

I took the bottle out into the full sunlight and held it up. The contents were that pale straw colour that denotes either one of the finest single malts or a healthy urine specimen. I had a suspicion they weren't the latter.

The bottle didn't have the usual liquor screw-top but a cork not unlike a champagne cork, fastened in place with a splotch of hard red wax. There was some kind of hieroglyph on the seal, a logo, but the wax had squished around it so I couldn't make out any of the details. For a label, the front of the bottle bore what seemed like just a scrap of paper torn off a larger sheet and hurriedly stuck on. Written on it by hand was one of those long, complicated Gaelic words that look like the monkey's been at the typewriter again. I hadn't the remotest idea what it meant. Probably DRINK ME.

I broke the seal and squeaked the cork out, sniffed. Decidedly not a urine sample.

"Quinn!"

I looked around, then up. At the top of the slope down which we'd come, Tania was standing, waving at me. The breeze was pressing her dress flat against one side of her body; on the other side the dress's long feathery tail was blown out like a flag, becoming progressively less discernible the further it was from her until finally, I could see, it was the gauziest of clouds in the silver sky.

She saw that she'd caught my attention, and beckoned.

Quickly, touched by an irrational guilt, I wormed the cork back in and started to put the bottle down by the Bothy door, but she gesticulated wildly with her arms that I should bring it with me.

Relieved that my beloved was still here, in whatever form she might now be bearing, I almost ran up the gentle grade, arriving beside her hardly out of breath. One glance as I approached her was enough to tell me that the slightly tipsy giggler of the Bothy was gone, replaced by the severe monarch whose eyes held too many years.

I almost tripped over the little wooden sign in the grass. Someone—Tania?—had turned it around, so that now it faced the valley, and myself. I hesitated briefly, expecting the wording too to have been altered, but it still read:

ABANDON YOURSELF
ALL YE WHO ENTER HERE

For a moment it struck me that the message had it wrong this time—I was, after all, not entering but leaving—and then I shook my head. The sign was perfectly correct. I was entering a world that was far smaller than the one I'd been visiting. Yet, for all that, the instruction made little more sense than it had the last time. How could I abandon myself? Why would I want to? Had I abandoned myself in the valley and not realized I'd done so? Was it myself that I had to abandon, or my self—my selfhood?

I opened my mouth to ask Tania, who presumably knew the answer, but then I remembered the stern way she'd told me I should stifle my questions, just be.

But human beings aren't really human beings unless they're inquiring about everything around them. Without realizing it was a question, I said, "Where are James and Ellen, Alison, the others?"

I expected a snapped response, but instead Tania smiled.

She reached out and with a long fingernail, almost a talon, tapped the side of the bottle I held.

"They're in here," she said. "Where they've always been."

What she'd said didn't seem to have any meaning, but I didn't dare push my luck and probe further.

"Now, Quinn, it's time for us to go back to a place where this day can end."

She turned away from the valley. Somehow her dress shifted on her body so that it was still the same as before, one side close against her and the other petering off infinitely into the sky.

I took the hand she held out to me, and kept pace with her as she halfwalked, half-skipped away across the field with the violet-tinged grass and the multicoloured flowers. Yet again we were surrounded by birdsong and by the little rusty insects we'd first encountered when we'd driven into the sun. Was it these insects, not unseen birds, that were the ones chirping and trilling? Or were they not insects at all but the actual bird calls themselves, visible and tangible in this land of Tania's?

We tore across the grass, far more quickly than our legs could actually be taking us. I felt as if I were the camera strapped to the front of the express train in one of those old sped-up movies they used to show to impress small children, me among them. Faster and faster we went, until the low hills in the distance became little more than purple blurs, even though the grass-blades and the starry flowers on the ground beneath us were perfectly clear.

Tania turned to me, then glanced back over her shoulder. Without thinking, I followed her gaze.

Behind us the sky was growing dark. The great train of her dress seemed to belong to both of us, not her alone, as it spread itself across the swathe of night.

Earlier it had been the clouds. Now it was the moon and stars.

And:

"Damn that fucking idiot in the Volvo," said Tania, jamming her foot down on the brake.

All the way back through the outskirts of Glasgow, she prattled away about how good it had been to see her family after such a long time, how she was worried that her dad was looking so much older these days, how Alison had settled down a bit now she had a little one on the way. . .

I just let the words pass by me at a distance, much like the tenements and shop windows on the far side of the car window. Wherever Tania had spent the afternoon, it didn't seem to be where I had been. We'd driven out to some place in the back of beyond by the side of an anonymous loch, and we'd met the new inlaws and had a meal and watched Dad show off his new electrically powered lawnmower, and Alan had nicked his finger while carving the lamb—probably because he'd had a drop too much of the sherry while we'd been waiting for the recalcitrant potatoes to cook. A perfectly normal afternoon meeting in-laws, in other words. This surely must have been what really happened.

So then how the hell had I managed to hallucinate that we'd gone somewhere else entirely?

I didn't have much experience of hallucinations—although I'd smoked the occasional joint in Iraq and before, I'd steered well clear of anything harder, including the hallucinogens that were endemic in the camps—but it seemed to me that my experience had been far too vivid, far too complete, to have been simply a fever dream. I could still taste the frothy beer we'd drunk, still touch with my tongue the greasy scum the mutton had left on the back of my teeth. Yet . . . yet wouldn't those sensations be just the same if instead we'd had the cozy family visit Tania was describing? In themselves they proved nothing at all. Besides, the things I'd thought I'd seen—the shiny silver sky, the dress that became the clouds or the stars, the grass blades tipped with a colour the human eye couldn't encompass—surely none of these could have any existence outside of dreams, or fevers, or both?

By the time we'd handed over the car to the hotel valet for parking and made our way into the supremely gilt and polished lobby, I'd more or less succeeded in persuading myself that everything I'd undergone that afternoon had been a product of abnormal psychology. Perhaps I'd picked up a dose of food poisoning at one of the restaurants we'd been in, and that had made my mind play tricks on me. It was evident from Tania's still flowing chatter that I'd acted completely normally during the visit to her family, that no one had noticed me behaving in any way unusually—or, if they had, they hadn't commented on the fact to Tania. Perhaps they'd simply put down any apparent eccentricities of mine to the fact that I was a Yank—hell, a country that could have Il Buce as its leader must be straining at the seams with people who were a bit touched in the head.

As we waited for the elevator—the lift—I felt the weight of a bottle in my coat pocket.

" . . . and what was nicest of all, I think," Tania was saying, her fingers laced beneath her chin, her face glowing with happiness, "was that when Mum and I were alone in the kitchen coping with the dishes, she said how much she and Dad liked you, really liked you. They both fell in love with you, Quinn. They both think of you now as being truly their son. Mum was so funny. She told me, all very sober and pompous, you understand"—Tania dropped her voice into an appropriate caricature—"that, a fine man like you, I was to be sure not to be such a silly wee flibbertigibbet that I went and lost you. I just about died. I mean, she hasn't spoken to me like that since . . . "

"Tania," I said quietly as the elevator pinged to announce its arrival. We were the only ones waiting for it. "Tania, none of this is anything like what happened to *me*."

The almost manic vivacity stripped itself away from her instantly. In its place there came across her face an expression I couldn't at first identify.

Then I recognized it: *contentment*. What had confused me was its complete lack of correspondence to her words and her body language. Clutching my left arm and its lifeless hand, she pulled me into the elevator car and stabbed at the button for our floor, all the while continuing to yammer about the perfectly ordinary family reunion we'd enjoyed. She was sending me two messages at once, the more important one being the one that wasn't conveyed in her words: that I'd in some way lived up to her aspirations for me by remembering the truth of the afternoon, not the official account. I was the investigative journalist who'd come good, who to everyone's surprise had succeeded in weaseling his way behind the curtain of propagandist lies and got the scoop—only for some reason my editor wasn't allowed to congratulate me publicly on the feat.

The same forked understanding hung around us like a haze all the way along the plushly carpeted, tastefully decorated, forbiddingly empty corridor from the elevator to our room. Once we were inside, I expected her to open up to me honestly, but still she persisted in the pretence, moving briskly about the room, hanging up her coat, spending a couple of minutes in the bathroom peeing and sprucing up her face, talking incessantly about nothing that mattered. After I'd used the bathroom myself—"Look, Ma! No hands! Well, not really . . . "—I came out to find her sitting on the bed holding the pint bottle, turning it over in her hands, looking at it the way you look at a book you've already read. She must have fished it out of my pocket while I was doing my best not to spray the apricot floor-tiles.

"I can't read that," I said, sitting down beside her, reaching out to touch the crudely lettered label with fingers that couldn't feel it. "What does it say?"

"It's in the old tongue."

"Yes, darling, I'd guessed it was Gaelic from the way it looks like someone's sloshed their alphabet soup over the edge of the bowl."

Tania shook her head, not smiling, still looking at the bottle, not at me. "An older tongue than Gaelic, Quinn," she said so softly I could hardly hear her.

I narrowed my eyes, trying to think what languages might have been spoken in Scotland before Gaelic came along.

"Pictish?" I hazarded.

Now she did turn her head toward me. She smiled, but it was the saddest smile I'd ever seen on her face.

"You're getting warmer, husband mine, but you've centuries more to go."

I gave up. "What does it say?"

She looked at the label as if reading it again. "Near as it matters, it says, 'The Hard Stuff.'"

I tapped the bottle again. "Pretty potent, huh? A hundred fifty proof, sort of thing?"

"Potent, yes," she said, inclining her head. The warm glow of the bedside light paradoxically returned to her face some of that cold austerity I'd seen earlier in the day. "You'll be finding out soon enough."

"A single malt, is it?"

"More like a blend."

I was disappointed. To be honest, although I could tell the difference between Laphroaig, which I liked in small quantities, and Glenfiddich, which I thought was more like paint stripper than liquor, most scotches tasted about the same to me. But I'd been told countless authoritative times, not least by Tania herself, that the malts were the aristocrats, the blends merely stopgap measures or "cooking whisky." I'd expected a bottle with this provenance to contain something more exotic than I could have found in the room's minibar.

Tania could tell what I was thinking by the way I shifted my seating on the bed.

"It depends on what you put into the blend," she said, "how fine it turns out to be. I told you what was in this one, Quinn."

"Your folks?" I'd assumed her comment back at the valley's rim had been whimsical.

She nodded. "This isn't just a whisky we're giving you. As it says on the label, it's the hard stuff."

"It *smells* like scotch."

"Well, it would, wouldn't it?"

"Shall I get the . . . ? Oh." Sometimes even I myself forgot about my disability.

"Yes," she said, to my surprise. "You do the fetching. Just the one glass, though. You can manage that, can't you?" She cast her eye at my plastic hand, lying on my knee. "This is a drink you'll be having on your own, lover man. It's not one I can share with you."

Perplexed, I went and got one of the glasses from the bathroom. If I put my hand vertically above it and then jammed the rim between the thumb and the side of the index finger, I could carry it. The stratagem wasn't going to work for drinking out of it, though.

I put the glass down on the bedside table, shaking it free with a little difficulty. "Fill 'er up."

"Not yet, Quinn. You're not ready yet."

"Who says? It's been a long day, and an extremely confusing one— for me, at least—and I cannot remember a time when I've needed a belt more than now."

"Stay standing," she said, looking up at me as I moved to sit down beside her again. "It'll be easier for us that way."

I didn't know what she was talking about, but of course I did what she said.

Tania stood up and, facing me, pushed my jacket back off my shoulders, then worked the sleeves off my arms. The garment dropped to the floor. Then she got to work on the buttons of my shirt, which in due course followed the jacket. All the while, her fingers moved with an almost trancelike slowness, performing each action with the minimum of effort and yet with the grace and flow of some stately parade.

The net effect was to make me more rampant than I could remember being since my teens.

With the same exquisite slowness, Tania unbuckled the belt of my pants and worked the zipper down.

"A fine upstanding military gentleman, I see," she remarked with an affectionate little grin. It was the same cliché with which she'd teased me when first we'd undressed each other, years ago. Her hair brushed the side of my erection as she pushed my pants and shorts to the floor, but she didn't react in any way to the contact. Instead, kneeling there, she pulled the laces of my shoes untied.

"Sit down on the bed now, Quinn," she said.

I sat, and raised my legs to let her tug off shoes, socks, the rest of my clothing.

When she had me completely naked, still kneeling in front of me, she looked me in the eyes with that same sad smile I'd seen before. It was the kind of smile lovers or kin have when one of them is about to depart on a long journey.

She stood up and leaned across me, pulling the pillows out from under the coverlet and puffing them up against the headboard. I put my arm as much around her hips as I could, feeling the denimed curve of her rear against the soft skin above the tangled mess of scar tissue where my wrist had once been, and tried to pull her down to me.

"No," she said, quietly but firmly, like a nurse rejecting the advances of a bedridden lecher. "Not now, Quinn. Not now."

Once she had the pillows arranged to her satisfaction, she took a pace back from the bedside.

The words were like a splash of cold sea spray on my face.

"What do you mean? Won't you be here? Where are you going?"

"It's where *you're* going that matters, Quinn."

"I'm not going anywhere. I'm naked as the day I was born, woman. I'd get arrested. Particularly with . . . "

Tania glanced at my tumescence with a sort of weary but loving tolerance: men will be men, they think with their balls, what can you expect?

"It's been pleasing to see my old friend back in the landscape again," she said with a dry little chuckle. "Seems a shame to waste it, but . . . "

She let the word hang.

"Later?" I said.

"Aye, later, maybe. Have you not got yourself settled yet? You've got some serious drinking to do."

Not until I was arranged to her satisfaction on the bed, with my back against the pillows on the headboard, would she speak again. By this time my penis had quietened. I'd begun to realize that this whole . . . whole *ceremony* had far too much of the nature of a farewell about it.

"Where are you going?" I said again to her, this time putting it into my voice that I was wanting an answer.

"Oh, just somewhere around."

"Where?"

"You don't need me any longer, Quinn."

I struggled to sit more upright. "What are you trying to tell me, Tania? Are you leaving me? Is that what you and your mother were really talking about in the kitchen? Or wherever. I know I've been a bastard to live with ever since Iraq, but . . . but this afternoon taught me something—this whole trip to Scotland has taught me something. I can feel the old me, the old Quinn, coming back, and he's here to stay. Now's not the time to give up on me, darling—I promise you . . . Or"—it wasn't credible, but it was the best straw a perplexed and bleeding man with a plastic hand could find—"or is there someone else I don't know about?"

The cruel monarch was suddenly back in the room, her eyes a green blaze of fury. When she spoke her words were clipped into arrows of ice that pinned me to the pillows.

"That is a question you should never have thought to ask, Quinn Hogarth. You have demeaned me, and I do not take kindly to that."

And then she relaxed her shoulders again. "No, darling. There's no one. I love you as much as I ever have—more, if anything. Believe me, this is all because of the love I have for you. If I loved you any less, I'd . . . well, I'd not have wasted the . . . the opportunity you presented me." She bit her lip, eyes dancing. "To put it in the politest possible terms."

Despite myself, I smiled too—more in relief that I'd escaped the full force of her regal ire than anything else.

"And now," she said.

Tania didn't complete the sentence, but, her movements crisp, reached for the bottle by the bedside and twisted its cork out. She sniffed the open top, appreciating the fumes, then poured the pale amber liquid into the hotel's tooth glass.

When she'd done and the tumbler was full to the brim, there was still about an inch left in the bottle. She looked at the remaining liquid accusingly, then very deliberately tipped it, too, into the glass.

It all went in, but the glass didn't overflow.

"Wait a moment," she said, and went to burrow through one of the drawers, pulling out the screw-topped plastic drinking cup I'd barely used since our arrival in Glasgow. For a moment I thought she was going to decant the liquor into it, but instead she just pulled out the straw.

"You'll need this, at least at first," she said, popping it into the glass. Still the meniscus held and there was no overflow.

"Kiss me," I said. "You owe me a kiss. Please."

"Before I go," she replied. "I'm not gone yet."

I knew I should be doing something more by way of protesting—I should be leaping from the bed and having a showdown with her, or going on my bended knee to plead with her—but it was as if there was something hypnotic in the air, so that all I could do was follow the flow of events with a sort of unhappy complaisance. She was the one who was in entire control of what would happen. For me to try to redirect things would be not just a challenge to her authority but a disruption of the natural order. I had the sense that all this had been written down before somewhere, and that I—and, for that matter, Tania—had no choice but to follow that unread script. A tiny part of me rebelled against this uncomfortable tranquility, but I ignored it as I would have ignored a butterfly on the field of battle: something irrelevant whose prettiness I might have the time to appreciate later.

So I watched her lethargically as she neatly folded my clothes and piled them on the ottoman that sat in front of the window table. She unravelled my socks and tucked them neatly into the openings of my shoes, then placed the shoes side by side under the ottoman. Lastly she came across to the bed once more and, assuming no disagreement from me, unstrapped the sad pink prosthetic from my arm. She placed the parody of flesh on top of the heap of my clothing.

Then she stood facing me, her hands cupped together like a virgin's in front of her crotch.

She took two quick, determined steps to the bedside, as if concerned her resolve might desert her, and looked down on me where I sat.

"I believe you requested a kiss, sir," she said with mock coyness.

Her lips were fire on mine.

I don't mean what the words would mean in a purple novel. I felt as if I were being kissed by and kissing flame. The pain was nearly as intense as I'd felt when I'd first come stumbling back out of unconsciousness after the device had exploded in front of me in Falluja, but where that had been hostile agony this was exquisitely pleasurable. Her tonguetip flickered against mine and I almost screamed, but still I forced myself against her.

Then she was on the far side of the room, standing by the door, her hand on its handle, half-shadowed because the weak glow of the bedside lamp barely reached that far.

"Drink, Quinn," she said, gesturing with her head to tell me what I should do.

I leaned to my side, fumbling the bent plastic straw around with the stump of my arm until it pointed toward my lips.

I took it into my mouth, my eyes still on Tania's silently standing figure.

"I've enjoyed beyond words having you as my husband, Quinn," she whispered. "My sweet lover. But you no longer need me."

Before she'd finished speaking she'd turned the handle of the door and was gone into the anonymity of the hotel corridor.

Before she'd finished speaking she'd turned the handle of the door and was gone into the anonymity of the hotel corridor.

I was a mist, a haar, that clung close to the land, creeping into every last one of its crevices, becoming almost absorbed by it yet retaining my own self, my own separateness. I became the inverse of trees, taking their shapes into myself, their convexities being reproduced with perfect fidelity as concavities within me. Flying birds and running animals—human animals among them—were streams of their passage through me. Stones and mountains formed new parts of me, too, as did valleys and the shore.

None of them paid the least bit of attention to my presence. I had been here not forever but for far longer than any of them had. I was simply a part of reality to them, like the air they breathed. As with the air, I was invisible. As with the air, they could not be if I were gone.

Formless, I had all forms. Formless, I was able to make of myself any form I chose, following whatever was the whim of my moment.

In this particular moment of mine I watched myself deciding that a part of me should be thickened, twisting streamers of intangibility coming together in a swirl and coalescing around each other in countless layers to create physical essence where before there had been none. The creation emerging from the mist, taking shade out of the greyness only I could see, had two legs, two arms, a head, a momentary identity, a name.

That name was Quinn, and the creation talked—I could see it doing so, even though I couldn't be troubled to listen. I did, however, bother to give it the power to see through my eyes, hear with my ears.

There were others like me. I knew this in the same way the small creatures knew of me. It had always been so. Like me, they toyed with their world, creating and destroying, most of eternity just playing. At our edges we blended with each other, enriching each other, delighting in each other. But not all of us did this, not always. Some chose the route of dying.

Through my eyes the Quinn creation could see one of these entering its death throes. It was taking physicality around itself, binding itself in an armour of steel to defend itself from all that was not itself, even though it had no attackers. I watched, passive, as it did this. I knew what would happen to it next—we all did. Self-caged, unable to bear the surrounding weight of its idiot armour, it would shrink, growing ever more bitter and miserable as it did so, like an old man seeking impotently to destroy all around him rather than confront the failure he has made of his life. The entity had become engrossed by its own madness, the madness that fed it and fed upon it. There was nothing any of us could do to save it.

The Quinn creation, however, wished to try.

Had wished to try.

Seeing it through my eyes, he saw the infeasibility of the task. Feeling its dying through my emotions, he was able to strip himself of his pity. The entity had not been struck by death, but had instead chosen of its own free will to die, and the manner of its dying. Through stupidity it had embraced insanity. Existence does not tolerate stupidity long.

We watched the stupid, shrinking, dying entity, did the Quinn creation and I. Perhaps there was a chance for it, perhaps it could save itself. It was difficult to care, although I sensed the Quinn creation retained some vestige of caring.

Certainly the Quinn creation, the name-taker, as it melted back into me—abandoning its self as it discovered its selfhood was all that had held it back from being truly free, truly individual, truly something other than just another faceless unit in a millions-strong temporary flock, truly everlasting—possessed enough of the compassion which I did not have for the one that was dying to be a name-giver as well as a name-taker. It gave the self-condemned, self-armoured, self-narrowing entity a name.

The Quinn creation, its shared thoughts fraying with regret, called the dying entity Fortusa.

I awoke with what I believed at first was the hangover to end all hangovers. My plastic beaker, empty, had found its way into my naked armpit. I squinted painfully against the grey light streaking in from the station; neither of us had thought to draw the curtains last night. Barely audible, like thunder beyond the mountains, a voice announced that a train for a destination was now boarding at a platform. The tiny noise made the spiritual silence, the utter Tania-less loneliness of the room— of the cold hill side—all the more profound.

I swung my legs over the side of the bed, got to my feet, swayed. No wonder the liquor was called The Hard Stuff: it had a kick like nothing I'd ever drunk before . . .

Yet my vision was clear. My mouth was no less fresh-tasting than on any other morning. My stomach wasn't unsettled.

The pain in my head didn't come from the liquor—or, at least, it did, but not from the alcohol. The pain was from the still-healing surgery the dream had performed in my mind.

Dream?

That had been no dream. It had been a glimpse, for the first time in my life, of reality. Reality makes us, moulds us, nurtures us or rejects us, but it is also made by us, by all of us, even though we are unconscious creators.

The incisions in my mind would heal soon. Already the stitches could be pulled out.

Half an hour later I was at the hotel's reception desk. The clerk glanced at my hands, my plastic hands, as I leaned on the counter in front of her. The left one was now accustomed to me; the right was still an intruder, but I wore it this morning anyway. It held my room card-key.

"My wife—she seems to have gone missing."

The receptionist raised an eyebrow, smiling. "Perhaps she'll still be at breakfast, sir, or in the . . . "

I shook my head impatiently.

"She's gone. I know that. Did she check out, or did she just . . . go?"

Frowning now, the receptionist checked my card-key, then turned to her keyboard, tapping a few times as she called a new display up on the screen.

"We have you registered as a single occupancy, sir. Perhaps, ah . . . "

"It's all right. Forget it."

I walked away.

Part of me knew the futility of what I was doing, but there was still enough of a part of me stuck in the old ruts that I felt compelled to go through the formalities.

I made towards a pay phone, then realized I'd never be able to get the coins into the slot. Back upstairs in my room, I picked up the ballpoint pen in my mouth, ready to tackle the phone with it, then let it fall again. If I really tried, I had enough control over my artificial hands to . . .

That was when I realized I'd dressed myself. Not just dressed myself but strapped on the hated plastic prosthetics. Which had I done first? How the hell had I strapped on the prosthetics before I'd strapped on the prosthetics . . . ?

Distraction by the realization, I froze for a full minute, perhaps longer. Then I sat down on the bed and shuffled my way out of my shoes. Standing up again, I went to the closet and tussled with the door until I had it open. From the row of my shoes there I selected a pair of slip-ons, and slid my feet into them.

Back on the bed, I clumsily pressed the 0 for an outside line, waited for the dialling tone, then with care hit the 9 and the 1 and the 1 again.

I put the phone back on the receiver before the ringing had time to start.

What the hell had I been doing? It wasn't 911 for the cops in this country: it was 999. Tania had told me that on the plane, and repeated it once we'd arrived in Glasgow until she was sure I had the information firmly imprinted on my brain. In my distraction I'd succumbed to an old habit.

But wasn't everything I'd been doing for the past few minutes just exactly that—succumbing to old habits? I knew that Tania had gone, and I had a slowly clearing understanding of why she had. I wasn't going to be able to find her unless she wanted to be found, which she didn't. What was the point of all this rigmarole I was putting myself through? Why was I still reciting the lines of the play when the curtain had long ago come down on the final act?

Sitting on the bed, I let my shoulders sag. Packing the suitcases would be a bit of a nightmare, but I guessed I could always heftily tip one of the hotel's maids to undertake the chore for me. Half the stuff I could leave behind anyway, although I found I was irrationally reluctant just to dump Tania's shoes and clothing and general clutter—if they were still there—into the room's wastebins. Even if I took everything home with me—yes, that was what I would do—the journey would be manageable. The hotel's valets or the taxi driver would get the baggage into the taxi, and at the airport I could use one of their trolleys or find a handler to cope. At the other end, in Newark, things might get a bit more difficult, but not if I explained my plight at the Glasgow check-in desk and asked them to signal the details through to their counterparts in the States. And from Newark International I could get a taxi all the way home, screw the cost. My wallet was fat with notes in both currencies, and my credit cards were—thanks to Dad's allowance—in reasonably healthy shape. The trip was going to be a challenge, all right, but it was all perfectly feasible . . .

My thoughts ran down like a clockwork toy.

Old habits again. My first impulse had been to try to track Tania down. Once I'd accepted that this was a fruitless endeavour, my next urge had been the primitive one of scuttling for home as fast as I could go. But home is more than a place, more than a geographical location, more than a set of names and empty symbols. There was a place where I'd lived my whole life, but it had been usurped by nameshifters—by people who seized the names of things, changed their meaning, and pretended they still meant the same. Freedom, on their lips, had become synonymous with slaughter and repression, democracy with the law of the concentration camp. The house in which I'd dwelt, whose every corner I'd thought myself intimately familiar with, had been invaded by thieves, and now I was on the outside gazing in through the window, watching them smash up my property. Whump—there went the microwave. Zip—and a razor sliced through one of the pictures on the wall. Crash—there went the valueless but infinitely valued glass vase Aunt Millie had given me before she died. And all the while the fire the usurpers had lit was blazing merrily in the middle of the living-room carpet, fueled by the chairs and the coffee table . . .

The place I thought of as home wasn't home any longer—not *my* home.

I lay down on top of the bed, its coverlet still in disarray from where I'd slept on it last night. The pillows were slightly damp from when I'd been sweating into them, but they were comfortable enough. I put my plastic pseudo-hands behind my head and stared up at the ceiling. There was no need to go scurrying back to the States just yet. The cash and credit cards I'd been planning to use to finance my dash for the solace of familiarity might just as well fund a few extra nights here in this station-side hotel—that's what they'd been intended for in the first place, remember. We'd sampled only a couple of the Indian restaurants, and there must be hundreds more in Glasgow for me to pick among. Was it not the case that Dali's painting of the crucifixion hung in one of the art museums here?

If I ran away, my flight would be a mourning. To mourn Tania would be fully to lose her, forever. If I stayed here a while longer she'd always be . . .

Around.

I wondered where that train had been departing for.

Every day as I arrive at my office, having climbed the last flight of stairs, I pause in front of the glass case that stands just inside the main door. I touch the top of the case, and perhaps it's true that I feel what I think I can feel: the cool smoothness of the glass against my artificial fingertips.

No. Of course that can't be right. The prosthetics I wear these days are much better than those dreadful pink plastic ones I once so loathed, but even they can't perform miracles.

The office is in one of these big old residential houses in Grampian Way, in one of the posher parts of Glasgow. Before that it was, briefly, the room over a garage. I've moved up in the world, and nowadays no one seems to notice I'm not Scottish. For four years I've been spearheading a charity devoted to organizing the endeavours of lawyers internationally to get the inmates out of the concentration camp at Guantánamo Bay. We win a few, we lose a whole lot more . . . but at least we do win those few.

I'm paid enough of a salary that every Saturday there's enough left over for lunch at an Indian restaurant. Oh, and for me to have been able to send back one of Dad's allowance cheques before he stopped sending them.

Inside the glass case is a life-souvenir that is one of the reasons I'm here.

The pair of shoes that long ago I pushed off my feet in a hotel bedroom, and have never worn since.

Their laces tied with perfect bows.

As I pause by the case this morning, I hear, rippling down the corridor, a sound that is one of the other major reasons why my home is in Glasgow, why I'm doing what I'm doing. A cascade of dearly loved laughter. As is almost always the case, she left our somewhat seedy flat before I did this morning, to get to work as early as she could. She's on the phone to a potential donor, perhaps, chatting him up for a few hundred or thousand euros extra, or perhaps it's a moral rather than a financial squeeze she's putting on someone: from time to time we gain the ear of a significant legal or political figure here in my chosen homeland, and then there can be a spurt in our achievements.

I thought I'd lost Tania forever, back on that first morning after she'd told me I no longer needed her and I'd accepted her gift of The Hard Stuff. She said she'd always be near wherever I was, but I hadn't believed her—I'd assumed she was talking purely figuratively. What neither of us recognized then was that the day might come when she'd realize that, though I might no longer need her, she might find herself needing me.

She found me again—easy enough to do, because I was hardly likely to hide from her. And of course I was waiting for her return.

Her name is Alison now, and she has dark, thick, curly hair rather than fine, straight and pale. She's a couple of inches shorter and a few years younger than she was before, and her accent is broader, but I knew her for Tania the moment I set eyes on her, that day in The Record Exchange on Jamaica Street when we were both trying to browse through the Savourna Stevenson CDs at the same time. Should I have had any uncertainty, I needed only to look into her eyes, which are brown sometimes and green sometimes but always with behind them the sense of an infinite past. We have a baby on the way. I eagerly anticipate the day when she'll announce that it's maybe time for her to take me to meet the folks.

I pat the top of the case one last time, smiling at the sound of her laughter, before I head down the passage to whatever Fairyland the new day brings.

John Grant is the author of some seventy books, both fiction and nonfiction, and a recipient of Hugo (twice), World Fantasy, *Locus*, Mythopoeic Society Scholarship, the J. Lloyd Eaton Scholarship, and Chesley Awards, as well as a rare British Science Fiction Association Special Award. His most recent novel is *The Dragons of Manhattan*, currently being serialized in *Argosy*. His most recent nonfiction book is *Discarded Science*, about theories and hypotheses that have fallen by the wayside (or should have). A recognized authority on animated movies, he is married to Pamela D. Scoville, Director of the Animation Art Guild; they live in New Jersey with a quartet of rescued cats.

CREDITS

Special thanks to the editors who originally selected and publications that first published these stories.

"Follow Me Light" © 2005 by Elizabeth Bear was first published on *SciFiction,* edited by Ellen Datlow on 01.12.05.

"A Maze of Trees" © 2005 by Claudia O'Keefe was first published in *The Magazine of Fantasy and Science Fiction,* August 2005, edited by Gordon Van Gelder.

"The Shadowed Heart" © 2005 by Catherine Asaro was first published in *The Journey Home,* edited by Mary Kirk, ImaJinn Books.

"Walpurgis Afternoon" © 2005 by Delia Sherman was first published in *The Magazine of Fantasy and Science Fiction,* December 2005, edited by Gordon Van Gelder.

"A Knot of Toads" © 2005 by Jane Yolen was first published in *Nova Scotia: New Scottish Speculative Fiction,* edited by Andrew J Wilson and Neil Williamson, published by The Mercat Press.

"Calypso in Berlin" © 2005 by Elizabeth Hand was first published at *SciFiction,* edited by Ellen Datlow on 07.13.05.

"A Hero's Welcome" © 2005 by Rebecca York was first published in *The Journey Home,* edited by Mary Kirk, ImaJinn Books.

"Single White Farmhouse" © 2005 by Heather Shaw was first published in *Polyphony 5,* edited by Deborah Layne and Jay Lake, published by Wheatland Press.

"Fir Na Tine" © 2005 by Sandra McDonald was first published in *Realms of Fantasy,* February 2005 edited by Shawna McCarthy.

"Magic in a Certain Slant of Light" © 2005 by Deborah Coates was first published on *Strange Horizons,* 21 March 2005, fiction edited by Jed Hartman (Senior Editor), Susan Marie Groppi, and Karen Meisner.

"A Treatise on Fewmets" © 2005 by Sarah Prineas was first published in *Lone Star Stories,* August/September, edited by Eric T. Marin.

"The Hard Stuff" ©2005 by John Grant was first published in *Nova Scotia: New Scottish Speculative Fiction,* edited by Andrew J Wilson and Neil Williamson, published by The Mercat Press.

JUNO BOOKS: Fiction Beyond the Ordinary
www.juno-books.com

Twelve Steps From Darkness by Karen E. Taylor
Laura Wagner came close to destroying her own life. Now her hard-won new life is threatened by something malevolent and uncanny.

Euryale by Kara Dalkey
Fantasy and romance deftly woven into a story of gods and monsters, dark secrets and strange omens. A mysterious veiled woman comes to Republican Rome to find the answer to a riddle.

Master of Shadows by Janet Lorimer
Ariel McPherson finds legend crashing into reality when she meets a mysterious stranger, Louvel. Is she in danger of losing her heart to Louvel . . . or her life?

Unveiling the Sorceress by Saskia Walker
Secret love and forbidden liaisons mix with the deadly implications of the enemy's plans in this sensual story of danger, passion, and intrigue with the exotic allure of 1001 Arabian Nights.

Wind Follower by Carole McDonnell
Satha, a dark-skinned woman from a poor clan is enslaved in her own land. Her husband, the wealthy young Loic, is blessed by God, but a rebel against the spirits.

Dark Maiden by Norma Lehr
A grief-stricken mother becomes a pawn in a battle between the forces of Light and Dark.

The Sarsen Witch by Eileen Kernaghan
Earth-witch Naeri plots to overthrow the horse-lords and restore her ancestral lands in a tale of magic, megaliths, and bronze-age high adventure.

House of Whispers by Margaret Lucke
Novice real estate agent Claire has a chance to sell a spectacular oceanview home, but when spirits speak and frightening images invade her dreams, she must take on the challenge of solving a tragic mystery.